TAEJIN

14318-BRAD

TAEJIN

A Novel

R.H. Brady

To order additional copies of this book, contact:
Xlibris Corporation
1-888-7-XLIBRIS
www.Xlibris.com
Orders@Xlibris.com

CONTENTS

For Jane Elizabeth

In Deepest Gratitude

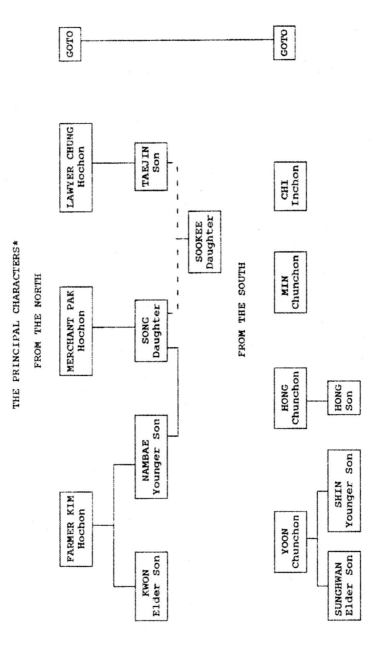

THE PRINCIPAL CHARACTERS*

FROM THE NORTH

FROM THE SOUTH

* Listed by place of first appearance.

SEOUL—1910

"They must not catch us. Hurry."

"I cannot move faster. It is difficult when you push so." The forward porter was perspiring freely, his face purple with exertion in the August heat.

"The Japanese have the courtier. He is being arrested," puffed his companion.

They stumbled along, ricocheting frantically, carelessly through the crowds of people. Their burden, a long and ornately decorated metal box, glistened in the sunlight.

"They will be after us in a moment," worried the man at the rear.

"They do not know where to seek us," replied the other.

"But he is a member of the king's court."

"A setting sun," panted the forward man. "Tomorrow the Japanese will annex us and put an end to the Yi Dynasty. Of what value is a court without a king?"

"Or an imperial treasure?" He snorted, then became serious. "Hurry."

The forward man did not reply. They steered an irregular course, unplanned, selected step by step as they grunted their way toward hiding. Seoul, a sprawling mother, gathered them lovingly to her breast, tucked them protectively into the obscurity of her mass. People, each scurrying in his own panic, enveloped them as would

busy surf, and they submerged determinedly into the inconspicu-
ousness of vast numbers of souls.

Behind them their trail became instantly as conjectural as folk-
lore. Men and women, children and the canes of beggars tamped
it away in their busy travels. The hills of the city watched, seeming
to smile. The valleys, the dwelling and trading places, ignored
them and seemed to forget.

THE NORTH—HOCHON

In an area near the sea west of Pyongyang nestled the village of Hochon. It was a small village, not sufficiently near the coast to permit commercial fishing. The soil, however, was black, rich. The principal economy was agriculture.

The village itself was a cluster of thatched roofs, huts more than houses. Each was surrounded by a wall which guarded a courtyard. Within the yard stood barrels of kimchi and an occasional crude cage of chickens. Water kegs abounded, making each home a world almost unto itself. Outside, the streets were narrow, their surfaces packed earth strewn liberally with debris. The people, old and young, passed their lives as had centuries of their ancestors. The old, learned ones walked slowly, garbed in white and wearing tall, cylindrical hats. The laborers worked their fields, developing a stoop early in their lives which accompanied them to their graves.

"Kim," called the boy. "Come help me with my father's crop."

Kim turned and walked toward his friend. "I cannot, Chung. My father has told me I must help him with our rice. It is setting time." He spread his hands. "It has been the same every year, but this year he made me sow the beds. Now the seedlings are ready. They cannot wait."

"But we have done the setting together every year," protested Chung. "Always I have worked in the paddies with you and you have helped me with my father's cabbage fields."

Kim laughed, poking Chung in boyish fashion. "You just want

help so you do not have to smell the stench of the excrement for so long." He held his nose in gleeful mockery. "It smells."

"But it has been fun."

"Yes," admitted Kim, "but my father has said we are no longer children." He stopped, thinking. "Perhaps if you asked him he would allow it."

They stood together, two boys racing on toward adolescence, anxious for manhood yet still unwilling to surrender the dubious boyish pleasures of working together.

"Yes," replied Chung. "My father will not object. I will ask your father for you." He eyed his friend impishly. "I am not afraid of him."

Suddenly, the two broke into a run, laughing, darting competitively along the narrow, raised path of the dike. On either side of them stretched geometric fields of water, clear, awaiting the plugging of the rice shoots. During the next several days all the family's members would descend into water some five inches deep, forming a crude line as if to advance and skirmish with nature. Then, bent at the waist, they would grasp the long, slender seedlings near their base, thrusting them down through the water and into small, closely spaced mud mounds below the surface, three to each mound. The motion would be continued, row after row, hour after hour, until the entire watery field showed a sea of tiny green pimples breaking its surface.

Kim and Chung arrived breathlessly at a widened area of soil packed hard with years of plodding feet. At its center stood a crude hut of timbers and baked earth, very similar to those in the village. Surrounding it was the requisite wall, erected to protect against intruders. The boys slowed to a walk as they passed through the gate into the courtyard.

Kim's mother stood near the house, bending to ladle kimchi, a thick, heavily spiced gruel with a cabbage base, from a wooden barrel into a worn pot. She looked up only momentarily as the boys shuffled past her into the house, removing their slippers at the door.

"Father," began Kim at sight of the gnarled man, "Chung wishes to speak with you."

The man looked up, smiling briefly, then became wordlessly wary.

Chung swallowed. "Kim has told me you will begin setting the rice tomorrow. May I help?" He dropped to a woven mat, watching the man hopefully.

The father shifted position slightly and reached for a clay pipe nearby. "And would you then wish him to help you with your father's cabbages?" He nodded, familiar with their habit in recent years. "You will join us in the water, but you and my son will play more than work. You will not keep up with the others. Soon you will be gone, both of you." He grimaced. "Such antics are of no help. We must plant the rice."

Chung's face reflected his acceptance of the reprimand, but he forged ahead. "When we were children it was so, but now we become men. Kim is my friend. I wish to help him and his family." He looked seriously at the man. "I wish to help you set the seedlings."

The man nodded. "Then it must be real help. Farming the rice is not a game to be played only so long as you enjoy it. When it is no longer fun we must work at it still." He drew easily on the pipe, watching Chung. "What of your father's cabbage? I think he must need your help with his own crop. How can there be kimchi for the winter?"

"Kim is my good friend," replied Chung. "If I help him with his work perhaps he may help me with mine. We can be together, but we will work hard." He paused, but then his face lit with inspiration. "We are not like your neighbor, Pak. He has a son the same age as we. His son does not help him at all."

"Pak uses no discipline," responded the man. "I think his son must one day inherit paddies he will know nothing about. Pak thinks of his son as a child." He pointed at the two with the stem of the pipe. "You see? It is all play and no work."

"He is a boy in a skirt," blurted Kim, now brave, agreeing with his father. "He is afraid to dirty his hands."

"We must not be so hasty to judge others," said his father.

"But we are different," offered Chung. "Pak is lazy, but we are not. We wish to help, to learn. I will learn of rice, yet I will someday inherit my father's cabbages. Kim will inherit your rice, but if he helps me he will know of raising a different crop." He watched the man's face for a reaction, then nodded. "We played at it as children, but now it must be different. We wish to learn, and because we are friends we wish to help each other. Always we will be friends."

The man held up a hand. "We begin tomorrow."

"I shall come early."

"There can be no games. You and my son must work hard."

"We will work very hard."

The man nodded. "Then it shall be so for one more crop. But I warn you both. If you play at games it will not happen again.

Kim and Chung bounded to their feet and started for the door. Then, remembering suddenly, they turned and bowed low to the farmer.

"Where will you go now?" he asked.

"To the village," replied his son. "We will be ready to work tomorrow."

They bounded back along the dike, retracing their steps into the heart of the village. There they found others of their friends. They jostled and laughed with the group, then stopped at sight of another, walking alone.

"Pak thinks he is better than we," sneered Kim. "I think he must not wish to dirty his hands."

Pak's pulse quickened with apprehension. "I do not think myself better," he retorted, his voice high, strained.

"You are no better!" shouted Chung.

"Yes, I am not," he replied. He began walking away.

They followed him, taunting, and he quickened his pace, then broke into a trot.

"Look," laughed Kim in glee. "I think he must fear us."

"Yes," they chorused, leaping to the chase. "Pak. You are a coward, Pak."

A rock struck Pak on the hip. He winced, but ran faster now, limping. They were on him like wolves, relishing the pursuit. He glanced back quickly and saw they were gaining. Frantically, he ducked into an alley, then scrambled for a fence. He was half over it when they caught his ankle and tore him back into their midst.

"Pak is afraid," they taunted, shoving him. "He is a mouse in the darkness. He runs from us."

His eyes were wide in terror. "Do not hurt me," he implored. "I beg you not to hurt me."

"You see?" cried Kim, triumphant. "He would become a beggar."

"I am not a beggar, Kim. I wish to go to my home."

"Then go," replied Kim in disdain. "Go and beg from your father." He grasped his victim's arm and thrust him roughly against the fence. It creaked with the impact.

Pak reached, uncertainly at first, then leaped high, gripping the boards. As he tumbled over the barrier a tossed stick glanced from his shoulder. He knew they would not follow. Slowly, in loneliness, he scuffed his way through back streets to his father's house.

From then on he became more and more the target of pranks. He never fought back, instead seeking ways to escape the nightmares. He took long, lonely walks into the mountains, discovering treasures the others never knew, would not have understood. He never flaunted a beautiful rock, an unusual flower. Wrapping them carefully, he crept home through the dusk and hid them. In the quiet hours he sat and fondled them in admiration.

Then one day an event took place which changed his life. Shortly after the annexation he was rooting through the silence of the mountain. The afternoon was young, the weather not yet cold. The sun, though weakened in strength by the advancing season, still played against the colors of rock, foliage and the distant sea. The air was fresh, the breath invisible. To north and south companion ridges rose from the plain, crowding each other as if endowed with mighty shoulders, bulls against the sky.

As Pak strolled along, relaxed in the power and beauty of the scene, he glanced down and noticed footprints and scuffed earth around a fallen log. Immediately his wariness gripped him. He straightened, looked around at the surrounding underbrush, listening intently. There was no sound. He picked curiously at the heavy log, the evidence of fresh digging. The earth suddenly joined his peers, taunting him, beckoning gleefully at his fear. He dared not dig, would not run. At last, frustrated at his indecisiveness, he wept.

Almost an hour passed, and with it his tears. His hands grew cold and he cursed his timid heart. Then, in a flash of fury, he dove at the log. Tearing, heaving, scraping, he burrowed into the earth more now to escape himself than to satisfy a curiosity.

His fingers were sore, his knuckles bleeding, but he did not notice. At last he shrank back, metal before his eyes. He shuddered, then felt the stream of tears again.

"You shall not frighten me!" he screamed to the silent world. "I shall not run away from you!" Then, wrenched in sobs, he dug about the pit he had created, mindless of time, place, danger.

By late afternoon he had bared a chest, ornately decorated. He grasped a rock, attacking the hasp with wild, bold blows. At last it broke and the lid obeyed his touch.

He gasped in awe. Glistening in the sunlight was the most beautiful brocade he had ever seen. He reached down and felt it, almost with reverence. Then, gingerly lifting a corner of the material, he found others. They seemed to cry out to be seen. Completely absorbed, he dug his hands deeper into the box, then froze.

The shaft of metal was smooth, cold. He worked his fingers around it and drew it from beneath the folds. It was a sword, obviously old, yet the engraved figures along the blade and grip were breathtaking. Ancient warriors posed, interspersed between the great mountains and gushing waterfalls of the Sorak. Along the blade were other figures more finely etched in the gleaming metal.

He grasped the weapon with both hands. Though he could lift it, his adolescent strength was not sufficient to swing it. He rested it on the ground, examining more closely the beauty of its craftsmanship, wondering who could have done the work, where, how long ago. Then, leaning it against a tree, he turned to the greater comfort of the brocades.

Pak did not sleep that night. Little by little, in repeated trips, he moved his newfound treasure through the darkness to his home. Then, its contents safely hidden, he carefully reburied the vault.

Many months passed, but Pak dared not bring his treasure into the open. Once he faced the prospect of having to earn a living, however, necessity dictated greater realism. The thought of farming was repugnant to him, yet he lacked the confidence to apply for the professions. Many of his former antagonists had entered the trades. He knew he would remain their target if he did the same. He decided to become a merchant. The decision was difficult. Apprenticeships were difficult to arrange unless one had funds. He had none. He knew if he immediately displayed his silks for sale independently without having left Hochon he would be accused of theft. Then, guilty or not, he would lose them.

He decided to take a trip. He could then return, having ostensibly purchased the goods, and set up a shop to sell them. Once they were sold he would take the proceeds and buy more.

Pak set out on foot for the larger town of Nampo. As he wandered through the shops he was shocked. No merchant offered fabrics of the beauty of his, yet the prices were much higher than he had imagined possible. He moved on to Pyongyang.

The size of the city was awesome to a country boy. Activity chattered about him in an endless, confusing cacophony. Vendors called their wares to the world, tradesmen shouldered through packets of people in their anxiety to be where they were not. Ragged old women plodded certainly along their courses, oblivious of the passing people. Young women, their dress traditional yet somehow enticing, measured him with bold eyes. He stood bewildered, then wandered deeper into the throngs, unsure of his goal, unaware of where he might eat or find a place to sleep.

After several days of searching he located some fabrics of better quality than he had seen on the market previously. Still, they barely rivaled his. The prices were exorbitant. Pak's heart fell. It would be obvious to anyone purchasing his silks in Hochon that they were more valuable than he could afford. He realized he would have to convert them first into something he could believably sell in the village.

He returned to Hochon, packaged some of the fabrics and set out once more for Pyongyang. He proceeded directly to the district where he had seen the finer fabrics, braced himself with what little courage he had, and entered a shop.

It was cluttered, piled high with fabrics, brass, lacquered furnishings. The aisles were narrow and so cramped that Pak had trouble getting through with his bundle. The merchant watched as he slowly unwrapped the brocades. When he saw them his eyes widened. "Where did you get these?" he demanded.

"I brought them from Seoul," lied Pak. "I was going to give them to my mother, but when I returned home she had died."

The merchant picked one up and spread it out. "And now you want to sell them?"

"Yes, Sir," said Pak meekly.

The merchant riffled through them quickly. "I cannot pay much for these."

"How much?"

The merchant offered a price.

Pak began rewrapping his bundle. "I paid more than that in Seoul."

The merchant raised the price, but Pak continued wrapping. As he was tying the package the merchant made a higher offer.

Pak tucked the bundle under his arm and touched a bolt of the merchandise on the counter. Then, giving the merchant a silent look, he turned toward the door.

"Wait."

Pak stopped and turned.

"How much do you want?"

Slowly Pak returned to the counter. "Mine are better than those," he said, "but you offered me much less than their price."

The merchant sucked in his breath. "You must understand. I have to make a profit."

"You do not have to make that much profit from me," returned Pak, feeling braver. "I only want to get back the money I paid for them. I do not wish to make a profit from you."

"You do not have that many."

"I have more."

The merchant eyed him suspiciously. "How many more do you have?"

"I have many more."

The merchant reached for the bundle. "Let me see them again."

Pak unwrapped the silks and the merchant looked carefully at each. The young man watched him.

"Are the rest as good as these?"

"Yes."

"Will you sell them all to me?"

"I think it must depend upon the price."

The merchant named a new, much higher price. "But only," he added, "if you will sell me all your others."

Pak was pleased but did not show it. "I will sell you all my others if you will promise me as good a price for them."

"Good," said the merchant, digging into his pouch. He paid Pak and reached for the bundle. "Will you be back tomorrow?"

"I will return next week."

"Why must you take so long? I want them tomorrow."

"It will take me several days to get them. They are at my home."

The merchant looked at him suspiciously again. "Where is your home?"

"Far from here," answered Pak. He was nervous now, but dared not let him see.

"I think they are stolen," said the merchant.

"They are mine," answered Pak with uncharacteristic boldness. "I said I would sell them to you, but if you give me trouble I
will take them to someone else. Other merchants will be happy to
buy them."

The merchant nodded. "I will not make trouble for you," he
said. "Bring them to me. I can get a good price anyway."

Pak nodded and left. Once away from the shop he recounted
his money eagerly. He had never imagined he could realize such a
profit. Suddenly the city was not confusing or oppressive any more.
Hurrying, he left for Nampo, where he purchased a large volume
of cheaper goods, some fabrics, but others brass or lacquered handi-
crafts. He wrapped them carefully, anxious not to damage them
on his journey. Then, bent under an A-frame, he began the long
trek home to Hochon.

He stored them safely away, then bundled more of the silks.
Lastly, he wandered through the village, looking critically at the
merchandise on display, trying to locate a space where he might
offer his wares for sale once he had returned with a larger inven-
tory. Empty shops were not numerous, but he found one which
he felt would suffice.

The following week he returned to Pyongyang as promised.
This time he used his A-frame and took the remainder of the fabrics. The load, wrapped in rags, towered high above him but it
matched his heart in lightness. Plodding along the unpaved road,
he hummed to himself. At night he climbed into the hillsides and
slept.

He remained in Pyongyang only a few hours, long enough to
deliver the fabrics. Then, armed with far more money than he had
ever before seen, he passed through Nampo and purchased more
goods. Upon his return to Hochon he opened his small shop in
the center of the village. It was well stocked. The people chuckled
but bought from him. The other merchants watched and grumbled.
Pak remained apart from everyone and quietly reinvested his profits in his growing business.

He was aware, however, that the competition would become more fierce. The other merchants in Hochon, though few, had been in business for many years. They could, and would, squeeze him to the point of closing if he were not visionary enough to outmaneuver them. He lay on his mat at night and thought, trying to discern what might be the quickest and surest way to defend against them. He thought of his sword, laughing at himself for even considering such foolishness. Even now he doubted he would be able to swing it. Suddenly he sat upright. The sword!

He scurried from his mat and struggled across the fields and up the mountain. He located the hole, scraped at the soil to make the digging look new, and raced back home. Next morning, a look of hope painted across his face, he made his way to the courthouse.

A Japanese soldier stopped him as he climbed the steps. "What is that you have?"

"I have a sword," he replied brightly.

"Where did you get it? You know Koreans are not allowed to have weapons."

Pak, frightened, held up the blade. "I found it. I came to give it to the commander of the Imperial Militia."

The soldier looked at him suspiciously. "We shall see that you do. Come with me."

He led Pak down a barren corridor and into an office. An officer looked up as they entered and bowed. Then his gaze traveled down to the sword and he rose. "What have we here? A Hochonese bearing arms?"

The soldier started to speak but Pak blurted out ahead of him. "I found this sword and I brought it here to give it to you."

The officer was guarded. "To me? Why should you wish to give it to me?"

Pak became subordinate. "Because we are not allowed to own weapons. I found it on the mountain and thought I should turn it in."

The officer reached out and took the sword. As he looked at

the blade he inhaled deeply. He looked up again at Pak. "Do you know what this is?"

"Yes, Captain. It is a sword."

The officer was running his finger down the blade, almost with reverence, but did not comment further. "Where on the mountain did you find it?"

"I can take you there."

"By all means, you must. What were you doing on the mountain? Do you work there?"

"No. I am a merchant. After I close my shop I go for walks."

"When did you find this? Certainly you have not been walking this morning."

"Yes, I have not. I found it last night."

The officer sat down and jotted some notes on a piece of paper. "What is your name?"

"Pak. I am a merchant."

"Yes. You said that."

"I only began my business a short time ago."

The officer rose. "Assemble a squad," he ordered the soldier. "We shall go to the mountain and see where this was hidden."

"It was in a beautiful box. The box is still there."

"Good."

They hurried down the steps of the courthouse and across the earthen square. The other merchants watched and smiled. "Pak did not remain in business long," they chuckled. "Already he is in trouble."

"Perhaps he was stealing his merchandise from the Japanese." They laughed, relieved that the newest competition was no longer existent.

As they neared the hole on the mountain, the officer looked at Pak. "Do you know the value of the sword?"

"I do not deal in swords," he replied.

"It is a national treasure," continued the officer.

Pak's face froze in amazement. Perhaps he had done the wrong thing. If it were a national treasure he might have been able to sell it. They were now at the hole. The soldiers removed the box and opened it. It was empty. They gestured to the officer without speaking.

"That is all there was? The sword?"

"Yes, Sir."

The officer pursed his lips. "How strange. A box this large and nothing in it but a sword."

Pak felt a twinge of apprehension but knew they could prove nothing.

"Are you sure there was nothing else?"

"Yes. I am most sure. When I found it there was only this box with a sword in it. I was afraid someone was planning an insurrection so I took it home with me and brought it to you this morning." He looked repentant. "I did not know it was a national treasure."

The officer had knelt and was looking at the figures on the box.

"If it is that valuable perhaps it is the work of thieves," ventured Pak.

"Without a doubt," replied the officer. "Many items from the national treasure are missing. It appears the thieves were most busy in Seoul before the annexation." He motioned for the soldiers to bring the box and they began winding their way back down the mountain toward the village. "You may be rewarded for this," said the officer.

Pak concealed his exuberance with feigned surprise. "I think I should not receive anything. I did only what I knew was right."

The officer looked at him without smiling. "Not many in your country would have done the same. They are too busy resisting us."

Pak appeared pensive. "I did not do it in the hope of receiving a reward."

The officer nodded, still unsmiling. "But we should set an example. It would help to eliminate the resistance if we rewarded you. Perhaps a medal, money."

"I do not want that."

Now the officer was surprised. "What do you mean? Do you refuse a reward?"

Pak shrugged. "I cannot refuse an honor. I would not insult the emperor by refusing. I would rather serve him."

"How would you do that?"

"There is no warehouse in Hochon."

"Hochon is a small village. We are supplied from the larger centers."

"May I build a warehouse? It would save the Japanese the trouble of constantly shipping things to and from the other areas. I could keep things here for Hochon's use. I think it must help your soldiers and police."

The officer continued walking in silence.

Pak chattered on. "I am young. I have been a merchant only a short time but I wish to grow with Korea. I believe our country must grow most strong with the help of the Japanese."

The officer smiled. "It will become very strong. You may be sure of that."

Nothing further was said, but during the following weeks a great warehouse was constructed in Hochon. It was large, with an earthen floor, a heavily thatched roof. To Pak's surprise and delight, the Japanese supplied the materials and labor. His only requirement was to move in as manager once the construction was complete.

* * * * * *

"Chung!"

Chung had emerged from the Japanese Occupation Office. He turned, his spirits high.

"Kim. Come walk with me. I have received good news."

Surprise splashed across Kim's features. "What good news? I think there is very little of that now. Stop. Tell me."

"I must tell my father right away. I will tell you if you will walk to my home with me." He smiled happily, beckoning to his friend.

They walked impatiently through streets unpaved and rutted. The village, though small, was busy. They bumped ungraciously from vendor to vendor, shopper to errand boy. The clatter of carts spiraled about them, yet conversation was subdued, furtive. A population once effusive now seemingly endeavored to maintain its vitality, yet robe itself in whispers. The incongruity left them drained, frustrated, suspicious.

"Did they arrest you and set you free?" asked Kim cautiously, his squat legs hurrying to keep up with the taller Chung.

"I am to be sent away to study," replied Chung.

"It may be a trick. You know they are not to be trusted. Everyone knows they find it amusing to tease us. They play with us as a cat does mice."

Chung, still hurrying, shook his head. "I took an examination. They told me I received very high grades. They will send me to the university."

Kim snorted. "They will teach you to fight in their army but you will not be sent back to Korea. You will become the meat on a Chinese bayonet. You must keep their own from dying."

"They will teach me the law."

Kim was almost breathless, tiring from the pace and anxious with Chung's news. "Stop, my friend," he panted. "Wait." He held out his hand and the other youth slowed, the joy still radiating from his eyes. Kim motioned to a hummock beside the path. They were beyond the village and the mountains crept in on them through the clear air. Summer hummed about them and it was hot.

"It has been three years since they came. What have we seen during that time? They said they came to protect us, to allow us to grow as a nation. Instead, they have brought nothing but oppression. Our land has become a police state. We are prisoners in our homes, in our villages. I think there can be no success for a Korean."

Chung, anxious to go home, remained standing. "Pak is successful," he offered.

"Pak!" Kim spat it out derisively. "They have made him a puppet. It is a perfect example of their oppression. They will take those who are weak and make them strong. They will suppress those who have been our leaders and make them beg for rice. They will destroy our good and promote that which is useless, and in doing that they will weaken us. We will recognize ourselves only by the grass on which we walk, the huts in which we sleep. No longer will we be men, but slaves."

Chung shifted impatiently, started to speak, then hesitated.

Kim grasped a stick and tapped it on the ground. "They can do it only if they divide us. If we remain united against them I think they will not be able to destroy us as a people. They know that, Chung. They know the only way they can discredit our leaders is to pick us apart, to select a few and make them into puppets. Then, when we resist, they will say we are criminals, renegades. They will hold up the weaklings who have abandoned us for their own comfort and say, 'Look. These Koreans are successful. These Koreans love us, but these others are rebels.' With that, more of our people will turn to them, and more after them. At last only a few of the strong loyalists will be left."

"And they will swat us down as flies," interjected Chung. "Is that what you want, Kim? Do you wish to be brushed aside as an annoyance of the past? That is all any of us can become unless we act now."

"What would you do?" asked Kim in surprise. "Revolt? Would you rise up against them and drive them away? Their army has put down many revolts."

Chung sat now, tentative but absorbed. "Kim, they would kill us all. They have a large army and we have none. No, we cannot revolt, but we can preserve ourselves in other ways."

"Then you will not go to their university? You will not forsake us?" asked Kim excitedly.

Chung shook his head slowly, seriously. "I will not forsake our people, but I must go to their university."

"Why?" Kim was shocked. "They will change you."

"In a way, I will infiltrate them," Chung replied simply.

Kim was incredulous. "Infiltrate them?" He laughed. "You cannot infiltrate the Japanese. They are in complete control. It is they who will infiltrate you. They will gain control over your mind."

Chung gazed pensively out across the rice paddies. A farmer stumbled through water half way to his knees behind a monotonously plodding ox. The sun beat down and Chung reflected on the discomfort of the man's toil and the dubious relief the water afforded him. "What will become of him?" he asked suddenly, motioning toward the man.

Kim followed his gesture. "The farmer? He must work out his life in that same paddy. He will be oppressed by the Japanese and his crops will be confiscated, exactly like yours and mine. I think he has no hope for the future."

Chung nodded. "Yes. And if he goes astray, does not obey their laws, what will they do to him?"

"They will throw him in prison," moaned Kim. "If he is fortunate they will kill him."

"They will do these things to him because he has no understanding of the Japanese laws. They will be able to do these things to all of us because we will understand only that such things are rules to be followed, orders given and received. And when we are arrested we will have no way to defend ourselves against the interrogation, no way to represent ourselves in our trials."

"Yes," agreed Kim quickly. "You see? That is what I have said to you. We are their slaves. We have no way to defend against their oppression."

"So we must lose our crops to them today. Tomorrow our sons will go into their army, our daughters into their beds. They will tighten their control over us. Yes, it will be much worse than now. Our only protection will be to know their laws, their customs. If we know what to expect it will be easier."

"No," rasped Kim. "You are wrong. Knowing will not make it easier. It will only make the game more fun for the cat." His eyes narrowed as he glared at Chung. "Yes. You will join them because you fear them. But I will not. They will not subdue me. Never. I will become as the dragon. I will breathe my fire at them. You will see, Chung. They will not be here forever, and when they are gone, I will remain. I will win in the end."

Chung shook his head, but spoke quietly, ignoring the threat. "If we rely on their laws and their lawyers we will lose everything. They will interpret as they wish, as it best fits their needs, and we will be none the wiser."

"But if you go and learn, how can you help us? You will be watched, perhaps not even allowed to return."

"Perhaps that is so, but perhaps not. If I were a prisoner I would rather have a Korean lawyer interceding for me than a Japanese. Or no one. They are merciless, Kim."

"Perhaps you could advise us, tell us what they plan," suggested Kim hopefully.

"Perhaps I could keep our people out of prison," added Chung.

"And perhaps," said Kim slowly, "we would never see you again. You could be sent elsewhere."

Chung nodded. "And another Korean sent here. I think it does not matter. I would be helping our people somewhere." He rose. "I must tell my father."

"And I must tell the others," added Kim, also rising. "We wish you good fortune, Chung. May they return you to the people of Hochon in the future."

Chung smiled gratefully. "I shall try," he replied.

Kim put a hand on Chung's arm, gazing meaningfully into his eyes. "You have been my best friend, Chung. Ever since we were children you have been my best friend."

Chung nodded, smiling.

"Someday we will remember these years. We may not ever know our freedom as it has been. The Japanese are seeing to that even now. But we will remember Korea and take pride in what it has meant to be Korean."

Chung stared at him, moved. "Yes, Kim. They have been good

years. Now it is our challenge to keep our Korean people as free and safe as we can."

* * * * * *

Pyun was asleep when the pounding began at the gate. It was officious from the start, but only when it went unanswered did the soldiers begin shouting, replacing the fists with the thunderous crash of rifle butts against the wood.

Pyun's wife shook him in horror. "They are here. The Japanese have come."

Pyun, his head still dazed from sleep and numerous bottles of mokle during the evening, merely grunted.

"Husband," she urged. "Wake up. It is the Japanese."

The shouts were louder now. Pyun rolled over and sat up. "Would they beat down my gate?" he groaned rhetorically. "Why do they come at such an hour?" He rose unsteadily and wove toward the door, sliding it back quietly, watching.

"Pyun," shouted a voice. "Open your gate and let us in. We wish to visit with you." The language was Japanese.

Pyun waited, trying desperately to clear his head.

"Must we let ourselves in?" demanded the voice.

Moments later there was a scraping sound on the wall and a head appeared in the darkness, boosted to the top by others below. Pyun reached quickly for a walking stick which leaned against the wall inside his door. Then, with a growl, he dove into the tiny courtyard, meeting the scaling soldier with a vicious attack the instant he dropped to the ground. The man let out a yell and a moment later two more soldiers dropped into the courtyard to assist him. Bayonets gleamed in the moonlight as they prodded Pyun back. At last, flailing only weakly with his cane, he realized his cause was hopeless. He dropped the weapon, glaring silently at the intruders. One of the men reached for the gate.

"Good evening, Pyun," smiled the Japanese officer, entering grandly as if nothing had happened. "I hope you will forgive my visiting you at such a late hour, but I have been most busy in my office." He stopped and stared at Pyun for a moment. "I am Captain Goto, and I am the commander of the Imperial Militia. What do you think of that?"

Pyun said nothing.

"I have been hearing many tales about the people of Hochon since my arrival. I am told they do not appreciate the protection being provided them by my soldiers. Naturally, this has troubled me greatly, so I have been talking with several of the people in my great desire to learn the reason for this unhappiness." He reached into his pocket and withdrew a cigarette, lighting it slowly. "Pyun, you are not the first person I have visited, and you will not be the last. You are most important to my investigation, however, because you seem to have some very definite ideas. I have heard them all over the village. What do you think of that?"

Apprehension gnawed inside him, but he stared back at the officer with a blank expression. "I do not know what you are talking about," he replied in Hangul.

Goto placed his hands on his hips, raising his lip in a sneer. "What kind of noise is that?" He turned to his soldiers and asked again, "Did any of you hear a strange sound?"

The soldiers laughed.

"It sounded like those barbaric mutterings one heard in this place when we first came," mused the captain. "Such sounds have been banned for so long I find it difficult to be sure." He turned back to Pyun. "Are you not well? If you are not well we shall have a doctor examine you."

The soldiers were still laughing and Goto, encouraged by their enjoyment of the scene, continued. "Now, Pyun, it will be most difficult for us to visit if you do not talk with me. To stand there making all sorts of croaking sounds at me will do no good at all. If you are ill we shall have you treated. If you are well but do not understand our language we shall have you trained. It is all part of our protection of you and your people, part of the kindness of the Emperor." He turned to the soldiers. "We will go now. Bring him."

"*Anio!*" shouted Pyun. "I do not wish to go with you."

Goto stopped and looked at him, but only for a moment. Then, continuing through the gate, he motioned for the others to follow.

The prison cell was cramped, the floor earthen. The space was further restricted by the presence of a box overflowing with excrement. Five other prisoners shared the space, which resulted in none being able to lie down for sleep. Talking was forbidden, the rule enforced by an alert guard immediately outside the cell. Food consisted of a small bowl of cold rice and a cup of thin broth twice each day. The rice was infested with lice, the broth merely a cold liquid support for buttons of congealed grease which floated around the surface.

Five days after his arrest Pyun was separated from the others and led before the militia commander. Goto sat behind a large table, aloof and stiff. "Tell me of your displeasure with your imperial protectors," he demanded.

Pyun swayed wearily, trying to focus his sleepless eyes on his antagonist.

"Speak up," ordered Goto impatiently. "I have many things to do. I have no time to sit here waiting for you to humor me."

"I have nothing to say," muttered Pyun.

"What? Nothing to say to me? But you have been saying things to all the village for weeks, months. You have told everyone in the village how unhappy you are with all the kindness we are showing you and your people. You have called us names I will not even take the time to repeat. Certainly you must remember what your unhappiness is all about. I demand that you tell me now. If you do not tell me I shall become most unhappy, too, and that will mean you must become very uncomfortable. What do you think about that?"

"I have nothing to say," repeated Pyun.

"Dog!" exploded Goto. "The others have talked with me. They have told me why they are unhappy and we have been able to discuss it. They have discovered they were very wrong, that they were most happy after all. They had not realized how happy they were until we discussed the matter."

Pyun lapsed into silence, staring tiredly ahead at the wall.

"You may be interested to know that your friends have also told me the reasons for your unhappiness. They have told me of the things you have been saying about me and my militia. I wish to help you, Pyun. I would like to be able to send you from this room a happy man, a man who would recognize how very good I can be to those who are willing to talk with me."

"If you know what I have said I think there is no need for me to tell you. I do not wish to talk with you."

Goto leaped to his feet. "You have been tried," he screamed. "I have tried to talk with you. You are not worth my effort." He turned to the guards. "Call the village together. Assemble them all here, in the village square. I shall make a speech. I shall explain to them what this dog has done to them. Hochon will be most unhappy with him, because they will be punished for his insults." He reached for his cap and sword, strapping the weapon petulantly about his waist. "And bring his wife to me. Quickly. There are many Japanese soldiers to be comforted. She will be their whore. This man has no more need of her."

Pyun looked up at him in horror. "No," he screamed. "You cannot. She is my wife. She is to comfort me! Your soldiers cannot take her."

Goto paused and turned, staring dispassionately at the prisoner for only a moment. Then, breaking into a broad smile, he turned and left the room.

An hour later the square had filled with people. They looked at one another, wondering what had happened, not knowing the reason for the assembly. A ring of soldiers had formed to their rear, watchful and still. At last Goto appeared, behind him a pair of soldiers prodding the stumbling Pyun down the steps to the open area before the crowd.

The captain strutted to a point where he could be seen by all. Then, clearing his voice, he began his speech.

"The Emperor is saddened today. He has tried to bring peace and protection to the people of this village. He has sent me here to see that you are happy and contented, that you have no problems or worries. It has come to his attention, however, that some of the people of Hochon are not happy with his efforts to bring you happiness. Some of your people have been saying cruel and untrue things about him. It saddened me when I learned of these things, and I have tried to talk with those who said them. Many of the people who were unhappy have changed their minds. Today, however, I have found the one who has been stirring up all the trouble. I have found the man who has been starting the lies about us, the one who has been ungrateful to the Emperor for all his kindness. I have tried to talk with this man but he has refused to talk with me. He has insulted the Emperor and my soldiers for trying to make all of you happy. Naturally, I cannot allow this to continue. I cannot allow such a man to remain among such a happy people, causing hate and discontent to creep into your lives as a result of lies and false accusations. The others were merely followers, but this is a leader. The others have seen the error of their ways, but this man continues to level insults. It is so with all who would be creators of hate. I hope he is the only one, that this will be the only time I shall have to call you together for such a sad event. If you continue to be a happy people, there will be no need for us to repeat such a spectacle, but be assured that if the need arises I shall not hesitate. I am here to see that you remain happy." He paused thoughtfully for a moment. "Of course, I must be certain the soldiers remain happy as well. To make sure they do, this man's wife will provide comfort for them."

The woman, standing nearby in the grip of guards, looked aghast. "No," she whimpered. "Please. . . ."

Goto turned to the soldiers and flicked his wrist. Immediately they forced Pyun to his knees. He looked up at them, only now beginning to realize what was happening. He whipped his head around to see Goto drawing the sword. "*Anio!*" he shouted. "No!"

Goto said nothing, the sneer now broad across his features.

Pyun scrambled, trying to rise. The soldiers forced him down once more. The prisoner struggled in futility, spitting angrily at his captors. Then, as suddenly as he had become violent, he subsided, his voice a soft whimper. "*Anio.*"

The militia commander stepped forward, now preening with importance. The square was hushed, only the heat of summer crying out for attention. Then, with a grunt of exertion, Goto brought the sword crashing down on his victim's skull.

THE SOUTH—CHUNCHON

Murashige lay on the pallet, flushed, feverish. Occasionally a moan crept from his cracked lips. Otherwise he was still, the time measured by his quick, shallow breathing. The militia commander watched quietly for a few minutes, assessing the situation. At last the sick man turned his head and looked at the officer.

"Where is Yoon?"

"He is with the soldiers. They will watch him until your replacement arrives."

Suddenly, pleading anxiety glistened in the tired eyes. "Please do not replace me. I do not need another to replace me."

The commander leaned forward consolingly. "You must not worry. I shall send you home where you can receive better medical attention."

"No." The reply was forced, pained. "I must stay. I will be better soon."

The commander dismissed the thought. "I must have a healthy builder. I must have a man who can withstand this climate."

"I can," protested Murashige. I have been here five years, ever since annexation. Never have I been ill before." He reached weakly for a bowl of water near the pallet.

"Here. Allow me to help." The officer lifted the bowl to Murashige's lips, supporting the head with his other hand. The man sipped gratefully, then lay back.

"You see?" observed the commander. "You cannot even drink

water without assistance. How do you expect to oversee the workers?"

"I know I will recover soon."

"It will not be the same. Winter is already upon us. Your resistance will be low, even if you recover."

"Yoon will help me," whispered Murashige.

"Yoon? A Korean?" The commander sniffed. "Such a thought
is ridiculous."

"He has proved himself to be intelligent and reliable."

"I agree he has done so, with you watching him. He has
been very loyal to all of us. But he has never been tested on his
own. You must remember, Murashige, these people cannot be
trusted. The moment we are not vigilant he will probably steal
from us."

"I did not trust him in the beginning, but I have watched
him. He works hard and controls the laborers very well. He is an
excellent foreman." Suddenly he doubled up on the pallet in a fit
of coughing, his face deep red from the effort. At last, the spasm
over, he lay back and closed his eyes, breathing quietly.

The officer said nothing but watched patiently. At last, convinced he was asleep, he started to leave.

"Major Kometani." The hoarse voice was insistent.

"I thought you were sleeping," said Kometani, resignedly sitting once more.

"It is a matter of honor, Major," whispered Murashige.

Kometani was surprised. "Honor? What has illness to do with
honor?"

"My family is very traditional. It is most important. If you
send me home I will be disgraced."

"But you have done nothing wrong."

"If my family is shamed my home village will despise me. You
know that."

Kometani sucked his breath through clenched teeth. "You ask
much of me. To save your face in some nameless village you wish
me to jeopardize our entire program in the city of Chunchon."

Murashige's eyelids were heavy but he persisted. "I must do it. Can you not understand?"

The major nodded. "I understand. You would use this Yoon to save your face."

"With Yoon I can do the work even while lying here."

Kometani sat back, weighing the situation. "There is so much to be done. The railroad is of critical importance. Then there are the other projects, the buildings, the highways. This city has been isolated for too many years."

Murashige reached for another sip of water and Kometani helped him. The breathing was labored as much with anxiety as disease, the plea driven by passion. "Send Yoon to visit with me every morning and every night. Have him watched carefully on the work sites if you do not trust him. In a short time I shall be able to return."

Kometani rose. "One week. We shall try it for one week before we make a decision. But you must remember, my friend. If our programs fall behind the disgrace will be much greater than that of a small village. Any failure will be a disgrace to the Emperor."

Murashige nodded weakly. "I shall not forget."

The commander stepped from the building into the cold, pulling his coat more tightly about him. His pace quickened as he turned a corner toward the new rail terminal. In the yard, hundreds of men were bending with shovels, picks, hammers. The cold and snow made progress slow. The swath of the roadbed was widening almost imperceptibly. Ties were being wrestled into place at one end of the area.

In their midst an overseer was hustling from one group to the next. "Measure it correctly," he cautioned. "The timbers must be exactly aligned." He hurried on to the next group. "Is that area level?"

"Yes. We have inspected it."

"How well did you inspect it?" squinted the foreman. "I think you had your mind more on the cold than the work. It appears uneven on that corner." He pointed. "See? It has a hump. The earth must be absolutely level."

He turned and took a paper from a waiting aide. Scanning it quickly, he scribbled on the sheet and handed it back.

Kometani stepped forward. "Yoon."

The man wheeled abruptly and bowed low in greeting. "Good morning, Major."

"You know, I suppose, that Murashige is most ill?"

"Yes, Sir. I was told."

"I shall probably have to send him home to Japan soon."

Yoon showed his surprise. "I am sorry. I did not think it that serious."

Kometani nodded. "Of course, if I send him home there will be a replacement."

Yoon expected it. "Of course. I shall do all I can to help the new man."

Kometani was serious but not threatening. "I am sure you will. In the meantime you are responsible to see that all the projects progress smoothly. I will not tolerate any of them falling behind, particularly the railroad."

"I shall not embarrass you, Major," Yoon assured him. "The projects will continue on schedule."

"I want you to see Murashige regularly," continued the major, not seeming to hear him. "You will visit him every morning and every night. Keep him informed of everything which happens. Follow his instructions very carefully."

"Yes, Major."

With a curt nod Kometani was gone. Yoon turned to his aide. They spoke quietly for a few moments, then parted and the aide made his way into the city.

* * * * * *

Chunchon is situated midway across the peninsula somewhat northeast of Seoul. It occupies a flat valley kept fertile by a river which tumbles down from Hwachon. After coursing past the city it continues south for several miles, then ducks furtively behind a mountain ridge to the southwest. Thus free of the city it hurries westward toward a rendezvous with the River Han.

Rising from the center of the valley is a single, bulging mass of a mountain which lingers in solitude some two thousand feet above the valley floor. The city nestles lovingly against its lower slopes, as though some long forgotten people took pity on the lonely outcast, sitting away as it does from the ridges of the north and west, the mighty Sorak range to the east.

While previous invaders of Korea had spent their concentrated horrors on Seoul and the other major cities, Chunchon had been largely ignored due to its isolation. The Japanese, however, were different. Their soldiers permeated every village, every lone rice cottage with their rule. The people of Chunchon grumbled but did not resist. Gradually they learned to hate but did not rebel.

Yoon had been one of the earliest to seek employment with the Japanese. When the occupation office was first opened he had risen early. The Japanese construction supervisor, seeking a foreman, found Yoon's name at the top of the list.

"Do you speak Japanese?"

"Yes, Sir."

"What do you know of construction?"

"I have built things."

Murashige snorted. "Such a reply tells me nothing."

Yoon looked confused. "I have built houses."

"I am not seeking builders of mud huts. Such things are for wasps and the animals of the river."

Yoon was demeaned. "I have worked on buildings in Chunchon."

The supervisor was not impressed. "What do you know of building railroads?"

"We have never had a railroad here. We are very isolated in Chunchon."

"Your reply does not answer my question."

Yoon began to perspire. "I know nothing of building railroads. I have never been away from Chunchon. No man in the city knows how to build railroads."

"Do you know many of the men in the city?"

"Yes, many. I have always lived here."

"What has been your past work? Be specific."

Yoon began enumerating.

"The construction. Tell me about the construction."

He took a deep breath and began describing simple laboring tasks.

Murashige began making notes. "You will report to me here tomorrow morning. I will explain your work to you then." He stroked his forehead in boredom. "I must make do with the best of a poor lot. You may as well be the first."

Yoon rose, excited. "Thank you. Thank you very much."

Murashige looked at him without warmth. "I shall expect you to work very hard and follow my instructions exactly. We have no patience with anyone who cannot do as he is told."

"I will," Yoon said. "I will learn quickly."

Yoon became preeminent by default. When few others applied for work they were conscripted. Only those who had enlisted became foremen. Yoon learned meticulousness more than construction, intimidation more than leadership. By the time Murashige had fallen ill much of his earlier apprehension had evaporated in the face of Yoon's performance.

The railroad was pushing eastward from Seoul. Murashige's responsibility began at the bend of the river south of the city and carried to a point some miles north. From there the Hwachon area was building a spur north while the Inje command was assigned responsibility for a line up the Soyong River to the northeast.

The aide approached the building in which Murashige lay. A soldier stepped forward. "You do not belong here. What do you want?"

"I have been sent here to receive instructions from the construction supervisor."

"Murashige is ill. No one may enter."

The aide looked perplexed. "But Foreman Yoon has sent me. Major Kometani said Foreman Yoon is to act for the supervisor while he is ill."

"Are you Yoon?"

"No. I am his aide."

The soldier gave him a look of disgust. "Go away. Go back to your work."

"I cannot. Foreman Yoon has sent me. I cannot return until I talk with the supervisor."

The soldier looked at him suspiciously, then stepped back. "Kimura," he called over his shoulder.

There was an answering call from inside and a moment later another Japanese appeared at the door. "What is the trouble?"

"This man claims to be Foreman Yoon's aide. He says Yoon has sent him here to talk with Murashige."

Kimura turned to the aide. "What is your name?"

"Min."

"Only Min?"

"Yes."

Kimura reentered the building. Min started after him but the soldier took his arm. "You will wait here."

Soon Kimura returned. "Follow me."

They walked down a corridor and into a small, dimly lit room. Murashige lay on a pallet.

Min bowed low to the ailing man and stepped back.

"Is this the correct man?" asked Kimura.

Murashige nodded and Kimura left.

"What do you want? Is something wrong?"

"Nothing is wrong, Supervisor. Major Kometani came to the work site and told Foreman Yoon he would be in charge. He told the foreman to come and talk with you every morning and every night."

Murashige smiled weakly, fleetingly, then became serious. "Why did Yoon send you now?"

"He received the instructions and wishes to know if there is something you want him to do before he comes here tonight. He would not leave the construction site when the men are working."

Murashige sighed, relieved. "Tell him to inspect each of the projects today. I must know if there are any slow areas, especially on the railroad construction." He paused, tired. "Tell Yoon not to forget the headquarters building."

"Yes, Sir."

Murashige was quiet, looking at him.

"Is there anything more, Supervisor?"

Murashige shook his head slowly. "There are other things but I must tell him myself. They are not important for today. Tell him to come here this evening." He choked momentarily. "Tell him to bring the construction schedules and the supply list."

"Yes, Sir."

Murashige dismissed him with a tired wave of his hand. Min turned and went out to the corridor. Kimura was there, very close to the door. Together they walked to the building entrance.

"Tell your man Yoon to come himself next time." Kimura was plainly antagonistic.

Min merely glanced at him and went down the steps into the snow.

"If he sends you again I will not let you in," called the soldier.

"Yes, Sir," called Min, breaking into a trot in the direction of the rail terminal.

* * * * * *

"Why do you come to me with such tales?" exploded Yoon, looking angrily at the foreman.

Hong, nervous at his wrath, nonetheless continued. "We tell you because he is the real thief. Ahn would rob you of your position, your life." He looked anxiously out from the construction hut into which he had drawn Yoon. "The others agree. All your other foremen are with you. Only Ahn would make trouble."

Yoon squatted. "Then it appears I must do something. I think I must rid myself of this animal."

Hong remained standing, silent now, and waited.

"Has he gone to the major with his stories?"

"I think he has not had time. He was first trying to take us with him."

"Why?"

"When Murashige was taken ill everyone thought it would be only for a short time. Ahn was most annoyed when the major made you the temporary supervisor but he thought it was not for a very long time."

Yoon looked up at the foreman, his face expressionless. "Does it disappoint you that I have remained in the position longer than you had expected? Or is it that you are concerned for Murashige's health?"

"I am most happy to work for you," returned Hong with passion. "It is Ahn. Ahn is the one who is trying to cause you trouble."

"I will complete the railroad," growled Yoon. "The supervisor will not be back among us. It is already spring."

"Ahn told us he would rather work for a new Japanese than for you."

"Then we shall give him the opportunity," rasped Yoon. "We shall arrange for him to work for the Japanese every day for the rest of his life." He smiled. "I think the true thief will soon be discovered."

"What will you do?" asked Hong.

Yoon looked at him, still smiling. "You should be asking what we will do. We shall do it together. All of us."

Hong shifted uneasily.

"There is a shed behind Ahn's house. It shall be found by the Japanese, very full of construction materials from the new headquarters building. It is his project. It should be easy to convince the Japanese to look behind his house."

"What will you do?" asked Hong again.

"We will remove materials from the headquarters and place them in Ahn's shed."

"But he will hear us. I think he will hear the noise and come from his house to expose us."

Yoon watched the tiny rivulets of the thawing earth dancing past the door. "Then we must decide how to remove him from his house while we place the materials in his shed."

"But how are we to remove the materials from the headquarters building? There are many guards."

They squatted in silence, thinking. The sky was clear, warm, sharp in its contrast with the mud around them.

"There must be a diversion," said Yoon. "The guards must be lured away from the building."

"It must be very carefully planned," cautioned Hong. "Anything which would draw the guard from the building would draw other soldiers. There could be a riot. They would kill many of us."

"But if it were not something evil which lured them away there would be no danger from the soldiers. If there were to be something they would enjoy, a celebration, they could be distracted for a short time."

"There are no celebrations in Chunchon. The Japanese would soon put an end to any celebration by the people of Chunchon."

"They would not stop a celebration which was complimentary to them. If it were something they enjoy back in Japan they would not stop it."

"But then our own people would have nothing to do with it."

Yoon watched him. "Is there not something we all have in common? The Japanese and the Koreans?"

Hong hung his head. "Neither the Japanese nor the Koreans would ever admit to having anything in common."

"You are wrong, my friend. We have the railroad. We all want the railroad to come to Chunchon." He scurried to his feet. "You must arrange for the materials to be moved to Ahn's shed. I will prepare the other details."

Yoon talked with Murashige, then hurried to the office of the militia commander.

"I do not understand such a request," said Kometani, beginning to laugh. "A bon dance in the spring?"

Yoon tried to ignore the ridicule. "Yes, Honorable Major. We understand it is most unusual."

"It is not unusual, it is ridiculous. A bon dance is a summer celebration. I think such an affair in the spring merely emphasizes ignorance."

Yoon did not retreat. "We wish to celebrate the progress of the railroad. We have worked through a long and difficult winter. The laborers have been very cold, but they have worked hard. The railroad is ahead of schedule. I think a bon dance would encourage them."

The major scoffed. "Would you enjoin the spirits of our ancestors at the wrong season of the year?"

"Major Kometani, a bon dance need not be religious. I think this must be a secular celebration. It is a custom we share in common, your people and ours. I wish them to see also the common benefit of the railroad. It will mean a better life for the people of Chunchon. If they recognize this sharing, even through a bon dance, I think the production will increase." He sighed. "There has been too much difference between our people."

Kometani's expression had changed to one of interest. "Where will you do this?"

"In the square at the front of the new headquarters building. Soon that will be the central square of Chunchon. It would be wise to make them consider it so now. It will make later changes easier, I think." His expression was full of hope.

Kometani nodded condescendingly. "You must remember one thing. I shall surround the square and your bon dance with militia. At the first sign of resistance or insurrection I will show you no mercy."

Yoon bowed silently, respectful of the man's power.

"Tomorrow night. Make your plans for tomorrow night." He stared at Yoon, distrustful, and started to speak. Then, thinking again, he merely sat and reached for his papers.

* * * * * *

Major Kometani stood at the edge of the crowd, watching
with interest. The soft glow from paper lanterns caressed the square.
At the center rose an enclosed tower. At its base was propped a
huge drum, its head being struck authoritatively, and the rim with
gentle taps, by a costumed elder. Around it, slowly, like a snake,
wove a thin line of dancers. "You see, Major? We have succeeded,"
exulted Yoon. "Many people have come out."

"Yes, but only a few of them are dancing."

Yoon nodded. "The rest are curious. Sooner or later all of them
will be participating. More people will come out for such things
in the future."

"I will be impressed only if it results in greater production. I
have no time to conduct such affairs merely to humor them."

"I think we will not be disappointed," said Yoon quietly. He
wandered off through the crowd, looking. Soldiers were everywhere.
Around the edges of the crowd they craned their necks to see the
winding line of dancers. Yoon looked toward the new building
under construction, large and dark behind the people. The guard
was not in view. He circled around the perimeter of the onlookers.

"Where are you going?" The soldier was brusque, threatening.

Yoon drew up haughtily. "I am the director of the bon dance.
I have come back to ask the militia if they are enjoying themselves."

The soldier was ashamed. "It is much like home."

Yoon relaxed, looking around. "I know. It must be difficult for
you to stand here at the rear. I am sorry they will not allow you to
join us."

The soldier was more at ease now. "But they will not. We
must remain alert."

"A most regrettable situation," said Yoon, moving on. He kept
his eye on the construction site all the way along that side of the
square. There was no guard to be seen. Yoon was certain the man
would be among the soldiers along the back of the crowd watch-

ing the festivities. He began working his way into the crowd again, intent on seeing Hong's signal. A half hour later Hong stepped into the center of the dancing area and joined the line circling the platform.

Yoon took the cue and approached the major. "Sir, it is obvious they enjoy themselves, but we must be certain they are wide awake for tomorrow's work. Would it be possible to end the festivities now?"

The commander yawned and motioned to a young officer. "Tell them it is finished."

"Yes, Sir." He moved off toward the platform. "Stop the music," he shouted. "The bon dance is over. Go home."

The people looked at him in disgust, but slowly began sifting out of the square.

* * * * * *

Major Kometani looked up as Yoon entered the room. "Is something wrong?"

Yoon bowed quickly, agitated. "Yes, Major. I am told one of the foremen has been stealing."

Kometani, not startled, sat back calmly to hear him out.

"My aide is outside. He has brought this matter to my attention."

"Which foreman is it?"

"Ahn. He is the foreman for the construction at the new headquarters building."

Kometani started in alarm. Ahn had talked with him earlier in the morning to suggest Yoon should be watched carefully. "Have the stolen goods been recovered?" he asked cautiously.

"No, but Min tells me he can lead your soldiers to them."

"What has this Ahn been stealing?"

"Construction materials."

Kometani still watched him.

"And tools."

The major rose. "Bring your aide to me. I wish to hear this for myself."

Yoon went to the door and motioned Min into the room. The aide bowed a greeting to the officer. Kometani motioned him to a seat.

"Tell the major what you have told me," ordered Yoon.

Min nodded uncertainly. "I saw Ahn taking materials and tools from the headquarters building. He is suggesting others do the same on their jobs. He plans to sell them to a friend in Seoul."

Yoon painted disgust across his face. "Did he think I would not find out? Did he think merely because I am a new supervisor I would not learn what he was doing?"

"He had. . . ." Min stopped.

"Answer my question." Yoon was impatient now.

"Ahn plans to have you arrested," murmured Min.

"Arrested? Me?" Yoon snorted. "Why did you not tell me this before? Why do you wait until we are here with the major?"

The aide looked meekly at Yoon. "I did not because I was afraid you would be angry with me."

"Angry? Of course I am angry. I must know about these things. I will not tolerate thieves in the. . . ."

Kometani held up a hand. "Please do not shout and scold. Your aide is demonstrating loyalty. You have discovered and re-ported a criminal to me. If this information is true you are in no danger." His gaze was calm but penetrating. "Min, you have told me Ahn is taking materials and tools. You say he is planning to sell them. Then you say he is planning Yoon's arrest. Why does he attempt such things? No one plans arrests except me. I am the commander."

Min bowed his head. "Ahn has said Yoon is driving everyone too hard. Ahn does not like it. He plans to have you replace Yoon. He hopes to be the one. Then there would be no one standing in his way. He would have one of his friends appointed to replace him on the construction of the headquarters and he would still be able to take what he wished."

"How many have joined this conspiracy?"

"I think no one, Major."

"No one?" Kometani raised an eyebrow. "Why would no one support such a carefully planned scheme?"

"I think they would not because everyone is happy to see the railroad coming into Chunchon. We think Yoon can do it faster and better than Ahn because he is loyal to us and to the Emperor. He requires us to work hard but he treats us fairly. He has no favorites."

Kometani nodded and rose. "I think we must find our foreman's treasure."

The others rose to follow him. As they left the building Kometani called for soldiers and the group started toward the headquarters building site.

"Where has he hidden these things he has stolen?"

"They are in an old shed behind his home," answered Min.

They marched on in silence, the only sound the clanking of the soldiers' combat kits against their hips. As they reached the construction Ahn looked up in surprise. "Good morning, Major," he smiled, bowing. He turned and bowed perfunctorily to Yoon. "Is my project to be inspected this morning?"

Kometani motioned the soldiers forward. "Arrest the thief."

They grabbed him quickly, twisting his wrists high up between his shoulder blades.

"Me?" he whined. "Why do you arrest me?" He jerked to pull himself free, then gasped in pain.

"Now," announced Kometani, "we shall have a look at the shed."

"What shed?" blurted Ahn in genuine surprise.

Kometani gave him a withering look and the group started off again. When they arrived at Ahn's house the soldiers spread out. "Here," came a call from around a corner, behind the house. "I have found it."

They followed the voice, arriving as the soldier slammed his rifle butt against a door. The wood, old and weak, shattered.

Kometani strutted forward, looked inside and emerged smiling coldly. "So. You thought you were to make a fool of me." He glared at Ahn.

The prisoner looked back, panic, worried consternation now distorting his already pained face. "What? What have you found which makes you believe me a criminal?"

Kometani merely nodded at the soldiers. "Take him away."

"But I have done nothing!" The scream echoed futilely through the busy morning.

Kometani turned to Yoon and his aide. "You have done well. The Emperor extends his gratitude."

* * * * * *

Kimura ran down the steps to the staff car.

"How is he?" demanded Kometani, brusquely returning the salute.

"He has seemed better for several days but I think it is very bad this morning."

The major strode toward the steps and into the building with Kimura almost at a trot to keep up. "Has the doctor remained to talk with me?"

Kimura winced. "He was called away for an emergency. He is not very hopeful. We have been trying to keep the fever from returning." He shrugged disconsolately. "We have not been successful."

Kometani shot him a look of disgust. "I think you spend too much energy attempting to control the fever. You should be concerned with what causes it. This illness has lingered much too long and still you have no answers."

Kimura looked helpless. "We do not know what else to do for him."

"You should be more concerned with what you can do for me, for the Emperor."

They had reached the entrance to Murashige's cubicle. Inside, the room was only shadows. Murashige still lay on the pallet but his weight seemed to have wasted into the matting. He looked up as they entered, managing a weak smile for the commander.

"Good morning, Major," he whispered, trying to raise his head.

Kometani knelt beside him. "Lie still. You must not try to move too much. It will tire you."

The look in the man's eyes indicated it made little difference. "The projects?"

Kometani looked at him silently for several moments, wondering at the man's determination. Finally he smiled sympathetically. "They are ahead of schedule."

"The railroad?" The effort of speaking the short questions was exhausting, yet there was a look of excited hope in his eyes.

"I have said it is ahead of schedule. But you must forget that. I think it is time for you to go home."

There was another whisper, inaudible.

The major took the withered hand and bent closer. "What did you say?"

Murashige closed his eyes tight with the pain, then opened them again. "When?"

Kometani did not understand. "Do you ask me when you are going home?"

The sick man shook his head. "Railroad," he rasped. "Completion."

"Three more days, I think. It will be four at the most."

Murashige nodded. "Now it is time."

The major raised an eyebrow, saying nothing.

Murashige labored with the words. "Home. Replacement."

Kometani leaned closer. "But what of Yoon?"

"Replace him now. Get Japanese. . . ."

Kometani shook his head. "I cannot understand you. Before you wished to stay. You wished for Yoon to be the supervisor."

The look was pleading now. "Japan. Japan." His body shook with a fit of coughing. The hand reached out, grasping at the air, then relaxed and fell to his side. His face was peaceful.

Kometani watched for a moment longer, then motioned for Kimura. The medic stepped forward and knelt next to the commander, feeling for the pulse. Finally he looked up and shook his head. Kometani nodded and rose. "I wish to have this place cleaned out right away. There is a terrible stink in here."

"Yes, Major."

The commander walked quietly from the room and down the hallway to the door. Reaching it, he stopped and looked for a long moment at the mountains, the flatness of the valley, the luxury of spring. Bustling activity swirled around the cantonment area. Finally, with resignation, he proceeded down the steps to the waiting car.

* * * * * *

The day was warm, sunny, as though orchestrated on cue for the occasion. People began gathering early, the old shuffling purposefully along in the wake of skittering, curious children. They swarmed around the terminal, overflowed along the glistening rails. Then, their places claimed, they settled into a hushed waiting.

The militia arrived in formation, uniforms neat and weapons menacingly clean. Commands were barked as their columns pierced the crowd, and they filed their way with the precision of chain around the sea of ragged souls.

The hush returned, broken only by the occasional shouts or laughter of children. At last, far down the track, a whistle sounded. It was high pitched, shrill, far away. A murmur spread hopefully among the people. Only the soldiers were unmoved. The whistle sounded again, still distant.

Kometani stepped forward to the edge of the platform and leaned over, looking. Only a small speck could be seen, far beyond the rice, a telltale plume of smoke trailing busily behind. The commander turned back toward his staff, then saw Yoon and his foremen at the edge of the crowd. He approached them, a formality in his step. "You have done well. The Emperor is pleased."

Yoon bowed low. "We are honored by your kind words." He indicated the others. "We have been talking of Supervisor Murashige. He will be most proud today."

Kometani looked at him without expression. "Murashige is dead."

Yoon's eyes widened. "When did he die?"

"I have forgotten," replied the commander, bored. "It matters little. I have a new Supervisor of Construction now."

The foremen looked at Yoon, questioning that he had not told them. Yoon stammered, but could not find the question in his shame.

Kometani was perceptive. "Ah," he soothed. "You must not lose your face with your foremen. I have told no one. You are appointed." Abruptly he turned and strutted back to his place with the staff.

The whistle was close now. The crowd surged forward to see. Soldiers hurried busily back and forth, pushing them clear of the tracks. Then, with hissing and a clanging bell, the engine slid into the terminal, its string of cars behind.

Kometani stepped forward, bowed low, and grasped the hand of the first officer, a general, who stepped from the train. They smiled and walked together to a stairway rising up the side of the building. As they reached a landing a collective groan went up from the crowd along the tracks. From the cars were dropping hundreds of new Japanese troops.

Police whistles blew from the foot of the steps. The people turned to see. Kometani was holding up his hands for quiet. Gradually all sound subsided.

"People of Chunchon, we honor the Emperor today. This railroad is a tribute to his Imperial genius. It will provide most notable progress for this city." The crowd was silent, shocked. The general stepped forward on the landing, high above their heads.

"The Emperor wishes to show his gratitude. He has therefore promoted the commander of the Imperial Militia in Chunchon to the rank of colonel and doubled the size of his militia." He looked triumphantly at Kometani. Once more they bowed low to each other. The general turned to an aide, taking a small box from him. "Colonel Kometani, with this decoration you are now installed as the Commander of the Imperial Militia for the entire Gangwondo Province."

The crowd shifted uneasily and some at the rear began to move away from the gathering.

"Stop them," cried the general. "They must hear this last. Do not allow them to leave until they are dismissed."

The soldiers standing across the rear of the crowd raised their weapons. The people looked at them fearfully and turned back to the terminal.

"Colonel Kometani has proved his value to the Emperor. The railroad has been completed ahead of schedule. Therefore, the quotas for Chunchon are now raised, as befits a provincial capital. The new quotas will be announced throughout the city. They will be a greater glorification of the Emperor." He stood back authoritatively.

Kometani assumed a serious air. Holding up his arms, he cried, "Banzai."

"Banzai," rose the reply from the soldiers.

"Banzai," shouted Kometani.

"Banzai," answered the soldiers.

"Banzai," screamed the officer again.

"Banzai," echoed his troops.

Kometani stood severely at attention, proudly viewing his domain. Then, stiffly, he descended the steps behind the general and entered a waiting staff car.

THE NORTH—HOCHON

Horror had spread throughout Hochon, and with it a growing disdain for Goto and his militia. The people developed subtlety as the only means of resistance. An apparent eagerness to answer questions while withholding particles of information became an art. Soon this evolved into the hiding of other things. Vegetable crops gradually became smaller. Rice dwindled slightly from season to season.

At last Goto lost patience. "It is becoming worse," he growled. "Each year production decreases a little more. There is no reason for it."

"The conditions have been excellent," agreed his deputy.

"Then they are hiding their crops. They are ignoring the levy. What do you think about that?"

"Perhaps we must make an example of one of them. If we catch one with rice in his pockets and make a public display of him it may not be necessary to do much more."

Goto sat back, puffing easily on his cigarette. "Perhaps we should do much more. Perhaps we should clean them all out, eliminate all the thieves."

The deputy nodded. "Where would you like me to begin?"

Goto rose and walked slowly to the window, a faint smile painted across his face. I believe we can start at random. It does not really matter whom we select. All of them are guilty. I think only the degree of guilt will vary from farmer to farmer." He turned.

"Go out into the village and arrest the first farmer you see. Bring him to me."

The deputy stood, silent, watching him.

"Well, what are you waiting for?" demanded Goto.

The man shrugged, bowed and left the room. Within an hour he was back, a farmer held securely between two soldiers.

Goto looked up with pleasure. "You have done well." As he transferred his attention to the captive his mien became severe. "What is your name, farmer?"

"Kim."

"Why have you been withholding your crops from us, Kim?"

The farmer looked back at him in shock. "I have not withheld my crops," he protested.

"Do not lie to me, farmer. I have much evidence that you have been withholding great amounts of your crops for several years. You have been selling them on the black market to make yourself rich."

"I have not," protested Kim incredulously. "I have always met my levy."

"Kim," continued Goto, his voice softening abruptly to a near whisper, "I am not a blind man. I am very intelligent. That is why the Emperor sent me here as the commander of the militia. Also, I am very strong. I will not tolerate lies and thievery. What do you think of that?"

"I have never stolen my rice," protested Kim again.

Goto smiled faintly, having now learned the farmer's crop. "We shall see," he replied. "I shall be most interested in your attitude after you have been my house guest for a few weeks."

"Try me," burst Kim. "Give me a trial and show me the evidence. If there has been a thief taking the rice it was not I. Perhaps your soldiers are the thieves. Perhaps they stole it to make themselves rich. Perhaps it was the great merchant, Pak. Perhaps his wealth was not enough for him." He stopped, out of breath, panting at Goto.

The commander eyed him with interest, a brief smile of satisfaction flitting across his face. Then he motioned to the soldiers. "Take him away. Show him to a guest room."

"I want a trial. I want a lawyer to represent me."

"Wait," said Goto evenly, holding up his hand.

The soldiers stopped.

"He says he wishes a lawyer and a trial." Goto strolled slowly toward the prisoner, contemplating him. "Yes. We shall have a trial. It shall be a most complete trial, one which all the village can see. There shall be lawyers, everything." He turned to the deputy. "See that proper lawyers are assigned. I think this will be most amusing." He waved to indicate the interview was over.

"Captain." Kim's voice was passionate.

"What more could a thief ask of me?" Goto stood with his hands on his hips, glaring at the farmer.

"I wish to have a Korean lawyer."

"Absurd," exploded the commander impatiently.

"Men from Korea have been trained in the law. One from this village went away to study." His voice was thin, strained. "I want a lawyer from Korea."

Suddenly Goto smiled. "That will take time. Much more than if you were to accept a Japanese lawyer."

"I wish to have a lawyer from Korea," repeated Kim.

Goto strode quickly to the desk. "Take the fool away," he snapped. "We shall find him a counsel from Korea."

The soldiers led him away to the prison. As he was thrust into the cell he vomited. A day later he almost begged for reconsideration, a Japanese lawyer who would get him more quickly out of the subhuman conditions. Then, remembering Chung's purpose in going to Japan, he braced himself in resolution and vowed to wait for a counsel from his own country.

The days plodded one after another across his world, cold, heartless, exhausting. The food, at first unpalatable, became an anxiously awaited event of each day. When it arrived he grasped it eagerly, consumed it ravenously. He lost weight. He lost track of time. Cellmates came and went, but he was never allowed to con-

verse with them. Though they had known each other for years
their only greeting was a furtive look, carefully shielded from the
greedy eye of the guard.

When the days had faded into uncounted weeks he wavered
again, and again Chung's admonition reinforced him. Yet, as the
rats foraged boldly through the cell he wondered if his request
would do him any good, if a Korean lawyer trained by the Japanese would be able to help.

At last he was removed from the cell and marched hastily across
the prison compound. The air was crisp, cool, and his breath fanned
out before him like an elusive feather.

"Where are we going?" asked Kim.

He received a resounding slap from one of the soldiers. "Prisoner, you are in no position to ask questions."

They walked on in silence and entered a stone building at the
end of the enclosure. Along the corridor were many doors, all closed.
They approached one at the end.

"Come in," called a voice in answer to the knock.

A soldier opened the door and they shoved Kim forward with
such force that he landed in a heap before the table.

"Wait outside," ordered the voice.

The sound of the soldiers' feet receded and the door latch
clicked.

Kim, sore, tired and now frightened, slowly raised his head
and looked into the eyes peering at him from behind the table.
Suddenly his heart began to pound. He half rose, then fell back in
disbelief. "Chung. So long. So many years."

"Yes, Kim. So many years."

The entire world seemed to whirl through his mind. Chung
appeared well, perhaps even happy. A twinge of resentment flick-
ered through Kim but was soon gone, replaced by a glimmer of
hope. He looked up and a faint smile crossed his face. "So you
were right when we last talked."

Chung returned the smile. "We spoke of many things, Kim.
About what was I right?"

"You have not forgotten. You realized even then what would happen. Remember? You said it that day on the dike. If we are arrested it is better to be defended by Korean lawyers than the Japanese."

"You are right, Kim. Particularly in the case of false charges. With our own people watching the law none of us can be convicted of false or inflated charges. I have always believed that."

"Then it should be simple for you, Chung. Get me freed of this ridiculous situation. I have not even been home since my arrest."

Chung paused, looking intently at Kim. "As I said, my goal is to see that no one is convicted of false or inflated charges. How false are the charges, Kim? How inflated are they?"

Kim rose and leaned on the table. "They are lies. All lies."

"What proof do you have of that?" asked Chung.

"Proof?" Kim searched his friend's face in futility. "Would you ask me for proof? The charges were made by the Japanese. That should be sufficient proof. They want too much." He paused, fighting for control. "I am a poor man. My crops have always been small but they have taken half of whatever I have been able to harvest. My family has gone hungry, my wife, my sons." He glared at Chung. "I wonder if you even recognize how life has become in your old village. You once spoke of freedom and safety for us. I think you have forgotten. The Japanese call it a treaty of protection but they are using us as slaves. If they had invaded us and plundered it would be no worse. And now what is my good friend doing for me?"

"I have not forgotten, Kim," shot back Chung. "But our world is changed. Our lives, the lives of all Korea, cannot turn around and go back, Kim. But you have not answered my question. The charge is that you have withheld rice from the Japanese. Either you did or you did not. What is the truth?"

"We are Korean. These charges are Japanese. You said you would protect us from Japanese tyranny."

"The law is the law, Kim. Did you withhold rice from them?"

"Yes. Yes, I withheld rice. I am Korean, not Japanese. I will not give to them at the expense of my family."

"Then you admit your guilt," said Chung quickly, a tone of finality in the statement.

"Chung, you are my defender, yet you talk as if you were their lawyer. You misinterpret your whole function. You must convince them the whole thing is a mistake. You must tell them you have searched my home, that I have done no wrong. You must convince them their informants are wrong." Kim turned and paced the floor in frustration. Then he wheeled and pointed a finger at Chung, screaming. "You are my defender. You are to represent me, not the Japanese. What do you plan to do to save me?"

Chung remained calm. "I shall do all I can. To begin with, however, we know you did withhold rice. Then we shall point out to them it was a misunderstanding. You did not mean to do it. Perhaps we can convince them much of the missing rice was stolen from you. There are many thieves."

"Yes. Japanese thieves have taken over our land. There are many thieves."

Chung ignored the outburst. "In Hochon many thieves prey on their neighbors. We will tell them. . . ."

"The thieves are the Japanese," emphasized Kim.

"Nonsense, Kim. Can you not see that you are only going to get yourself in more trouble with this stubborn line of reasoning? The Japanese may not be liked here, but they are still the rulers. We cannot deny that. Their laws must be obeyed or the entire village will suffer." He threw up his hands dejectedly. "I have been trying to point this out to you, Kim, but you will not listen. Every new charge brought against you will make it harder. Every time you resist, one new charge will be added. I cannot help you if you insist on insulting them each time you see them."

"Then you will do nothing to save me? They call me a thief. Can a man steal from himself?"

"I will not lie to save you, Kim. I will try my best to defend you, but I will not lie."

Kim leaped up, purple with rage. "Lie. You are a lie. You are lying to yourself."

He surged forward, diving at Chung. The table overturned and Chung leaped quickly behind his chair. Instantly the door flew open and the soldiers rushed in.

As Kim was dragged from the room he was still screaming incoherent curses over his shoulder at the stoical Chung.

Lawyer Chung made his way through the chill of the village to the courthouse, turning over in his mind the various courses of action open to him. That he should have been returned to Hochon for duty, even at a special request, was unusual. He did not wish to jeopardize this good fortune by being aggressive on Kim's behalf. On the other hand, Kim had been his friend since childhood.

He was troubled further that Kim's natural antagonism had been so fortified by such an officer as Goto. The man obviously was a tough, much different from the Japanese Chung had met previously. He had set an early example in Hochon with an execution. Now he seemed determined to solidify his control over the people through more punishment. It seemed not to matter whether or not the man was guilty. Kim was a foil, a means to an end.

A further consideration was the effect a harsh sentence would have on the population. Now they felt oppressed. How much more would they take before some underground organization sprang up to challenge the Japanese authority? If he were to be of any help to his people, as well as to his Japanese benefactors, he had to keep unrest in check to avoid any possibility of insurrection and at the same time suggest a realistic solution which would discourage further violations. Resistance would surely mean annihilation of the village.

With these thoughts Chung made his way up the steps of the militia headquarters. Turning the corner, he approached the door of the militia commander.

"Yes?"

He opened the door and saw Goto seated behind his desk. "Ah. Come in, Chung. Come in." Goto rose and circled his desk.

Chung stepped forward into the room and bowed low. Goto returned the greeting and they relaxed.

"As I recall," said Goto, "today is the day you are scheduled to meet with the farmer, this Kim. He should have had time to consider his position by now."

"I had a discussion with him this morning."

Goto brightened. "Good. I trust there will be no further difficulties."

Chung winced. "He is a very unhappy man, Captain."

"Is he unhappy about his stay in our prison?" He smiled sneeringly. "Or is he unhappy that he may very well die?"

Chung reached out and accepted the cup of tea a soldier handed him.

Goto looked up. "That will be all, Yamauchi. Leave us alone."

The soldier bowed low and exited. Goto sipped his tea in silence for a moment. "Chung, this village is a great problem for as small as it is. If it were Songnim or one of the larger cities, even a provincial capital, it would be more understandable. But in a village like Hochon such resistance is most unusual."

"I think there have not been very many cases of insubordination."

"You are right. There have not. But only because of my iron rule, that is most certain." Goto sat back with a satisfied smile. "Before I was assigned here there was a certain element of this village and the surrounding country which sought every opportunity to resist us." He gestured. "But then, you know all these things, do you not? You are from this village."

"Yes, Captain, but I think my record of service indicates I and my family have always been most loyal to the Emperor. We have never participated in such resistance."

"Oh, I did not mean you or your family have been disloyal." Goto dismissed it with a quick wave. "No, there are most reliable reports about your loyalty. But it is the collective attitude of the people here which keeps me alert. Consider Kim, for instance. I am told he has always been a passive resister at the very least. He has ignored the courtesies of our culture, conveniently looked the other way when honors were due, grumbled whenever he was cornered into obeying a rule." He stopped and studied Chung. "You must be of approximately the same age. Did you know this man before?"

"We were children here together. Our fathers were neighbors."

"How did he react when the Imperial forces first arrived?"

Chung shifted uneasily. "He was like the rest of us. We were surprised. We were not as aware of the situation as the people in the large cities. News travels slowly in Korea."

"But what was Kim's attitude?" pressed Goto.

"I think he did not believe it would be a permanent annexation. He somehow seemed to believe the Yi Dynasty would rise again and remove the Imperial forces. But he cannot understand why such a large percentage of his crop must go to the Emperor."

Goto scoffed. "That is ridiculous. Before we came a large percentage of his father's crops were going to Yi? Does it make a difference whether the rice goes to Seoul or to Tokyo? His father never saw the rice again once it had been shipped to Seoul."

"Kim does not understand such things. He knows only that the Imperial forces came to Hochon and forced him to learn a new language, which he does not speak too well, incidentally. He is not very intelligent."

"He is the kind of vermin we will be well rid of, believe me. What do you think of that?"

Chung pursed his lips. "That is what worries me."

Goto looked his question at the lawyer silently.

"I do not believe you should get rid of him. I think we can better use him as an educational device."

"Precisely why I want to get rid of him. Consider the last execution, the disposition of the man's wife. The population was most impressed."

"I was not here then, but I am told they were frightened and somewhat sickened." Chung shook his head pensively. "I believe it would be much easier if the people knew we were firm, but at the same time fair."

"I think you are trying to save an old friend." Goto was smiling.

"No. I have already told Kim that I will not lie for him. I think the best way to solve the problem is to change his and the village's attitudes."

"There is no way to change their attitudes."

"Perhaps there is. Already they know you have no compunctions about executing a criminal. Now, suppose they were also to see that you would be lenient if the prisoner were more repentant, shall we say. In the other case, for instance, the man was eliminated for sedition, if I recall the records. I think he was not executed for withholding his crops."

"That is exactly what I mean. They are most aware I will not tolerate sedition. Now I shall teach them another lesson. This time they shall learn my views on thievery. If they learn the lesson well I will consider leaving the others alone. If they do not I shall arrest more, many more."

"But Captain. May I suggest you consider the extra work which will result for the militia? It might even require additional support from your higher headquarters. I think the colonel might be displeased with that.

Goto shifted and leaned forward. "Chung, there is much merit in what you say. If you were Japanese I would never question your motives. However," he chanted easily, "as a Korean, you must prove your worth to me. And as a Hochonese, you shall be scrutinized very carefully." He sat back, as if becoming comfortable for the presentation. "Tell me your plan for this Kim."

"If Kim is executed I think people will feel sympathy with his wife and sons. They will wonder when their turn will come. But if Kim is allowed to live, to go on and farm his paddies, you could confiscate a larger percentage of his crops. However, the people will conclude there is a way to keep some of their crops legally. An infraction will mean hungrier mouths until the next harvest, but not starving mouths. You might even let Kim stay in prison for a period of time. If there were a delay in the trial, then Kim were assessed a larger percentage of his present crop as a sentence or fine I believe he would be impressed enough to abide by the rules in the future. You could impress on him how fortunate he is he has not been executed." Chung sat back, exhausted.

Goto poured another cup of tea for him. "You realize this is not the way I work. I am a most strict officer. I will not tolerate anyone trying to hoodwink me." He sipped his tea. "However, I suggested you should tell me your plan. I hope, for your sake as well as Kim's, it will work as you say. My greatest desire is for your people to be happy and safe. That is why we are here, to protect you. If you can prove to me that you can keep this village happy and safe you may become more of an asset to me than you realize. If not?" He gestured as if in dismissal.

"When do you wish the trial to be conducted, Captain?"

"Whenever you say, Chung." He smiled and nodded mockingly. "I am at your command. What do you think of that?"

Chung grimaced inside but his face remained expressionless. "Very well," he said. "I shall set the date for two months from today. That should give Kim ample time to consider his most unfortunate predicament." Chung rose, bowed low and left.

Kim had been returned to his cell. He did not see his lawyer again for three days. The soldiers kept his arms and legs shackled with heavy chains that day.

"Why do they bring me here chained like an animal?" he demanded of Chung when they were alone again.

"Perhaps it is because you are proving you cannot be trusted."

"Someday," hissed Kim, "I shall kill you. You will die for what you are doing to me."

"I am not doing anything to you, Kim. You are doing much to harm yourself. I have faced much trouble because of your rebellious attitude."

"I think you have not known a day of trouble in your entire life," scoffed Kim.

Chung went on. "Do you recall the last person who was arrested for being rebellious?"

Kim hesitated. "I remember, but you were not here then," he growled finally. "You were away becoming Japanese."

"He was executed." Chung bit out the words. "His wife was taken as a whore for the Japanese soldiers."

"Those things happened because he made speeches against them. I have not made speeches. I have tried only to feed my family."

"The militia commander considers you a thief. He plans to execute you now and take your wife for the soldiers."

Kim felt a wave of cold fear creep through him. "When?" he whispered.

"He plans to do it immediately after the trial. In the village square like that last one. He plans to call all the village together and make a spectacle of you and your wife in front of your friends."

Kim's eyes were wide. "And you? What are you doing for me?"

"You must learn to control your temper. Every time you are rude to him, refuse to answer a question, give a hateful look to one of the guards, they will make note of it for your trial. You must become a most obedient prisoner or I can do nothing for you."

Kim was near a whimper now. "I think you are doing nothing to save me. All you do is preach to me."

"I believe I can save you, at least from the execution. I do not know about anything else now. It will depend on you, on your attitude during the time remaining."

"Will they leave me here?" Kim was whispering, not from a desire for secrecy, but from emotion.

Chung spread his hands. "Perhaps. Perhaps not."

"I do not like this place," spat Kim.

"It all depends upon your attitude. You could be executed or you could go free. The militia commander plans to execute you and I want him to free you. It may be necessary for me to bargain to keep you alive."

"If I were free perhaps I could move away. Perhaps I could go to Seoul, Pyongyang. Anywhere." Tears were in the corners of his eyes as he rehearsed the names of places he had never seen.

"Kim." Chung offered the name gently, trying to restore his attention.

The farmer looked at him, saying nothing more.

"You are a marked man, Kim. They have studied your reactions to every little thing which has happened since they first came. They consider you a troublemaker. If you escape this trouble they will haunt you. The first thing you do which they do not like they will execute you for it. Make no mistake. You will not be allowed to go away. You will be watched day and night. Your crops will be inspected. Everyone you talk with will be questioned most carefully so they may learn what you are saying. One thought against them, one word, one act of disobedience or even dislike, and they will put an end to it all. In the village square, with all the people of Hochon watching your disgrace."

Kim's eyes were narrow with hate. "This is what you have done for me? This is how you protect the people of Hochon?" He swept his arm in an arc. "Look at the mountains. They take the timber. They leave no trees to protect us from the rains. The water will run off and drown us. They steal our rice, our cabbage. And when we try to steal it back they kill us.

"You are not required to accept what I can do. You may continue your present attitude and be executed. They can take your wife for the soldiers. You have asked me to help you. I thought keeping you alive and perhaps getting you out of the prison was helping you. I thought leaving you with enough food so you did not have to steal was helping you. I think that is not enough for you. You demand more. You wish to drive the Japanese away all by yourself." He leaned forward. "They will not go, Kim. Nothing any of us can do will make them go away."

Kim was silent for a long time. He sat hunched over and stared intently at Chung. "I shall do it. Not today or tomorrow, but I shall drive them away. And when I do, Chung, there will be many men facing firing squads and many weeping widows in Japan." He shrugged resignedly. "But for now I will do as you say. I will not fight them and I will not embarrass you. You are one of them now, and I will not make you lose your face with your new nation. While I do it, though, remember what I have told you. I will have revenge, Chung."

Chung watched him rise, slowly, sorely.

"Send me to the mountain now. I will cut away the timber for you and your Japanese friends.

Through the next weeks, as he chopped, he swung each blade toward an imagined Japanese throat. At night he dreamed of revenge. By the day of his trial Kim was outwardly a subservient Hochonese farmer wishing earnestly for an opportunity to reform. Within, he was a revolution waiting to explode.

As he was led to the courthouse he caught a glimpse of his wife standing nearby with a pair of soldiers. His blood went cold. Then he looked past her and into the faces of the others. "Tomorrow," he thought. "Tomorrow I shall begin. But today I must become free to join you." He yielded willingly to the urgent grasp of the soldiers hurrying him up the steps and into the courtroom.

Before him sat Goto, severe and still. At a small table off to the side was Chung, and opposite him at another table, a young officer who fiddled self-consciously with his pencil. The soldiers marched Kim to the center of the room. He had started his bow of respect to the court even before they told him. Goto noticed and cast a quick glance at Chung.

"The charges," read the young officer in a high, almost adolescent tone. "Kim. . . ."

He heard the name and it somehow seemed they were talking about another man. He strained to understand the words but his mind would not respond. Goto was nodding at the young officer and looking at Kim.

"How do you answer, farmer?" Goto was formal.

"I am most sorry. I am guilty."

Goto sat back with satisfaction. "It seems your time in the

forest has helped you learn to think properly. Perhaps you have discovered the errors in your life."

"Yes, Sir," Kim said again, almost eagerly now.

"Kim, my impulse was to sentence you to death. I did not believe you had the intelligence to be useful to Hochon any longer." He paused and stared at his prey. "Perhaps I was wrong. Perhaps you can learn to be a decent citizen after all."

"I will try," he said. "I will try to be a good citizen for my people."

"And," prompted Goto, "for all the people of the Empire."

"And for all the people of the Empire," added Kim somewhat less willingly.

A hush had come over the others. As his gaze wandered back to Goto the captain was intoning his sentence in a caterwauling voice reserved for official pronouncements. " . . . seventy-five per-cent of your recent crop. You will serve ten years in prison, work-ing for the Emperor, where you will learn the greater values of the most gracious Imperial protection. Meanwhile, your wife will leave your house and spend her days comforting the Japanese soldiers. They are far from home. It is good for them to be entertained and comforted in this far-away place." He paused, then resumed the chant. "Also, you are sentenced to die before a firing squad. . . ."

"What?" his mind screamed. "How can that be?"

" . . . if you should be caught in any further deviation from the laws of the Empire or of this Imperial Militia."

Kim almost collapsed. He looked at Chung, who stared back at him without emotion.

"Take the prisoner away." Goto rose. Kim stood transfixed, numb. Then the soldiers were prodding him from the room. When they burst through the door into the sunlight there was a slight commotion among the group beside the shop. He slowed mo-mentarily to gaze at his wife, wondering whether she and his sons would survive without him. Then, roughly, the soldiers grasped him and dragged him off toward oblivion.

THE SOUTH—CHUNCHON

Yoon sat authoritatively behind his desk. "Colonel Kometani wishes to know what you would like most to do as a career."

Min, who had remained standing since entering the office, shifted his feet slightly. "I think I do not understand."

Yoon smiled, rising and motioning the aide to a seat. "The colonel is most impressed with your loyalty to him and the Emperor. He believes such dedication is worthy of reward." He took a seat next to Min. "It was the Ahn affair," he said softly.

Min brightened. "But I did only what you told me to do."

"Ah," chanted Yoon, wagging a finger at him, "but you must always remember how it appeared to him. My instructions to you then are best forgotten today. Now, tell me. What would you most like to do?"

Min cast about helplessly, searching vainly for an answer. At last he shrugged, smiling weakly at the supervisor. "I wish only to work for you."

"Min, you are not very ambitious," Supervisor Yoon scolded. "This man has much power. He can send you to school. He will make you what you wish to be."

"Will he make me a man of power and influence?" Min looked impishly at the supervisor. "Will he give me a life of ease and comfort?"

The supervisor laughed. "He wishes to educate you. How you put it to use would be a matter of concern to you."

Min's mind was whirling. "Supervisor, I do not know what to decide. I have never thought of such things. I have learned only from my father." He paused, looking sheepishly at the supervisor. "And from you."

"But you are intelligent."

"I do not know what to say."

"Then I shall recommend."

Min looked up quickly.

"I shall recommend that you be trained as a schoolmaster."

Chagrin darted through Min's chest. "A schoolmaster? Supervisor, I think I would not become a very good teacher in the school. I told you I have never been in a school."

"Do you question my wisdom, Min, merely because you have never been in a school?"

Min looked only momentarily chastised. "I could become a man of influence in the school."

Supervisor Yoon rose. "One never knows what he may be able to achieve until he tries. Consider me. Until the Japanese came I was a common laborer. I had no education and no hope of becoming anything more. The difference between me and those who still labor out there was a single day, a single decision. I applied for work with the Japanese."

Min sat listening, unmoved.

"The others did not. They knew they would be put to work by conscription so they did not apply." He spread his hands in finality. "When the Japanese sought foremen they turned to those who had demonstrated an interest in the future instead of resentment for the past. I was made a foreman and I worked diligently. One requires only opportunity to achieve success, and much of that we create for ourselves."

Min shifted, uneasy now. "What of construction? I have worked with you. I know more of construction."

The unschooled supervisor tensed. "I suspect you would wish to return to Chunchon after your training. Colonel Kometani is generous with our people but one day there will be a new com-

mander in the province. He will wish to change Kometani's policies. I think he will bring in a Japanese construction supervisor."
He bowed his head, affecting concern. "Yes, even I will be demoted."

"Then what of commerce? I could become a merchant."

Supervisor Yoon breathed easier but looked with concern at
the aide. "You would become a simple vendor? One needs no education to become a vendor."

"But I would. . . ."

"Vendors are many and worthless. A schoolmaster has influence over the lives of many."

"Supervisor, I know it would be most difficult for me. I would
be required to teach Japanese doctrine. I am no worshiper of the
Japanese. I would not be able to do well as a schoolmaster."

"Any worthwhile endeavor requires courage," snapped the supervisor. "Each of us must do things we dislike. They are best
accepted quickly, committed to routine and ignored. Otherwise, I
think we would live a very difficult life. However," he said, returning to the desk, "I shall explain to Colonel Kometani that you do
not wish to be educated."

Min leaped from the seat. "Supervisor. I have not said I do not
wish it. I am filled with surprise, with great honor. Please. Do not
tell him I refuse."

Supervisor Yoon stopped. "Then what would you have me tell
him? Shall I explain that you are indecisive?"

Min swept an arm through the air. "It is only that I know
nothing of being a schoolmaster."

"They will teach you, Min. They will send you to Japan and
teach you."

"Japan?" gasped Min. "Would I not be sent to Seoul?"

"Japan," repeated the supervisor. "There are no facilities in
Seoul for the training of new schoolmasters."

"How long would I be kept in Japan?" blurted the aide.

"You would stay for several years. You must learn much to
become a schoolmaster."

Min sank back into the chair. "When would I be sent away?" he whispered.

"Very soon, I think," answered Yoon, softening now that he controlled the younger man once more. "Perhaps in three days."

"Would I return to Chunchon?'

"You may apply," replied Yoon. "Those who apply, who are willing to try, often succeed beyond their expectations."

"I shall," announced Min almost defiantly. "I shall come back to Chunchon."

* * * * * *

The house was meager but clean, well kept. Yoon stood in the doorway to welcome his guest. They bowed low to each other. "You bring great honor to my house." Yoon placed his hand on Min's shoulder and led him into the room. "Come. We must sit."

"Thank you, Supervisor. You have been a most gracious bene-factor. Have you been well?"

"Oh, yes. I have sons now. They will be students in your school." He gazed admiringly at the younger man. "Did you enjoy your years in Japan?"

Min laughed. "It is much like Chunchon, only worse. There are more Japanese there."

Yoon smiled. "It is of little concern, this political thing. You are now a schoolmaster." He poured some rice wine. "That is the most important thing, I think."

"Yes. Now I have been indoctrinated and can pass it on to all the innocent children of Chunchon." He shook his head. "It is much different than I expected. I always thought schoolmasters were dedicated men, that the dedication was to the children. I have thought about all the things people told me when I was young, before I went to Japan. The Japanese taught me one thing and you taught me another. They told me to love Japan and be loyal to the Emperor. You advised me to question them and be loyal to myself.

Neither of you, though, told me to care about the children for their sake. It seems nobody cares about them."

"Of course we do. We care what they become. We care what they think, these future adults, and we try to make them think the way they should. They must inherit this world we have, you know. Their whole purpose in childhood is to grow up. It matters not where in the world you go. You will always find it the same."

Min smiled. "Supervisor, you have never been out of Chunchon, yet you know these things as well as if you had been there in the classroom in Japan. However, I do not agree with their teachings. They call me a professional man. I am not, you know. I am really a craftsman. I am a whittler, a carver. I did much reading while I was there and it is as you say. The world over, people raise their children and they send them to school. They call it education and tell themselves they are doing it for the good of the children. But it is not education at all. It is more a matter of inculcation, and it is for the good of the adults, not the children. It consists of training them to observe our values and reflect our views. In that way we can be certain the world will stay as much the same as possible throughout our lives, and when we grow old we will not be required to face the shame of a totally new type of society. We will be able to keep things much the way they have been all our lives. We need not admit that the world we have now may not have been best. We need not admit our failure. We go to bed and we create these little tools, these little carvings which we then polish into what we need to protect us."

"They must learn. I think they do not know what is good for them. We do, so we teach them."

"Many apologies, my benefactor, but I understand it differently. It is not a matter of us knowing what is good for them because we do not. We know, or think we know, what is good for us. That is what we teach them. Consider carefully what I say, Supervisor. You and I are in the productive years of our lives. We look at the old or we look at the young. In reality both of them are liabilities, yet we spend our energies on the young. The morning ones. The old are the evening people. We respect them because we must live with our consciences, because it is the custom to honor them. We must. But once they cease to be productive do we really care about them? I think our real concern is for the young, and yet the whole time we are teaching them we are not really caring about them either. It is only a desire deep inside which says we shall try to make them like us so we will not be required to be like the ones who are old today. It becomes our frantic grasp at immortality. It is a vicious cycle, this life thing. I think it is most unfortunate that we cannot win. When the little carvings I polish and inculcate with the ideas of our society grow up they will not care about the evening people today. We will be customarily respected, but their basic concern will be their own insulation from change."

Yoon was overwhelmed, shocked at the younger man's desecration of the aged. "Is this what they have taught you in Japan?"

Min shook his head. "I think if they knew I feel this way I would be in a prison cell, not a schoolroom."

"I think there are enough problems between the Japanese and the Korean thought to last you a lifetime. If you become concerned with the old and the young you will never have any peace."

"I am not troubled by it, Supervisor. It is my philosophy. It is what I believe. The only task left to me now is to apply it."

"I do not understand you."

"Do you remember our conversation before I left for Japan? I was having many doubts. I did not believe enough in myself, and yet I was hoping to be a man of great influence."

Yoon nodded, still perplexed, shaken.

"You told me I should have courage. You told me of your own rise to the position of foreman and said if I would try I could succeed beyond my expectations."

"I did not intend that you try to ignore the old. They are our wisdom, our ancestors."

"I agree. They are our wisdom and I shall learn from them." Min was forcefully serious. "I intend to make my desires realities. I shall try and I shall have courage. All these children, these little tools, may be a dream for their parents, that futile clutch at immortality, but to me they will be different. The parents will fail, but I will not. I shall use these same tools to create my influence, to build some comfort for my later years."

Yoon was frustrated. "You must have some plan," he said hoarsely. "Tell me your plan."

Min leaned forward. "May I trust you, Supervisor?"

Yoon scoffed. "You ask a ridiculous question. Of course you may trust me." He reached across and poured more wine.

Min accepted it with a preoccupied nod. "There was a philosopher many years ago who said a man is the sum of his experience. Please consider mine. I began as a laborer. Most fortunately, I learned construction while I worked for you. Then you assisted me most graciously and now the Japanese have made me a schoolmaster. I am responsible for the polishing of the young people of Chunchon. Perhaps in the future it can be more than just these here. For now, however, my first task is to convince the Japanese I can teach their doctrines effectively to these children. I must be the craftsman for the Japanese, not for the parents. But the doctrine really is not important because it is futile. These children will appreciate the useful things I teach them, not the doctrines. You taught me practical things, and I extend you my respect. The Japanese taught me doctrine, yet I do not respect them. But if I convince them of my loyalty, my ability, I will gain credence as an educator. And one day I shall have greater authority. I shall control the programs of education. That is when I will become influential because my students will be loyal to me above all else. They will respect and honor practicality." He looked seriously at Yoon. "I think the Japanese will not be here forever. I think they will not be with us during our entire lives."

Yoon leaned forward with interest. "What is to stop them? We have no way to defeat them. We cannot drive them away."

"You know what has been going on in other parts of the world. Consider the World War. Some very significant strengths were displayed in that war. Then consider the revolution in Russia. I tell you, Supervisor, communism will be a most awesome force in our lives. When the Japanese are required to worry about the United States in the Pacific and the Russians to the north they will not be able to strangle Korea the way they do today. I think they have bigger and more pressing problems on the horizon."

Yoon's eyes were bulging, aghast. "Do you tell me one of those nations is to fight with Japan?"

"I think they will not only fight with Japan. I believe they will defeat Japan."

"And what will become of Korea then?"

Min spread his hands to suggest triumph. "We will return to self rule. That is when all my years of accumulated influence will become so very important."

Yoon was not that sure. "What is to prevent Russia or the United States from coming to our land as did the Japanese?"

"I think they must become too busy watching each other. I think they will not have time to conquer such a small place as Korea."

Yoon became silent. His wife entered and set some bowls in front of them. His two sons came into the room and bowed low.

Min looked up. "Well, are these the first two? Are these to be two of my charges?"

Yoon snapped back from his thoughts to reality. "What?"

"I asked if these are to be two of my charges."

"Oh. Yes. They are my sons. I told you I have two sons. They are Sunghwan and Shin. You will be teaching them."

Min mistook his preoccupation for concern. "Oh," he said with an attempt to dismiss alarm, "I think you must not worry about it. I do not flog my students. Particularly the sons of my friend and benefactor."

The sons remained silent. Yoon's wife continued to serve the food without speaking.

Yoon changed the subject. "Kometani arranged your assignment here."

"I must visit him. I owe him my gratitude."

"He is not here," replied Yoon flatly.

Min's eyebrow shot upward. "Oh?"

"He was made a general. He has been sent to the Kwantung Army in Manchuria."

"Were you then demoted? You told me you would be replaced by a Japanese when Kometani left, that it was useless for me to study construction."

Yoon shook his head, smiling now, his position secure. "I have remained supervisor."

Min looked at him uncomfortably, remembering the conversation years before. At last he shrugged. "Do you know the headmaster?"

"He is cruel."

"So is life, Supervisor. So is life. It all begins with our exit from the womb. Certainly the rest of life is cruel. The school, the government, even our health. We would only be suggesting something which cannot be if we treated the children any differently in school than they will be treated for the rest of their lives."

* * * * * *

The students sat before him, wondering, already cowed.

"I tell you you are most fortunate. Not all have this opportunity. Most of your kind are working in the fields. It is only because we suspect greater intelligence in you that you are here. Do not disappoint us." Min glared pompously over the room. "I must make one thing clear before we begin. Only Japanese will be spoken. You must not think because my name is Min you will be permitted to use Hangul. Do not attempt to revive the Yi thought in my classroom. Remember, if Yi were still in power you would receive no education at all."

The students cast quick, cautious glances at one another.

Min took note. "The only communication permitted in this classroom will be from me to you or from you to me. In other words, you will not talk among yourselves. You are here to learn and I will be the one to teach you. You have no need to learn from each other."

He rustled through some papers, then looked again at the group. "Before I begin, each of you will rise and tell me your name."

They remained motionless, no one willing to be first.

"Come, come," he snapped. "One of you must have a name." His eye fell on Yoon's youngest son. "You. You must not sit there like stone. Tell me your name." His voice was disarmingly kind.

The boy rose. "Shin."

Min continued. "Is that all? Only Shin?"

"I am called Shin," repeated the boy. There was a giggle behind him.

Min stepped rapidly past Shin to grasp his older brother by the hair. "Do you find something amusing?" He yanked, bringing the boy to his feet.

"No, Schoolmaster." His look had turned quickly to fear.

"Then why do you laugh?" He shook the boy.

There was a whispered but inaudible reply.

Min leaned forward, shouting in his ear. "I cannot hear you!"

The boy twisted, trembling. "Because you already know him," he repeated.

Min thrust him away sharply. "I know no one in this room. No one. Is that clear?"

"Yes, Schoolmaster."

"What is your name?"

"Sunghwan. I am his brother."

Min stood back and surveyed the room. "I think you must learn quickly. When I ask for a name I wish to hear a useful name. Familiarity is of no use to me." He turned back to the older boy. "Do you hear?" he screamed.

"Yes, Schoolmaster." Tears of humiliation filled his eyes.

"Well, Sunghwan," announced the schoolmaster, "when you enter my classroom I know you from nowhere else. Is that clear?"

"Yes, Schoolmaster."

Min glared at the class in general. "There is no favoritism in this class. We have only one favorite, and he is the Emperor. No one else." He stalked back to the front of the room. "Now that we know these two, who is next?"

Several boys shifted position but no one rose.

"How about you?" Min shouted, pointing to a boy next to Sunghwan.

The student started, then almost leaped to his feet. "Hong, Schoolmaster," he shouted.

Min folded his arms and smiled. "That is the way each of you will respond. Each time you are called upon to recite, each time you speak in my classroom you will follow Hong's example."

The others were ready now, almost anxious to announce their names to this new stranger, this man from their fathers' generation whom they were forbidden to know.

*　*　*　*　*　*

"Min, I have been asked to make a recommendation to the Supervisor of Education." The headmaster motioned to a chair. "Please sit down. I wish to discuss it with you."

"Does it concern me, Honorable Headmaster? Have I done something wrong?"

The headmaster smiled. "You have been my most effective schoolmaster for several years, Min. Always I have been able to rely on your teaching and your discipline." He poured tea and sat back. "I have recommended that you be promoted."

Exploding with excitement inside, Min strove to control his outward reaction. "I am most honored by your consideration, Headmaster."

"I wish to instruct you, however, that basic changes are now required in your treatment of your students."

"Have I not been severe enough?" asked Min in apprehension.

"Quite the contrary. A schoolmaster is expected to be severe, to make them attentive. As a schoolmaster I was the same. My discipline was legendary. However, a headmaster must fill a somewhat different role. He, as the superior, must be understanding. He must not baby them, but he must be willing to hear their problems, show them a degree of sympathy. Quite simply, it is a safeguard against total resentment." He lit a cigarette, inhaling deeply. "Of course, such an attitude could present a problem in your case."

"What problem, Headmaster?"

"You are a Korean. At times through the years I have almost forgotten the fact, but you are a Korean. If you, then, are too gentle while the Japanese are severe it could be construed as your reversion to nationalism. Quite simply, it could foster resentment rather than averting it."

Min leaned forward in sincerity, anxious to be reassuring. "Honorable Headmaster, I shall not allow it to happen. The people of Chunchon know me as a strict disciplinarian. I shall listen attentively, even be more understanding of circumstances, but I shall not show them preference. I shall not. . . ."

"Min."

He stopped, curious.

"You will not be remaining in Chunchon."

"Where, then?" he breathed softly.

"You will be assigned as headmaster of the school in the village of Gapyong. It is around the mountain to the west toward Seoul. It is a small school, but of course so is the village. The headmaster there has met with an accident. There is only one schoolmaster remaining. We cannot promote him to headmaster yet. He is too young and inexperienced."

"Are they not afraid to make a Korean the headmaster in such a place with no Japanese to oversee his teaching? In Chunchon there would be the Supervisor of Education. In this Gapyong there will be no one."

"You will not be alone in Gapyong," broke in the headmaster. "You will have assistance, observers. There is the militia. They will be your friends." He studied Min carefully. "You have a difficult task, Min. Your people will not trust you because you will be in a position of power with the Japanese. The Japanese will be cautious of you, at least in the beginning, because you are Korean. Only if you are both firm and understanding with all of them can you avoid problems."

"And if I fail?"

"Very few of your people have become headmasters. You will be one of the first. Quite simply, your failure would be construed as a failure of your people to measure up to our very high standards. I suggest that you not fail."

Min swallowed. "When will I be sent there?"

"Next week. I think you should go there as soon as possible."

Min left the school and wandered into the autumn. The hills and mountains roared with color which cascaded brilliantly to the floor of the valley. The air was brisk, bringing an echo of the foliage to his cheeks. He walked for several hours, alternately elated at his good fortune and apprehensive of its constrictive implications. At last, bone tired, he made his way to his room and slept.

* * * * * *

Shin bounded excitedly into the house. "Father, the schoolmaster is going away."

Yoon looked up in surprise. "When? Why?"

Sunghwan emerged from another room, happily expectant.

The younger boy dropped to the floor near his father. "He is to be made a headmaster. He will go to Gapyong in a week."

The father reached for his pipe, trying to control his anxiety. "Why has he not come to tell me? Am I no longer his closest friend?"

"He will come, Father. I know he will come. I think he is very excited now. He learned only yesterday. He must wait until he becomes calm."

"Tell me when he comes so that I may be away," sneered the older brother.

Yoon turned to him angrily. "I think you must be more courteous toward my friends. You should be happy for him."

"I am happy for me, for my friends. He has been cruel to us for too many years," replied the son.

"Father," cried Shin. "I must go and tell Hong. He will be most happy for the schoolmaster."

Yoon nodded pensively and the boy was gone. The father turned to his eldest. "Why do you so hate my friend? You should honor your schoolmaster."

The boy, rapidly outgrowing his adolescence, bristled. "My father, he is a Japanese in his heart. He hates us, his own people."

"That is not true, Sunghwan. He works for the Japanese, as do I. Many could call my heart Japanese as well."

"But you are different," protested Sunghwan. "You only work with the Japanese to stay alive. You do not really believe in them."

"I think neither does Min," said his father.

The son scoffed. "Does he not believe in them? He is worse than the Japanese themselves. He is worse than any of the Japanese schoolmasters."

Yoon smiled. "And you hate him not so much for that as for his punishment of you on that first day many years ago. Think back. Is that not so?"

Sunghwan nodded. "I have hated him ever since."

"He did you a favor. You began hating him and it became a deep hatred of the Japanese." He shook his head. "I hope your brother has been as fortunate."

Sunghwan snorted. "He loves him."

"He admires what he thinks the schoolmaster is. He does not really know him."

The boy was puzzled.

"Min may be the most loyal Korean in the entire city. He is duping the Japanese. Oh, he has been more severe than they expected of him, but he has succeeded in fooling them. They believe he is blindly loyal to them." He chuckled. "What he has really been doing is making a good impression on them. He has believed they would then promote him to a position of power and responsibility. It has been successful."

"Yes, it has been successful," replied the son. "He has taught the loyal Korean students in the school to hate him."

"And to hate the Japanese along with him. It is most unfortunate he could not teach the adults of Chunchon as well."

"He has not succeeded with Hong and my brother."

"Hong?"

"Your foreman's son."

"What of him?"

"He is as bad as my brother. Both of them wish to study in Japan."

Yoon looked at him in surprise. "How long has this been their desire?"

"More than a year."

"Have they made their applications?"

"I think they cannot because they are too young. But Hong wishes to study construction engineering. Then he plans to return to Chunchon."

Yoon's eyes were wide. "But what would he do here? There is only my appointment."

"Yes. There is your appointment." The son waved a finger toward his father. "Perhaps the schoolmaster has been trying to fool the Japanese, but he has fooled many students as well."

"And your brother. What does he wish to be?"

"A soldier." He laughed. "Can you imagine that? My brother wishes to become a Japanese soldier."

The father scoffed. "He may have that opportunity whether he wishes it or not. But that is ridiculous. They would not educate him. He would become a slave, doing their dirty work, the tasks their own people do not like."

"Father, I think you and I perceive this well. My brother does not. He believes they will educate him, make him an officer."

Yoon slapped his knee in disgust. "Why have you not told me this before? Have you talked with him about it?"

"I have tried, Father, but he will not listen to me. He thinks everything the schoolmaster does and says is correct. He admires his cruelty. The schoolmaster is so flattered at the way his chosen favorites admire him he cannot see what he is doing to them."

Yoon sat back in disappointment. "You should have told me this before. Why did you not do so?"

The son shrugged. "Schoolmaster Min is your friend."

"And you are my sons." He rose and began pacing the room. "I must do something. I must talk with your brother. He must realize he is falling into a trap Min set for the Japanese." He looked at Sunghwan. "It was not meant for the students, you know. It was for the Japanese."

"I think it does not matter. The damage is done."

"I shall make your brother understand."

"It will do no good. The schoolmaster has been teaching him for all these years. It is too late to change him now."

Yoon glared at him. "Then why did you not tell me before? You should have told me when I could have done something about it."

"You have heard him talking, my father. You must have suspected."

"I did not. I thought Min was using discretion when he was working with the students." Suddenly the impact of it struck him. "He has done it," he growled. "He has done what he swore he would do."

Sunghwan was startled by the viciousness in his father's voice. "What did he swear to do?"

The father's eyes were mere slits. "He swore he would use the children as tools. He wished to become a man of influence, a man of power. He planned to use the Japanese and the children. He swore he would use them as a bridge to his own success."

"He has concealed his plan well, Father," admitted the son, a new respect creeping into his voice. "He has been cruel, which has convinced the Japanese he is not a nationalist. He has selected a few special students and persuaded them the Japanese life is most desirable. With such a record he has been promoted." He paused reflectively. "No!" he shouted, shaking his head. "He could not hate the Japanese as you say. He is one of them."

Yoon growled again. "He is an animal. He has used my son for this." He slashed the air with his hand in frustration. "And Hong. He has used Hong as well. Tell me," he ordered, swinging around and facing his son. "How many of the other students has he lured to the Japanese?"

"He has persuaded many for the Japanese, but not all of us. Many of us hate him because he loves those who make us slaves."

"He does not. I know him. I arranged for him to go to Japan. He did not want to go because he hated them. It was most difficult for me to convince him."

"I think he did not hate them after he returned from their land."

"No. You are wrong. After he returned he told me of his plan. Min believes they will not be with us for a long time. He merely wishes to use them until he can achieve an influential position, until they trust him and no longer watch his every move. Then, when they are gone, he will remain. He will be considered a man of great wisdom by our people. He will be a leader."

"But he cannot if our people hate him."

"He will not do it in Chunchon. He will merely gain their trust here and be sent away for his promotion. He will use the people and children very differently when he is sent away."

Sunghwan scoffed, not believing. "Father, it is you he has made the fool. How would he drive the Japanese away?"

"He has studied. He knows. He has told me Japan will fight a war with the United States and Russia. He believes Japan will not win and we will be returned to self rule."

The son listened with interest. "If his prophecy is correct he is a very wise man to do what he does today. He will have that influence, first in a village, but later in cities, the entire nation." He lapsed into a thoughtful silence.

Yoon groaned and leaned forward, looking at his son, this adolescent almost a man. "Has he now captured you as well? First your brother admired this animal for what he thought he was and you hated him. Now you have learned what he really is and you admire him. When I talk with your brother and tell him what has happened he will hate the schoolmaster for really going against the Japanese." He slapped the floor. "I am your father. When are my sons to respect me? When will my thoughts begin to mean something to my sons?"

Sunghwan looked at his father, alarmed. "Do you not think it is good for a man to become influential?"

"He will not!" Yoon sprang to his feet again. "He promised he would not, but he has used my sons. I will not allow it. He used the two of you as an experiment in furthering his own goals."

He raced to the door and burst out of the house in fury. Sunghwan started after him, but stopped. Then, in resignation, he turned back into the house.

The schoolmaster looked up from his desk and smiled with pleasure as Yoon entered the empty classroom. "Yoon, my friend. I am honored to see you here."

Yoon sneered. "You have ruined my sons." His voice was gravelly with rage.

"What?" Min rose and started toward him, then stopped as the level of Yoon's rage became apparent to him.

"You have ruined my sons," repeated Yoon. He slammed a fist into the podium as emphasis.

Min backed off and motioned to a chair. "I do not know what you are saying." He pulled the chair forward toward his visitor. "I would never ruin anyone's sons, certainly not those of my best friend."

Yoon grasped the back of the chair, swaying. "You predicted you would do it. When you returned from Japan you predicted you would do it. Even before you went, you were interested in but one thing."

"My esteemed supervisor," said Min, a slight tremor in his

voice, "you confuse me with such talk. Please sit down and tell me what is troubling you." He indicated the chair again and Yoon sat.

"It was I who arranged your positions, both before and after you went to Japan. How could you have been chosen for the training if I had not helped you?"

Min sat tentatively on another chair. "I agree. I have always been most grateful to you for all you did for me."

"Then why did you ruin my sons?"

Min realized there was more to the problem than he was able to see. "How did I ruin your sons?"

"Greed. It was your greed that did it."

"Did what? My dear Yoon, you must be more specific. I do not understand what you say."

"I shall explain." The rage was gone, but not the anger. "My youngest son wishes to go to Japan and join their army. He even believes he can be an officer. He developed such an idea from listening to you here in the classroom." He studied the face of the younger man. "You said years ago all the children are is tools. Tools for the adults to polish into what they could use for their own ends. It was easy to listen to you then because I did not realize what it would mean to me within my own family. I did not realize you intended to use my sons as two of those tools."

"I have not done so."

"You have. You said you wished to make a name for yourself with the Japanese, even though you hated them, and be promoted to a position of influence. You and your greed. Power. And now you have convinced my son that he should be a Japanese soldier."

"I have never suggested he become a soldier."

"You must have done so. And my foreman's son. He wishes to go to Japan to become a construction engineer."

"I have not suggested that to him."

"Min, do not lie to me. Lie to the others. Lie to the Japanese, but do not lie to me. I have done too much for you."

Min was beginning to perspire. "And your oldest son,

Sunghwan. What can you say I have done to ruin him? He is one of the most hateful students I have ever had in my classroom."

"Yes. You are right. And what made him hateful?"

"I do not know. I only know he hates the Japanese."

"And you have ridiculed him for it."

"I have punished him when necessary, just as I would any other student who did not follow my rules."

"You made him hate the Japanese. That was good. But what you neglected to do was inform him how you really felt about them. You let him think you were a loyal servant of the Emperor. He has learned to hate you for it. Now, today, he learned the truth about you and suddenly that hate has turned to admiration." He glared at the schoolmaster, waiting for a reply.

Min stammered. "I think I do not know what to say."

"How will my younger son feel when I talk with him about this? What will he think of his great schoolmaster when he learns all you desire is to become powerful by duping the Japanese, that you really feel no loyalty to the Emperor at all?"

Now Min turned pale. "I think you would not do such a thing. Do you realize if you tell Shin he will go directly to the Japanese? If he goes to them I can never be promoted to the school in Gapyong."

Yoon sat back and smiled, enjoying Min's discomfort. "I think that is so. You will be destroyed by the very tool you have used. Is that not the way you consider my son? You took this tool and carved and polished it, and when you were finished it was to serve a purpose. Not for me nor for Chunchon, but for you. My son. It was his zeal, his love for the Japanese which you, as you call it, inculcated into him which was to earn you that promotion. The headmaster considered your progress. He noticed all the students you had won over to Japan and your new position as headmaster of the school in Gapyong was to be your reward." He pointed a finger at Min. "That is what you have done to my son."

"If you tell Shin about this it will only make him more loyal to them. He will go and tell them. They will reward him. It will make him a hero. He will be theirs for the rest of his life."

"He is already lost. There is no way I can change that."

"And me. Your friend. For all these imagined crimes you would have me thrown in prison. I will be tortured, you know. They will torture me to death as an example to all the others."

Yoon nodded. "You will receive exactly what you deserve."

"Yoon!" Min rose. "You must stop. I am to be promoted."

"I think you were to be promoted."

Min reached to the table, took a pitcher of water and started to fill a glass. As he did so some of the water splashed onto the floor. "Oh, forgive me. I am sorry. Did it splash on you?" He leaned over to look at Yoon's foot, then grasped it quickly and flipped the older man to the floor. Yoon landed with a thud. Min moved quickly, lifting the chair high in the air to bring it crashing against the supervisor's skull.

He was quick and thorough as he arranged the scene. Then, crying with panic, he ran from the room calling for the headmaster.

* * * * * *

"He came to visit me, but then, he is my friend. He was once my supervisor, you know. Before I went to Japan to study I was his aide on the railroad construction project. We have always been friends." Min looked at the headmaster and the soldiers who had rushed into the room.

"And what happened here?" asked the headmaster curtly.

"I was sitting here at my desk preparing my lessons for tomorrow. I heard a noise and looked up. Yoon was there, coming into the room to congratulate me on my promotion. I began to rise and welcome him when he slipped. There, on the water. It had been spilled there, I think. A most unfortunate accident. When he fell he struck his head on that chair. It was a hard fall, very bad." He shook his head. "Is he badly hurt?" He looked hopefully at the headmaster and the soldiers who were bent over Yoon's body.

One of the soldiers looked up at him incredulously. "He is dead."

Min let out a groan and reached for the headmaster. "It cannot be."

"It is most obvious." The headmaster led him out of the room to the corridor. "Are you certain that is all that happened?"

Min glanced at him in alarm. "Yes, Honorable Headmaster. Of course."

"I thought I heard loud voices coming from this part of the school." The headmaster was walking slowly, watching Min from the corner of his eye. "Are you certain there was no trouble with Yoon?"

"I am most sure," answered Min quickly. "I have told you we were good friends. Both his sons have been my students. The younger one remains. He wishes to join the Imperial Army."

"What of the other son?"

"He has left the school. His father and I have spent many hours discussing that one. We wished to help him but he appears to have a mental problem."

The headmaster eased. "That is most unfortunate. Perhaps the younger one will restore the family's honor."

Min sighed inwardly with relief. "I think he will become a most loyal soldier."

They had reached the headmaster's office. "Perhaps your move to Gapyong will help you to forget the loss of your good friend."

Min's pulse pounded but he dropped his eyes. "Yes, Honorable Schoolmaster."

* * * * * *

Shin, nearing his house, paused. A large crowd of people was gathered before the gate. Everyone was talking. At sight of him they quieted. He quickened his pace and darted past them into the house.

Before him his mother was weeping. As she saw him she reached out, clutching him to her, sobbing.

"Mother, what has happened?"

Slowly she drew back, looking at him through welling tears. "Has no one told you?"

The boy was confused. "Told me what, Mother?"

She sobbed again, deep, wrenching. "Your father. . . ." She looked at him again. "Dead."

His ears rang. The word reverberated through his mind, as if trying frantically to escape, to be gone from him. "Dead?" He looked about him and saw his brother lying in a corner away from them. He looked at his mother again. "How?"

She fought to regain her composure.

The boy broke away from her and ran to his brother. "Say it is wrong," he screamed. "You must say it is a mistake."

Sunghwan lifted his head. His eyes were red. "It is not a mistake. He was killed this afternoon. In the schoolroom."

"No!" He rolled away from his brother and looked again at his mother. She still knelt, sobbing, unable to accept the loss. He rose and raced from the house, diving through the sea of faces so well known, yet so strange to him now. Once free of them he dashed off in the direction of the school. When he bounded up the steps and into the classroom it was empty. Turning, almost in panic, he raced down the corridor to the headmaster's office.

As he burst in the aide leaped up to grab him. "Stop! Where are you going?"

Shin looked at him, then sobbed and pulled to free himself. The sound of the opening door stopped him. The headmaster stood stiffly before them. "What do you want, Shin?"

The boy looked at him. "Say it did not happen," he sobbed. "Please say it did not happen."

The headmaster stepped forward consolingly, placed a hand on his shoulder and said nothing.

The boy looked into his eyes and knew. The tears were hot, sticky. Finally they subsided. The headmaster took his arm and lifted him to his feet, then led him to the door.

* * * * * *

The staff car was waiting, the driver idling the engine.

"Remember, you must not be too harsh," warned the headmaster.

"They will be trying to use me because of my name."

The headmaster grimaced. "I think you must handle that problem quickly and efficiently."

Min smiled. "They shall learn to honor the Emperor." He looked around once more at the familiarity of Chunchon. "It is time to go."

The headmaster grasped his hand almost with fondness. "I wish you good fortune."

They bowed from the waist and Min climbed into the staff car. His salute and smile were lost in the driver's impatient acceleration.

The road wound south, following the river. They rode in silence. A sentry at the bridge started to raise his arm, then tiredly waved them on. At last they sped around the bend at the foot of the valley, the craggy cliffs rising insistently from the right of the road and disappearing into the hovering clouds. The river coursed along on their left, at times shallow and dashing violently about the rocks. Later it was deep, still, moving with a confident assurance toward the west.

When they approached Gapyong the river darted away to their left, joined by another gushing out of the village. Min looked across at an open field near the junction of the two streams. It was flat, dry. Farther back, a grove of trees stood as sentinels against the encroaching hills. He wondered if it were as attractive during the rainy season, or if the bulging rivers would claim its broad, beckoning beauty. He had little time to ponder. They had entered the village and the driver slowed to a stop before the school.

The sound of the brakes magnetized first the school, then the village. No sooner had Min stepped down than he was surrounded by the young, the curious. He reached back into the vehicle and removed his satchel.

"May I carry it for you, Headmaster?"

Min looked down at a boy, perhaps ten. "I have not come to Gapyong to gather servants, but to teach," he announced so that all might hear. "I think I must bear my own belongings."

The boy backed off in disappointment.

Min looked over the group of people, a measure of dignity hiding his pleasure at the adulation. "I am most honored by your kind reception," he said slowly. "However, I have come to do the work of the Emperor. I think he must be pleased if the people of Gapyong do the same."

Slowly at first, they began moving away. Silently. As they drifted farther from the car a low chatter of evaluation began.

Min watched them go, pleased. Then, as he ascended the steps to the school, the staff car turned around in the square and drove away toward Chunchon.

When he entered his office a young man stood facing him. He bowed low.

Min returned the bow and set down his satchel. "My name is Min. I am the new headmaster."

"Honorable Headmaster, my name is Watanabe," returned the other. "I am your schoolmaster assistant."

Min stalked commandingly around his desk and sat. "How long have you been here, Watanabe?"

"Almost a year."

"Almost a year." Min studied him without warmth. "What have you learned in almost a year?"

Watanabe was perplexed. "I think I do not understand you," he stammered.

"Then you must learn. I am a most easy person to understand

because I speak directly. I have no time for playing with word games."

"Yes, Honorable Headmaster."

"Then answer my question, please."

"I have learned never to trust a Korean."

Min bit his tongue, almost reacting with instinct rather than intelligence. "Then you have learned well," he replied. "How many students are in the school?"

"Seventy-two, Honorable Headmaster." He was still standing, but now Min indicated a seat. The Japanese crossed the room and sat.

Min leaned back in his chair. "Watanabe," he said easily. "I am not a waster of time. Therefore, I think we must discuss our problems right away and have it done with. I will begin with mine. My name is Min. I am a Korean. Also, I am the headmaster. I think it will not be easy because of our traditional teaching methods. Schoolmasters are severe, headmasters understanding. It would be most unfortunate should our students misunderstand my more calm approach to their predicaments as Korean nationalism. I am very severe by nature."

"You are faced with a most unfortunate situation, Honorable Headmaster."

"I agree, but it is not uncontrollable. I shall merely be required to practice extreme caution. I shall be understanding to a point. Any attempt on their part, however, to take advantage of my name will result in the most severe punishment. I shall expect you to emphasize that fact in your classroom." He sat back and eyed the other. "Now you may tell me of your problems."

Watanabe cleared his throat, still unsure of Min's true attitude. "It has been most difficult to teach all of them alone. I am grateful you have come."

Min waited. "Am I to assume," he asked at last, "that you have experienced no difficulties beyond those? There are too many students?"

"Yes, Honorable Headmaster."

"That is most strange," mused Min. "I would have thought a village the size of Gapyong would have produced more than seventy-two students."

"Not all of them are qualified for an education."

"Not qualified?"

"They were tested, Honorable Headmaster," added Watanabe.

"Not qualified for the trades? Not qualified to be trained in the law? I think I do not understand the term 'not qualified'."

"The former headmaster believed education should be reserved for those who are loyal to the Emperor."

Min nodded thoughtfully. "I agree, to a point. However, we must think of the usefulness of the others. Not to themselves, mind you. To the Emperor."

"They are. They work."

"Where?"

"In the fields."

"And what of the trades? Who does the building, the merchandizing?"

"We do. The Japanese."

"That, Watanabe, is where the error lies. Why should we use good Japanese soldiers and craftsmen to do menial work which these people can learn to perform? I believe our principal purpose here should be to create an ability in these people to perform the manual labor for the Japanese. The Japanese should be the overseers, the foremen. They should not be required to labor while a vast surplus of manpower languishes in the fields."

"The former. . . ."

"Come. Come," interrupted Min. "Please do not talk to me of the former. The former headmaster is no longer with us. I am. From now on, it will be my policies, my ideas, and my rules which will govern the education of Gapyong. It is a decision which has been made at a much higher level than this. And I promise you, I have no intention of failing. In fulfilling my requirements I plan a rapid advancement for you, Watanabe. We shall expand this school. We shall have two, even three times as many students as there are now. More students will require more masters. When they arrive you shall be my senior assistant." Without waiting for a reply he rose abruptly and proceeded into the first classroom.

The students looked up apprehensively as he marched to the front of the room. He stood stiffly, drawing a deep breath of satisfaction. "Now let us begin."

THE NORTH—HOCHON

Merchant Pak smiled and bowed low at the gate. Lawyer Chung and his wife returned the bow and, their young son remaining close, followed their host into the house.

Pak's wife and daughter bowed and the woman motioned to chairs. The room was well furnished with beautiful, lacquered furniture accented by rich brocades and elegant pieces of art. Hand woven silk screens served to separate the parlor from the low dining table. Highly polished brass accented finely carved tables, while ancient ceramic vases hid furtively in the corners.

"I have heard the farmer's life was spared." Pak settled beside the lawyer.

"Yes, but he is most upset. I think he expected I would free him entirely. He is not very grateful."

Pak snorted. "What would have happened had you not defended him?"

Chung shrugged. "Goto would have executed him. It was his plan to offer Hochon another gruesome spectacle such as he provided with Pyun."

"Kim is a bully. He has no intelligence so he lives his life as a bully."

"Yet he does not understand when others are the same." Chung was quiet for a moment. "I think I was such a bully as a boy."

Pak waved it away. "It is different in childhood. What we were as children did not determine what we became as adults." He eyed

Chung cautiously,. "I had no desire to spend my life as a farmer like my father, yet it was interpreted as cowardice. But I have built my comfort as a man. I think you were popular with the others only because you did not shrink from the fields. You were considered a part of them then, yet you have risen above them."

Chung shifted uneasily. "But I am not above them. I merely learned the law to protect them. If I had not I think Kim would now be dead. The people ascribe greater importance to me than I really deserve."

"But you escaped the fields, just as I."

"Yes. Just as you."

"Then you must understand. We have a better life. We escaped the fields."

"Perhaps they do not wish to escape the fields. I think Kim would be most happy to return to his paddies." He sighed. "Each of us has a function. They grow the food we eat. You store and distribute it. I protect them from exploitation. I think the only difference is that there are fewer of us and more of them. It does not make us better than they."

Their children were sitting, listening, though the mothers were talking of other things.

"Song." The merchant motioned quickly to his daughter, not wanting her to see his embarrassment. "You may go and talk with Taejin. I think the conversations of fathers do not interest eight year old children."

The girl rose, looking uncertainly at the lawyer's son. She was frail, almost emaciated, yet her eyes were bright, expressive. "Come, Taejin. I will show you my room."

He followed her. "Have you known the farmer?" he asked when they were alone.

She shook her head. "My father is most careful to keep me away from them. Do you know them?"

"No. I have not lived in Hochon. It was my father's home when he was a boy, but I was born in Seoul. We were brought here only because the farmer was to be tried."

"Then must you now leave?" Her young face was anxious.

"I think the captain of the militia will keep my father here. I have heard my father say the captain liked his work."

"I am glad." The moment she said it she dropped her eyes, wishing it had not slipped out.

"Why?"

"I do not have friends," she confessed.

"I know no one." He paused. "You are the first I have met."

"Hochon is a small village. My father takes us to Songnim and Nampo. Once we went to Pyongyang." She looked at him proudly.

"Has he taken you to Seoul?"

"He said he will take me there soon."

"It is much larger than Pyongyang."

She ignored the boast. "Perhaps your father will take you there, too."

He changed subjects abruptly. "My father has said there will be a war."

Her face showed shock. "Where will it be? Will it be in Hochon?"

"It will be in China," he announced authoritatively, having gained control of the conversation.

Fright flashed across her face. "Will they take our fathers?"

"I think they must be needed here. Perhaps they will take farmers."

"Where will they take them?"

"To China. To the fighting."

"But who will grow the rice?"

"Women and children will be sent to the fields."

"Must my mother become a farmer? Will I be sent to the fields?"

He affected bravado. "I think we must do our part. I am not afraid to work."

Song's mother entered, summoning them quietly. "We must eat."

The girl looked anxiously at her mother. "Taejin has said there will be a war."

The mother hurried them along, casting a quick glance at the boy. "Come. There is bulkogi, beef. We must not talk of war."

Song recognized her mother's gentle rebuff and said nothing further. But later, as the lawyer led his family from the house, the boy spoke quietly to her.

"You are my first friend in Hochon."

Song smiled. "You are my only friend, Taejin."

THE SOUTH—CHUNCHON

The large, rectangular yard in front of the school was flat, grassless. The youth of Chunchon, students as well as those not deemed qualified, were packed into its area. On the steps stood a Japanese officer, one they had not seen before.

"I am Major Goto," he shouted. "I am the new executive officer of the Gangwondo Province. I am new to your province but I am not new to Korea. I have been here for many years, serving as militia commander in the village of Hochon, far to the north. Since I am not new to your customs I am also not new to your tricks. What do you think of that?" He paused, surveying the silent and apprehensive crowd.

"China has offended the Emperor!" The words exploded from him, frantic, vindictive. "In Peking the Chinese bandits kidnapped some Japanese soldiers at the Marco Polo bridge. It was a clear provocation. Naturally, we have punished them for this insult, but unless we arm rapidly the Chinese will attempt more of these atrocities. They may attempt to mount an invasion. If they do, it will be directed at Korea."

Feet shuffled in place and looks were exchanged, questioning glances which wondered at their fate. Around the perimeter paced soldiers, watchful and waiting.

"My first duty in your city," continued Goto, "is to conscript many of you for service in the Imperial Army. Most of you will go. If you work hard and fight well against the Chinese troublemakers you will be fed and clothed. If you do not you will likely be shot. This is the first day of the conscription. Each of you will be registered before you leave here today. From that point on you will not leave your homes, your classrooms or your assigned labor. If we look for you we must be able to find you immediately."

Deep in the crowd Shin nudged Hong. "You see?" he whispered. "Now I shall enter the army. Two months ago they would not have me. Now they will invite me to join." Pleasure radiated across his face.

Hong was pale. "It is good for you, but my predicament is most unfortunate. I took examinations. Now they will put me in the army and send me off to China. I think I will never receive my education."

"Your situation could be worse," soothed Shin.

Back in the crowd stood his brother, squeezed tightly in the pack. He strained to see what was happening at the front. A line of young men was beginning to ascend the steps, disappearing into the school. A lump tightened his throat. He was convinced he would soon be dead.

At the entrance the officer barked instructions to the soldiers and strode into the building. Sullen faces watched him as he stalked down the corridor and into a room. The front of the line was at the doorway, waiting. Inside, soldiers and clerks were chattering among themselves.

"What are you doing?" he demanded. "Do you not realize we have a train to fill by five o'clock? Get on with it."

"Yes, Major," answered the leader and motioned toward the door. The first man moved forward as the major proceeded into a back office.

Out in the corridor whispers were darting back along the line. "He has said they have a train to fill by five o'clock."

"I thought he said we are to stay where we may be found. Today is only registration."

"Yes. That is what he said outside. It is only more of their lies. They bring us in here and it becomes something different. We will go from one room to another and finally end up on a train without ever seeing the front of the school again." The speaker sneered with disgust.

Suddenly he felt a steel grip on his arm and was yanked from the line. He glanced up sharply to see a Japanese soldier grinning maliciously at him. "I see we have a troublemaker already. Perhaps you are a sympathizer with the Chinese." He motioned for another soldier. "Call the major. We have a dissenter."

The other man nodded and hurried off in the direction of the office.

"I am not a dissenter," protested the young man. "I was only talking with my friends."

"Friends? You have friends? Perhaps we should take them along with you to see the major." He looked around expectantly. "Which of you is a friend of this dissenter?"

The others shrank back, none willing to be seen.

"You see?" chuckled the soldier. "You only thought they were your friends."

There was commotion down the corridor and the other soldier returned, followed closely by the major. "What is this?" demanded the officer. "I am told you wish to see the front of the school again."

"I was merely making a joke while I was waiting," trembled the youth. "I would be most honored to enter the army."

The officer motioned for the others to follow, starting toward the front entry of the building. At the top of the steps he stopped. The soldiers and the prisoner stood behind him. The major held up his hands.

"We have here," he shouted, "a man who demands to see the front of the school again. He believes it will give him courage." He glanced at his prisoner, who was being held tightly by the soldiers. "He is a dissenter!" he screamed. "He thinks we would not allow him to see this city again once he was inside the building." He motioned for more soldiers. "I tell you," he continued, "I shall always give you what is best for you. This dissenter wishes to stand here and admire the front of the school. Fine. He shall have the opportunity."

He wheeled and motioned for the soldiers to take the man down the steps. They dragged him to a gaming post, trussing him tightly against it. Quickly they wrapped a rope across his forehead, securing his head in a position facing the school.

"Now," shouted Goto. "He will have the pleasure of admiring the front of the school for a period of three days." He started back toward the entry of the building. "Make very certain he watches it constantly," he called back. "Provide him with incentives."

Moments later a soldier dashed out of the building with a pail of water and a ladle. Steam was rising from the water. He dipped the ladle into the pail and poured its contents over the man's head. The prisoner screamed, writhing in a vain attempt to free himself. He could not move. The soldier laughed and poured another dipper of water over his head. His skin was beet red from the scalding.

"Look at your school," laughed the soldier. "Is it not beautiful?" Again he applied a ladle of the steaming water. "Each time you look away you will receive another incentive." Then, casting a superior look at the crowd, he called, "If you doubt our sincerity, look at this criminal as you pass. The same reward could be arranged for you." He set the pail on the ground at the man's feet and stood back to watch.

Those in the yard drew back, circling as far as they could from the victim as they moved toward the school. The soldiers forced the lines to pass within a few feet. Though they tried not to look, they could not help themselves. The grotesque, bulging eyes were pained, the face now a purple mass. Weak groans sounded from him incessantly.

Shin was horrified. This was so totally alien to his previous experiences that nausea struck him as he passed the man.

Hong, behind him, saw him retch. "Do not look," he whispered.

Shin stiffened and swallowed hard. "He deserves it," he said aloud.

A soldier looked, wondering if it were an epithet.

"He deserves it," Shin said again, louder. "Anyone who would not fight the Chinese deserves to be punished."

The soldier stepped toward him. "What is your name?"

"Shin."

The soldier whipped out a notebook and scribbled the name. "You learn your lessons well."

"The Chinese would have done worse to him. He should have been willing to go." It had worked. The nausea was gone.

The soldier stepped back along the line, listening and watching the others.

Shin climbed the steps to the school and wound with the line down the corridor. At last he stood before the desk. The clerk looked up. "So you are the valiant Shin."

Shin looked at him in surprise. "Yes, Sir."

The clerk rose. "You will come with me." He led him into a back office, where Goto sat stiffly behind a desk, writing. He looked up. "Is this the man?" he asked the clerk.

"Yes, Sir."

The major nodded, dismissing him, and motioned Shin to a seat. "Your name is Shin?"

"Yes, Honorable Major."

"I am Major Goto. I was surprised to hear of your outburst in the yard. Were you not worried about the reactions of the others to such statements?"

Shin shrugged. "Why should I worry, Honorable Major? I attempted to join the Imperial Army before. They would not allow it then."

"Would not allow it? Why not?"

"They said they would not trust a Korean."

"Why were you so anxious to join the army?"

"I have wished to join ever since I was a boy."

Goto was patient. "You have told me how long, not why."

Shin was embarrassed by the error. "I have wished to join because I learned from my father that we should try to be like the Japanese."

A look of surprise flitted across the major's face. "Really? And who is your father?"

"He is dead now, but he was the construction supervisor for Chunchon for many years."

"The construction supervisor? A Korean? How did that happen?"

"He was a foreman for the Japanese supervisor, but then the supervisor died. My father completed the railroad for Colonel Kometani."

"Do you mean General Kometani?"

"Yes, Honorable Major. He was promoted to general."

"Then perhaps that is where your desire to be a soldier originated," suggested Goto.

Shin nodded. "My schoolmaster also said it would be good for me."

Goto sat back and lighted a cigarette. "And who was that?"

"Schoolmaster Min."

"Another Korean in a major position? What in the world was the general thinking of?"

"Min is a good schoolmaster, Honorable Major," defended Shin.

"I am certain he is," agreed Goto quickly. "I shall look forward to meeting him."

"My apologies, Honorable Major, but he is not here now. He was promoted."

Goto lifted an eyebrow. "Promoted?"

"Yes, Sir. He became headmaster of the school in Gapyong."

"Is that not the town at the far side of the mountain?"

"Yes, Honorable Major."

Goto was near shock. He had believed such cases as Merchant Pak and Lawyer Chung to be relatively isolated. The few educated Koreans were watched very carefully, kept subordinate. "So this Min told you to join the Imperial Army?"

"Yes, Honorable Major."

"Why did he do that?"

"He was very loyal to the Emperor. He taught us to respect the Emperor and be loyal to Japan."

"Did he have the same effect on all his students?"

Shin shook his head. "Most regrettably, Honorable Major, not all. But many of us realized he was right."

Goto sat forward with interest. "Do they all wish to join the Imperial Army?"

"No, Honorable Major. Some wish to study in Japan. My friend Hong is one who wishes to study."

"What does he wish to study?" Goto asked.

"Construction engineering. He has already taken the examinations but he is now in the line out there," he said, motioning toward the outer office. "I think he must go into the army now." He looked anxiously at Goto. "How soon may we leave?"

Goto spread his hands. "Some will leave today. Others may not leave for a week, perhaps longer."

"May I leave today?" he implored.

"It depends upon the registration and processing." He eyed the youth before him. "Why? Do you have that great a desire to be gone from here?"

Shin swallowed hard. "It is because I talked with the headmaster a long time ago. I asked him how I could become an officer in the Imperial Army. He said it was impossible. He said I must be a Japanese citizen."

Goto nodded.

"I wish to go to Japan and become a citizen, a subject of the Emperor."

"Let us see how you perform in your basic training."

Shin was so excited he almost leaped from his chair. "Do you mean there is a chance for me, Honorable Major? I could become an officer?"

Goto smiled patronizingly. "There is always a chance. I would not consider it a probability, but yes. There is a slight chance."

Shin sat back, grinning happily in relief. "Thank you, Honorable Major."

"I think you must not thank me. It has not yet been accomplished. It will be the grace of the Emperor which will make you an officer if it does happen. And the Emperor's grace is bestowed only on those whose performance is most high." He rose. "For now I think you must proceed with your processing or you may remain in Chunchon for the rest of your life."

* * * * * *

Tanaka, the construction supervisor, leaned forward. "I told Hong I would present the request to you on behalf of his son. Hong is a very faithful foreman."

"It appears there are many faithful Koreans here," replied Goto dryly.

"Hong has scored very well on his examinations," continued Tanaka.

Goto poured more tea. "I have never before heard of such a loosely run province," he said, shaking his head. "Why, even in Hochon, the village which was my first command, we had no such permissiveness. It is most fortunate you have not had a rebellion."

The construction supervisor set down his cup. "Chunchon is not a small village. It is a large city."

"I think it is not that large."

"There are many from whom to choose in a city this size. Loyal ones will be found. General Kometani believed the best way to control the people was to give them the responsibility as long as they did not abuse it. I understand there were many people who questioned the way he operated until he proved it would work."

"And where did he develop that philosophy?" snapped Goto.

"I am told it was from my predecessor, Yoon. The supervisor stopped and thought. "No, that is incorrect. It was the man before him really. A Japanese by the name of Murashige."

"What did he have to do with it?"

The supervisor took another sip of his tea. "It was a matter of pride. You see, he became ill. Ultimately, he died of his disease. He could not face going home to Japan with his task unfinished."

"What was the task? I think these construction projects are constant. Was there one which was more important than all the rest?"

"The railroad. Apparently, Murashige felt he must complete the rail line before he could go home with his respect."

"Did he complete it?" asked Goto with sincere interest.

"I am told he died three days before the railroad was completed."

"Then he was unsuccessful. Kometani must have sent him home by that time."

"That was very interesting. General Kometani allowed Murashige to remain here in Chunchon. He lay on a pallet and each morning and evening he issued orders to Yoon, the Korean foreman who was then acting as construction supervisor. Then Yoon went out and did what Murashige told him to do."

"That should not have taken much ingenuity on his part."

"Murashige convinced the general it did. He wanted to save his own honor."

"And when the railroad was complete it earned Kometani a promotion, so he made Yoon the permanent supervisor out of gratitude."

"Yes."

"And Yoon was the man who preceded you in the position."

"Yes."

"That is most strange. There was one of the young ones we were processing yesterday in the conscription. His name was Shin. He said his father was the construction supervisor here before he died."

"That is the one," said Tanaka enthusiastically.

"It must be a dangerous position. Your two predecessors have both died in office." He grinned. "Does that not make you nervous?"

The supervisor smiled. "It will take more than this position to kill me."

Goto was serious again. "This Yoon seemed very loyal. Why?"

"That is how Chunchon is different from your village in the north. Yoon was very loyal to the Japanese. Not only that, but he had an aide in the early years. It was when they were building the railroad. Yoon arranged for this aide to be sent to Japan to study. He came back several years later as a schoolmaster. He was loyal, too. So when they needed a headmaster in. . . ."

" . . . Gapyong, they sent him. What do you think of that?" Goto looked pleased, the supervisor, confused.

"How did you know?"

"I have told you I talked with Yoon's son yesterday." He rose and started pacing the floor. "I am most uncomfortable with this situation."

The supervisor looked curious. "What causes you discomfort?"

"I think it is much too smooth. There is too much apparent loyalty here, and too much success. It smells rotten. I do not trust any of them."

The supervisor rose and followed the major in his pacing. "But there has never been the slightest question about any of them." He stopped and thought for a moment. "Wait. Yoon's oldest son was different. He always sulked about the Japanese."

Goto stopped and turned. "Is he still here?"

"He is unless he was conscripted yesterday."

Goto smiled and sat down again, pouring himself another cup of tea. Offering one to the supervisor, he asked, "What was so strange about his attitude? That is the way the Koreans think. Perhaps it is a case of this other son not being quite so cunning as the one with whom I talked. He shows his true feelings, his father and brother did not. And this schoolmaster. I believe that was another case of misjudgment. I do not know the man, but I think he may not be quite the loyal man he appears."

The supervisor shifted his position, returning to his original topic. "Do you mean, then, that you will not allow the Hong boy to go to Japan to study?"

Goto laughed. "No. Of course not. That would alert all the criminals. No, Hong may go to Japan. And this Shin who wishes to become an officer may go on with his plans, since he will have to complete his basic training with valor before he can even be considered for commissioning. I shall merely alert Tokyo of the situation here and they will keep a most careful eye on the two of them. If Shin does not become an officer he will blame the people in Japan and we will still have the opportunity to trap the cell here. As for the schoolmaster, I think I must talk with Colonel Hieda about him. I think the area commander will agree it is most necessary to slow him down. He could do much harm if he is allowed to continue teaching these children. If he is that subtle, we have no idea what things he is teaching when he thinks we are not watching him."

"Then I think the only one left is the other son."

"Yes. The other son." Goto set down his cup and stood. "I shall plan something special for him. If he is as antagonistic as you say he is I think he can be a most graphic example for the rest of Chunchon. It would be a logical arrest to make. He does not seem to have the intelligence to cover his tracks."

"But Major, suppose they really are loyal. Suppose they are leaders in making the rest of the people of Chunchon more loyal to us, causing them to create less trouble. Would not our causing such difficulties for these few incite a rebellion?"

Goto smiled sardonically. "I should enjoy an opportunity to show them the force of our weapons."

Tanaka rose from the chair, shaking his head. "May I tell Hong his son will be going to Japan or should I allow it to go through normally?"

Goto paused and thought. "I think it would be best if you told him. Allow them to think it was their influence, their cunning which obtained this for the boy. It may throw them off their guard." He sat once more, smiling pensively.

Tanaka watched him, expecting more. Finally, realizing the major was merely entranced, perhaps planning how he would proceed with their annihilation, he turned and left the room.

* * * * * *

The militia commander at Gapyong looked up in surprise as Major Goto strode in. "Good morning, Major." He rose and bowed. "You honor my command."

"Good morning, Captain." He glanced around the room. "What did you say your name is?"

"I am Captain Amioka, Sir."

"Fine, Amioka. I am Goto, the executive officer of Gangwondo Province."

The captain was impressed, yet curious. "Please have a seat, Sir. I shall order tea." He clapped his hands and sat near Goto. "This is an unexpected honor, Major. Is there something I can do to help?"

"I am concerned for your school," confided Goto. "I understand you have a Korean headmaster here."

Amioka nodded. "Yes, Sir. He came here from Chunchon two years ago."

"Do you like him?"

"He is doing excellent work. Watanabe, the junior schoolmaster, reports to me regularly."

"You realize, I hope, there is a questionable side of this Min." Goto's look was piercing.

Amioka showed his surprise. "I have not realized, Honorable Major. No one has told me."

"How long have you been serving in Gapyong?"

"Three years." The tea came and he poured for Goto, then himself.

"Then you have been here since before he came and you have never even suspected Min was working behind your back. Amioka, I am amazed at this entire province. The more I see the more

shocked I become. Everyone here is so trusting of the Koreans."
He sipped his tea. "I can tell you from long experience, it is wrong."

"But, Major. I have had him watched since the first day he
arrived. I talked with Watanabe. He has been most careful to report everything to me."

"What do you mean by everything?"

Amioka was becoming nervous. "Watanabe tells me what he
says, what he does, the material he teaches in his classes, his whole
attitude."

"And what of his friends? Have you checked on who his friends
are?"

"I think he does not have any."

Goto was surprised. "Has he none at all? That is odd, would
you not say, not to have any friends?" He sat back casually and
lighted a cigarette. "Or is it that he only sees them quietly, when
no one knows? In other words, my friend, I wonder if he has formed
some sort of underground here. Some sort of organization which
will work at crossed purposes with us. Then he could be as loyal as
he wished during the day and be stabbing us in the back each
night. And we would be too hypnotized by his most exemplary
teaching methods to notice."

Amioka became defensive. "He has been watched. There has
been nothing about his habits which would lead us to believe such
a thing was happening." He stopped and considered the senior
man for a moment. "Please tell me, Major, what it is that makes
the provincial headquarters believe such a thing is happening."

"There is strong evidence of collusion between this man and
several in Chunchon," replied Goto.

"Collusion for what purpose?"

"They wish to further the fortunes of several closely connected
individuals in a certain select group."

It was too vague for Amioka. "I think I do not understand
what you mean, Major. Perhaps it is because I am out here in
Gapyong and away from the central command. I do not know
these other men you mention and I see no contact between any-

one and Min. All I see is what he does at the school. That appears to be most loyal to our government."

Goto sat back, undaunted. "Perhaps I should tell you some history. It began when they were building the railroad many years ago. A certain man by the name of Yoon appears to have begun this den. He formed it with one of his assistants by the name of Hong. They took advantage of a chance illness of the supervisor of construction, arranged for Yoon to be named acting supervisor while the man was dying, and managed to make the position permanent. I have not yet had the time to investigate the circumstances of the supervisor's death in detail, but I suspect the death was not natural. I intend to explore it further. Regardless, when Yoon became the supervisor, Hong immediately became his lead foreman."

"But was the headquarters not aware of that?"

"Apparently the headquarters personnel were too busy arranging their own promotions. During the time Yoon was acting supervisor he had an aide. This aide ran all sorts of errands for Yoon, including carrying messages back and forth to the sick man, the Japanese supervisor."

"So the supervisor knew only what he was told by this Yoon and his aide?"

"That is the way it appears. Now, I find this very interesting. The supervisor died only three days before the railroad was completed. Yoon was named to the permanent position and his aide was sent off to Japan to study." He leaned forward. "Amioka, it smells. I believe the aide was being rewarded for his extraordinary service to Yoon."

Amioka refilled the teacups. "And how does this concern my headmaster?"

Goto sat back and placed his hands on his knees in triumph. "Min, your esteemed headmaster, was the aide. What do you think of that?"

"Then you suspect he performed the crime? He murdered the supervisor?"

"I suspect he played a major role in the death of the supervisor. Consider the facts. Yoon and Hong wish to become strongmen. If they could eliminate the supervisor they could control all the construction in Gangwondo Province. From there they could provide positions for those loyal to them, or deny positions to their enemies. If someone failed to cooperate they could be assigned to more difficult labor. Our two headmen could control it all."

"Is that what has happened?"

"You must wait. I am not finished. Consider my hypothesis for a few moments. The only barrier in their path was the Japanese supervisor. If they murdered him and were caught, they would be executed. If they could arrange for someone else to do it they would have no worries. If their servant succeeded they could reward him through their influence. If he failed they could have him eliminated, preferably before suspicion turned toward them. Provided they worked quickly enough they could succeed and appear to be heroes in the process."

"You believe they succeeded?"

Goto spread his hands. "Murashige, the Japanese supervisor, died. Yoon and Hong received their promotions. Min received his reward. Yes, Captain Amioka, I believe Min murdered the construction supervisor."

Amioka evidenced admiration. "You have been in Chunchon only a short time, Major. How did you discover this so quickly, especially when no one has ever suspected it before?"

Goto tried to look matter-of-fact. "Most fortunately, I have excellent intuition. It began through a chance meeting, but from there my intuition has solved the mystery. You must remember, I have spent many years in Korea. I know how they think. I know what to look for."

"But was General Kometani not the commander in Chunchon when all this was happening? I think I would not wish to be the one to suggest he was negligent."

"Yes. Kometani was the commander during the building of the railroad. He was promoted to colonel when the rail line opened.

Later, when the provincial headquarters building was completed, again ahead of schedule, he was promoted to general and transferred to the Kwantung Army. He has become very famous since those days."

Amioka thought for a moment in silence, then looked up at Goto. "I ask your pardon, Honorable Major. I think I do not understand how Min is operating today in Gapyong."

"I believe he has maintained his contacts in Chunchon. I think Hong did not become the leader of this syndicate when Yoon died. I think Min became their leader. I want him watched far more carefully now than he has been in the past. I wish to shower eyes on him like the snows of the winter. I wish to know where he goes, whom he sees, even what he eats. I wish to be kept informed about what he is teaching the students in the school and what effect it is having on their thoughts. Quite simply, I wish this schoolmaster turned inside out so we may inspect him in the most careful detail. What do you think of that?"

Amioka suddenly appeared to agree, placating his superior. "Major, I will keep you informed. I have been curious about this man ever since he arrived. The first day he was here he ordered Watanabe to do things as though he were one of the schoolboys. Watanabe was most embarrassed."

"Why did you not do something then and there?"

"I did not because I decided to wait a few days and see if it continued. It did not, so I talked with Watanabe. We decided it must have been brought on by a Korean being given an unexpected position of authority. Never having had one before, he might have been expected to act as he did."

"It will be a great pleasure to me the day we shoot him. I shall prove he murdered the construction supervisor. When I do we shall have a grand festival for the execution." Goto paused contemplatively, then continued, strengthening his hypothesis for Amioka. "Yoon and Hong had sons. Shin, Yoon's son, wishes to become an army officer. Hong," he smiled craftily, "wishes to study construction engineering. I did not wish to do anything hastily so I told

Shin it would depend on his performance in training. That should keep him busy. As for the other one, we shall allow him to go for his schooling. After that, we certainly can arrange for him to be assigned to a place far away from Chunchon when he is graduated. Thus, we shall be most certain the dynasty of Yoon and Hong comes to as sure an end as did that of Yi."

Amioka nodded. "And what of Watanabe? Shall I inform him of this?"

Goto smiled cunningly. "No, I think you should not tell him now. Later, perhaps. If this Min is as clever as he appears he could trick Watanabe into telling him of our plans." He rose. "His time for heroism will come."

A month later, however, Watanabe was called to the headquarters during classes. Headmaster Min was waiting when he returned. "Who was that you went to see?"

"A Major Goto. He is the new executive officer for Gangwondo Province."

"And what did he want with you?"

"He was on an inspection tour," lied Watanabe. "He wished to discuss the school as part of the inspection."

"Well, why did he not ask for me? Is the fact I am Korean forever to be a curse?"

"I have no idea, Headmaster. I only know he wished to talk with me."

Min shrugged and turned away. "It really makes no difference. We have an excellent school here. The curriculum is very good. It is a credit to the Japanese system and is beginning to provide them with much assistance in the trades." Suddenly he stopped, thought, and turned back to Watanabe. "Tell me, did he mention that I am a Korean?"

Watanabe looked at this man who, for all his pomp, had been a highly effective headmaster, a good friend. "Yes, he mentioned it."

Min nodded. "I think he must wish to replace me as headmas-

ter." He dropped into his chair, then looked dejectedly up at
Watanabe. "That is what he plans, is it not?"

"Headmaster," evaded Watanabe, "I wish you to know I respect you. I have a most high regard for the way you run the
school. The day you arrived you were harsh with me, but I know
why. I knew even then. Since that day you have been a most fair
superior. I have tried to work hard and well for you."

"You have done very well, Watanabe. I could not have asked
for a more loyal man."

"Headmaster." Watanabe was plainly troubled.

"Yes," answered Min without looking up.

"You will not be headmaster much longer. I have been ordered
not to tell you that, but I feel I must say it. The major is in a very
vindictive mood."

Min looked up, angry. "But why is he angry with me? Why is
he not angry with some of the slackers, the ones who are trying to
avoid their responsibilities? I have always tried to do things the
way they wished."

"I do not know him. Today was the first time I have met him.
I think he must be a very willful person." He paused. "Even Amioka
does not trust him."

"And what does he plan to do with me? Am I to be put out on
a labor detail?"

Watanabe wrestled with his conscience. "He plans to execute
you." Suddenly he was agitated. "He plans to try you for murder
and execute you. If he learns that I warned you I will be there with
you before the rifles."

Min was staring at him in horror, the color drained from his
face. "What does he say I have done?" he whispered.

"He believes you murdered a construction supervisor in
Chunchon."

He thought of Yoon, a cold chill running through him. He
wondered how the man could have learned. There had been no
witnesses.

Watanabe was still talking. "I believe it is most unfortunate, but Major Goto has spent several years in Hochon, a village of the north where such things are common. There is much oppression in the north."

"There is much oppression everywhere in Korea," whispered Min. He looked up imploringly at Watanabe. "When does he plan to arrest me?"

"I am to watch you and keep him informed. He wishes to know everything you say and do, who the people are you visit."

"Why? Does he plan to arrest others as accomplices in this imagined crime?"

"I think he wishes to create a spectacle. He plans to make a festival of the trial and execution."

Min looked up at his assistant. "Do you believe I would do such a thing?"

Watanabe was emphatic. "I do not believe his charges. If I did, I would not be telling you this. But you have been my friend."

"Have I any hope?"

Slowly Watanabe shook his head. "Most unfortunately, none at all."

Min stared at the floor. "Then I must disappear."

"It will do you no good. He will find you. When he does he will claim your running away is proof of your guilt."

"I think it better than if I stay here. You said yourself I have no hope at all. I think there is no sense in remaining here and letting him shoot me." He glanced around the room, panicked. "No, I shall escape while there is still time. But I must ask your assistance. Do not tell him I have gone until tomorrow. I must have twenty-four hours. If I have that he will never find me."

"But where will you go?"

"It would be better if you did not know."

"I shall have to tell him, you know. I shall have to tell Captain Amioka. He will have to put out a search party."

"If you do not tell Amioka until tomorrow morning he cannot do any more than the major."

"But how do I keep it from him?"

"I think you must tell them you saw me in my room. Tell them I was in my room at ten o'clock tonight. It would be entirely reasonable for me to have departed during the night. In that case, the logical place for them to look for me is in the mountains above the valley. They will never suspect where I really intend to go."

Watanabe was curious. "Where is that?"

Min looked at him sadly. "If I tell you they can force the information out of you. No, as I have said, it is better if you think as they do. I would go to the hills above this valley."

"But you cannot leave Gapyong now. It is daylight. You should be in the school."

"I must. Do not worry about it." He stood, looking fondly at Watanabe. "Someday I hope you will see me again, but not as an accused man. When you do, please remember me as a friend."

"I can only remember you for what you are. You have truly been a friend." They shook hands, then bowed low in mutual respect. A moment later Watanabe was alone in the room.

Min moved rapidly. After sauntering casually through the town he dashed for cover. Several miles away, he dove into the river and, swimming strongly against the current, soon dragged himself up on the opposite bank. Tired, he crawled into the brush and rested. It was not yet noon. An hour later he was moving again, walking steadily but not frantically now. His course was eastward toward the Sorak Range. If he could get into its foothills they would have a difficult time finding him.

By nightfall he was far into their protective crags, picking his way slowly through the rocks northward. Until he could arrive at a plan he intended to hole up in the mountains and wait. It was summer. He could subsist on berries if necessary.

He found a vantage point, deep in the brush, from which he could watch Chunchon below him to the west. He had now completely circled the city from Gapyong. It was the least likely spot for the Japanese to search for him.

At midmorning he saw a staff car race up the highway from the direction of Gapyong. The dust rose in a cloud from its wheels.

It was impossible to tell who or how many were in the vehicle. He waited. Within minutes of the car's arrival in Chunchon a convoy of trucks departed down the same road, moving away from him. Min knew they were the search party, that now he had little to fear but the elements, the cold of the winter ahead. Certainly, if the Japanese intended to search the Sorak they would not do so for several days. By that time he would be far away.

The truck column was but a small snake now, far down the valley to the south and beginning to wind around the bend in the river to the west. He rose and worked his way along the slopes to the northeast, following the general direction of the Soyong river. Inje lay miles ahead. In the area between there was nothing but a series of tiny hamlets and isolated cottages nestled protectively in the draws.

He evaluated several locations for a hiding. None seemed right. He continued his course eastward, but slowly, cautiously. Days passed, then weeks. He ate berries, and once snared a small animal, which he ate raw rather than chance a fire with its telltale smoke.

Summer had gone when, near Inje, he climbed a gorge to the south. The mountains rose sharply now, almost vertical in their beauty. Towering waterfalls tumbled hundreds of feet through the clear air from their overhangs above. Then, spattering onto the rocks below, they joined the stream of others from farther up the gorge to leapfrog their way into Inje.

The climb was tedious, precarious. He stumbled frequently, grasped rocks until his hands bled. Then, in the distance, he heard a sound. He shrank into the underbrush and listened. It was the regular impact of an axe on wood, reverberating in the crisp air.

Carefully, he crawled forward. The sound grew louder, but still he found no one. It was almost half a mile before he discerned movement through the trees. He crept closer.

The woodsman was alone. Leaning against a tree was an A-frame which he was piling high with small logs and branches. Beside him lay an old blanket which he would use as padding for the load against his back. Next to it lay a heavy coat, his protection against the advancing autumn.

Min looked hungrily at the blanket and coat. He would need such protection for the harsh winter ahead. He made his decision quickly. Selecting a club from the deadfall about him, he circled his prey. Then, with a scream, he sprang out at the unsuspecting woodsman.

The startled man had only begun to turn when the bludgeon struck his face. He died instantly. Min wrestled the A-frame onto his victim's shoulders, then carried him to the cliff and pushed him over. He could not even hear the impact when the body struck the bottom.

He returned to the site of the man's cuttings, gathered the coat, blanket and axe and made his way farther into the wilderness.

Mists hung damply about him. There was a chill in the air, and he began watching for shelter. The rock faces were pocked with small impressions and caves, yet many were not accessible. At last he saw one on the far side of the gorge. It appeared to be deep and was covered by vines which hung down over its face from the growth above. It took him six hours to reach it.

He tested the strength of the vines carefully. One broke but the remainder held. Gathering several together, he wrapped the blanket around his shoulders and pulled the coat over it. Sliding the axe through his belt, he swallowed hard for courage and began the precarious descent toward the mouth of the cave.

While the opening was small, the inside was considerably larger. Penetrating some forty feet into the cliff, Min was certain it would provide him ideal protection, not only from discovery, but from the elements of the harsh Sorak winter as well. His only problems would be scarce food and the danger of building a fire.

It was dark. Even in the afternoon, when the rays of the descending sun shone against the face of his cliff, the protective vines cut off most of the light. He was hungry, yet his exhaustion was more pronounced. He piled his blanket and coat in a corner of the cave and lay down. Moments later he was fast asleep.

* * * * * *

"What do you mean, he is gone?" exploded Goto. "Where has he gone?"

Watanabe was shaken. "There is only one place he could have gone. I think he must be in the hills north of the town."

"Did you notify Amioka?"

"Yes, Honorable Major. He has a search party there now, but he says he must have more help if he is to be successful in capturing the man."

Goto rose and screamed for his men. "Assemble a battalion. Send them to Gapyong immediately. A prisoner has escaped." He turned exasperatedly toward Watanabe. "Now, Schoolmaster, perhaps you will tell me why he might have thought it necessary to leave Gapyong?"

"I do not know, Honorable Major."

"I think someone must have said something to him. I think he would not suddenly leave the town when you say he has never done so before. You must think that unusual, do you not?"

"Yes, Honorable Major."

"Did you watch him yesterday?"

"Yes, Honorable Major. I was with him after school until late in the evening."

"What happened then?"

"I left him at his room and went back to my quarters."

Goto folded his hands and thought. "Are you certain you said nothing which would have alerted him?"

"I said nothing, Honorable Major."

"And Amioka? Did he see Amioka?"

"I think he did not, unless he saw him during the school session."

Goto leaped from his chair. "Then how could he have learned my plan?" he screamed.

Watanabe recoiled. "Perhaps when you sent for me at the school. That may have been the time. He is the headmaster. If his assistant is called in by the provincial executive officer he would probably wonder at the reason. Perhaps someone followed me and eavesdropped on our conversation from outside."

"Well," mused Goto in a moment of calm, "that establishes his guilt. If he were innocent why would he find it necessary to run away?"

Watanabe remained silent.

There was a knock at the door and a captain entered. "Major, the battalion is ready."

"Then why are you standing here? Get them on the road to Gapyong."

"Sir, are you coming with us?"

Goto looked at his watch. "Start them moving. I shall follow in my staff car. Meanwhile, if you arrive there before me, report to Captain Amioka. He already has a search in progress."

"Yes, Sir." The officer bowed and left.

"Who is attending to the school today?" He was glaring at Watanabe again.

"No one, Honorable Major. There were only two of us."

"Then what are you doing here? Is the education of Gapyong to come to a halt because a criminal has escaped? A criminal goes free and suddenly there is a school holiday. I think you have devised a most effective way to encourage a crime wave, a lack of respect for the Emperor."

"I shall depart immediately, Honorable Major."

"I think you should not expect to remain in Gapyong much longer. I intend to arrange for both you and Amioka to be transferred back to Japan. There is little you can do of any use here in Korea. I consider you both ineffective."

Watanabe blanched. "Yes, Honorable Major." He bowed but it was not returned.

The search continued for days. The mountains north of Gapyong were combed. From there the hunt moved eastward to

Chunchon. The city was searched from door to door with no success. Hong was grilled unmercifully to no avail. Min had disappeared like a star at daybreak.

Bulletins were dispatched to all commands in Korea. Initially,
each commander made a cursory search of his area. Then, with the
approach of autumn, their ardor waned and Min became a thorn
only in the side of Goto.

He brooded. He had never been made to look the fool before.
He was accustomed to being obeyed, always seeing his campaigns
through to a successful if grotesque end. Thus, to be so frustrated
by an elusive man whom he wanted on an elusive charge was particularly irritating.

"Goto, you leave me no choice but to interrupt your investigation." The area commander was terse.

"Honorable Colonel," preened Goto, unheeding. "I shall have
the criminal very soon. I have learned where he is hiding."

"I think you are not listening," rebuffed Colonel Hieda. "I
have reviewed the evidence in this investigation."

Goto smiled. "I am most honored, Colonel. My experience
and intuition have led me to discover his corruption."

"Your experience has betrayed you. Your intuition has caused
much embarrassment in my command. This foolishness must stop."

For the first time Goto recognized the senior man's displeasure. "But, Honorable Colonel, I have seen much of this sort of
thing before. I uncovered many criminal plots in Hochon. These
people come from the same stock. The Koreans cannot be trusted."

Hieda ignored him. "In my review of this situation I have
learned many facts. Murashige died many years ago. The medical
records indicate he was a very sick man. Our present advances in
medical science indicate it may have been cancer. General
Kometani's log states that Yoon was most well qualified for the
position to which he was assigned. He was highly intelligent. He
learned rapidly and well under Murashige." He paused, lighting a
cigarette. "Yoon and Hong were friends. This was most natural.
They worked together. And now for this Min." He snorted deri-

sively. "He was loyal to General Kometani and the Emperor in the face of a great crime wave in Chunchon. There was much thievery. He might well have joined with the criminals and reaped handsome profits at the expense of the Emperor. Most fortunately for us he did not. He observed the criminals and turned them in. It was for this loyalty he was rewarded."

Goto squirmed, trying to save his face. "I think he hoodwinked General Kometani very well with his trick. It was part of his scheme."

Hieda stubbed out the cigarette in disgust. "I think you must rest. You are of no value to me in your present state of mind."

"A most constructive suggestion, Honorable Colonel," replied Goto quickly. "May I go to Seoul?"

The colonel brightened. "You become perceptive, Major. I think you will benefit greatly from a rest in Seoul. The women there are much better than the wenches of Chunchon."

"And," replied Goto, his spirits buoyed, "the hunting will be most productive."

"You confuse me."

Goto smiled, sensing a veiled approval from the commander. "I shall return with Min in chains."

Hieda rose abruptly. "I shall not allow you to further embarrass this command in such a way. You will not seek out Headmaster Min."

"But, Honorable Colonel, he is in Seoul. My intuition. . . ."

"Then you shall not go to Seoul." Hieda paused to quiet his agitation. "I have told you I wish you to rest. It appears you will not do so in Seoul. I shall offer you a final alternative. You may go on a hunt of a different kind. In the Soraksan. You may rest there for five days. I shall hear no more of Headmaster Min. You must be content to hunt in the Sorak and return to Chunchon. To disobey me will cause me much displeasure and I shall send you home in disgrace."

Goto stared, disbelieving.

"You will leave immediately," snapped the colonel, bowing curtly.

Inje was cold with late autumn. The higher altitudes of the Sorak were colder still. Min had left his cave early, hoping to snare food. Now, some distance up the slope from the gorge, he stopped. A weak sun was drifting inconsequentially higher in the sky. It provided light, if little warmth.

"What do you seek this high in the mountain?"

Min wheeled to see the officer standing easily beside a tree. The muzzle of the weapon was following him.

"I am a woodsman," Min replied quickly. "I am seeking new areas from which to gather faggots."

The officer smiled and moved toward him. "We shall see," he said arrogantly. "What is your name?"

Min glanced nervously at the weapon. "I am Chang."

"And do you know who I am?"

Min tried to ignore the easily recognized rank. "You are a soldier."

"I am a major," corrected Goto quickly. "I am Major Goto, executive officer of the Gangwondo Province. What do you think of that?"

Min immediately bowed low, the easier to hide his panic.

Goto swung the weapon in an arc. "Do you live here in the Sorak?"

"My humble cottage is in a valley many miles from here," Min replied.

"Why do you come so far in search of faggots?" pressed Goto.

"The hills near my home are bare, Honorable Major," explained Min. "I must go far to find new areas and to snare food."

"Ah, then you are also a hunter," observed Goto.

"I hunt only to feed myself and my wife, Honorable Major."

"Then you must know where to locate game," concluded Goto. "You shall serve as my guide."

"I shall be most honored," bowed Min. He pointed along the rising ridge to the south. "I think it will not be difficult to find game farther up. They often water at the top of the gorge."

Goto nodded and slung his weapon casually over his shoulder.

"Where is your camp? If you are far from your home you must have a camp."

Min shook his head. "I sleep only on the ground, Honorable Major. I have no need of a camp until the snow comes." They began making their way through the forest. "Do you come to the Sorak often, Honorable Major? I think you must be too busy to come here often."

"I have come to hunt, to relax," replied Goto importantly. "I am a seeker of criminals. When I complete an investigation I seek relaxation."

"A most worthy occupation," agreed Min, apprehensive. "Have you recently solved a crime?"

Goto looked at him sharply, then relaxed as Min plodded onward in apparently easy unconcern. "Yes. My intuition has led me to solve a most flagrant crime. I have traced a schoolmaster who murdered a supervisor of construction."

Min waited, then prodded Goto's silence. "Did you execute him?"

Goto smiled. "I have not done so yet, but I shall. I have only recently learned he fled to Seoul. I shall arrest him immediately after my hunt."

Min's pulse was racing. "I am most honored to serve as guide for such a hero, Honorable Major."

Goto smiled with satisfaction. "I have much experience with your people," he boasted.

Min looked at him, raising an eyebrow. "Oh? Then you have served our province for a long time?"

"No. I am new in Gangwondo. I have been many years in Hochon, a place far to the north."

Min pointed to his right. "I think we must move closer to the gorge."

Goto turned with him. "Is there a watering place so high?"

"The source of a waterfall, Honorable Major, must be from the top. There are many waterfalls in the Sorak."

They reached the edge. Together they looked down, both awed

by the magnificence of the sight. Far below them the floor of the gorge was rough, a jagged surface strewn with rocks and logs which peeped furtively from the rushing water of the stream. From either side of them fell curtains of water which sang their way gleefully to join with others at lower levels. Then, melded, they danced their way down the beckoning flume toward Inje. "Do you not find our mountain beautiful, Honorable Major?"

"I shall consider it most beautiful when it fills my belly," replied Goto impatiently. "Where is the game?"

Min looked past him. "Behind you now," he said quietly.

Goto turned quickly, swinging the rifle from his shoulder. As he did Min swung hard, quickly at his throat. The dropped weapon skittered away and Goto fell, then struggled to rise, to reach the firearm. Min hastily snatched up a stick, felt it crunch as it broke between the other's shoulders. Then, diving, he kicked the rifle into the gorge.

Goto raised his eyes slowly, stunned. "Who are you?" he gasped.

Min smiled, now wielding a stouter club. "My name is unimportant. I am a friend of schoolmasters."

Goto's face tightened. "You are Headmaster Min," he hissed. He shifted and Min waved the wood over him.

"I suggest you do nothing foolish, Honorable Major. I should not like to kill you. You have lost your face. I shall allow you an honorable death."

"You will die," rasped Goto. "You will face a firing squad."

"But who is to arrest me now, Honorable Major?" leered Min. "I think you must first arrest me before you may execute me."

Goto sneered. "When I do not return a thousand soldiers will search these peaks. They know where I have come."

"They will not find a criminal. They will find only the body of a careless major killed in a fall. Your death will be considered a most unfortunate accident."

"You are a wanted man. They will seek you out as my murderer."

"I?" laughed Min. "But you have told me you have proof I fled to Seoul. I think they will not seek me in the Sorak."

Suddenly Goto rolled to one side. Min brought the club down, too late. The major sprang upward, a knife glistening in his hand. Min swung the club again but Goto was on him, driving the blade deep. The schoolmaster groaned and fell, dragging the other man with him. They rolled, Goto withdrawing the blade and thrusting again. It struck metal and glanced off, piercing his own body. A look of horror flashed across Goto's face. He grasped frantically at Min, but slid uncontrollably toward the precipice. Min watched him with hazy eyes as the officer drifted agonizingly from view. All that remained was the ringing, futile scream as Goto plunged to the rocks far below.

* * * * * *

It took Min several days to work his way down to the Soyong River. Then, keeping careful cover, he sought the isolated cottages he had seen on his way into the area weeks before. He approached one.

"What do you wish from me?" asked the peasant suspiciously.

"I must have help."

The man looked at him, haggard and limping. "Bandits?"

"The Japanese."

The man looked around to be sure they were not being watched. "You must come inside."

Min hobbled through the gate and into the hut. "Do they come here often?"

"They come only when they wish to steal from us." There was hate in his voice.

"Is there a place where I can hide if they come while I am here?"

"Yes." The man did not say where. "Where is your home?"

"Sokcho. The fishing place."

"Why do you come this way?"

"They stole my fishing boat." Min feigned anger. "First they took the fish, then my boat. When I protested they put a bayonet in me."

His host clicked his tongue and motioned to his wife. "Bring some hot water." Looking back to Min, he asked, "When did you eat?"

Min was aware he was gaunt, not only from the wound but from not having eaten well. "I stole in Inje. Other than that I have snared small game."

"Today you shall have rice," the man said without smiling.

"What are they like here?" Min asked.

"It is bad, but I think it is much worse in the cities. There they have no freedom. They are very close to the militia. Here in the country I think it is too much trouble for them."

"What is your work?"

Again the man gave him a suspicious look. "What does it matter? The only things we are allowed to keep are the faggots we collect in the mountains. If we catch game they seem to know it and take it away from us."

Min affected incredulity. "Then how do you eat?"

The man smiled wanly. "We have little."

"I have fished all my life."

"We will get you well. Then you must move on. It can be very dangerous here for one who does not know the mountains. One of my neighbors disappeared several weeks ago. He has never been found, and he has worked in the Sorak all his life."

"Does anyone know what happened?"

The man looked at him in disgust. "How could we? I have told you he has never been found."

"Has anyone gone to look?"

He shook his head. "I do not work in the Soraksan. I remain closer to home."

The woman had come with the hot water and they stooped over him, dabbing at the wound. "You have been wounded most seriously. It will take much time to heal."

They dressed the wound with clean cloths, then led him to a pallet. "Lie here," said the woman.

"I cannot. I must go."

The man touched his shoulder. "You must stay a few days. Then you should go."

Min could not be convinced. "No. I must find a place where I can hide. You said I can do nothing here. I must find a place where I can hide and do something useful."

The man scoffed. "Where would that be in Korea? The Japanese are everywhere."

"There must be a place farther inland. I shall go to Seoul. I will be able to lose myself in Seoul. There are too many people for them to watch."

The man nodded without agreeing. "You must do as you believe. I think you must find difficulty in the city, but you must do as you believe. You shall eat before you go."

Min looked at him and nodded. "Yes. I shall eat."

"Good." the man motioned once more to his wife. She stepped down into the earthen kitchen and he heard the rattle of utensils. A moment later the sound was replaced by another. The man looked up sharply, then beckoned to Min. "The Japanese. Come."

He led him into the kitchen and indicated a floor burner, an opening in which the fires are kindled to keep the floors warm. "Crawl in here. Stay close to the wall," he whispered.

Min bent and squeezed into the space. It was sooty with use, hot. The hatch closed behind him. He groped in the darkness, then began slithering on his stomach into one of the larger ducts leading under the main portion of the house. Footsteps sounded above his head, then the squeak of the gate.

"What is your name?" The words were spoken in Japanese.

"Oh."

"What do you do, Oh?"

"I gather faggots in the forest."

"Where do you gather your faggots?"

"In the forest behind my house. On the mountain."

"When was the last time you were in the Sorak?"

There was a pause.

"Answer. The Soraksan."

"Two, perhaps three years. I do not work in the Sorak."

Min heard footsteps scuff through the courtyard and enter the house. Now they stood directly over his head.

"A Japanese officer has died in the Sorak Pass."

There was a momentary silence, then, "That is most unfortunate. Is he one of the officers who has come here?"

"He was the executive officer for Gangwondo Province."

"I knew no such man."

"One of your neighbors was found near the body."

"Did he kill him?"

"No. Your neighbor has been dead for several weeks, the officer only a few days. It seems strange. Two deaths in the same location. First your neighbor, then the officer."

"How did they die?"

"If you know nothing it does not concern you."

Min shifted uneasily in his cramped quarters.

"I know nothing of such things," announced Min's host. "I thought my neighbor might have been lost in the mountains. I thought he would find his way home."

"We shall find him," said the Japanese. "If your neighbor was murdered we shall find the criminal." The footsteps receded into the courtyard and the gate slammed shut. The footsteps returned to the house and moments later the small hatch opened.

"Come out now," commanded Oh.

Min worked his way back to the opening and Oh grasped his heels to pull him into the kitchen. "You heard?"

"Yes."

Oh looked at him levelly. "Were you in the Sorak?"

"I only passed it on my way along the river valley."

"And you were never questioned, even around Inje?"

"Yes, I was not."

Oh handed him a bowl of rice. "You must eat this and go.

There is no room here. If the Japanese come again and find a stranger we will have much trouble. It is enough misfortune to go hungry without being arrested for harboring a criminal."

"I am not a criminal," protested Min.

Oh did not answer, but went about eating his rice.

"I do not know where to go."

"That is your problem. You said you would go to Seoul. Go there."

Finishing his rice, Min handed the bowl to the woman and rose. "Thank you for your kindness to me. I shall not forget you."

"I think you must forget," answered the man. "I wish you to forget you ever saw this cottage or anyone in it."

Min pulled the coat on and hobbled to the door. He had taken only a step through it when Oh shouted at him. "Wait."

Min turned wearily.

"That coat. Where did you get the coat?"

Min was startled, but tried not to show it. "It is my old sea coat. I wore it at sea for many years."

Oh nodded with excessive interest. "I think it must be a very popular coat. My missing neighbor owned one exactly like it."

"There are many in Sokcho."

"His wife made it for him," countered Oh. "She never made coats for the fishermen in Sokcho." He moved a step closer to Min, then stopped as Min brought out Goto's knife. He flashed the blade menacingly at the retreating woodsman.

"Go," pleaded Oh. "Please go away and leave us."

"I think the moment I go you will be running for the Japanese. No, I think I shall remain safe. Your woman will go with me."

The woman moaned in horror. "Please. Leave me with my husband. He will say nothing."

Min still stood with the point of the blade aimed at the woodsman. "Tell your woman she must come with me."

The man stood frozen in place.

"You have your choice, woodsman. Send her with me or watch her die."

The woman began crying. Suddenly the man lunged at Min, ignoring the knife in his fury. His outstretched arms closed about Min's neck, then relaxed as a horrible, contorted expression wrenched his face. The blood spurting from his belly poured out on the floor as he sank, his eyes already glassy.

The wife screamed. Min grasped her arm. "Be quiet and help me."

"I will not help my husband's murderer," she spat.

"You will help me," he growled, "or your death will be much slower. There will be much pain."

She looked up at him, pale with terror.

"Come," he rasped. "We do not have all day."

She bent and began dragging her husband's body toward the door.

"Where are you going with that?"

"I must burn him," she answered, still tugging.

Min reached out and thrust her away from the corpse. "Would you attract the Japanese? Place him under the floor."

"I must burn him," she whimpered. "I must free his spirit."

"You will put him beneath the floor," he shouted. "Do it quickly. We must go."

She began crying again, but dragged the body into the kitchen. Together they stuffed it into the opening.

"Clean up the mess," Min ordered. "Make the house look the same as usual."

She scampered for a pan of water and a brush, then knelt and began wiping the blood away, eyeing the knife warily. When it was done Min motioned her toward the door. "I think you must wear a coat. It will be cold in the nights."

She reached to a hook by the door and took down a wrap. Then, together, they walked from the house and across the road. Soon, having forded the Soyong River at a shallows, they climbed into the higher elevations and began working their way northwest toward Hwachon. Circling the village widely, they changed their course to the southwest.

"Where are we going?" she asked.

"Far away," he answered.

"I will return," she hissed. "I must return to free my husband's spirit."

"You will not talk so much," he growled.

She lapsed into silence. Two days later the town of Gapyong lay below them. Min looked down at the houses, the school. Life appeared to be progressing normally.

"Do you know this town?"

"No," he lied.

"Then why did we not go around it as we did that other one?"

"Because I must learn exactly where we are."

"Why did you kill the officer?"

"He murdered my brother."

"In Sokcho?"

"In Hochon. Far to the north."

"I think you lie. He was from this province."

"He was in Hochon before. He was most cruel."

She looked at him warily. "Then you are not from Sokcho?"

He laughed without humor. "I have never seen Sokcho."

"Then you are the one who killed our neighbor," she exclaimed. "Why should I help you? You killed our neighbor and you killed my husband."

Min was casual. "I know nothing of your neighbor."

"You wear his coat," she snapped. "You killed him."

"I found the coat."

"You lie."

He struck her.

"You lie," she hissed again, her lip bleeding. "You are a murderer."

"Would you wish me to murder again? Slowly?"

She gazed at him, suddenly curious. "How can you kill men you do not know? How can you kill without remorse, without sorrow?"

He studied her for only a moment. "I have a goal. I must

achieve my goal, yet they would kill me as quickly as I them. I could not then be successful."

"So you would kill men you do not know?"

"Your husband threw himself on the knife. He killed himself."

"And our neighbor?" she groaned. "You feel no more remorse than a tiger killing a gazelle."

Min shrugged. "He must fill his belly."

"And you killed to fulfill your goal?"

"It was expedient."

The day ended. Cold crept in on them through the darkness. The woman laughed. "You have not slept," she chided him. "The moment you sleep I shall run away. I think you cannot sleep and keep me."

"Then I shall tear your clothes and use them to tie you," announced Min.

She looked at him dubiously, then appeared resigned. "I will not run away."

"I shall be certain you do not," he promised. Grabbing her wrap, he slashed at it viciously with the knife, cutting it into lengthy thongs. Then, pulling her close, he lashed her to a tree. "Now you will sleep. If you try to escape I shall kill you."

She lay huddled against the bark, whimpering. Min's muscles were tense as he watched her. They lay without moving, cold, far into the night. At last her breathing indicated she slept. Min closed his eyes.

It seemed only a moment. She leaped so quickly he was caught by surprise. By the time he clutched at her loosened ties she was away from him, running through the darkness.

He leaped up, following her sound through the trees. It was useless. She was proceeding down the hill, at times quietly, confusing him, at others noisily, emphasizing the threat. At last, close to the village, he turned back up the hill in frustration.

* * * * * *

The woman was in rags. Captain Amioka looked up sharply as she entered his office. "What do you want, woman?"

"I have escaped from a killer in the night."

Amioka was doubtful. "And who is this killer?"

"The man who killed my husband."

"And where did he do this?" asked the officer patiently.

"Near Inje. My husband was a woodsman. He killed our neighbor, too."

"Why did you not run to the militia commander in Inje? Why have you come all the way to Gapyong?"

"Because the killer took me as a hostage."

"Then how did you get into the village?"

"I escaped."

Amioka sat back quietly, thinking.

"He also killed a Japanese officer."

The captain looked up, concerned now. "What Japanese officer?"

"I do not know his name. When the Japanese came to our house they said the officer was a leader of the Japanese in all of Gangwondo Province."

Amioka tensed. "Major Goto?"

She shook her head. "I do not know. I never heard his name. He died in the Sorak Pass."

Amioka was hastily scribbling notes. "When were the soldiers at your house?"

"Two days ago."

"Then why did you and your husband let the killer in after you knew there had been murders?"

"He was already there. He was hidden under the floor."

"And you did not tell the Japanese?"

"I could say nothing. My husband would not allow me to say anything."

"And he was murdered for his kindness?"

She began to cry. "I do not know why he brought the man into our house."

"Do you know his name?"

She shook her head. "He said he was from Hochon."

"Hochon? That is far north of here. What would he have been doing at Inje?"

The woman felt lost. "He had come to murder the officer."

"Where is your house?"

"On the road to Inje. There are only two. Mine is the one farthest from Inje. On the Chunchon side."

Amioka led her to the outer office and motioned her to a seat. "Wait here. I wish to review some details of Major Goto's death."

"You can capture him if you hurry," she blurted.

He turned back to her. "Where? Do you know where he is?"

"He is going to Seoul."

"Did he tell you that?"

"He told my husband he would go to Seoul."

"What was he doing when you escaped?"

"Sleeping. I escaped while he was asleep."

Amioka dashed into his office. His hand shaking, he telephoned the provincial commander. "Colonel, I have a woman here who says she has been a prisoner of a murderer. He has killed several people. She says he has murdered Major Goto."

"Where is he now?"

"She said he is going to Seoul."

"Where is he from? Gapyong?"

"No, Sir. He is from Hochon."

"Hold her. I wish to talk with her personally. I shall come immediately."

"Yes, Sir."

He hung up the phone and went to the outer office. "Where were you when you escaped from this man?"

"Up in the hills. Above the town."

Amioka turned and motioned for a militiaman. "Assemble a squad and try to locate the place. Perhaps we can discover a trail. If

we do it soon enough we may be able to arrest him before the
colonel arrives."

The soldier grabbed his weapon and dashed from the room.
"What did this man look like?"

"He was rough."

"Rough?"

"I think so."

"What more can you tell me about him?"

She shook her head, confused. "I cannot remember."

"Wait here," he said. "We shall talk more later."

* * * * * *

When Min turned back from the woman he moved steadily
westward toward Seoul. His progress was slow and he covered little
more than a mile. As dawn approached he worked his way down
the slope to the highway. Crossing it, he slipped into the river.

The water was cold, numbing. He waded in the shallows near
its edge and reversed his direction eastward toward the junction of
the two rivers near Gapyong. Occasionally a vehicle would roar
along the road. He crouched in the bushes at the water's edge,
waiting for it to pass.

Now he peeped up to the terrain next to the river. He found
himself staring across the open, flat area he had noticed the first
day he had been driven to Gapyong. Beyond, he could see the
town itself.

Crawling out of the water, he lay on the bank, hidden by some
low shrubs. Sleep came almost immediately. When he awakened it
was late afternoon. He was cold. He knew he must eat, yet he
dared not move from the hiding until dark. He waited, shivering.

When night came, he crawled up into the field. The lights of
the town were beckoning. Already he had decided which house he
would approach. The family had been kind to him when he was
headmaster, seeming to sense his dilemma. Also, their house stood
on the edge of town nearest him.

The sounds of the night enshrouded him. Traffic on the road was infrequent, but speeding when it passed. Guard posts had been set up on the road at the entrance to the town. He knew they were there to intercept him should he try to enter. Tense now, he stopped and watched the perimeter of the village away from the road. Not surprisingly, sentries were marching there as well.

He counted them and timed their marching of the posts. They were unusually close. It would be difficult penetrating them. His only hope was that they did not know, or had not surmised, who he was.

He crept closer to their paths until their boots were almost touching him with every pass. Then, assured of their cycles, he lay and rolled quietly across the trail after one had marched by his position. Finally, his heart pounding, he lay deep in the grass and caught his breath.

Long before dawn he was hidden behind some kegs outside the home of his acquaintance. The moment he heard stirring in the house he rapped quietly on the gate. They did not hear him. He rapped again. The activity in the house stopped and he knew they were listening. Again he rapped.

A door runner squeaked as someone left the house to enter the courtyard. He rapped again.

"Who is there?" came the nervous query.

"Headmaster Min. Please let me in," he whispered.

The bolt of the gate was slipped and a face peered out in the darkness. Then, assured of his identity, the man opened it wider and Min stepped in. Immediately the bolt was slipped back into place. The man said nothing, but beckoned Min to follow him. They moved quietly into the house and the door slid shut.

"Min. Why do you come here?"

"I am seeking someone who will listen to my story."

"They said you murdered a construction supervisor."

"I did not. He died in a fall. It was an accident."

"That is not what the militia said. There were many stories about you in the town the day after you disappeared. The executive officer of the provincial militia came all the way from Chunchon to make the speech and lead the search for you."

"He lied." Min accepted a warm cup of tea with heartfelt gratitude. "It is most sad that I was forced to leave Gapyong, but he meant to execute me. I knew there was no way I could convince him I did not do it."

His friend nodded. "It is easily understood. You had little choice in the matter. It is most fortunate you learned of his plans." He looked sympathetically at Min. "Where have you been? You do not look well."

Min smiled wanly. "I have been hiding many miles from here."

"But you look starved."

"I have eaten only what I could trap. I have drunk water from the streams."

The friend rose. "That will happen no more. Today you shall eat like a man." He went to another room and Min heard the low murmur of voices. Moments later he was back. "My wife will make food for you, but I think there is no need for you to hide now."

"I am deeply grateful, but I shall be wanted by the Japanese for the rest of my life."

"They no longer search for you. You must not worry."

"The moment they see me I will be arrested. They will execute me for something I did not do."

"I think they have cleared you."

"But the officer who came from Chunchon. . . ."

"That officer is dead. I think the others believe you are innocent."

Min shook his head slowly, but his mind raced with apprehension. "How can I be certain?" he murmured.

His host studied the worry on his face. "When the daylight comes I shall try to learn something for you. But for now, you must eat and rest."

"I am injured," added Min.

"How?"

"It does not matter," replied Min evasively. "It was an accident."

The man nodded, accepting it. "Major Goto made speeches about you."

"Did the people believe him?"

"I think the people did not know what to believe. For many months they believed he was wrong." He paused. "Until yesterday."

"What happened yesterday?"

"A strange woman entered the village. She said there is a murderer in the hills from a town in the north called Hochon. The woman was his hostage but she escaped and came to talk with the militia commander. The colonel even came here from Chunchon. He said the one from Hochon killed Goto."

Min was silent.

"The people are relieved. They did not want to believe you guilty, but many thought it could have been you. The Japanese believed so."

"I am not really guilty of all they say."

"I think you must allow me to take care of it. The people now believe you are innocent. Perhaps the Japanese will be the same."

When daylight had come he dressed and left the house. By noon he had returned.

"Our hopes were correct," he exulted. "The Japanese have cleared you. You are free."

Min's heart pounded, then fear gripped him. "How can I be certain? I think perhaps it is a trick. They have tried many tricks to arrest me."

"There are bulletins to the people of Gapyong posted throughout the village. They say Headmaster Min was unjustly accused."

"They say it to lure me out."

"They say you have fled in disgrace, but that the people should remember you as a good man, a good headmaster. They have even given you credit for the curriculum at the school. They say Gapyong would not have the good tradesmen they have today had it not been for your foresight."

Min scoffed. "I think they must also express a hope for my return."

"They suspect you are dead."

Min smiled, beginning to hope.

His friend placed a hand on his shoulder. "You must not be such a pessimist. The people of Gapyong like you. They like you because you really are what the Japanese say. You are a good schoolmaster. You were good to Gapyong."

Min shook his head. "I think it was not the people of Gapyong who wished to arrest me. It was the Japanese. I think it is a trick. They will publicize me. They will praise me. And if I come out of hiding they will shoot me." He nodded instructively at his friend. "I think so."

"If you have no courage you will be hiding in a kimchi barrel for the rest of your life."

Min pondered the situation. "You are right. I shall go. But I think you must be most careful, if they ask you, to say I have never left Gapyong. If they know I hid in the mountains they will find a way to shoot me for all those murders accomplished by someone else. They will wish to punish someone to avoid the shame of not catching the real criminal."

He dressed and left early next morning. As he passed through the streets of Gapyong people looked up in surprise, then smiled with encouragement. But when he climbed the steps to the headquarters two soldiers fell in behind him.

Min caught his breath and was tempted to run, yet he knew such a move would be futile. He entered the office of the militia commander.

Amioka looked up, an expression of triumph on his face. "Min," he smiled. "I am happy to see you again. Come, sit down. We shall have some tea and renew old times."

Min bowed, then sat as the captain poured the tea.

"Where have you been?"

"I have been in Gapyong."

Amioka was surprised. "Only in Gapyong? You have not left the village?"

"Yes. I have not. I was afraid to come out of hiding. The officer from Chunchon was going to shoot me whether I was innocent or not."

Amioka shook his head. "A most unfortunate situation. He has met with an accident, you know. He is dead."

Min said nothing, but accepted the tea.

Amioka continued. "We have many things to discuss, now that you have rejoined us, and yet I must make a journey today." He grimaced at the inconvenience, then stopped and looked up, an expression of inspiration crossing his face. "I know. You have not been out of Gapyong in many months."

Min glanced quickly over his shoulder. The soldiers were behind him.

"Would you not like to go into the countryside?" asked Amioka amiably. "An old woman lives there. Her husband was murdered recently." His expression became sad. "So many murders," he sighed. "There is much crime. Please come with me and keep me company."

"Yes," said Min without enthusiasm, cornered.

"Good," exclaimed Amioka. "I think there is no need to waste time."

They entered the staff car, one soldier driving with Amioka in the front, the other huddled beside Min in the rear. Min, already crestfallen, became increasingly morose as they drove. The route took them through Chunchon and up the banks of the Soyong River. A light snow had begun to fall, gently, silently. Gradually the road faded under the whiteness and only the supplicant branches of the trees lining the road suggested their path. They rode in silence, then slowed and turned toward the cottage. Smoke was wafting peacefully upward from behind the trees.

As they rounded the final curve of the lane Amioka let out a gasp. Min stared at the scene with mixed emotions. Before them, burning busily, was a pyre. At its top were the charring remains of the woodsman and, embracing him fondly, the body of his wife.

THE SOUTH—INCHON

Chi pulled his handcart slowly toward the tidal basin. The water was beginning to recede from Inchon harbor. In silhouette the Wolmido fortress mushroomed, the causeway seeming a giant tether to preclude its drifting away. In the wharf area ships began riding the racing water toward the Yellow Sea beyond, leaving the city to its hours of stench from the tidal mud before the next high tide.

Chi watched the departing vessels for only a moment, then descended a heap of rocks toward the trash strewn ooze. He was a slight man, young, gaunt. His clothes were rags, his face unshaven. From the left sleeve of his torn smock protruded a grotesquely deformed arm, a mere knot of a hand. Around the arm he had woven the cord of his sack, into which he now began dropping the dubious treasures he dug from the mire.

When the staff car approached he appeared not to notice. Bending farther, almost imperceptibly, he was below the level of firm ground. The men were no more aware of his presence than of the multitude of trash crate shacks crowding the sea wall.

The vehicle stopped and two men emerged to stand looking out across the harbor. "It must be a strong prison," ordered a voice. "I shall not tolerate an escape from this prison."

His companion shifted his feet and replied inaudibly. Chi slogged his way closer to the wall and huddled, listening, alert at word of a prison. Above him, near the two, curious children drifted close, awed by their appearance. A third man, the driver, threatened them away.

"I shall be most disappointed if a country boy causes me to lose a prisoner," continued the first voice. "Perhaps you can imagine the consequences of such a disappointment."

"Yes, Honorable General. I shall not disappoint you. I am most honored by this great opportunity."

General Enomoto snorted. "You would not be so honored were a Japanese available. You should be thankful to the Chinese. Only because they are creating a senseless and suicidal war is such an assignment made available to you. Otherwise we would have our own people doing this."

"Yes, Honorable General." He paused, nervous. "You have not said why you have brought me here to the harbor. Do you wish the prison constructed here?"

Enomoto measured him hawkishly. "You seem uncertain. Are you uncertain? If you do not think you can do it properly I can send for someone else. They can use you to great advantage in China or Manchuria."

"I only think the soil here may not be firm."

"Then you are questioning my judgment."

"Honorable General, if the soil is firm I shall be able to construct a fine prison here. If it is too soft I shall tell you. I would be most reluctant to build such an important prison on soft ground."

"Do not linger with your doubts about my judgment," snapped Enomoto. "I shall not long tolerate insults from a Korean."

The younger man nodded apprehensively. "I meant no insult, Honorable General."

"I shall not listen easily to a plea that my prison cannot be constructed here," continued the officer, seeming not to hear him. "As you can see, a large port has been built along the far end of the quay. If the soil will support that it will support my prison."

"It appears it took them much time and expense to construct such a port," replied the other. "I think the foundation where we stand was not so well reinforced. Only the sea wall was constructed to keep the tides from flooding the city."

Suddenly, without commenting further, the general turned and stepped into the staff car. The driver spun the wheel and the vehicle sped away, leaving the younger man standing disconsolately amid the slum abutting the spreading sea of slime.

With the sound of the receding car Chi peeked cautiously over the sea wall, then scrambled up the rocks. Before him stood the stranded man, neat in the uniform of the civil service, staring after the vehicle. "Will he punish you?" The language was Hangul.

Hong wheeled about, startled. "What are you doing here?" he demanded. "Why have you been spying on conversations which do not concern you?"

Chi bowed, smiling. "I am merely a poor forager. I was collecting after the tide when you approached. I could not help but hear."

"You should have left with the children. You should not have stayed here when the general arrived."

Chi's smile remained. "You have no face to lose with me. A man who burrows in the mud for his treasures sees and hears nothing."

"See that you remember. I should not wish to have such conversations known about the city by morning." He stopped, suddenly aware of the peril.

"The general would be certain you had talked," prompted Chi. He waved his healthy hand. "I have said you have no face to lose with me. I can be as loyal as you wish me to be."

"What is your price?" asked Hong evenly.

"I think we must not talk of price. You would insult me with such a question."

"Then what do you want with me?" asked Hong, suddenly frustrated.

"I think you are new to Inchon. You must have many questions."

"I have lived here all my life," snapped Hong. "I have no questions."

Chi laughed. "If that were so you would not have spoken to the general as you did. You would know how the sea wall was built. You would not have to study the foundation for your prison." He shook his head. "I think you are not from Inchon."

"It does not matter what you think." Hong turned toward the depth of the city.

"You must walk a great distance into the city of Inchon."

Hong kept walking. "It is not that far."

"The command building is far from here. It is on the Bupyong side. The east." Chi made no effort to follow him.

Hong slowed, then stopped and turned tiredly. "What is it you wish from me?" he asked again.

Chi moved closer now, the mud still dripping from his feet and legs. "I think only that you must trust me. I can help you. I can tell you things about Inchon which you must know to construct your prison more quickly."

"There is no need of such intrusive banter. Answer my question. What is it you wish from me?"

Chi became quickly serious. "My friends are many. They see much and hear very well. I shall keep you informed."

"My staff will keep me informed," sniffed Hong, turning again toward the city.

"It would be most fortunate for a newcomer to know things before his staff tells him. It could be beneficial to know before the Japanese." He shuffled forward to smile again at the confused Hong. "Your access to information may have a lasting effect on your success at Inchon."

"I should have you arrested," exploded Hong. "You come and speak to me in an obsolete language, offering me seditious information to use against the Japanese and my staff. You are an eavesdropper, a spy." He turned. "Yes, I shall have you arrested."

Chi continued his confident smile. "First you must find me in a city you do not know. I think you would not know where to look." He unwound the cord from his collection sack and set it on the ground. "I have offered you only friendship, an opportunity to perform your task better for the Japanese. For this you would have me arrested?" He shook his head slowly. "I have often helped the Japanese in the past."

"Then why do you address me in Hangul? Why do you hide in the mud from the Japanese?" He scoffed. "I have no need of what you offer. I have a very efficient staff."

Chi laughed. "You will see me again. I hope the general is not as angry on that day as he was this morning." He bent and retrieved his sack. "May the fortunes be kind to you." He started back toward the pile of rocks and began descending to the mud below.

Hong made a move as if to speak, then thought better of it and started once more toward the city. He had taken only a few steps when he stopped and returned to the sea wall. Chi was bent into the debris.

"What is your name?" called Hong.

Chi scoffed. "Would you have me tell you so that you may have me arrested?"

"I would have you help me," replied Hong. "I know little of Inchon. I lived as a boy in Chunchon. To the east, beyond Seoul." He was uneasy with the confession.

Chi shuffled at the mud, then resolutely began climbing the rocks again. "You may build his prison here," he said, reaching the top. "When the sea wall was constructed a great deal of care was taken with the foundation."

"How would an ignorant forager know what was done? I think you would not understand what they were doing."

Chi smiled confidently. "It is a most distinct advantage to my benefactors that many believe me ignorant." He shrugged, then became serious. "I think your first concern must be to return to your headquarters. I will help you. The general will think you most resourceful if you return quickly after being abandoned."

Hong was stopped. "Yes, I think so," he replied reluctantly.

"Then you must wait here," said Chi quickly. "I will return in only a moment." Dropping his sack into the handcart, he set off at a trot into the clutter of huts.

The children returned, staring hesitantly. Hong returned their gaze, first in equal curiosity, then with an air of superiority. They backed away a step, whispering among themselves. At last Chi returned, an ancient rikisha and jin hustling along behind. He grinned at Hong, motioning him into the seat, then issued clipped imperatives at the jin. The man nodded and they began bumping precariously along the earthen streets.

The route was rough, winding. Along their way vendors pushed carts of wares and services, chanting incessantly of sharpened scissors, repaired tools. Their cymbals and tambourines echoed a rising tattoo, the scissors snapping open and closed in rhythm.

Hong watched the robot of a man pulling him. He was old, seeming too frail to long sustain the pace, yet he did not slow. As they arrived at the headquarters Hong reached into his smock for money to pay him. The jin's smile was fleeting, and disappeared immediately. "Your friend would be most disappointed if I accepted your generous offer. I cannot." He bowed, lifted the tongs and wheeled toward home.

"Wait," called Hong.

"Your friend wishes you good fortune," called the jin over his shoulder. Then, turning a corner, he trundled into the crowd.

* * * * * *

"Where are your plans?" demanded Enomoto. "I wish to examine the work schedules."

Hong hesitated.

"Have you done nothing?" asked the general. "I have ordered you to construct a prison."

"There are problems at the site along the quay wall," said Hong softly.

"Problems? What problems?"

"Construction of the prison at that location must require the displacement of many families. I have been seeking an alternate site."

Enomoto slammed his fist on the desk. "You have been assigned to my staff as an engineer, not a sociologist. My sociologists carry rifles and bayonets."

Hong nodded. "Yes, Honorable General."

Suddenly, inexplicably, the general mellowed. "Please sit," he said, indicating a chair. "I think we must discuss success and its motivations."

Hong sat, uneasy.

"I perceive in you a softness, a gentle concern which would be considered most desirable in a temple. However, we are not monks and this, most assuredly, is not a temple. Hong, we are men of action. We are shaping the destinies of millions throughout the world. All people cannot be leaders. Most must be guided, manipulated, if we are to achieve our goals." His voice was instructive but kind. "I suspect you feel remorse for the filth of the quay wall. They are your countrymen and you are young. However, I must advise you that such empathy can only lead you to failure. The accomplishments of the world must go on. They will go on. If you spare these leeches of the tide, another will replace you. Your procrastination will merely cost you your opportunity at leadership."

Hong watched him, distaste for the words gnawing at him, yet he realized the challenge.

"All your life, Hong, you will face such requirements for sacrifice. Today it is a dilemma. Tomorrow, every day of your career, you will be confronted by such decisions. The test of your fortitude, indeed the measure of your success, will depend on your decision at the quay."

"But what will become of them?" agonized Hong.

"They are pith," replied the general easily. "Before they camped at the quay they burrowed in similar squalor in another forgotten den. Before that it was yet another. They are without either respect or ambition. We could install them in palaces and within a month the halls would be infested with slime and thievery. The doors would be broken and the furnishings reduced to bludgeons for use against their neighbors. It is a fact of humanity, Hong, that such creatures can never rise above their clannish mentality."

"But would you have me ignore them as humans?"

"If they were human we would develop a use for them. They are not. Therefore, we ignore them as we do the vermin of the seaport. The progress of our empire cannot falter each time we encounter an infestation of termites." He shook his head emphatically. "No. As they migrated to the quay, so will they migrate elsewhere. Their removal to create space for our prison will be but another of a thousand migrations. Your decision, Hong, must be whether to rise as a leader or join these maggots." He rose. "If you would become the leader you dream, you must learn to see such creatures for what they are. They are there to test your determination." He lifted a pencil thoughtfully from the desk, then suddenly slammed it down in fury. "You have kept me waiting a month, Hong, and shown me nothing. Delay me another month and you shall become a most unhappy man." He said nothing more, but turned as though keeping to a schedule and hurried from the room.

Hong remained standing in the cold reality of the man's power. The chair was soft, the desk imposingly large. At last he walked to the door and left the building. As he reached the sidewalk the people closed about him, anonymous, in their haste caring not that he existed. He looked for a staff car. There was none. At last he began walking, leaning through the people toward his office several blocks away.

"Good morning again, my friend. Must you still walk because of his wrath?"

Hong glanced quickly into the twinkling eyes of Chi. The man was hurrying beside him. "I go only to my office. It is a short walk."

"There are many rumors at the basin."

Hong continued his rapid pace, saying nothing.

"You could make many friends." Chi swept a quick look behind him. "Come and talk with them."

"There is nothing to discuss."

"If you do as the general wishes there will be much hate. People will die."

"I think you know nothing of the general's wishes."

"If you talk with the people no one will die. You may convince the general you have followed his wishes but the people will be prepared."

Hong remained implacable, stretched his pace.

"They will not be in their houses when they are scraped away."

"I think I may not build the prison there."

"You are without choice. The general has given you his orders. You must follow them. The people of the basin will be angry."

"I have not talked with the general," snapped Hong.

"Would you have your countrymen die to save your face?" Chi hurried forward, ahead of him, and searched his eyes. "He is a cruel man. He has no consideration for such people as live at the basin."

Hong slowed, his face still without emotion. "I will talk with you tonight, but not now."

Chi was equally expressionless. "My friend will await you near your home with his rikisha."

"You do not know where I live."

"I think if I know of your general's conversations I must have little difficulty with such simple information."

Hong quickened his pace once more and Chi fell away into the bustle of people.

The sun had sunk behind Wolmido. Hong left his office, having accomplished little beyond thought, speculation at Chi's ubiquitousness. Though dusky, the streets remained crowded. Hong threaded his way toward home, then stopped at sight of the rikisha. The jin grinned but said nothing. Hong moved quickly to the vehicle and they set off, the jin shuffling rhythmically between the tongs.

Soon they were among the basin dwellings, close to the sea wall. The tide was high, lapping hungrily at the clustered huts.

They turned a corner and the jin stopped, dropping the tongs and reaching to help Hong from the seat. He remained silent, but nodded toward a door. Hong walked quickly into the building, a bathhouse.

An attendant bowed hospitably. "You honor our establishment, Hong. Please follow me."

He drew himself up, ready to speak, then elected to follow her silently. She led him to a large yet crude inner court, then smiled demurely and indicated an enormous wooden tub. "I am Yong Cha. You will join your friend, please."

Chi already was immersed in the steaming vat. Beside him an attendant languished, slowly and sensuously washing him. Hong entered a cubicle and disrobed, then made his way to the steaming water. Yong Cha was waiting.

"Come, my friend," smiled Chi. "It is a most relaxing place to discuss your dilemma."

Hong stepped down, the heat startling his pulse. Gradually the girl led him down until he squatted shoulder deep in the vat. Yong Cha settled beside him and began the ablutions.

"Have you considered our discussion of this morning?"

Hong, distrustful, looked away. "How did you know of my discussion with the general?"

"A simple deduction, Hong. We have seen much of the Japanese. General Enomoto is not a very resourceful man. Therefore he could be expected to behave most traditionally."

"How have you learned my name?"

"A natural question is most quickly answered. At the government buildings the name of a Korean is not considered privileged information." Chi smiled easily.

Hong now looked at him for the first time. "Then should I not be extended the equal privilege?"

"Of course," replied Chi, laughing. "I am Chi. I am a forager."

"I think you occupy your time at more than foraging."

"It is a matter of interpretation. Most questioners are satisfied merely with the activity. Few would concern themselves with the objects for which I dig."

"Then you may consider me differently. I am most interested in your true goals."

"I have sensed it from the beginning," replied Chi. "You are an astute man, yet you live this most frustrating dilemma. You are a forager, as I, yet your goal is success, power. Because the Japanese represent the root of power you have allied your professional life with them. Your dilemma, however, lies in the fact you are Korean."

"Many are Koreans," scoffed Hong. "Many of our people have become educated by the Japanese. We work diligently in the pursuit of their goals."

Chi nodded emphatically. "I agree. There are many renegades from the spirit of our people. But I think their attitudes are much different from yours. They are only greedy, heartless men. You are not."

Hong looked at him in surprise. "How can you say that? I was educated by the Japanese, just as the others. They did not force me to go. I asked. I took examinations. I begged them. They have made me only what I asked to become."

"But it is different."

"Why?"

"What have the others asked? The renegades?" He peered seriously at Hong through the steam. "They have asked to become soldiers, to be handed rifles and bayonets."

"That is not true. Our men have been conscripted. Those who wished to go before were rejected."

"Some were rejected."

"Most."

"But they did wish to go, did they not? Even before they were conscripted they wished to go and collect their instruments of oppression. And the others, those who have learned the law." He sneered. "They have returned not as protectors but as prosecutors. Those trained as schoolmasters have begun shaping the minds of our children. They would make them Japanese children, Japanese men."

"And I am a builder of prisons."

"You are a builder," nodded Chi. "I agree. That you must now build a prison is most unfortunate, but I think your principal goal is to build for us, not to tear us apart."

"I shall do as I am told."

"But you have not done so. You have delayed, procrastinated. I think you have made the general most angry."

Hong looked at him again, irritated. "What do you know of my conversations with the general?"

"I have deduced much," explained Chi simply. "If I am wrong I think you will leave this place and I must soon be arrested. But perhaps I am correct. I have studied the general carefully. As I have said, he is not a very resourceful man. He has attained his rank by following the line of least resistance. If some were cruel, he was more so. In the face of his shortcomings he has risen to his high rank through a diligence in excesses."

He was talking rapidly now, seemingly anxious to reach a specific goal of thesis before Hong could interrupt him. "The day he brought you to the quay, that day we first met, he made it most clear he wished his prison constructed where our homes now stand. It was a very typical action indeed. I expected the machines to appear the next day, but they did not come. Each day after that we waited but nothing happened. It was then I realized your dilemma, your real concern for our people. I knew you were not an oppressor. It was most natural I should deduce the relationship between you and General Enomoto."

Hong stared, then nodded slowly. "You must realize, Chi, there is little more I can do. I have tried very hard to save your homes. I cannot."

"But you can help us."

"How? What can I do? I think if I try to do anything for you the general will not approve. We shall all be placed in a most compromising situation."

"Give us information and time," replied Chi, rising and stepping from the vat. His attendant dried him gently yet thoroughly, then began massaging him as he stretched on a mat.

Hong followed him from the water and felt the strength of Yong Cha's hands rubbing him dry. "What information could I give you?" he asked.

"Tell us exactly where you must build this prison. You will not require the entire quay area. Tell us where you must remove homes so that we may move what we can. Do not let them take us by surprise."

"And if I cannot?"

"You can," replied Chi. "You can warn us when they will come. I think you would do that for your people."

Yong Cha was massaging him now, still silent as though unconcerned. He looked at her. She was studying her work. "I do not have much time," he said. "I must show much progress very soon."

"How soon?" asked Chi.

"I must clear land and begin the foundation in only a few days."

"Will you show me where you must clear?"

"What will you do?"

"We will move our homes in the area you must use."

"I think such moving must require much time. I cannot wait long."

"May we have a week? Will you allow your people a week to protect their lives and homes?"

"Where will you go?" evaded Hong.

"We must move farther along the basin."

"And if the sea wall there does not hold?"

Chi raised up and waved the attendant back. "I think you would not allow us to make such an error of judgment." He was looking squarely at Hong, not smiling, waiting for a reply.

"It is dark. We cannot see well enough in the night."

"Then I think we must look with the sun."

Hong nodded, at first tentatively, cornered. Then, in animation, he agreed. "I will do it," he exploded. "I will work with you, but you must work equally with me."

Chi watched him, concerned.

"Enomoto must have his pleasures. His thirst for our pain must be satisfied. We can give him that and be done with it. It will cost us nothing."

"How?" demanded Chi. "Must we sacrifice lives to his appetite?"

"Only time. Effort. I think all the people of the basin must work, but the general will never be the wiser." He was off the mat now, gesticulating in his nakedness, suddenly caring, knowing his people.

"And if he learns?"

"He must not learn."

Chi's voice was quiet, but not without passion. "You wish leadership. I think if you achieve this you must become a hero among our people. There will be no question of our loyalty to you."

Hong hurried to the cubicle, reached for his clothes. "I shall return in the morning. Have your jin waiting."

Chi showed his surprise. "The jin? Will the Japanese not wonder if you use a jin? Perhaps a staff car would be more discreet."

"And the Japanese driver would advise Enomoto of my every move." He shook his head. "The jin will be better. Early. Have him come very early."

Chi nodded and began dressing.

"And now for our attendants," said Hong. "What consideration do we owe them?"

Chi started to speak, but Yong Cha motioned quickly. "My only consideration can be my continued availability to serve you. I ask nothing more."

Hong looked quickly at Chi's attendant. She dropped her eyes and said nothing.

"Very well." He stopped only for a moment, looking at the cripple with a new purpose, an air of having already achieved a goal never until now recognized. Then, with a purposeful bow and a gesture of courage he stepped out into the night.

* * * * * *

Through the next week the quay wall was a blur of activity. Dwellings evaporated, only to reappear miraculously at the farthest extremity of the slum. The children played as usual, yet their adults grew curiously quiet. An atmosphere of expectation spread and hovered like a pall over their lives.

The door of Hong's office flew open. "When did you do it?"

Hong looked up quickly, then rose and bowed to the general. Enomoto stood, hands on hips, awaiting a reply.

"I think, Honorable General, I do not understand your question." He glanced nervously at a wooden chair and attempted to regain his composure. "I am most honored by your visit, Sir. May I offer you a seat, tea?"

"Of course," replied the general. He crossed the tiny office and sat, glaring up at the still standing Hong. "I have asked you a question. When did you do it?" He waved a hand impatiently. "The quay wall. How did you manage it?"

"I have had the area cleared this week, Honorable General."

"I know," replied Enomoto. "I had hoped to watch the extermination. Yet I was not told when the heavy equipment would be working. Perhaps you will explain why."

"I was not aware you wished to observe, Honorable General. I was merely aware you wished the area cleared. I have done it."

"You used no equipment," observed Enomoto.

"I used people. They are indolent. I believed it more economical to use the resources at hand."

The general paused, the hint of enjoyment beginning to flicker at the corners of his mouth. "I went there this morning," he said at last.

Hong did not reply.

"I went there with the intention of replacing you. Perhaps you do not understand your function. Do you understand it?"

"Honorable General, my function is to construct your prison."

"My prison?" Enomoto rose. "Your function is to keep me informed of progress on the construction of the Emperor's prison. You are to see that its growth continues without faltering." He sat once more. "How did you force them to do it?" Enomoto's thirst for entertainment had returned.

Hong was evasive. "I think no man will long remain in opposition if he realizes he has no chance of success."

"That is nonsense. They have opposed me ever since I arrived."

"I offered them an opportunity to move or be moved, Honorable General. Apparently they have experienced the latter at some time in the past."

"Are you telling me you used no force to remove them?"

"None was necessary."

Enomoto's humor changed once more. "When will the prison be completed?"

"In approximately six months, Sir," replied Hong.

"Six months is too long."

"I think we must not work the laborers longer."

"Hong, perhaps you must work them day and night. They already know how to sleep. Teach them to work." He stood. "Three months. I shall give you three months, no longer."

"I think I must have more laborers to complete it so quickly."

"Then use more. Conscript more." He had reached the door, but now stopped. "The only more I will not approve is more time or more money. You are forbidden to pay them more. If you conscript more, each must receive less." The door slammed and Hong returned weakly to his chair. He started to sit, then changed his mind and reached for his cap.

Arriving at the basin, he walked out onto the expanse of cleared land. It was level, would require little preparation. He looked toward the huts along the perimeter. Even the children were not in view. He began walking, gradually faster, until he burst among the shacks. Those in the alleys watched him, saying nothing. A chilling restlessness permeated the entire basin. He nodded. The greeting was not returned.

At last he came to the door of the bath. Yong Cha answered his knock. "Where is Chi?" he demanded.

She motioned him quickly inside. "I think he is looking for you," she whispered, closing the door. "The Japanese were at the basin this morning."

"The general has told me," he replied. "Send someone to find Chi. I must talk with him. We have very little time."

She padded into a back room, then returned. "They will find him. I think you must wait here."

"Why? What has happened? Is there trouble?"

"Come," she coaxed, ignoring his question. "You must relax." She led him to a mat and motioned him down. "Perhaps you would enjoy tea?"

He nodded impatiently. "But what has happened?"

She called softly to another room, ordering the tea, then knelt and began massaging his shoulders in strong, penetrating strokes. "I think you have not looked at the far end of the basin today."

"I have come here only now. I have seen the cleared area only. The people do not speak to me. Even the children run and hide."

She said nothing further but continued the massage. He seethed, frustrated. Another girl brought the tea, then disappeared as silently as she had come. At last there was the sound of voices and Chi hurried into the room.

Hong looked up quickly. "Where have you been? What is happening?"

Chi dropped dejectedly at his side. "You have tried. I have been talking with the people, telling them you have tried."

Hong leaned toward him in exasperation. "I have tried to learn what has happened. No one will tell me. Only Yong Cha will speak to me."

"The Japanese came this morning."

"I have been told that much."

"The general was with them. At first he came alone. In his staff car." He accepted a cup of tea in his good hand. "Then he became angry. I think he was anxious to find nothing done and to replace you. He called soldiers. They examined the soil but there had been no heavy vehicles there. There was no debris."

"Then I think he had what he wished. The area is prepared for construction."

"He wished blood," spat Chi. "They proceeded through the basin seeking the new homes, the displaced people. When they found them at the far end of the quay wall they pushed them into the water." He shook his head. "Many are homeless. Some are missing."

Hong, speechless with horror, merely stared.

"They have no place to go."

"We must help them," groaned Hong. "We must assist their reconstruction."

"I think they will not trust another effort to help them. They have been badly beaten."

"We shall find them more materials. They can rebuild."

Chi laughed despairingly. "They will be watched too carefully."

Hong lay back on the mat but waved Yong Cha away. "He has prepared his revenge for me as well," he said. "He has told me I must complete the prison in only three months."

Chi took no notice.

"The project should require six months," he added, staring disconsolately at the ceiling. "I think he must wish very much for me to fail so he may discipline me."

"And if you do not fail?" asked Chi flatly.

"I must fail. I cannot work my laborers day and night. That is his wish. He will always wish more."

Slowly Chi turned to him. "Would you be permitted more workers?"

"More workers but not more pay. If I conscript more workers I think each must receive less."

"And if you do it?"

"I cannot."

"What will happen if you do it? If the prison is completed in three months?"

Hong shrugged. "I will be assigned elsewhere."

Yong Cha reached and poured them more tea. The other attendants were gone.

"Then we must do it," whispered Chi. "We must complete the work on schedule." He leaned forward. "If you do it I think you must receive another important assignment. You will become a most valuable man in their eyes."

Hong watched him hopelessly.

"If you are valuable to them, others must be valuable to you."

"I cannot take the basin with me. When I go the people here will be left behind."

Chi was speaking faster. "But those who motivate them, those who make it possible for you. I think you must be loyal to them." He nodded toward Yong Cha. "She has nothing here, and I think I am not considered a friend by many here now. We have nothing to keep us here. Once the work is done there will be only more oppression. The people will hate us more."

"And for that reason there will be no support. They know there will be no gratitude."

"If they thought otherwise it would be different," said Chi.

"How could they think otherwise?" scoffed Hong. "We have told them otherwise if the land were cleared. We have told them their homes would be spared. Now you have seen the results."

"Then we must convince them again." He shrugged. "They can be convinced. We shall tell them the Japanese are sorry their homes were destroyed. It was a misunderstanding. If they will work hard their homes will be replaced. They will be reconstructed for them."

"And they will know better."

"Today they have nothing. They have lived for centuries sucking at the nipple of hope in empty promises. They will never be any different."

"You would do this to your own basin? To the people you have known all your life?"

"Each man must make his own step upward. One must accept his opportunities as they present themselves." He stared ominously at Hong. "If we do not convince them I think you must be punished most severely by the general. It is a matter of survival, yet you cannot do it alone. You must rely on those of us who would assist you."

"What would Yong Cha do? How would she help me?"

Chi smiled. "The watchdogs must be distracted from time to time."

Yong Cha smiled knowingly. "I think the women of the basin must be most helpful if we are to succeed."

Hong rose and drained his cup, now recognizing the qualities of which the general had spoken only days before. "We must work quickly. There is little time to lose." He turned to Chi. "You must go to them now. Tell them what you will."

Chi nodded and hurried to the door. "Yong Cha and the jin will be our messengers. The jin can find you and Yong Cha can find me." He stopped, looked meaningfully at Hong for a long moment, and was gone.

Yong Cha stood looking at him. "Have you time to talk with me?"

He nodded.

"Please come to the tub. You must relax." She took his arm, urging him. "We can talk there."

He looked around. "What of the others?"

"They are gone. They will not come back until I send for them."

He hesitated. "I think I must go and tend to the prison."

"Chi will arrange things. You will have much time to tend to the prison, but for now you are too upset." She smiled, now more friend than masseuse. "Come."

He succumbed, and shortly was immersed in the steaming tub, Yong Cha soaping him gently.

"Why are you not angry?" he asked suddenly. "You are a part of the people here."

She continued washing him. "I know you could not help it. I know you tried to save the people of the basin."

"But they are angry," he retorted.

"They do not understand. Not yet. Chi is telling them. My girls are telling them. I think they will not be angry with you for long."

He lay back, felt the warmth of the water relaxing him. Yong Cha continued washing him, gently but insistently. Gradually her hands stopped and she studied his face. He turned his head and looked at her. "How long have you lived here?"

"Since I was a girl," she replied.

"And why have you befriended me?" He watched her eyes. "This is only your business."

She was quiet for a moment. "It is my business, but I do not work for the clients. My girls go to the tubs."

"Then why do you do it for me?"

"You are different. You are not like a customer." Her eyes were boring into him now.

"And the first time I came here you came to the tub, but you knew nothing of me. Why?"

She smiled. "I had planned one of my girls for you."

He frowned, puzzled.

"Then, when you came in, I changed my mind."

"Why?"

"I did not think one of the others should be with you and Chi. Your conversation would be too important."

"And what of the girl who was with Chi?"

"She is his close friend. She would say nothing."

"But you felt you should not let another do me?"

"Yes."

He was quiet for a moment. "I am glad."

Her eyes were down again now, not looking at him but sensing his seriousness. He reached out and touched her in the water, tentatively at first, but when she did not resist, with more boldness. He cupped her breasts, and felt her thigh brush his. Gradually, the full length of her body floated against him, her breath coming at a faster pace. He wrapped her in his arms with desperation.

When it was over they left the tub and he lay on the mat while she dried and massaged him.

"Do you feel better?" she asked softly.

He reached up and stroked her face. "I think one does not feel better when others are suffering."

"But you are suffering also. You are suffering for them."

"There will be more suffering. I do not think the general will allow anyone peace. I am learning he is a very vindictive man."

"Perhaps we will not always have to be here." Her eyes were sparks now. "Perhaps when the prison is finished we could go away."

"I will be sent away," he said. "If the prison is completed on time I will be sent to another assignment. If it is not, I may find myself in a prison."

She let out a whimper and threw herself next to him. "We cannot let that happen." She held him tightly. "We will find many people who will work."

"But I cannot pay them. The general has said he will give me no more money to pay them."

"Trust in us. Trust in your friends. We are not many, but I think Chi and I will be able to get them to work."

They were quiet for a long while. At last, he rose and began to dress. She lay watching him, then stood and donned her robe.

"You are a very beautiful woman, Yong Cha."

She smiled. "I hope you will never forget me, Hong. I wish to be with you when you leave Inchon."

Fully dressed now, he reached out for her and held her close.

"May I go from Inchon with you, Hong?"

He did not reply, but drew himself up with the challenge ahead and strode from the house.

* * * * * *

The prison opened without fanfare. One day there were work-men, the next, prisoners. The people of the basin stared in wonder as the scrawny men were unloaded from the trucks and led into the enclosure. Many of them were Caucasians. They were gaunt, emaciated, yet they were tall and walked with their heads high, not with the customary downcast visages of prisoners.

"Americans," whispered an observer. "They are Americans."

"I think some are English and Australians."

The trucks droned on, a seemingly endless line, dumping their cargoes and rolling off once more toward the east.

Hong had received his orders two days previously. Immediately Chi and Yong Cha had disappeared, along with the nameless jin. Now, having gathered his few belongings, Hong began the short walk to the rail depot.

A staff car pulled to a stop beside him. He looked up into the smirking face of General Enomoto. "Where are you going, Hong?"

"To the train, Honorable General," he replied, bowing.

"Get in." The general turned his gaze straight ahead.

Hong climbed cautiously into the car. The vehicle accelerated.

"I was most disturbed that you did not come to say goodbye to me, Hong."

"I did not think you would wish to see me, Sir."

"Nonsense."

"I think you do not approve of me, Honorable General."

"You merely required an education," replied the general. "I provided it."

"I am most grateful, Honorable General."

"When you ignored the courtesy I thought it necessary to seek you out. I wished to congratulate you. It was a most significant achievement for a Korean."

"Thank you, Sir."

"There was trouble at the basin this morning. Out by the sea wall."

Hong said nothing, waiting.

"It appears some of the laborers were seeking you. They wished to be paid."

"They were paid yesterday, Honorable General," he replied.

"They were also seeking a man and a woman. The man is a cripple, they say."

"There are many cripples along the basin."

Enomoto waved it off. "It is of little real consequence. I instructed you many weeks ago in the matter of manipulation. You learned quickly the proper place of these vermin." He smiled. "We have paid them more. They demanded and we paid them. It cost us several hundred rounds of ammunition."

They had reached the terminal.

"Your assignment in Seoul is a most important one. I have arranged it for you. Practice well the lessons I have taught you and you may one day rise above the curse of your ancestry." He nodded impatiently as Hong stepped to the curb.

The ride from Inchon to Seoul, though not of great distance, was long. He sat, frozen with the horror of his success and stared at the flat, changeless scenery creeping by. In the distance he could see mountains, tall, imposing. They seemed to draw no closer, the train huffing methodically through Bupyong, Kimpo and Yongdongpo. At last they trundled across the Han River and steamed into the city's southern terminal.

The first person he saw was the jin. "Chi has found a house. He awaits your orders."

Hong looked at him blankly, subduing his disgust at the turn of events. "Tell him I shall contact him once I am settled and have reviewed my assignment."

"The woman wishes to see you as soon as possible. Yong Cha. She has a home for you."

"*Taedanhi comsahamnida.* Thank you very much." He turned abruptly and hid his face in the teeming mob.

THE CONSCRIPT

Shin had left Chunchon in ecstasy, confident he would soon enter a commissioning program in the Japanese army. However, upon his arrival at the training center he was shocked to learn he was to receive no special treatment. Rather, he was treated with the same derision as the other conscripts. When he was not singled out for officer training he asked a sergeant about the situation. The man laughed. Stung by the rebuff, Shin gathered his courage and vowed to earn his way through performance.

His graduation from training saw him posted to China with hundreds of his fellows. His grit and determination earned him decoration after decoration. Promoted for his valor, he was transferred to the Philippines, where his bravery finally won him his long sought commission on the battlefield at Bataan. He was personally singled out for decoration by General Yamashita. Thereafter, he fought valiantly on island after island across the Pacific. At last, however, he was returned to Korea, where he was named the guard commander at the prison at Inchon.

Shin was mortified. His return to Korea merely highlighted his local ancestry. The Japanese treated him with condescension. He responded by placing grave, even cruel, restrictions on the guard force, may of whom were Korean. No longer were they permitted to visit the hot baths during their off duty time. Instead, Shin ordered that they be drilled and trained for combat. The program quickly developed into a repeat of their basic training and caused grumbling and low morale. Prisoners were even more mistreated than was the norm. Guards who shirked their duties were punished mercilessly.

The colonel who commanded the prison became gradually aware of the discontent. He summoned Shin for counseling, only to find his enthusiasm for the training infectious. The colonel's superior, however, was a general who took particular exception during a visit to the poor treatment of the Japanese among the guard force. At last, with the escape of a prisoner, Shin was held personally responsible and demoted. It was more than he could take. Chagrined, he gathered his documents and decorations into a small pack. Then, his face and self respect lost, he stole away and was not seen again. There was a search, but with the end of the war at hand, it was called off for more urgent matters.

THE NORTH—HOCHON

"I will not be afraid if they send me to fight in the war." Taejin was carrying a yoke, from each end of which dangled a bucket. Two other young teens were busily ladling the excrement to fertilize the vegetables.

"Then I think you must hurry and grow," replied one. "I have heard the Japanese are losing many battles. The war will be finished soon."

"No. They will win. You will see."

He crept forward along the row, keeping pace with his companions. In neighboring rows other villagers, both youngsters and women, were progressing alongside them.

"You love the Japanese," sneered the ladler. "Your father is their puppet."

"He is not," shouted Taejin. "He has defended our people."

"He has sent them to prison. Look at the mountain. It is bare of trees. My father has told me there were many trees before the Japanese came. They have made the prisoners cut them down and take them away."

Another broke in. "Your father has provided the labor. He has made sure the Japanese had many men to help them."

The buckets were empty and Taejin stepped aside, replaced by another carrier. He made his way back along the row to the wagon for replenishment. Song was there, a scarf wrapped tightly about her face in an attempt to block the offensive odor.

"I have heard you arguing with them," she said.

"They have insulted my father."

"It will do no good to argue, Taejin. They treat me the same. I think they would wish to see you go to the war because of your father."

"And I will go."

A look of fright crossed her face. "Please do not say such things, Taejin. You have been my only friend for the last six years. If you are sent away I will have no one to talk with."

He painted her a wan smile. "I shall not speak of it again." He began refilling the buckets.

"May I work with you?" she asked.

"I think we must work where they tell us. We do not have a choice." He finished, shouldering the yoke.

"I will go back with you." She followed him as he returned to the rows.

Taejin replaced the empty yoke bearer and the ladlers had just begun working his buckets when there were shouts from the area of the wagon. They turned. Workers were dancing and cheering.

"Song," he said. "See what it is all about."

She started toward the wagon, but other workers were racing toward the rows.

"The Japanese have lost!" they shouted. "The war will be over!"

Song turned to Taejin, a look of disbelief on her face. Slowly, he removed the yoke from his shoulders and set it on the ground.

One of the runners approached their group. "The Americans have dropped a great bomb in Japan," he shouted, gasping for breath. "They have destroyed an entire city with one great bomb." He ran on to announce the news to other groups.

Militiamen were arriving, leaping from their vehicles, their weapons high. There were no more Japanese. They had long ago left for the fighting. These were Koreans. "Go back to work," they shouted, fanning out to encircle the field. "You must go back to work."

"Why?" yelled the workers. "The war will be over. Japan will be defeated."

The militia advanced on them. The workers ignored them.

Suddenly there was an agonized scream at the wagon. All shouting stopped as they turned to look. A militiaman was yanking his bayonet from a still figure on the ground.

The other militiamen closed on the workers. "You must go back to work," they growled.

"But you are Koreans," shouted a worker from deep in the crowd. "Would you kill your own countrymen?"

"Arrest him!" shouted the leader. "Bring him to me."

The young worker, perhaps thirteen years old, was dragged forward.

"Take him away," snapped the leader.

Taejin stooped and raised the yoke to his shoulders once more. Song stepped forward and began ladling the excrement from his buckets onto the plants.

"What will happen to us now?" she whimpered.

"Be quiet," he warned. "They are in a most vicious mood."

She nodded and continued ladling in silence. Others around them did the same. The banter was over, the mood broken. Only the odor rose in the summer heat.

"Taejin."

He could see she was in trouble. "What is wrong?"

"I think I will be ill."

Quickly he set down the yoke and went to her. Tears were streaming from her eyes and into the scarf.

"Come," he said, taking her elbow and urging her away from the rows. "You must rest."

As they approached the wagon a militiaman stepped into their path, brandishing his weapon with bayonet fixed. "Where are you going? You were told to go back to work."

Taejin slid his arm around her shoulder. "She is ill. I am taking her to rest." They continued walking, moving to pass him.

The bayonet prodded menacingly into his chest. "She may rest at night. Now you must work. There is much to be done."

Song's eyes were wide. "Please. Do not hurt us."

"Go back to work."

Taejin tried to turn her, keep her from looking toward the wagon. It was too late. She was staring in horror at the body of the boy they had bayoneted. He lay where he had fallen, a grotesque contortion frozen permanently into his face. Suddenly she began retching. Taejin grabbed her, trying to keep her from falling.

The militiamen were on them in an instant. "You! Return to work immediately or we shall arrest you."

Taejin tried to ignore him but strong hands were gripping him now, tearing him away from her.

"She is ill," he shouted.

"That is obvious. You must return to work. We will take care of her."

He looked around as they thrust him back toward the field. They were leading her to shade, pushing her down to sit.

"Is she your sister?" growled the militiaman.

"No."

"Then why do you concern yourself for her?"

"She is my friend."

Nothing more was said, and he picked up his yoke. The other workers had progressed beyond him. He made his way to them.

"I think the merchant's daughter takes after her father," said one of the boys.

Taejin said nothing.

"You were trying to get out of work because of her," said another.

He ignored their taunts. As soon as his buckets were empty he made his way back to the wagon to refill them. Song was now lying on the ground under a tree.

"Do you feel better?" he called.

She nodded and waved weakly to him.

When he returned to the field he moved to a different row. More militiamen had arrived. They were moving among the workers, taking their names.

"You will listen!" shouted the leader when the lists were complete. "You have caused us trouble today. We now have your names. If you cause more trouble we shall come to your homes and arrest you. You cannot hide from us." He looked around at the group. "Work is finished. Go to your homes. Do not congregate in the village. If you do you will be arrested."

The women and children left in silence, shuffling toward the village. During the next two weeks each day was the same. Then, through the stillness of the night came an eerie squealing. The people awakened, hurrying to their gates. The sound became louder, spiraling into a roar of engines, still accompanied by the squeals.

The militia were nowhere to be seen. At last, a column of tanks roared around a bend at the far end of Hochon and squealed its way into the square. Trucks followed them, troops dropping from their beds as they came to a stop. The men were large, many of them caucasians. On the sides of the vehicles were painted large red stars.

* * * * * *

Farmer Kim, now free of prison, welcomed the Soviets with open arms. Every day of his confinement he had imagined the oppressed people, the downtrodden, the rats scurrying through life seeking a crust of bread and hiding from bright lights. He had listened each day to their moans, railed year after year as they achieved little from their labor. Now he listened intently to the first speeches and became vocal in their support. He felt he had found that great equalizer for which he had yearned so long. He visited the headquarters of the party and requested literature and further instruction in socialist thought. He talked with more of the people of the village, telling them their years of unrewarded toil were over. He preached against those who had built estates and assured the poor that these homes had been built at their expense. He slept little and worked diligently, and when the local People's Committee was formed Kim was one of the first men appointed to serve.

He reveled in the appointment, vowing at last to elevate his family into a measure of comfort as a sort of unspoken compensation for their years of deprivation. His first thought was for his two sons. He was determined they would now have what they wanted, be treated with more than moderate deference.

"The People's Committee has canceled all contracts," he announced grandly to his motherless sons. "Imagine that. None of the young women of Hochon is now to be held to any marriage contract which was made while the Japanese were here."

Kwon, his elder son, scoffed. "What need do I have for a woman? I would rather work with you in the party. If I rise in the party I will be able to have the comfort of any woman I wish. For now I will work as you have worked, my father."

The farmer smiled. "If that is your wish, I am proud beyond my dreams. But should you change your mind you have only to name the woman and she will be yours. I will see to it."

Nambae, the younger son, shifted uneasily, saying nothing.

"Well, Nambae, I think you must not think as your brother thinks. You seem nervous."

"I have seen the daughter of Merchant Pak, Father. I would like you to arrange for me to marry Song."

Kim sat back and laughed merrily. "The merchant's daughter?" He laughed again. "It would give me great pleasure to deliver her into your bed."

The young man brightened, but said nothing.

"Why would you wish to marry such a woman?"

"She is very beautiful, Father."

"She is a child," scoffed his brother.

Nambae bristled. "She is fifteen."

"She is too frail. Always she has been but a straw in the wind."

"She was frail as a child. She is no longer frail."

His brother showed his disgust. "You could have any woman in the village. Our father has said it is so. I think you must wait and think. You will not want such a sickly one when there are so many others who are older and healthy."

Farmer Kim waved him to silence. "If she is young I think she will grow older. I do not consider that a problem." He grinned. "The merchant fears for his life, you know. Always, he has feared for his life. Even when we were boys he was afraid of the rest of us. That is how he became a merchant. He was afraid to work in the fields with the rest of us. He played trickery with the Japanese and they made him a merchant. He could not have done it if he had not had the Japanese to do it for him." Kim laughed again. "You see? It would please me to take his precious daughter from him for you." Suddenly he was serious. "Are you certain, Nambae? Are you certain you want the daughter of such a spineless one?"

"Yes, Father. But can you really arrange a contract? I have been told there was a contract for her to marry Taejin, the lawyer's son."

Kim spat. "They are canceled. I have told you." He was pensive only for a moment. "Yes. That would be very interesting, stealing a contract from the great lawyer." He rose. "I think the merchant must still fear me. I shall give him a good reason to remember why."

"Shall I go with you, Father?"

"No. I shall do it myself. There is no need for the bridegroom to be present for such things." He rose. "By the end of the day I shall have it arranged."

In only a short time Kim was at Pak's door. "I have come to talk with you about your daughter, Merchant."

Pak peered at him, suspecting.

"Come, come, merchant. Are you not going to invite me to enter your house?" He glared accusingly at Pak.

"Please. Come in, Kim." The merchant backed away from the door and motioned the farmer inside. "May I offer you tea?"

"That would be most gracious of you, Pak." He stared at the merchant for a moment. "I was remembering today of the days when we were boys. You were a farmer in those days, just like the rest of us. Your father was a farmer."

Pak waved to his wife for the tea and sat. "Yes. My father was a farmer."

"But," continued Kim, "you were not content to be one of us. You did not want to work in the paddies like your boyhood friends."

"I had an opportunity to become a merchant. It was thrust upon me by the Japanese."

"Oh?" Kim smiled disarmingly. "I did not know the Japanese had forced it upon you. You must have been very unhappy with the Japanese. They robbed you of an opportunity to work hard in the fields with the rest of us."

"Yes."

Kim laughed. "Well, I have come to offer you a chance to rejoin your old friends. I have come to arrange a marriage contract between your daughter and my younger son."

Pak paled. "But she has already been contracted to marry the son of Lawyer Chung."

Kim scowled. "A contract which means nothing. You know that all such contracts arranged under the Japanese have been canceled. This is a new order. I think you must not dwell on things as they were before. All that is dead."

Pak persisted. "The lawyer and I hope to arrange a new contract. We still hope to marry my daughter to his son."

Kim sucked air forcefully through his teeth. "Then I think you must change your mind, Pak. The lawyer is not a man to make your relative. He is nothing now. You will gain nothing for yourself or for your daughter by marrying her to his son." He spread his hands matter-of-factly. "On the other hand, were you to marry her to my son I think you should be very happy with the results. After all, not many of those who worked for the Japanese will be able to continue in the same work with the government of the people." He stood. "I wish you to think about that until I return. I would not want you to make another foolish mistake with your life."

With that he was gone, but the next morning he returned. "Well, Pak, have you thought about what I have told you?"

The merchant was steadfast. "The lawyer and I will try to arrange another contract of marriage."

Kim made no effort to enter the house. Glaring at Pak, he spat, "I think if you wish to keep your warehouse you must reconsider your position. I am a member of the People's Committee. I have a great deal of influence in Hochon now. I can see to it that you remain the warehouseman for Hochon. But you must be willing to do something for me in return." He leered at Pak. "That should not be too difficult for you to understand, Pak."

"I will think about it," replied Pak.

"See that you do, Comrade Pak. See that you do."

When he was gone, Song emerged from the next room. "Father, must you do this?"

Pak looked sadly at his daughter. "I think the farmer will give me little choice."

"But Father. I have thought I would be married to Taejin. I have been promised to him."

Pak shook his head. "I am afraid, Daughter, that if the farmer does not have his way life shall become very difficult for us all."

At last Song and Taejin discussed the situation openly between themselves. At first she hid her knowledge.

"Are we not to be able to marry as our families wish?" she pouted, clearly worried.

"What of our wishes?" he countered.

Song turned away from him, blushing demurely.

"I think we must wait until it is determined how we are to live. My father was a lawyer for the Japanese. There are those in Hochon who hate him and would now seek revenge."

Song looked up quickly, concerned. "Do you think your family will be harmed?" she asked.

Taejin shrugged, trying to appear nonchalantly brave. "I think we cannot judge that yet. I think it will be a matter of who the leaders are."

She looked furtively about her, though they were alone at her father's warehouse. "Do you think my father will be in danger?"

Taejin shook his head. "I think he will not be in as much as my father. No one else in Hochon can tend to the warehouse. No one knows administration."

She scoffed. "It would not be difficult for them to bring someone in to replace him. It would be a simple matter to replace him with one of their own."

Taejin was dubious, not knowing how the situation would affect the merchant, unsure of how to reassure her. "I think we must wait and see," he said lamely.

"And what of us?" she pressed.

"I think we must wait and see," he said again. then turning, he gazed into her eyes. "Song, I want you to become my wife."

Song dropped her eyes, blushing again. "I would like that. I would like to be your wife." She hesitated, then looked up into his face anxiously. "But they have canceled the contract. Why would they allow us a new one?"

Taejin hesitated, uncomfortable with her question. "Individual cases might be different," he faltered. "They canceled all so as to eliminate the old government and all its influence. They wanted nothing to remain." He straightened, gaining confidence. "Do we worry without reason? Perhaps a new contract could be arranged under the new government."

Her doubt was obvious. He reached and took her hand consolingly. They began walking, lost in thought, deeper into the warehouse. Hugh bins of rice enveloped them, rising high toward the roof.

Suddenly tears crept down her cheeks. "I hope it will be so. But you have said you worry for your father. Others already have approached my father. I have listened from hiding. They tell him he must change his mind. They tell him your father no longer has influence." She looked quickly up at him, speaking honestly but not wanting to hurt, alarm him further, yet knowing she must be frank. "They tell him he will keep his warehouse if he arranges a marriage to another. I think he is most worried."

He had stopped abruptly, angered. "Who has said this?" he demanded.

"Several men."

"Who?" he demanded again.

She began sobbing louder now, shaken by his anger. "Taejin, please do not be angry with me. I cannot tell you if you become angry."

His face twisted with emotion, yet he softened. "I am sorry to frighten you, Song." Impulsively, he drew her close and held her to him. "I worry that I may lose my father. I worry that I may lose you." He stroked her shoulders lovingly, then gently urged her head to his chest, his fingers in her hair.

She did not resist, but returned his embrace. "I am afraid you will do something foolish if I tell you. I do not want to cause them to harm you."

He absorbed her apprehension. "I will do nothing. But I must know who these enemies are. I must know who would think ill of my father and who would threaten yours."

Her body moved with the sobs, warm and urgent against him. "It was the farmer. Kim."

"Would he have you for one of his sons?" he asked in alarm.

"He would have me for Nambae, his younger son," she replied softly.

Panic shot through him, insistent, threatening. She held him tighter, feeling his arousal and sensing it in herself.

"But you cannot be his," he moaned. "You must be mine, Song. You must be mine."

She turned her face upward and searched his eyes. Then his lips were on her, kissing her, seeking her lips, her eyes, her ears. Slowly, they made their way to a bin. His hands read her body, stroking her into response. Gently, without words, he released the smock from her shoulders. She watched him, breathing deeply. Then, totally detached from the world around them, they slid softly into their oneness. The crimson of her innocence seeped tranquilly into the rice mountain, unbeckoned except by love, unrecognized except by passion.

* * * * * *

Next day Kim returned to Pak. He wore a new air of confidence. "Pak, I think the time has come for you to tell me your decision. I have made arrangements."

A knot tightened in the merchant's stomach. "What arrangements? I think I must take part in any arrangements."

"Then you agree to a marriage?"

"I have made no decision."

Kim measured him. "My son will make a very good husband for your daughter. After all, is he not the son of an official of the people?" He paused. "You see, Pak, you have a problem. You continue to think in the old way, the way which is now dead. You think in terms of farmers and merchants and such. But, you see, in the new order we are not necessarily what we were in the old. For instance, in the old order I was, indeed, a farmer. But in the new I am not. I am a government official. Other people may feel more comfortable being just what they were in the old order, all the while reaping the benefits of the new. I think that must be very good, if that is what they wish. However, such people must recognize that it is not business as usual, so to speak. In the old days you became a merchant because you made an arrangement with the Japanese. Now I think for you to remain a merchant you must make an equal arrangement with the people." He studied him. "I am offering you that opportunity, Pak. I am giving you the opportunity to remain a merchant. You and I can agree on a marriage between my son and your daughter, and I can make certain you remain the merchant and warehouseman for Hochon. It is that simple."

Pak bowed his head in despair, knowing he had no alternative. If he refused, Kim would ruin him, and why not? They had never been friends. The farmer had envied him all their adult lives because of the warehouse. Even before that there had been antagonism. And, after all, was Kim not right? Perhaps he could reap benefits from such a union. "When would you wish the wedding?" he asked quietly.

Kim smiled triumphantly. "Why, as soon as possible. I think there is nothing to be gained by waiting. I think we could arrange it for next week or the week after. The sooner the better." He stood and reached to Pak. "I am certain you will be happy with the results of your good sense."

The wedding took place two weeks later, but there was no celebration. Contrary to the old custom of congregating well wishers, the new order dictated merely a recognition and signing of official documents before members of the People's Committee.

* * * * * *

Nambae was obviously distraught as he entered the room. His father looked up, perplexed.

"Father, I have married a tainted woman."

Kim was shocked. "What do you mean? How is she a tainted woman?"

"Song is not a virgin. She was not a virgin when we were married."

The committeeman bounded from the mat on which he had been sitting. "Are you certain, Nambae?"

"Father, I am most certain," shot back the son. "I think there must be an annulment. I think the merchant must be exposed for making a bad contract. He dealt in damaged goods."

"I shall kill him," growled the father. "I shall make him wish he had never been born!" He paced angrily. "Who has done this?" he demanded.

"I think it must be Taejin, the son of the lawyer," replied the son. "There was the marriage contract under the Japanese. I think they could not wait."

The father said nothing, musing. "I think the merchant was not careful enough. He was too intent on other things." He was watching his father anxiously. "Father, I think we must declare to the village that he dealt in a contract with a tainted daughter as the prize. We have been duped."

"Yes," exploded his father. "Declare to the village that a member of the People's Committee allowed himself to be tricked by the wily merchant." He flung his arm in the air furiously. "And then our leaders will conclude they have made a bad choice in appointing me to the committee." He measured his son. "I have reason to believe I may soon become the chairman of the committee. How will that look? What will the provincial leaders do when they learn their choice for chairman has been so easily disgraced?" He stopped and glared at his son. "I have lost my face, and it was you who caused it to happen."

"I, Father?"

"Yes, I think so. It was you who chose the woman. You looked only at her face. You asked me to arrange the contract, and I did that for you because I am becoming an influential person." He gathered in his breath. "You have shamed me!" he screamed.

Nambae shrank back, fearful now of his father.

Kim was whispering now. "I shall not be shamed in public. I shall not lose my face. I am soon to become even more powerful than I am now, and to lose my face would mean it would not happen." He straightened and spoke emphatically. "No. You chose the woman, and you shall keep the woman. I will deal with the merchant, and I will deal with the lawyer and his wayward son. But the village and the provincial leaders will never know."

"But Father," pleaded the son. "Must I spend my life married to a faithless woman?"

"Yes. You chose her. You must live with her. You must forget she is tainted." The committeeman stared at his son for a long moment, then left the room.

Nambae hurried to his home and confronted Song. "You have tricked me," he shouted. "You are a tainted woman."

Song recoiled at his fury, yet did not reply.

"We shall shame you. We shall shame your father. I think your father will no longer be the warehouseman for Hochon!"

His wife regained her composure. "The marriage was forced upon me, upon my father."

"You have been with another man and you did not tell us. Your father did not tell us."

"I did not want to marry you."

"You had no choice in the matter."

"Then you should not complain with what you got."

Her husband advanced to strike her. "You will not speak to me that way again, woman. You are my wife. You will treat me with respect."

The slap had stung, but she stood her ground. "And must you not treat me with respect as well?"

He slapped her again. "A whore is not worthy of respect. You are a whore!"

"Then annul the marriage," she shot back. "I think you must be very careful not to live your life with a whore."

"Who was he?" he hissed. "Who has done this?"

"It does not matter, my husband," she smiled. "You have called me a whore. I think a whore must be most indiscriminate."

He slapped her again. "I will not put up with such insolence." He reached and tore her clothes from her in a single swipe. "You will learn submission. You will learn to be discriminate." He was stepping out of his clothes. "Last night I was surprised to learn you are not a virgin. Today you will wish you were." He grabbed her and threw her to the mat, forcing her legs apart. "At least you will bear me a son."

She was panting with the struggle. "I cannot," she moaned. "I am pregnant."

He stopped as if shot. "Who? You must tell me who."

"It does not matter. You have called me a whore. I think a whore cannot know who." She reached out for her torn clothes, but he stopped her. "I was willing to be your wife, but you had no consideration for me. Now you say you will annul the marriage and shame me and my father. Do it. I cannot bear you a son until

I bear this other child." She laughed. "I think you will not wait that long."

He had risen and was dressing. A moment later he bounded out the door.

"Father, I have worse news." he shouted as he entered his father's house.

Farmer Kim merely looked at him, now loathing what the son had done.

"She will have a child by this other man. We must do something." He was panting in his fury. "The marriage must be annulled and the Pak family exposed."

"No!" shouted his father. "My career is just now beginning. It will not be destroyed by you losing our family's face. You will keep her."

"And what of the child?" wailed his son. "What of her bearing this other man's child?"

"I think you must raise it as your own," replied his father evenly. "I shall punish this Taejin and his family, but you will say nothing. I will not lose my face! I will not lose my opportunity to be chairman of the People's Committee."

* * * * * *

It was a crisp October morning. The air was still and its chill quickened the steps of those who had risen early to face the day's challenge. Lawyer Chung's wife was preparing rice as he pulled his smock about him. Suddenly there were shouts in front of the house and a banging at the gate.

His wife rushed into the room in alarm. "The street is filled with men."

"Are they soldiers?" he asked quickly.

"Some are, but not all."

Chung walked quickly to the front of the house, as he did so hearing the banging repeated at the gate. Turning quickly, he said, "Be prepared for anything and stay with Taejin. He will protect you. I shall see what this is all about." He went out into the crisp but cloudless day.

The banging continued now, insistently.

"Yes," he called. "Good morning. I am coming."

He opened the gate and stepped back.

"Ah, good morning, Chung. It is a pleasure to see you again, to see my old friend after so many years." Standing in the opening was Farmer Kim.

Chung looked quickly over Kim's shoulder and saw that his military escort was far larger than necessary. "Good morning, Kim."

"I was just passing this way and it occurred to me that in all these years you have never once invited my sons to your home. They no longer had a mother since you and your friends had sent her to whore for the Japanese, but you took no further notice of that. It must have slipped your mind. Of course, I was busy elsewhere and could not have come, and you were busy with the Japanese." He brushed past Chung and strode toward the house. "Is the tea hot?"

"Of course."

"Good. Then we shall visit." Kim turned to the soldiers. "All of you. Wait here. I must visit with my old friend before we go on." He turned and entered the house. Once inside, he looked appreciatively around the room. "You have a beautiful home here, Chung. Let me look around at the rest of it before we talk."

"I think we are not prepared for company at this time of day," answered Chung, knowing it would not matter.

"But, have you not heard?" asked Kim in feigned surprise. "The people never sleep. Only the light changes. The people are always awake."

After walking admiringly through the house he returned to the parlor. "Now we shall visit." He sat at the low table and looked expectantly toward the door. "Well, where is the tea?"

"What is it you wish from me, Kim?"

"Wish? What do you mean by that? I wish some tea and an opportunity to visit with you. We have not seen each other in a long time. It is time to renew acquaintances. To bury past differences, as one might say." He smiled at Chung, but without warmth.

Chung's wife brought them tea and disappeared.

Kim looked up at Chung. "Come. Sit down with me." He gestured to the floor.

Chung sat.

"It has occurred to me I have never thanked you for what you did in my defense. You saved my life. I believe that is the way you put it. I thank you."

"You are welcome."

"And I hope to be able to return the favor." He lit a cigarette. "No, I do not hope. That is an incorrect statement. I shall return the favor."

"Thank you."

"You see, Chung, you have been apart from the people of Hochon for many years. How long has it been? Thirty years?" He shook his head in mock sorrow. "That is much too long. Of course, the Japanese made you do it, but then, I told you they would. I told you they would infiltrate your mind. And as a result, you see, you became Japanese. That was most unfortunate."

"I worked very hard to keep our people free of their tyranny."

"Of course you did. You kept me free, did you not? Well, I was not exactly free, now, was I? But you kept me alive. All you charged me as a fee was my rice. You extracted my fee in rice. And, of course, my wife. Is that not so? You extracted my fee in the form of my wife, my rice and labor."

"Your wife and your rice were taken from you by the Japanese. I merely kept you alive."

"But not out of prison. I did nothing wrong, yet I was made to wait a long time for my trial and to serve ten years."

"It was most difficult to get them to do anything quickly."

"Except to take our crops and to execute our people, innocent people," prompted Kim. "And to take our wives and daughters to comfort their soldiers, as they called it. That was not entirely true, was it, Chung? What they did was turn our wives and daughters into whores for their pleasure." He paused. "But even that is not wholly true either. Your wife was not taken. Nor were the wife and daughter of the merchant, Pak." He shook his head. "Oh, what good care the Japanese took of their friends, the lawyers and merchants."

Chung remained silent and watched him, wondering what his intentions were. It began to appear he too was going to spend some time in the prison.

"Nevertheless," Kim continued, sweeping it all aside, "all that is behind us now. We hold no grudges in Hochon. We wish to put our village and our people back together again. And that includes you, Chung."

"Thank you," Chung answered, without emotion.

"So we thought the best way we could do that was to return things to the way they were before the Japanese came in the first place." Kim studied him, an amused expression on his face. "Most regrettably, there are certain things which cannot be reversed. An education, for instance. One cannot turn to the world and say, 'Here is my education. Take it back. I do not want or need it anymore.'" He laughed at his own wit, then became serious once more. "But there are other things which can be returned, such as material things." He watched Chung carefully.

The lawyer said nothing.

Kim looked around the room. "All of this is Japanese doings. Before they came you were one of us, and we have come to welcome you back among us. To forgive and forget. We thought you would want that, to be a part of us again."

Chung swallowed hard, knowing he was about to lose everything.

"So we have decided that you should be returned to our midst in grand style. We shall move you into the house which was your father's, and you may begin farming the land again. You see, under the People's Republic there is really no need for lawyers. It would be most wasteful of a strong man." Kim was chuckling with glee now. "You know, I have just remembered when the Japanese came to the homes of our people to arrest them. They came much as I came today, though I did not mean for you to be alarmed. I was merely passing by with my friends. But when the Japanese came to our homes they banged on the gate in much the same way. Except when they came into our homes they did not sit with us and visit as we are doing now. Instead they beat us. All about the head and shoulders. In our courtyards they knocked us to the ground and sat on us. It was terrible."

"They were not a gentle people, as some would have the world believe."

"They were not. That is true. But then, is gentility not a matter of degree? A matter of interpretation? Of course it is. The fact that they beat us and then accused us of such crimes against them was most ludicrous. And yet, they helped us. Even that time in the prison helped me. Did you know that?"

"I am sorry. There was nothing more I could do."

"Oh, I meant that not to scold you. Not at all. I meant what I said. My time in the prison helped me. Otherwise I would not have seen the people and their needs as clearly as I do today. Before the prison I saw only myself, my own needs. I did not see the people. Then while I was in the prison I realized that all the people had needs. And if each person started out with the same things it would all be much better in the end. Society would be better. There would not be all this fighting and bickering to gain material things because everyone would be equal. And because of that we could all work together to provide for everyone's needs and all the people would be better off. They would be truly happy. That is what I have worked for. And now," he said, sitting back and opening his palms upward, "that is what we have. Are you not happy we have achieved it?"

Chung felt cornered. With the soldiers lounging in front of his house there was little he could do but agree. "I am most happy."

"Good. Now let us decide what is to be done with your beautiful house. Actually, I am told that people who work in the government, attending to the affairs of the masses, should live near their work. Perhaps one of our government officials will be moved into this house. But then, since you now have your father's house you will not need this one anyway." He sighed. "Yes, it is most fortunate the way things have turned out."

"Who will live here?" asked Chung, mechanically curious.

"That is an excellent question, Chung. It seems to me that your house would make a most appropriate headquarters for the People's Committee." He sat back and thought for a moment. "Yes. That would be a very good idea. This room, as a matter of fact, would make a very good office for the chairman. He could live in the other parts of your, excuse me, the house and be near his office to serve the people many hours a day."

"The chairman of the People's Committee?"

"Yes. Would that not be appropriate?" He smiled. "Of course, you will gain much favor with the committee by donating your house to the people for such a purpose. Imagine how grateful they will be."

"But the chairman is a Russian."

Kim looked surprised. "Have you not heard? We no longer have a Russian chairman."

Chung was shocked. "Than who is the chairman?"

Kim looked triumphant. "I am."

Chung gulped. "You?"

"Yes. You recall our talks about it. Yes, I am the chairman. I thought it most complimentary of them to select me. After all, it would have been bad to keep someone from the outside in power the way the Japanese did. We have no need for outsiders. We do not even need a militia."

"Then who are the soldiers?"

"Korean. Every one is Korean. It is better that way. They understand the problems of the Koreans. And when they see a problem, or I see a problem, we can go about solving it together for the good of the masses. Do you not agree that is the best way to solve our problems? We should solve them ourselves. We have no need of foreigners to solve our problems."

"Yes. Without a doubt that is better."

Kim looked at his watch. "It is late, and we have much work to do. It is best we all get started." He stood and turned to face Chung. "Your work today, Comrade, will be to move to your father's old house. I shall leave some of our comrades here to help you." He walked to the door, then stopped and turned. "Of course, you will take only what you absolutely need. The extra material things you have will be donated to the people. Certainly you understand."

Chung stood at the door and looked after him for a long moment.

"Lawyer."

Chung turned and saw the soldier. "What do you want?"

"We must hurry. There are many things to be done. You had better begin. You, your wife and your son will do the work. My comrades and I will watch most carefully that you fulfill the chairman's wishes."

Chung walked through the house. His wife appeared from a shadow, and with her, Taejin. "We must move," he told them.

"We know. We heard." There were tears in her eyes.

"Father, must you surrender to him?" The young man said it with a hint of disgust. "I think he is not worth your spit."

"I have no choice. He has left soldiers here to be certain we move today and take nothing they want."

"I think we must find out what is happening in the other towns," continued the son. "I think there must be a revolution against them."

Suddenly he was knocked to the floor. Above him hovered a soldier brandishing a bayonet at him. "Are you a revolutionary?" sneered the soldier. "Perhaps you would like to express your views to Chairman Kim."

Taejin said nothing, but tried to rise. The bayonet pricked insistently into his chest. "You will stay where you are!" The soldier nodded to the horrified lawyer and his wife. "Do as you were told," he ordered.

The lawyer and his wife began gathering what belongings they could under the watchful eyes of the soldiers.

Taejin was led from the house by two of the guards and marched away. Upon his arrival at the prison he was taken before a people's magistrate.

"What is the charge?" asked the man tiredly.

"Sedition against the people, Comrade Magistrate," replied one of the soldiers.

The magistrate looked at the young Taejin with renewed interest. "And what seditious acts did he perform?"

"He was plotting and preaching revolution, Comrade."

"Revolution?" The magistrate smiled. "Was he too weak to participate in the last one? I think if he were interested in becoming a revolutionary he could have done something then." He waved his hand at the guards. "Take him to a cell. Let him think about his timing. Surely, he must have been a sympathizer with the Japanese."

"How long must I remain in the prison?" blurted Taejin.

The magistrate scowled. "I think you are not in a position to ask such impertinent questions. The people will decide your fate at your trial."

"And when will I be tried?" persisted Taejin.

The magistrate did not reply, but motioned to the guard. "Take him away."

* * * * * *

Chairman Kim strode importantly into his son's house. "Where is your husband?" he asked.

Song merely glanced at him. "I do not know. He does not tell me where he goes."

"I think tomorrow he must take you to the court of the people's magistrate. You should begin to learn about the court system."

"I have no interest in the court system. I have a house to keep and a husband to serve."

Kim smirked. "I shall send him a message. I shall tell him to take you to the court tomorrow. You should find the cases most interesting."

Song immediately became wary. "Why should I find them so?"

Kim passed it off. "If you are to be in the family of the People's Committee Chairman you must find all such things interesting. And educational. We must not forget they are so."

"Who is to be tried?" she pressed, more apprehensive.

"Oh, it matters not who is to be tried. That is not important. I only think you should understand the system of the people's justice. One day it may become most important to you." He looked around the room. "This is not a very clean room. I would suggest you keep it more pleasant and clean. Perhaps your husband would spend more time here if it were more presentable." He turned quickly and departed.

Next morning Nambae hurried her out of the house. "Come. My father says you must learn about the people's courts. Today is a good day to begin."

"Why is your father so anxious that I go to the court today? I think I could go at any time. I do not feel well today."

"My father says your bastard child cannot be an excuse for your failing to learn about the people's government. I agree with him. Come. We must hurry."

As they entered the courtroom she shrank back, stifling a cry. Seated in the prisoner's box was Taejin. He was shackled, with a guard at each shoulder.

Nambae made no notice of her reaction. He took her elbow and guided her to the front row. "Here we shall be able to see and hear well."

"I think you are most cruel, Nambae. You know he has been my friend all my life."

"Oh? I did not know." They sat, and she stared at the doomed Taejin.

"Why have you done this to me?" She was whispering it without looking at him, fury on her face.

"We have thought you might wish to see him for the last time.

You should be aware of what a criminal he is." Nambae was looking around the courtroom with an air of importance.

Moments before the trial was to begin Farmer Kim entered. He strode to the front of the room and took a seat on the other side of Song. "I am pleased to see you were so anxious to attend this trial, Song. You will learn a great deal about the justice of the people."

Song looked straight ahead, saying nothing.

"Come, come," urged the chairman. "Certainly you remember how to say good morning?"

"*Anyanghashimnika*," she answered, mechanically, not taking her eyes off Taejin.

When the trial began it was quick and efficient. There were no motions and countermotions, only a listing of the charges. These had been expanded to include sedition, inciting to riot, and other general crimes against the people.

"Why has his father not come to the trial?" she hissed at no one in particular.

Chairman Kim raised an eyebrow. "His father? The lawyer? What does he know of the people's law? No, it is much better that he is not here. He would only get himself and his son in greater trouble."

The magistrate began speaking. "I have heard the evidence in this case. I wish to compliment the law officers who brought this criminal to justice. I think we must make all the people of Hochon aware of this man's crimes. It will be a good education for the masses." He looked sternly at Taejin. "You will rise."

Taejin labored to his feet and stood with his head bowed.

"Prisoner, you are now sentenced to be confined in the prison mine at Hyesan, where you will perform hard labor for a period of thirty years. You will be paraded through the streets of Hochon so that all the people may see you and know what happens to criminals who would plot and preach against the masses."

Song watched him as they led him away. A man so good. A man she loved. She was certain he would not survive.

THE SOUTH—GAPYONG

Min had aged. Always tall by Korean standards, he was now beginning to gray. It gave him a distinguished, learned appearance which he nurtured carefully through his dress and mannerisms.

When Shin climbed the steps of the school Min looked at him with vagueness.

"Schoolmaster. Do you not remember me?"

Min looked harder. "Shin. My student Shin." He looked at the uniform of the captain and his eyes filled with tears. He gesticulated anxiously. "Come in. Quickly."

Shin slipped through the doorway and Min closed and locked the barrier carefully. He turned, appraising the younger man. "The war is over and you have returned."

Shin smiled proudly, yet deferentially to the teacher. "I have sought you first. I have not even gone to Chunchon."

Min nodded. "It is wise, Student Shin," he replied, starting purposefully toward his office. "You have many medals. If the Americans were to see you in your uniform I think they would have many questions."

Shin, following him closely, passed off the comment. "The Americans will be more concerned with the generals, the actual architects of the war. I do not worry about them. I think I must be more concerned about the Koreans."

They entered the office. "Have you done wrong?" asked Min, surprised.

"I think," he said evasively, "the ineffective soldier of the army which wins must be hailed the hero. The bold soldier of that which loses will be derided. Our people hated the Japanese. I think such hate does not die quickly."

"But the Japanese took you much in the manner of a conquered vassal. You had no choice. I think you must not worry for the Koreans."

Shin smiled, interested, hiding his fear of the Inchon guards. "It is a curiously fortunate turn of events, this war. You have made a most significant point, Schoolmaster. Korea, regardless of the outcome, could not lose this war. If the Japanese had won we could have celebrated with them. We were part of their nation. Now that they have been beaten, however, we find ourselves in an equally comfortable position. We have been oppressed by Japan, forced to fight beside them. The world must pity Korea. The vanquished are still the victors."

"Then if the Koreans are to be pitied I think no one will punish you for your forced participation." Min got up. "Come. I shall take you to my bungalow. You shall see the setting. It offers many comforts for the soul as well as the body."

They walked from the school, casually strolling along the streets of Gapyong. Min nodded sagely at passersby but did not stop. Soon they were outside the town, seemingly unconcerned as they approached Min's field beside the river. Then, turning, they approached the grove of trees. Min stopped, smiling. "Is it not beautiful?"

Shin walked forward a few steps, then stopped. "It could be a cottage for a woodsman, a tradesman. You have done well, Schoolmaster."

Min nodded emphatically. "We shall stay here. You may contemplate your future in peace."

"Yes, I must think of the future," said Shin, approaching the bungalow.

"And I think, the past." Min, perceiving, had not moved.

Shin turned. "What of my past? My past has been only with

the Japanese. Always I was forced to fight. I was conscripted in Chunchon."

But you became an officer. You have many medals."

"They mean nothing now." He opened the door, entering with Min now close behind.

"What have you been doing?"

Shin turned to him, only mildly irritated. "Schoolmaster, you have been most kind to me. I am honored and grateful, but I think you must not ask me of my past again. I have come here so that I may contemplate my future."

Min advanced slowly and sat. "I have always advised you well, Shin. I shall do so again, but I think I cannot if you will not discuss such matters with me." He gestured toward Shin's uniform. "I think you have performed many heroic deeds to be elevated to such rank. It has been but ten years since your conscription."

Shin hung his head, thoughtfully silent. At last he looked up. "I was placed in some situations which proved most awkward. They assigned me difficult and dangerous tasks. I was watched carefully. Had I made one wrong move they would have disciplined, even executed me." He looked meaningfully at the aging schoolmaster. "Even that would not have ended it. They would have arrested those who helped me attain the rank. Even you, Schoolmaster. You taught me. You were expected to have given me a thorough education in loyalty to the Japanese. You too would have been arrested."

"Where did you fight?"

"In many places. I fought in many battles."

"And you have many medals. I think they did not quickly honor an unwilling soldier. They would not promote an average Korean to the rank of captain."

Shin turned and viewed the room, ignoring further discussion of the subject. "You have obtained a most sturdy cottage, Schoolmaster. Was it a gift from the Japanese?"

Min laughed. "The Japanese knew nothing of its existence. It is new, though it appears worn and used. It was the final act of my students. They built it during the final days when the Japanese were worried with other things."

"Where did you obtain the materials?"

"I have said the Japanese were preoccupied with other things." He contemplated Shin. "Did you perform what the Americans are labeling war crimes?"

Shin tensed once more. "The Japanese expected many things of me. But I have said I think the Americans will be looking for the generals, the people who planned such things. They will not be interested in the soldier in the trench."

Min nodded reflectively. "They expected many things of everyone. You have said you were coerced. You had no choice in these matters. Many others did the same in their assignments, even here in Korea. There were very few of our people who trusted them, who felt a real sense of loyalty to them." He stopped, watching for Shin's reaction.

"I felt loyalty to them, but only to prove their attitudes about our people a myth." Shin looked at the schoolmaster more anxiously, almost with pleading in his eyes. "You knew their demands. You were the one who taught us all those years in your classroom. 'The Koreans are inferior,' you said. 'You must not speak Hangul. You must adore the Emperor.' Schoolmaster, you were their mouthpiece."

"Did you ever consider my reasons?"

Shin looked at him as though the question were rhetorical.

Min leaned forward, almost in supplication. "Did you believe I loved them? Did you believe your father loved them?" His face became fiery with passion. "We hated them."

"But you taught us most convincingly."

"I had no choice. Life was for me as it was for you in combat. It was the only way I could achieve my greater goal." He gazed off at the distance, pensively. "I predicted this."

Shin looked at him in surprise, waiting.

"I predicted it to your father many years ago. You were a small boy. I predicted this war and its outcome most accurately."

Shin, so long immune to awe of others, now looked at his old schoolmaster with a measure of admiration. "How could you have known, Schoolmaster? Certainly there was more to your prediction than this. You have said you hated them, yet you worked most diligently teaching their doctrines."

Min smiled. "When they sent me to Japan for my education I read much more than my assignments. I spent far more time in thought than was required. Had they realized what I was really thinking I would have been disciplined, perhaps imprisoned."

Shin was becoming impatient. But what were your thoughts? What led to this prediction?"

"I considered World War I. I considered the revolution in Russia. Great new world powers were created in those years, powers which were allying themselves most loyally with the traditional powers. Japan, if she continued her course of aggression on the mainland of Asia, was certain to come into a most unfortunate confrontation with one or all of them. I knew the Japanese would be strong, but I did not believe they could fight a protracted war against all of them and win. I knew they would need Korea for her manpower. The conscription was certain to come. It was unavoidable. I made my plans accordingly."

Shin was captivated. "What were your plans? What is this greater goal you have mentioned?"

"I had no intention of serving as a soldier for the Japanese. Yet, I knew if I resisted them they would make me one of the first to go." He was now firmly in the grip of his ego, ignoring the efforts of Shin's father and the others who had helped him. "I decided to join them. The best way to attain a measure of power was to become a schoolmaster. They would always need me here in Korea. They needed men here to prepare their human tools of war."

"Is that what you considered me, Schoolmaster? Was I only a human tool of war?"

Min shook his head. "Many of the others, perhaps, but not you. You were most intelligent. You had common sense, yet I suspected an element of craftiness in you. Good craftiness, I think.

Well intentioned, but craftiness all the same. I believed you would become an officer." He looked up and a glint of pride swept through him. "You see? I was right. You became a heroic officer."

"But all for a losing cause. You have said you knew the Japanese would lose. Was that your goal, to see them lose the war?"

"Of course not," scoffed Min. "My goal was power, influence. I was poor as a boy. I was determined I would never return to that condition. The teaching has been merely a means to an end. Schoolmasters are influential. They mold entire populations. This was merely a route by which to achieve power."

Shin leaned back on an elbow, entranced.

"Now, as I predicted, the Japanese are gone. We have endured many years of their domination but they are gone. I think Korea must now return to self rule."

Shin laughed with a hint of derision. "What has occurred during the past two weeks? The Americans have occupied one half of the country, the Russians the other. It will be only a replacement process. The Japanese will be replaced by these other two giants. I think they will have little need for soldiers from among us."

Min smiled. "That also was part of my prediction to your father. I think these two are to be most worried about each other. They will become involved with Korea only as a trophy. It is the law of the jungle. The bucks fight to the death and the doe is the prize. Korea, along with the rest of the world, will be the prize."

"And where will you achieve your power then?" Shin tossed a pebble toward the field. "I think you must have difficulty becoming powerful under the Americans. I think they will be cautious of a man who was a leader for the Japanese."

"I was not a leader."

"You were a schoolmaster. You were one of the influential ones."

Min nodded, agreeing but flattered. "You must admit I have laid for myself a very solid foundation. I began under the Japanese in Chunchon, performed as they wished and expected me to perform, and was promoted to be their headmaster here. In Chunchon I was faced with many challenges. They did not yet trust me. I knew that. But I also knew if I could be assigned a school of my own where I could establish a curriculum with only enough of the Japanese ideology to keep them satisfied I could build a fortress. I accomplished it. I was moved to Gapyong. It is a small town. People always have learned only from their fathers. Building trades?" He laughed. "There was no learning of building trades in Gapyong. They erected shacks and mud huts, nothing more. They farmed rice and watched their houses tumble into the water with each year's flooding of the rivers. Public buildings? Gapyong had none. But I have taught them. Now they have the knowledge to go anywhere in Korea and obtain work. These students of mine, yes, and former students too, will build a Korea for this century. They will be trade leaders all over our nation. They know they would not have that knowledge without the foresight of Min. And now I have an entire village filled with grateful people who are most ready to follow my suggestions."

"It has been a great accomplishment, Schoolmaster," agreed Shin, "but what will happen now?"

"We must watch these Americans," warned Min. "I believe they will begin distributing great amounts of money around the world. They are a most wealthy nation. They are the victors, but they are tired of war. I believe they will distribute money instead of bullets. A double standard will emerge throughout the world. In nations such as Russia, position will represent power. In the United States money already is the measure. The Americans will use their money as a weapon. The Russians have very little money, so they would be most happy fighting. But the United States will donate their dollars and attract everyone into their debt in exchange for a better standard of living. In a very short time the Russians will face a front so solidly built on American dollars they will be unable to challenge anyone."

"And you, Schoolmaster? Have you a plan to obtain some of those dollars?"

Min grinned. "I can see no reason for allowing such power to go elsewhere."

"Then do you think the Russians will lose to the Americans?"

The schoolmaster evaded him. "Any great change will not come until after my lifetime. Therefore, I shall not worry about it."

"But how can anyone overcome this powerful dollar weapon?"

"It is most simple," replied Min. "If you are given money by a man when you have none you are most grateful."

"Of course."

"You are grateful even if it is only a loan."

"Well, yes. I think if I have none even a loan is welcome."

"And you will be loyal to this benefactor, whatever he asks of you?"

Shin hesitated.

"You see? I think already you are unsure. You hesitate to answer. Why? Because when you accepted that money you yielded a measure of your self respect, your freedom. You wish to have a clean financial slate, to believe the money is really your own. But deep inside you know it is not. Therefore, you begin pretending it is. You hoodwink yourself into believing you earned it on your own merit. In that way you are able to maintain your respect." He raised a finger instructively toward Shin. "Ah, but then suppose there comes a world crisis. The creditor comes to you and requests your support. Oh, he does not wish your dollars. He has many dollars. He desires your men, your blood. You become uncomfortable but you feel an obligation. Yet, at the same time, you begin to resent the grip that creditor has on you."

"I think perhaps one must rebel at such a time."

"Perhaps. But I think the creditor is too intelligent to allow that to happen. He senses the resentment and he perceives you are worried about having to repay the loan someday and donate your men in the meantime. I think at such a time he displays great magnanimity. 'We shall terminate the loan,' he says. 'You shall never be required to repay it. It is yours. Keep it. Be only my friend.' Does this not pose an entire new set of circumstances? You owe him nothing. You are independent, or so you believe. He has transformed the dollar allegiance into an ethical allegiance. You are relieved, free. You are no longer his vassal. You have received his dollars and he does not ask you to return them. You may take them and build your economy. Suddenly you are a respectable power." He smiled. "That power is built on money, not position."

"And I think the Russians must still face a solid front of opposition."

"Yes," nodded Min. "For awhile they must contend with such a front. But then you progress a generation. The borrower who became the freedman passes into history. The new generation has become secure in its self esteem, but every time that former creditor suggests you do something for him your heirs have seen you respond most willingly. At last a most critical question arises. 'Why?' ask your heirs. 'Why must we send our men, donate our lives because a nation on the other side of the world tells us we owe it to them?' The former creditors say, 'But we gave you affluence. We gave you millions, billions of dollars. You owe us your loyalty in return, your support. I thought we were friends.' I think the new generation will become most reluctant. They will say 'You told our fathers they owed you no more money. You told them they were not expected to repay it. You asked only that we be your friends. We are your friends.'"

Shin shifted. "I think they will say friendship requires manpower."

Min nodded. "But you reply, 'I have a most productive economy. I have resources, factories. I shall be most happy to trade with you, but for a fair price. I wish to receive parity for my production.' He will come then, that onetime creditor, and appeal to your sense of ethics. That is when your resentment will reach saturation. You will learn to hate him. I think the first time you have an opportunity you will turn on him. He has been bartering your blood and that of your ancestors for many years. Now I think you must watch for your opening. When it comes you will barter his. It will be your only course back to self respect." He shrugged. "It happens with individual people. I think it must happen with nations. Shin, this is my prediction. The United States possesses the money and the motive. It will happen as I say, but I will not live long enough to see it. You must watch it yourself. One day you shall see I was right."

"But how would the Americans use our men? Our blood?"

Min spread his hands. "Look at our nation today. We are divided. At least under the Japanese we were a single entity. But now the Russians are occupying the northern half of our nation and the Americans are in the south. It will be only a matter of weeks before they are gone. Perhaps months, but in a very short time they will be gone." He shook a finger again. "But you will see that they will have put in place Korean soldiers to fight their battle for them. The Americans do not want to have the Russians facing Japan across the Sea of Japan with no buffer zone to protect them. They will keep their soldiers in Japan and call them their occupation forces. They will create an army in Korea to protect against the Russians. Then, the Russians will create an army in the north to face the Korean army of the south. You see? They will then use the Koreans to protect them. It will be our blood which will spill if we desire to put our country back together again as a single nation. But is that not what every Korean will want? To be a reunified nation?" He smiled. "Of course. We are one people, but we have been divided into two. The great powers will pit brother against brother, uncle against nephew. And they will not care, just so long as they are able to consider our nation a buffer to protect their occupation forces in Japan. They have defeated Japan, but now they will become friends. The Americans will give the Japanese much money to rebuild their nation which the Americans have torn apart. But as I have said, they will tell the Japanese they are their friends. It is we, the Koreans, who will suffer. We will be the ones to spill the blood of our sons to protect them."

"Then we will soon build an army." Shin was beginning to feel enthusiasm. "And the officers of that army will be those who have learned their skills in, should we say, another army?"

"It would seem the likely thing, Shin. Why should we begin

all over again when we have experienced warriors within our population?"

"Then perhaps there really is a place for me. Perhaps I could become an officer in the new army of Korea. I could be fighting for my own country the next time."

Min was hopeful. "Let us hope there will be no fighting. Let us hope our men will only face the army of the north and not have to fight with them."

"And your power? What of your power, if these things are to occur as you say, Schoolmaster?"

Min smiled. "Only the problems will occur in the future. I think the money must begin arriving very soon."

"Then I think you must move quickly to place your school in a position to receive this money earlier than the rest."

"I have given much consideration to the school in Gapyong. It is a government school. If we are to form a new government I think the schools must become most busy attempting to inculcate new ideas into the coming generation. The schoolmasters will be too involved with ideology to teach a useful curriculum. My strength, my prestige in Gapyong had its beginning in the curriculum, not the ideology, and I think that is the way it must remain. I have taught them useful things. I have taught them the trades. They have appreciated that."

"I think you cannot continue such a curriculum now."

Min nodded. "I cannot in the public school. However, a private school would be a most profitable venture."

Shin's eyes widened in surprise. "A private school? I think such a school must cost much money. You must be giving out money which you do not have and there can be little coming in until you are established."

The headmaster smiled slyly. "I think there must be many opportunities. We must only seek them." He indicated the bungalow in which they sat. "This cost me nothing."

"Then I think you have stolen your opportunities."

"Are the Japanese to return to reclaim them?" He laughed. "My students constructed it as a training project."

"But what of your school? Where will you build it? The Japanese are no longer here. I think you cannot steal more materials from them."

Min was unconcerned. "The materials still exist. Only the Japanese have gone away."

"Then you will steal them as you did before?"

The schoolmaster wagged his finger at the young man. "You must remember, Shin, that American wealth is the result of free enterprise. They have achieved great profits from their system. I think they must look most favorably upon a poor Korean schoolmaster who wishes to contribute to the rebuilding of his nation by preparing the tradesmen in a free enterprise. A private school is a business. They admire business. They will support it."

"And will they also provide materials for it?"

"They will provide money. I think they will expect me to use it for materials and labor to build the school."

"Then you will have no funds once the school is completed."

The aging man chuckled. "In practicing free enterprise I shall not forget the lessons I have learned from being born a Korean."

THE NORTH—HYESAN

The spring thaw was beginning to take effect in Hochon and other areas of peninsular Korea. At Hyesan, situated far to the north near the Manchurian border, it remained bitterly cold.

The morning of Taejin's arrival it was still dark. He looked out from the door of the cattle car in which he and his fellow prisoners had been transported north and saw the long line of colorless men plodding toward the mine. Around them was a high, barbed wire fence. Its posts of heavy timber were dug firmly into the ground. Towers stood at the corners of the enclosure and patrols with dogs prowled outside the fence.

"Hurry," screamed a guard. "There is no time to be wasted." He was scurrying back and forth in the car, urging the new prisoners on to greater speed as they fell forward onto the snow. In his haste he came upon an old man, feeble and frail. The man was not rising, but lay shivering on the floor.

"Up, I say. Get up." He prodded the man with the butt of his rifle but the old man did not move. The guard glanced up quickly to see if others were watching. Several were. He drew his bayonet and prodded the old man once more.

There was a whispered groan from the old chest.

"Did you say something to me?" shouted the guard. "If you speak to me, speak loudly and clearly. There is much noise in the camp."

The old man groaned again.

"I will give you one more chance. Speak up."

Again there was only a groan.

Standing, the guard shrugged, swung the butt of the rifle against the old head, and sank the bayonet to the hilt in the railing chest. He withdrew the blade sharply, wiping off the blood on his victim's ragged coat. Then he turned.

"You and you," he shouted at Taejin and another prisoner. "Get rid of the trash."

Taejin looked down at the body at his feet. Suddenly he was very nauseous.

The guard screamed behind him. "Move. What do you think you are doing to my carriage? Move. Get the trash out of here. Do not get sick in here or you may join your dead comrade." As if to make his point more emphatic he prodded Taejin with the point of the bayonet.

Taejin looked up at the other prisoner. Their eyes met only for an instant before they bent together and heaved the old man off the train. The guard still shouting behind them, they dropped into the snow.

More guards were there and all were screaming their instructions. The prisoners were formed into a line and marched off in a frigid shuffle toward some crude buildings at the far end of the compound. Then there was a call behind them.

"Who is responsible for this mess?"

They dared not turn.

"Stop. Stop them all. I will ask once more. Who is responsible for this putrid mess on my platform?"

The line had come to a stop and the men waited apprehensively for the pounding feet to catch up. Now the steps slowed.

"I want them. The two responsible for the mess back there. Who dumped that body on my platform?"

Taejin hoped all the prisoners looked enough alike to shield him. They did not.

The guard was behind him now. Apparently he was peering into each face along the line in an attempt to find him.

"You!" He screamed it. Taejin noted that it was the same excitable guard who had been on the train. "You are one of them. Get back there. Clean up the garbage." He moved forward to the next man. "And you. You are the other one. Oh, we have a pair in the two of you. Get back there with your comrade." He motioned threateningly with the bayonet, which was still fixed on the end of his rifle.

The man fell in next to Taejin and they began the cold walk back toward the train.

"Do not walk side by side. Never walk side by side in this camp. You will always walk one behind the other. When you are told to change position you will do so while facing away from each other. Never look at your comrade. It is forbidden to look at your comrade." He was dancing about them as they walked. Taejin had stepped out to the lead position.

"Hurry. Hurry. I have no time to wait for you to meander along. When I say for you to hurry that means you must run, for if you do not I shall be forced to punish you. Hurry. Hurry."

Taejin leaned forward and broke into a trot. He could hear the other man thumping behind him. Taejin wondered about the old man. What could he have done to warrant being shipped off to such a place at his age and in his state of health? Who was he? From what part of the country had he come?

Now they were at the body.

"What do you want us to do with it?" asked Taejin.

"What? What? You idiot. Carry it with you. You must take it with you when you go. You do not leave garbage on my platform."

Taejin reached down and grasped the withered wrists. Feeling his companion's tug at the other end, he rose and started off through the gloom.

The line of new prisoners had begun moving again. They fell in at the end of the line and shuffled along, their burden swinging between them. Soon they approached a line of buildings, more properly huts, constructed of tarpaper and old lumber. The line came to a stop.

Orders were being screamed at the front, off in the darkness. Taejin decided they would be repeated for those at the rear who could not hear. He leaned down to place the body on the ground until it came time to move again.

"Do not put it down." The voice was deep and threatening, next to his ear. "You must hold it."

He straightened.

"Are you a murderer?" The guard stepped into his vision.

"No."

"Then why do you carry such evidence?"

"I was ordered to carry it."

"You must address me properly, prisoner. Have you no manners?"

"Yes."

"Yes, what?"

"Yes, I have manners."

"Yes, Comrade Guard," tutored the voice.

"Yes, Comrade Guard," corrected Taejin.

"Now, about this evidence. Where did you kill him?"

"I did not kill him, Comrade Guard."

"What is your name, prisoner?"

"Taejin, Comrade Guard."

"You are a marked man, Taejin. I will return for you."

Taejin shuddered as the guard crunched off through the snow into the darkness. The line began moving again, then stopped. The orders from the front of the line were becoming frenzied now. Taejin peered past the line, trying to see what was happening. There was flurried activity, but he could not discern its cause. The line moved again and stopped. More shouts. He looked forward again and saw the prisoners being stripped of their clothing. Once a group was standing naked in the snow a pair of guards would run them off and the line would begin moving again.

"All of you. Remove those rags." The voice was near him. He peeked over his shoulder, then lowered the old man to the ground and began removing his clothes. It was cold. He wondered how many would die here. Would he himself die here? He began to suspect that before long he would wish to die.

A guard was approaching. "What is this?"

"This is the body of a prisoner who was killed on the train, Comrade Guard."

"And you are the one who killed him?"

"No, Comrade Guard. I did not kill him." He was shivering in his nakedness.

The guard turned to Taejin's companion. "Then you must be the one who killed this man."

"No, Comrade Guard."

The guard's look changed to one of surprise. "Is he your father?"

"No, Comrade Guard."

The guard looked down at the body. "What are his clothes doing on?" He pushed his face close to them. "Remove his clothes," he shouted. "I have said everyone would remove his clothes." He stood back and watched with mild satisfaction as Taejin and the other reached down and began disrobing the corpse. When it was done they straightened.

"Now you must take him with you," rasped the guard.

Taejin did not move. His companion was beginning to moan.

The guard looked quickly at him. "What is that sound?"

Only the moaning sounded from behind Taejin.

The guard approached the man. "You must be the guilty one. You have killed him."

"I did not, Comrade Guard," choked the prisoner.

"You are a liar," shouted the guard. "You have killed him or you would not be moaning like this." He turned and called another guard. The man came up at a trot. "What is the matter, Comrade?"

"We have a murderer here." He motioned toward Taejin's companion.

"I am not a murderer," screamed the prisoner.

The guard struck him hard. "We have a special place for murderers. Come with me."

They yanked at the man and he let out a cry as he was led off to a tree stump some fifty yards away in the graying dawn. Taejin saw him climb onto the stump and watched the guard gesticulating at him. Then, in a weak but audible voice in the cold air, the man began chanting desperately. "I am a felon," he cried. "I am a felon."

"This is not the theater," shouted a guard. "Move."

The remaining prisoners began hurrying across the compound where the others had gone before them.

"Do not forget your luggage," a guard shouted at Taejin. He stopped and looked. The guard was pointing at the old man's corpse. Taejin stooped and picked it up. Then, stiff and cold, he carried it off across the yard. Behind him, tolling crisply through the cold, his companion's voice continued its monotonous, chanted announcement. "I am a felon."

* * * * * *

The munificence of nature hovered expectantly about them, seeming to beg for recognition, to soothe their constant agony. To the north rose Manchuria's towering Changpai Range, to the east and southwest the great Mantap and Sanmaek peaks. Resplendent in white, each vied with its neighbor to display the greater beauty, present the most awesome view. Between them, in contrast, the infant Yalu gurgled the first tentative steps of its ancient journey toward the sea. The prisoners did not notice. By noon they had been dressed, billeted, and formed again in the central yard.

"You will be divided into two groups," announced a senior guard. "One group will labor in the mine fifteen hours each day." He paused and stared hawkishly along the line. "The second group will be our housemaids. They will keep our home beautiful. Also, when the main shift is sleeping, the housemaids must assist by keeping the mine in production."

Along the rear of the formation strolled other guards, watchful, their hope of finding a deviant obvious in their cold eyes.

"When you are summoned to work you must not linger. If you tarry too long on your bed we shall infer you are rebellious. Those who rebel will be punished. When you eat you must eat quickly. You are here to work, not to become overfed. Five minutes will be allotted for each meal. You will be expected to consume all food given to you. If you do not eat we shall infer you are rebellious. Those who rebel will be punished." He looked along the line again, gauging the effect of his words.

"Prisoners in this camp do not walk. You must run. There is much work to be done and if you do not move from place to place quickly you may be unable to accomplish your share of the work. Those who do not accomplish their share will be considered rebels."

He pivoted abruptly and marched stiffly from view. The other guards moved forward, shouting, pointing, threatening. Two groups were formed, the first ordered quickly into the mine. Taejin, included in that group, found himself packed tightly into a dank tunnel and prodded down an endless ramp. Ahead they heard the sounds of toil, the incessant shouts of guards. He strove to shrink into the crowd of prisoners, to achieve anonymity through their numbers. Within two days the ploy was useless. The guards learned their names quickly.

Back on the surface the opposite shift was faced with easier tasks but worse conditions. Its men found themselves in constant close contact with guards who shoved, cursed and punished with obvious pleasure. Each seemed a madman who forever created situations in which the prisoners were pronounced guilty of a multitude of imagined crimes.

They worked, ate and napped their way into the routine, a race of men at first lost to their families, then to society, and finally, inexorably, to themselves.

* * * * * *

"Husband, what can we do? I think it is only a matter of time before the farmer sends his soldiers for you."

The lawyer looked forlornly at his wife. "I think we must try to get to the south. I think we can be safe only if we escape Hochon."

"But why can we not go to another village? I think it must be very dangerous if we try to go to the south." Her face was pleading, frightened.

"If we go to another village in this part of the country they will find us. They are creating lists of all the people. No travel is permitted. If we were to go to another village there would be questions." He shook his head. "No, there is no place in the north where we can be safe. We would be caught and sent to prison. Perhaps they would even kill us. I think we must go to the south."

"But how, my husband? I think it must be very difficult. I have heard the border is patrolled." She bowed her head in quiet sobs.

He reached for her, trying to console. It was to no avail. She cried herself to sleep as he lay staring into the night.

Kwon rose from his headphones. He hurried importantly to his father. "I have found the reason to arrest the lawyer," he exulted.

Chairman Kim looked up in surprise, a smile cracking his face. "What have you found, Kwon?"

"The lawyer plans to defect to the south. I have heard it in my listening device!"

Kim leaped up. "Then we shall have him arrested. He shall go to the prison." He laughed, striding about the room in triumph. "A defector. Are there others?"

"No, father. Only Chung and his wife."

"She is of no use to us. It is the lawyer I want."

The soldiers swooped down on the defenseless Chung, locking him unceremoniously in the prison which had hosted Kim so many years before.

"Why am I under arrest?" demanded Chung.

"Quiet. You will learn in due time." The guard snapped the lock and strode away from the cell.

"But I have done nothing," protested Chung, shouting at the empty corridor.

Thereafter the only people he saw were the guards who brought him food. He tried to talk with them, at least to learn why he had been arrested. They would not answer.

The day before the trial was to begin he was removed to Pyongyang. The moment the journey began he knew he was doomed.

Kim had already arrived. He strode arrogantly through the streets. The throngs of people scrambled to get out of his way. He was jubilant. He was convinced he had developed the case which would finally elevate him above the rank of chairman in a small provincial village.

The trial, as usual, was short. Chung, in addition to defection, was accused of crimes against the masses for a period of thirty-five years. He was subdued. Kim sat in the court and hardly looked at the defendant. He poured out a tale of oppression of the people which Chung had perpetrated throughout the Japanese annexation. The magistrate nodded in sympathy with each new charge. Finally he sentenced Chung to life imprisonment.

After the trial was over, Kim hurried to the Secretariat of Provincial Organization. The secretary rose and advanced to shake his hand. "Comrade, you are a hero of the people. I congratulate you."

Kim bowed low. "Thank you, Comrade."

"Come. Sit down. We must become acquainted." The secretary indicated a chair and the two sat.

Kim, beaming inside, kept up a stolid facade. "I believe this will complete the education of the people of Hochon in the benefits of the new order."

The secretary laughed. "Not only the people of Hochon, Comrade Kim. Diligence such as yours educates all the people everywhere throughout the People's Republic.

Kim nodded confidently. "I am happy I was able to contribute, Comrade."

"You have indeed, and you shall again, Comrade."

Kim's eyes widened. "Again? Is there something more I can do?"

"We have so many programs. It is a great problem keeping abreast of them all. Consider your defector, Chung, for example."

Kim bowed his head. "That was a most shameful thing to have happen in my village. But I caught him," he added quickly.

The secretary brushed it aside. "It happens in other places as well. But perhaps you did not realize we already have plans for stopping such things."

"May I be a part of your plans, Comrade?" asked Kim eagerly.

The secretary threw back his head in laughter. "A part of them? You, Comrade Kim, shall be a central participant."

Kim caught his breath in anticipation. "What can I do, Comrade? I will do anything for the advancement of the revolution."

The secretary gave him a long look. "I have studied the files of the Hochon cases most carefully. You have some very dedicated workers there. They are excellent investigators for the Party."

Kim thought back to Hochon. Other than his soldiers his strongest supporters and workers were his sons.

"I was most interested to learn," continued the secretary, "that the two most faithful are your sons. What are their names?"

"My sons names are Kwon and Nambae," answered Kim, now suddenly fearful that his sons would be promoted rather than himself.

"Yes, those are the names. They were instrumental in the criminal investigation of each of your cases, if I recall."

"In a minor way, Comrade," said Kim, passing it off. "They follow my orders without question."

"Of course. But their dedication is the type which can be of great assistance to the People's Republic."

Kim's stomach was churning with apprehension. "Are you suggesting they are to be recognized?" he blurted.

"All three of you are to be publicized. In different capacities, of course, but then, they are younger than you and have many more years left in which to serve the masses."

"What will our assignments be, Comrade?"

"I said a few moments ago we have plans for stopping these

defections to the south. At the same time, however, we must obtain as much information as possible about their plans. We must be aware of the strengths and weaknesses of the south."

Kim, puzzled, said nothing.

"Our plan is to train your sons. They will be schooled in every aspect of the collection of data from the enemy. Of course, we know they will do very well in such training. You have given them excellent background."

Kim hardly heard the secretary's words. "And what will my assignment be?"

The secretary held up his hand. "You must be patient. I will come to that. First, as I said, your sons will be schooled. Following that, they will be ordered to infiltrate this underground path to the south. Once there, they will report back and we shall merely move in and choke off this boulevard for malcontents." He looked pleased. "Others have done the same, you know. Your sons will not be the first. Since only a few get through to the other side, however, we must train and dispatch many."

Kim, still preoccupied, was unmoved. "But my mission. What will my mission be?"

Suddenly the secretary looked sad. "That, Comrade, is the difficult part of the operation. If a man were any less a servant of the party he would become most upset. But you, Comrade? I know we have no worries about you."

Kim's patience evaporated. "What, Comrade? What is expected of me?"

The secretary, ignoring his anxiety, continued calmly. "As you must realize, the government in the south is most cautious about those who defect. They are very suspicious that we are placing agents in their midst. Naturally, they will be even more suspicious of two men whose father has become such a hero of the masses. Therefore, we must allay their suspicions. We must make them believe the defections are real."

Kim was puzzled. "How can that be done?"

"That is the difficult part," sighed the secretary. "Consider what happens in the case of many criminals. Their families are arrested. Of course," he nodded, "in your Chung case you did it in reverse. You wanted the father but you arrested and tried the son first."

Shock stabbed through Kim.

"Obviously, the same must be true of you. But remember, it is all for the good of the Party. We must get our agents into the south. We must convince their government they are true defectors. The only way to do that is to mount a manhunt for them. At the same time we must arrest you for not training them well enough in socialist thought. We will bring you to trial and convict you. You will be placed in prison."

"No," shouted Kim. "Not prison. I have worked too hard for the people to be sent to prison." He became supplicant. "Do not send me to prison, Comrade."

The secretary tossed up his hands in resignation. "Forgive me, Comrade. I can see it is too much to ask of you. I had thought you a true hero of the people, anxious to see our cause succeed." He rose and strolled to the window, looking down on the restless city. "I think we must return you to Hochon and have done with the matter." He turned slowly, eyeing Kim coolly. "Of course, you will be watched carefully by the new chairman of the Hochon People's Committee. We must be most skeptical of those who are not willing to give all they have for the Party."

Kim was panicked now. "Wait, Comrade. I am a good friend of the Party. I wish to help the masses."

"But you do not wish to help them enough to go to prison for them," snapped the secretary.

Suddenly Kim realized he had no choice but prison. Once he returned to Hochon he would be followed day and night. They would never leave him alone until they had created a case and arrested him. "Comrade, I am sorry if I seemed angry. In reality it was fear. Every man knows fear, especially if he has already been in prison. I spent more than ten years in prison. But I am not unfaithful."

The secretary sat down again, calm, poised.

"If giving my sons to the people will help the Party, take them," moaned Kim. "If I must go to the prison, send me. But please do one thing for me, Comrade. Do not send me to a place where the conditions will be bad."

The secretary sighed. "Comrade, I think you will not find your sentence worse than anyone else's."

Kim bowed his head, defeated. The secretary said nothing more, but watched the chairman's transformation progress before his eyes. Moments ago strong and willful, he now became merely a biological specimen. At last he breathed deeply and looked up at the secretary, his eyes uncertain. "I shall return to Hochon, Comrade. Do what you can for me, as I shall for you." When he was gone the secretary rang for his deputy.

"Did you hear?"

"Yes, Comrade. I extend my apologies for doubting him and your judgment."

The secretary chuckled. "For a few minutes I thought you were right. I thought he would refuse this, and of course, if he had it would have exposed him as the opportunist you had thought him. Then we would have had no choice but to have eliminated him."

* * * * * *

By the time Kim returned home his sons were gone. Kim sat in his office, an empty feeling in the pit of his stomach. Then, with resignation, he reached for the telephone and placed a call to the Secretary of Provincial Organization. "Comrade, I am most sad to report there has been a defection in my village."

"Who was it, Comrade Chairman?" asked the secretary brusquely.

"Two people," answered Kim uncomfortably.

"Two? How could you permit such a thing to happen? I had been told yours was a model village."

"I am most sorry, Comrade Secretary."

"Who are they? I must have their names so we may issue a bulletin for their arrest."

Kim swallowed hard. "They are my sons, Comrade."

"Your sons?" There was a pause on the other end of the line. "I thought you had a good relationship with your sons. I thought they were investigators for the party."

"They were, Comrade. They have always been good sons."

Only ten minutes passed before the police arrived. Kim was led from the house and placed in a car. To his surprise Merchant Pak was sitting in the back seat, locked in chains.

Pak looked up in surprise. "What are you doing here, Comrade Chairman?"

"Perhaps I should ask you, Pak. For what have you been arrested?"

Pak was trembling. "My daughter has disappeared. I have been arrested because they say she has defected."

Kim growled in anger. There was more to the situation than he had been told. "When did she disappear?" he rasped.

"This morning," replied the merchant in a whisper. "She was last seen in the company of your sons." His eyes darted fearfully at the policemen.

Kim emitted a throaty gasp of rage and lunged across the seat at Pak but a policeman pulled him back. "She is a harlot, Pak. She is a tainted woman. Not only was she a harlot, but she was pregnant when you married her to my son." His breath came in panting gasps of fury. "She lured them away," he shouted. "Where was she taking them?"

Pak shrank back from him. "I do not know what you are saying. I only know the police came and arrested me. They told me Song had defected."

Kim merely looked at him in disgust. The car raced out the road toward Pyongyang. Spring was tumbling into the heat of summer, yet the rains had not begun. Dust choked them, stung their eyes. To the side of the road they could see numerous farmers spearing their rice shoots into the water of their paddies. In other places oxen dragged crude farming equipment across the black earth.

At last the rural scene subsided before the spread of the city. There was no traffic to delay them and they were soon ushered unceremoniously into a prison. Kim never saw the merchant again.

Within days a public trial was readied. The morning of the ceremony Kim was paraded from his prison cell and moved to the Hall of Justice.

"Comrade prisoner, you fathered two sons. They have defected to the capitalist south along with a woman from your village who is married to your younger son. You, a government official, a servant of the great People's Republic, did not educate your sons very well. You have permitted defections from the village of Hochon. You are an enemy of the people."

It had begun. He hung his head in shame, and yet in pride. He listened while the magistrate and the prosecutor exchanged comments about the charges. His defense counsel sat totally still, listening to the proceedings with an impersonal expression of boredom.

"And now, Comrade. How do you plead?"

"Guilty, Comrade Magistrate. I am most guilty of all your charges."

The magistrate looked severely at him. "Do you realize what this means?"

"Yes, Comrade Magistrate."

"Very well. You are found as you plead. Guilty. You will be taken to the north, there to serve the people in prison for a period of ten years."

"Ten years," he thought. "I must serve ten years for trying to do good for the masses." Forlorn, he allowed himself to be led from the courtroom without sensing the surroundings. He was numb with fright. He realized he probably would not survive his sentence.

It was late. The city was black, and the prisoners in the sur-

rounding cells of the holding prison were snoring. Then he heard
the click in the lock.

"Prisoner Kim," a voice said softly.

"I am here." He rose with the resignation of the damned.

"It is time to go."

He followed the guard through the corridors, still in his daze.
He was led into a brightly lit room. He blinked. Then his eyes
focused on the Secretary of Provincial Organization.

"Comrade Secretary. Why are you here?" He looked around
the room. It was well appointed and clean.

The secretary smiled. "Congratulations, Comrade. You have
done well. You will be most happy to learn your sons are doing the
same."

Kim felt a surge of pride leap through him. "Thank you, Comrade Secretary. I am pleased to do it for the good of the people and
the Party."

The secretary nodded. "I am sure you are. And now it is time
for you to go. It is a long trip."

Kim bowed his head. "Yes, Comrade. I am ready."

"Of course," continued the secretary, "you go not as a prisoner."

Kim looked up quickly, an expression of surprise lighting his
features. "What do you mean, Comrade?"

"You have been appointed to the largest prison in our complex
to the north. You are now warden of the prison mine at Hyesan."

The hint of a smile began playing about the corners of Kim's
mouth. He dared not believe it. It must have been a dream. He
wondered if he were still asleep in his cell.

The secretary had risen. "Now come with me. I shall introduce you to your new leader, the Secretary of People's Corrections."

With an air of true comradeship, the secretary circled an arm
about Kim's shoulder and led him from the room.

* * * * * *

Through the first months of their marriage Song and her husband quarreled violently and often. Each could recognize the plight of the other, yet pride insisted that neither should yield.

Nambae, for his part, was so shamed by the turn of events and his father's unwillingness to seek an annulment that he lost all interest in his wife. He no longer found her attractive. In the face of his frustration he continued to accuse her, to growl constantly of what he considered her immoral past. This resulted in Song biting back as she had from the beginning, emphasizing she had not wanted to marry him at all. Invariably, the belligerence resulted in his beating her. She began to take a certain pride in her ability to infuriate him, wearing the consequent bruises as badges of her effectiveness. And yet, she worried for her baby, for what his violence might do to the child.

In time, Nambae realized there would likely be no change in her attitude, and with that, seriously questioned his ability to control her. At last he fiercely cautioned her that if she did not obey him as her husband he would take measures against the child, either unborn or later. Horrified, worrying that she had lost Taejin and now might lose his child, she gradually moderated and accepted his demands for the sake of the child.

Because of her pregnancy, Song did not fare as well in the concentrated training as the others, but she was considered ready when their deployment date arrived. The three melted into the teeming streets of the city and within two days Song reported a contact to the others.

"Are you certain it is not a trap?"

"Yes, I think it is good."

The older brother rose. "Can you take us there now?"

"No. Not tonight. He said we must come early in the morning." She hesitated. "He wishes us to bring money."

Nambae laughed. "That is impossible. We have no money."

His brother was cautious. "It is a typical trick. If we could pay them they would wonder where we obtained it. They would suspect us as agents." He looked meaningfully at the others. "We have no money. I hope you did not offer to find any."

"I told him we have nothing except what we steal."

"What did he say?"

"He said nothing further about it. He was testing me, I think."

He nodded. "At what time do we meet him in the morning?"

"We must be there at three o'clock."

"Then we must go now. We must not risk being caught moving during the curfew."

They gathered together what few things they had, tied them in small bundles and stepped out into the street. Song led them by a winding route through the city until they were close to the government buildings.

Kwon looked at her in surprise. "Here?"

She nodded. They backed into the shadows and waited silently.

Several hours passed. Then they looked up in apprehension as a police officer stepped into their corner.

"Are these the two?" he asked.

"Yes," answered Song. The surprise on her face showed she was as shocked as the brothers.

"Have you brought money?"

Kwon looked at him blankly. "For what must we have money? Are you to arrest us for breaking the curfew?"

The man laughed. "You are safe with me. I stole the uniform."

They let out a collective sigh of relief.

"When the curfew lifts in the morning an old woman will pass here with a basket of cabbages. Follow her, one at a time. When she stops, watch for a man with an A-frame. On it will be some lumber. Do not follow him, but watch the alley he enters. Fifteen minutes after he enters the alley, go there one at a time. The girl must go first."

Nambae started to ask a question but the man was gone as quickly as he had appeared. They settled back to await the dawn.

People had been on the street for almost an hour before they saw the woman. She made no notice of them, but hobbled along the pavement in a bustle, the basket of cabbages held tightly in her arm. After several blocks she stopped at the stand of a vendor. Quickly, they looked around for the A-frame. It was only a moment. The high pile of laths emerged from the crowd. As the man broke through the people and headed for an alley across the thoroughfare, Song started nonchalantly in the same direction. She passed it, then doubled back on schedule.

The alley was dirty, filled with trash. Somewhere in the filth a baby whimpered. She slowed, afraid. Then an arm reached out and beckoned to her. Startled, she flinched, then recognized the man from the night before.

"Are the others with you?"

She nodded without speaking. He led her to an old crate and motioned her inside. A few minutes later both the brothers were with her and the man was nailing the crate shut. Song huddled close to Nambae. There was a heavy lurch and they felt themselves being lifted precariously. They heard grunts and a muffled curse. Then the crate was sliding across a flat surface.

The roar of an engine preceded their movement. It was slow at first, but they soon accelerated and droned along a road. Three hours later they slowed and stopped. The vehicle backed and the engine became still. Moments later, the end of the crate pried free, they stepped out into the sunlight.

"Come. We must hurry," said a man they had not seen before. They turned the corner and were on a pier, a boat drawn up beside it. The man motioned them aboard and within three hours the coastline had fallen below the horizon.

It began raining, large bulbous drops which beat the sea smooth and reduced visibility almost to nothing. The three looked about them apprehensively but the crew smiled.

"Do not worry. There is no better way to escape detection on the radar than to become lost in a rain squall."

Somewhat reassured, they watched as the boat gradually lost

speed until it was almost dead in the water. Then the engines went still. Somewhere off to the side they heard a foghorn sound above the splashing of the rain. It was answered by their boat. Again the horn sounded, and again it was answered.

A quarter of an hour later the two vessels were together. The three made their way to the other boat. Engines were restarted, and the boat from the north disappeared into the squall.

Their new hosts did not speak. The boat turned, and soon they were speeding south. As they came out of the rain they saw a gunboat ahead. It flew the flag of the Republic of Korea.

* * * * * *

During his time in prison Taejin had seen many atrocities, watched many die. He had learned to say little or nothing at all. Anything he did say was in answer to direct questions from the guards. He had developed a vacant stare and a practiced anonymity. He worked steadily, if not hard, and asked for nothing.

The lessons had been taught rapidly and learned well. During his first month he was constantly taunted by the guards. Then, apparently having found newer and more interesting targets among the more recent arrivals, they began to ignore him. At first he had wondered about his companion of the day they arrived. Then, with experience, he looked for him no longer. He had seen many others set on the stump to chant their way into death. At first it seemed there was no reason to their selection of victims. Those who ascended the stump often had done nothing at all. After watching in horror for several weeks he discovered a pattern to the executions. They seemed reserved for occasions rather than crimes. When there was a reason to impress someone, particularly a new group of prisoners, inevitably someone would be singled out and destroyed. Then, armed with the example they had set, the guards emphasized to every prisoner in the camp that he could well be the next.

Some months after his arrival Taejin was moved to the auxiliary shift. Autumn had arrived and the worst of the year's weather was ahead. It was the least desirable time of year to be placed on the auxiliary shift. Those in the summer months could enjoy a few hours of sun and warmth each day as they went about their tasks. In winter they went without the protection of the earth in the mine, feeling instead the biting cold of the wind which raced down from Manchuria and Siberia.

The days were interminably long. He learned to take each day as it came, never looking ahead to the passage of time. With even a short sentence he would have gone mad. With his long one it was almost certain he would never live to see freedom.

If a prisoner became ill he was given one day of rest and care-less medication. If he was unable to work the following day he was executed as a malingerer. There was no board, no hearing. The guards merely dragged or carried him away and he was never heard of again. During the first year Taejin tried to keep himself healthy. After that he became as much a fatalist about sickness as he was about everything else. He ate his two bowls of rice per day, lost weight, developed strength in his back and arms, and slept the sleep of the dead whenever he was allowed near his pallet.

In the spring, after he had been returned to the main shift, the camp learned gradually that a new warden was in command. One day there had been a ceremony for the guards. The administration had repeated the ceremony so that all the cadre could attend. Those who watched the prisoners during these ceremonies were doubly harsh. Dogs were brought into the camp, not a normal procedure, to help guard them. Punishments were meted out liberally.

At one point a man on the auxiliary shift lagged too far behind his comrades in file. A guard with a dog was at the rear of the line.

"What are you doing, Prisoner?"

The man said nothing, but hastened his pace to catch up.

The guard bounded forward. "Prisoner, I have asked you a question."

"I am most sorry, Comrade Guard." The man cast a terrified look at the dog lunging at his throat.

"When a guard in this camp asks a question he must be answered," shouted the guard. "That is why you have throats."

One of his comrades at the front of the line had noticed the activity and brought the line to a halt. The prisoners were made to turn and watch the confrontation.

"I am most sorry, Comrade Guard," the man shouted more insistently.

The guard sneered. "Still you have not answered my question. I am tired of waiting." With a barked command he dropped the dog's lead. It growled menacingly as it sank its jaws about the man's windpipe. He had time only for a muffled cry, choked off at its source. The guards laughed gleefully as the dog continued to maul the prisoner. Then, realizing its victim was dead, it looked up quickly at the next man in line. The man shrank back but the dog was on him. The guards laughed. Then, with a bored attitude, the keeper called to the dog. It dropped the man and returned to heel immediately. The man was not dead, but two days later they executed him. He had been unable to report for work.

In the next weeks, discipline became even more rigid than it had been before. Prisoners were beaten, starved and tortured in addition to the regular executions. Attitudes changed, all for the worse.

Then Taejin learned the reason. They were in the labor line when he saw his father's old enemy. Warden Kim had not noticed him, but Taejin dreaded the day he would. From that moment on the uncertainty of life took on a new and horrifying dimension.

* * * * * *

The year had been long and Lawyer Chung's wife was lonely. She had not seen her husband since his arrest. Only rumors surreptitiously heard led her to suspect where he had been taken.

Now that Chairman Kim was gone she had no more antagonists in Hochon. There were new soldiers, a new chairman assigned from Haeju and the new chief of police. She did not realize

the perils which could result from trying to visit her son and husband.

Her plans were not elaborate. Stripped of all her possessions
by Kim and the Party, she owned no treasures but memories. Thus,
with her meager belongings wrapped in a rag, she left Hochon for
the long walk to the north. Her only known goal was the prison to
which her son had been sentenced.

Winter turned to spring, and it was late May before she reached
Hyesan. Her feet were swollen and cracked, her face drawn with
hunger. All along her route she had melted into the trees or crowds
of people to avoid being seen by soldiers or police. Thus far she
had been fortunate. No one had recognized her for the stranger
she was.

She entered the city of Hyesan, wondering where the infa-
mous prison was located. She wandered and begged. In the evening
she found another old woman perched on some boxes near the rail
terminal.

"I heard shots last night." She watched the other woman carefully to see if her introduction of the subject would bring a reaction.

"It was only the prison. They were probably shooting some
more of them."

"I wondered if there had been an escape."

Her new companion looked at her in disgust. "If no one has
ever escaped before now, why should you think there was a chance
last night?"

The lawyer's wife nodded in agreement. "I know, but one can
always have hope."

"It would be useless," scoffed the woman. "If one escaped they
would shoot a hundred. It would be harder on the ones who were
left."

The lawyer's wife was unconcerned with the others. "I suppose if one were to escape he would have nowhere to go."

"Nowhere at all. He would climb over the fence and be forced
to come down the highway into the city. How could one of them

swim the river or climb the mountain?" She shook her head. "Yes, there would be no place to go."

They sat together silently for a long time. Then the lawyer's wife rose. "I must go."

The other woman looked at her. "Where would you go? It is easy to see why you are here."

Chung's wife looked at her in surprise, fright stabbing her heart. "What do you mean?"

The other woman laughed. "You are not the first who has wished to see one of them. Did you not know there are no visitors in the prison?"

The Chung woman braced. "I do not know what you are talking about."

The woman looked at her disgustedly. "Look at your clothes, your feet. The clothes are torn through wear. Your feet are old from walking. You have come a long way."

There were tears in the corners of her eyes. "Please do not turn me in."

"I? Turn you in? Why would I do that? What would it gain me?"

"Both my husband and my son are in prison. I have no one."

"Are they both in Hyesan?"

"No. My son is here. I think my husband is at Mampojin."

"How long has your son been here?"

"Two years."

"He is probably dead." The woman rose. "Come with me. You need food and rest."

There was panic in the mother's eyes. "No. I must find my son. He cannot be. . . ."

"First you eat and sleep," broke in the other, not concerned with her protest. "Then we shall try to find a way for you to see your son. But we must be careful. If we are caught he will be killed, and you with him." They started along the street away from the terminal. "Do you have money?"

"None."

"It is easier if one has money."

"I have no way to earn money." She was agitated.

"Perhaps we can find a way without money." They plodded through the city, winding through alleys and lanes until the woman finally turned into a basement, beckoning Chung's wife to follow her. She began preparing rice.

Chung's wife sat on the floor and leaned against a mat. "How will you arrange it?"

"I do not know that I can. I can only try."

"But how will you do it?"

The old woman stared at her intently. "You ask too many questions. Perhaps you are one of them."

"I am only anxious to see my son."

"Where did you come from?"

"Hochon. In South Pyongan Province."

"You have had a long journey."

"I am very tired," admitted Chung's wife.

"Well, tonight you may sleep. Tomorrow we shall see about your son."

Chung's wife did not want to antagonize her but she was curious. "How will you do it?"

The other woman looked at her again. "How can I be sure you can be trusted?"

She looked shocked. "I am not from them."

The woman placed a bowl of rice and chopsticks in front of her. "I have helped others. There are ways."

"I hope you may also help me."

Having eaten, she washed and lay on a mat, falling asleep instantly. When she awakened there was already a gray light in the sky. Her companion was gone. She rose and washed again, basking in the forgotten luxury, then looked outside in the alley. The woman was nowhere to be seen. She went back into the room and waited.

It was several hours before the woman bustled in. "You will see your son today."

Her heart leaped. "How? How have you done it?"

The woman looked at her severely. "That is not your concern. You have only to follow my instructions."

In the early evening the woman took Chung's wife out into the city. It was already dusk and they wound their way through streets lighted only dimly by widely separated streetlights. Soon they were out of the center and walking along a dirt road which paralleled the railroad tracks. On the side opposite the tracks the road was lined with tumbling shacks covered with tarpaper. An occasional wisp of smoke rose through cracks in the roofs. Children sat in the street, watching them. There was little conversation.

Approximately a mile from the city the woman led her into a path which bisected the road and proceeded off through an open field. In the distance she could see the barriers and watch towers rising through the strong lights which surrounded the compound. Every few yards along the perimeter there was a guard. Most of them had dogs.

The women crept along the edge of the lighted area. At the corner of the compound they turned with the fence, keeping the same distance from the lights. Soon they were against the foot of the mountain. Her companion led her up through the brush and closer to the fence. Then, apparently having reached a challenge point, she stopped.

They waited almost an hour. Then, coming out of the forest they saw a guard. He hurried to them, occasionally looking over his shoulder.

"Come with me, please."

They followed him farther up the mountain. Then, stooping down, he opened a trap door in the ground. They descended a ladder and crawled through a passage. At its end were lights and a sickening stench. The guard rose and peered at Chung's wife carefully. "Taejin?"

"Yes."

He turned and motioned to a door. "Do not visit too long. We could be captured at any time. We would all be executed."

She stepped forward toward the door and opened it. On the floor at the other side of the room sat her son. She let out a cry and ran to him. He blinked in utter surprise.

"Why are you here, my mother? Are you a prisoner?"

She hugged him and wept silently.

He held her off and looked at her face. "Have they arrested you?"

"No. I am fine. I wished to come and visit with you."

He could not believe it. "Prisoners are not allowed to have visitors here. How did you get in?"

"I was helped by a friend," she replied, sniffling back the tears.

"How did you get here from Hochon?" he asked, incredulous.

"It was a very long walk."

"And my father? Where is my father?"

She was quiet and serious now. "Your father was arrested soon after you were sent here. They tried him in Pyongyang. I am told he was sent to Mampojin."

Taejin's face twisted with rage. "Why? What did he do?"

"He did nothing. He was most careful to do and say nothing, but Kim arrested him. They took him away and I have never seen him again." She looked at his thin features and wondered at his aged appearance. "Are you given enough to eat?"

He laughed scornfully. "We are given two bowls of rice each day. We work in the mines fifteen hours a day. Many die."

"Kim was arrested too," she said.

He started to speak, then waited.

"His two sons defected, along with Song. All three of them defected to the south and the farmer was arrested as a result. He also was tried in Pyongyang and sentenced to prison."

"They lie," he hissed.

"No, it really happened," she said, nodding emphasis.

He took her shoulders firmly in his hands. "Mother, the farmer is warden of this prison."

She stared at him in shock. "That . . . that could not be."

"But it is, my mother. He has been here almost three months.

They have played a trick. It is most probable his sons are agents in the south today." He pounded his fist into the earthen floor. "It was all merely a trick to make the south think they were defectors."

"Are you certain, my son? Have you seen the farmer here?"

"I saw him one day at a distance. I have not talked with him. I think he does not remember I was sent to this prison. I must be thankful for that. I had no trouble recognizing him when I saw him."

"I cannot believe this. The trial, the sentencing. Did they promote him to this as a reward?"

"Kim would do anything for a reward, for a promotion. I believe he would wish to be party chief someday but he is too old and too ignorant."

"You must escape," she blurted. "You must get out of this place."

He looked at her sadly. "There is no way I can escape. There has never been an escape from Hyesan."

"You must go out the way I came in. You must do it, Taejin."

He held her and patted her shoulder sadly. "Believe me, my mother. There is no way out of Hyesan."

She pulled away and sniffled back her tears, calmer. "I am going to Mampojin when I leave here. I shall try to see your father."

"I wish you good fortune, but you must not do anything dangerous."

"It does not matter now. I am miserable every day. If they were to shoot me what would it matter? Our lives are finished."

He sank back sadly. She was right. With her husband and son in prison she had no future except more oppression from the government. The situation would never improve.

There was a knock on the door. "Come," was the whispered command from the other side. "It is time to go."

She looked at her son once more. "I shall never see you again,

Taejin. I have loved you. *Anyangikesipsio*. Goodbye." She turned and shuffled through the door.

* * * * * *

Kim sat back and laughed. "That was most entertaining, Comrade."

The officer smiled. "I am happy you have enjoyed it, Comrade Warden."

"It was a performance without price. Better than all the others put together."

"I had not realized you were such a hero, Comrade. Sacrificing your sons must have been most difficult for you."

Kim smiled and shrugged it off. "If they had been caught or killed it would have been difficult, but they were not. It was a risk, but the revolution is built of risks. They must be accepted if we are to win the world."

"I agree, Comrade Warden, but the humiliation of arrest and a trial must have been most difficult for you to endure." His respect now bordered on awe. "Your family and friends must have been shocked."

Kim, his ego inflated by the adulation, turned philosophical. "No man can place himself above the cause of the masses. Sacrifice? Humiliation?" He sniffed. "Such things are the stepping stones of the revolution. We must accept them willingly, joyfully as a means to an end. The important thing is progress. What does it matter that we must step over the bodies of others? Today the People's Republic is strong because of sacrifice. Tomorrow all Korea will be united, and after that, the world. We cannot afford to be emotional, Comrade, if we would have it happen."

"This Taejin, Comrade. Do you wish us to administer the usual punishment?"

Kim sat back and mused. "No," he replied softly. "I shall handle this one differently. I want him to realize what he has done. I want him to know he has killed his mother and father. I want him to. . . ."

His voice trailed off, but a ray of inspiration lit his face. "Sacrifice."
He bounded from the chair. "That is the answer, Comrade. Sacrifice." He waved his arm frantically for the officer to leave the room.

* * * * * *

Chung's wife expressed gratitude to her companion and began
the long walk along the Manchurian border to Mampojin. The
road was unpaved but smooth. Gradually the Yalu River became
wider and the mountains fell behind her. She was only one day's
walk from Mampojin when the bandits found her. The moment
she saw them she knew. It was fortunate she was so frail, for she
died quickly. Her husband was shot the same afternoon.

Next morning Kim received a telephone call from the Secretary of Provincial Organization. "Congratulations on your plan,
Comrade. It has been studied by the leaders of our government
and approved as a stroke of genius. You may very well have made
possible an earlier reunification of Korea. Your plan makes an earlier invasion most feasible."

Kim was overcome with pleasure. "Your news is a most pleasant surprise to me, comrade. I am grateful for their acceptance of
my humble plan."

"You need say nothing, Comrade. Your actions for the Party
outweigh your words. The Chairman is most impressed with your
performance."

Elated, Kim sent immediately for Taejin, then sat grandly in
his office as the prisoner was led in. "Good morning, Taejin."

"Good morning, Comrade Warden."

"I trust you have been well since I saw you last?"

"Yes, Comrade Warden."

"I regret I have most sad news for you, Taejin. Both your mother
and father died yesterday."

Taejin went cold. It had been less than a week since his mother's
visit.

"Of course, had you not visited with your mother they would

still be alive. But then, you did have many things to discuss, did you not?"

Taejin bowed his head and said nothing, suddenly realizing they had let her visit him. It was not a clandestine thing at all.

"You realize you are to be punished as well for this infraction?"

Taejin rehearsed in his mind the conversation and the speculative statements he had made about Kim and his sons. "Yes, Comrade Warden."

"Your punishment will be different, however. All the prisoners at Hyesan will share it with you. I am sure your comrades will be most happy at the prospect of your fellowship."

Taejin remained silent, knowing the end result would be death.

Kim turned to the guard. "Return this animal to his cage."

THE SOUTH—SEOUL

Yong Cha rose at the sound of the footsteps. Moments later Hong stepped into the house. He wore the look of importance she had learned to recognize as a sign of victory. "Have you brought good news, Hong?"

He smiled, bracing tall. "I have met today with the leaders of our new government. I am to be installed in a most important government position."

Her eyes sparkled in pride for him. "Tell me," she begged excitedly.

He was stiff, uncomfortable in his western style suit. She helped him from the jacket, then handed him a lounging robe.

"The new government is most impressed with the construction I have achieved in Seoul. I am to be named a cabinet minister."

She drew in her breath sharply. "We must tell the others. Chi should know."

He held out his hand. "He will be told at my convenience."

Her broad smile waned gradually. She lowered her eyes and said nothing.

"My position will be most influential. I shall become wealthy."

She looked up but still said nothing, watching him carefully.

"Are you not pleased?" he preened. "I have survived the Japanese. It is a most fortunate honor. Most of the cabinet officers are arriving from the United States. They have been hiding there during the war. The Americans have been training them as a government in exile."

"I think you must learn much, and quickly," she said. "They will already have arranged their influence in the government. They will have made friends and allies."

Hong scoffed. "They must hold in high regard one who has remained here. I was not one who ran away. I stayed and excelled. They were most surprised to see my accomplishments upon their return."

"Have you not told them of the others?"

He looked at her, slightly irritated. "What others? I think others worked only as I directed them."

"Chi and the jin have been most loyal. Do you plan positions for them?" Her eyes were cautiously alert.

"Your principal concern should be for ourselves. The others have served their purpose. I have kept them from prison for their trouble."

"They can accomplish more. You have said you will be wealthy. I think they can help. All of us came here with you from loyalty."

"All of you came here with me to escape Enomoto and the animals of the slum."

"We deserve a reward for such loyalty."

He turned to her, his only expression one of superiority. "I have made you my wife. Is that not sufficient reward? You shall live in the comforts of my achievements."

"I mean no argument, Hong. You have been most kind to me."

"Then I think you must forget Chi and the jin. They are of little consequence."

"What have they done to anger you?" she asked, almost hesitantly. "Always they have helped. Never have they failed you."

"They are merely animals. They imposed themselves upon me at Inchon and have clung to me as leeches ever since."

"Am I also an animal of the slum? Am I a leech whom you would wish to dismiss now that you have become so important?"

He merely looked at her, stung.

"I think you would not be so important today if they had not helped you. I think you would not have completed the prison at Inchon if they had not lied to the people. Your animals of the slum worked only because of the lies."

"Have you learned what happened after the prison was finished?" He was caustic, disgusted.

She waited, suddenly apprehensive.

"They demanded the wages Chi had promised."

"Is that not why you removed us to Seoul? We had all agreed they would want their wages. We knew they would seek out those who had promised them."

"They were shot."

She gasped. "You had not told me."

"They were shot by Enomoto when they demanded what Chi had promised."

Her look became cynical. "I think you are making an excuse."

"Think what you wish."

"How did you learn?" she challenged. "Who told you they were shot?"

"Enomoto. He told me as I left Inchon to come to Seoul. The people had looked for you and the cripple. When they could not find you they went to the Japanese. Enomoto found the situation most humorous."

She was silent, reflecting.

"Does it surprise you? Did you think they would not seek the wages they were promised, the reconstruction of their homes? Or does it surprise you that the Japanese should shoot them?"

Tears welled in the corners of her eyes. "Why have you not told me before this?" she asked softly. "Why have you waited three years?"

"I wished to spare you the reality of their treachery," he replied curtly.

"You wished to use them still," she snapped, suddenly angry. "You knew the lie before it was told but you did not object then.

You have known lies since, planned them, told them, used them. You did not object because you were gaining great rewards. But now, suddenly, I think you do not like lies any longer. Now you do not need those who would tell them."

His blow sent her sprawling. She huddled in the corner into which its force had thrown her.

"You will not speak to me in such a way again," he whispered. "I have done many things, but I have been generous with you. I will not hear such vicious words from my wife."

Several days passed. Hong spoke little, Yong Cha less. At last he broached the subject again. "Have you seen Chi?"

She shook her head.

"The jin. Have you seen the jin?"

"I have seen no one."

He sat carefully and accepted the tea she had poured for him. "I have decided to provide a position for Chi."

She looked up, surprised.

"I have found I will be able to use my appointment most advantageously. I shall be able to arrange appointments for those I consider worthy." He sipped at the tea, awaiting her reaction.

"I think Chi will be very grateful."

"He will have an opportunity to make much money. I shall arrange for him to become the National Director of Orphanages."

Yong Cha rose and circled behind him. Impetuously, her strong hands began massaging his shoulders. They were stiff, the muscles knotted. "Does he know of your generosity?"

"I have not seen him."

"Have you also arranged an appointment for the jin?"

He shook his head. "Chi will have many opportunities to appoint others. I think he must arrange for the jin."

They were silent for several minutes.

"Husband."

He said nothing, waiting.

"I beg your forgiveness for my ingratitude. I was most rude to you."

He merely grunted, but reached up behind him to stroke her arm.

"Please forgive me," she whispered. "You are a very generous husband."

"You should tell Chi to meet me here this evening. Say nothing of our conversation. Also, I do not wish him to bring the jin. He must come alone."

She darted away from him, smiling.

"Do not go now," he called after her as she fled the room. "I would prefer to eat first."

"Yes, Hong," she called. The voice was drowned by her activity in the kitchen.

It was late when the door slid open and Chi stepped out of his slippers at the threshold. He bowed to Hong, then followed his gesture to a seat beside the low table. "Good evening, Hong. Your wife has said you wish to see me."

Hong nodded, blanketing his joy of success with a busy air. "It is most urgent that our conversation this evening be kept in strict confidence, Chi."

"You must never worry for my tongue," replied the other. "I am most honored that you continue to trust me."

"The war is over. What are your plans?"

Chi looked at him curiously. "I have made no plans."

"Why? I am no longer in the Japanese service. There will be no more projects of the kind I have done before." He watched as Chi balanced his tea to his lips with the good hand.

"I have waited to learn if you have need of me."

"And if I do not?"

Chi's eyes fell. "I shall go away. I shall seek food and a pallet by some other means."

"What have you heard of the new government?"

"I have heard they have been brought from the United States. I think they will be puppets."

"I think you are wrong." He said it calmly, almost inaudibly.

Chi cast him a sideward glance. "Have you heard news, Hong?"

"I think certain appointments may become possible. Of course those who receive favors must remain most loyal to those who arrange such things."

Chi's pulse quickened. "Is there a chance that you may receive such an appointment?"

Hong remained expressionless. "It is no longer chance. I have been appointed."

Chi broke into a wide grin, reached for his host's hand. "May I wish you good fortune, my friend?"

"It would be more appropriate that you wish such for Chi."

Chi sat back, stunned. "For me? You have arranged such an appointment for me?" He shook his head in disbelief. "I think you must be very powerful to arrange such a thing for a simple forager."

Hong waved it away. "It is important that you remain silent until I have made the necessary announcements."

"What is your position to be?" blurted Chi.

"I have been appointed a cabinet minister."

His guest let his breath out slowly. "You will be an important man in our government. What position could you have arranged for the humble forager?"

"I have arranged for you to be named the National Director of Orphanages."

Chi laughed. The sound pealed through the room, ringing, joyous.

"You will be a powerful man," added Hong, "but your responsibilities will be equally great. First, you will be responsible for all the orphanages throughout the nation."

"But there are none," protested Chi. "I am to be the director of a myth."

"Within the month there will be many, but they will be shabby, ill kept."

Chi, now more calm, looked curiously at Hong. "Would you have me suffer the disgrace of keeping stables for castoffs?"

"I would have you discuss a most pitiable situation with the

Americans who will be coming to our nation soon with their pockets full of money."

Slowly the import of the situation began to dawn on the guest. "Will I have the opportunity to appoint others?"

"Each province will have a director. Each of those directors will have several orphanages. Each of those will have a manager. Naturally, such appointments should be of great value to those who receive them."

"Who will make such appointments, Hong?"

Hong sat back, contemplating the other man. "I believe it should be the right, or if you prefer, the responsibility of the National Director to make such appointments." He paused. "Just as it is my right to appoint you to your position."

Chi stopped, looking at him, overwhelmed. "But Hong. I have no funds with which to purchase such an appointment from you."

"There are many ways in which such payments may be arranged," said Hong easily. "Of course, those who seek appointments from you must have the necessary desire."

Yong Cha entered and the conversation ceased until she had poured them more tea and departed.

"Our arrangement will be a matter of reports and percentages. You shall be expected to provide me with frequent and accurate reports on the state of affairs in the orphanages. I shall be most particularly concerned with numbers. In consideration of your appointment I shall consider you sufficiently grateful if you permit me to share your joys. The greatest of those, Chi, will be the generosity of the Americans."

The glow had disappeared from Chi's face. "I think I shall be ineffective, Hong. I know nothing of such things as orphanages."

"But I think you know much of orphans. The tidal basin of Inchon was a den of the nameless. Few had homes, fewer knew relatives. You have attained a high degree of expertise in this lucrative endeavor. You must remember, you have lived among them, created them. Now you shall have the opportunity to care for them and reap a profit."

The cripple was watching him, still dubious.

"America's heart bleeds for the orphans. They pay great amounts of money for their support. I think an astute man could be very successful at convincing them of the needs. An observant man will be most clever at presenting them a budget based on dollars and operating based on won."

"And my directors and managers? How do I find those with funds to purchase such positions? I think no one in Korea today has money."

"Chi, you and I have arrived at an arrangement. Today it is worth only our esteem for each other. Tomorrow, next year, the situation will be much different. I think perhaps a similar arrangement with others could prove happily beneficial to you." He studied the other man for a moment. "And to me."

"I know no one."

"After your appointment is announced you will be able to wear your title to the provinces. I think you will find many who would be your loyal friends." He rose, sober within the cloak of his power. "I think you must begin preparing well, Chi. You must think about what will make the Americans weep. When they arrive you must be most convincing."

Chi nodded, his enthusiasm growing. They moved toward the door. "Hong, have you considered the jin?"

"What of him?"

"I think he too has been loyal to you."

For Hong the meeting was finished. "The jin has been your aide as you have been mine. Perhaps in your gratitude you will determine a fitting reward."

* * * * * *

The interpreter was a sallow man, blonde and tall. Though his clothes fit perfectly he appeared ill at ease, almost hesitant. His Hangul was impeccable, his manners in strict compliance with a code obviously instilled through diligent schooling. Yet, he looked

at the sights about him in wonder and curiosity. Such surroundings had been unavailable in the classroom. Anxiously alert to the
conversation of the other two men, his eyes occasionally closed in
concentration as his mind processed a question from English to
Hangul, then delivered the reply.

They had met early in the morning. His superior from the
State Department and Chi had spent several hours in general discussion. Now they were driving, tour fashion, through the streets
of Seoul seeking out the back alleys, the mud huts by the Han
River, the crowded warrens of filth and disease in the inner city.

"But there wasn't that much fighting here, was there?" The
State Department official was aghast. "I just don't understand how
a country the size of this could have so many orphans."

The interpreter processed the words to the waiting Chi.

"Orphans," replied Chi, "are merely children with no parents.
I think they are not always caused by war, by the shooting and
bombs. Our nation was bound in the chains of Japanese occupation for more than thirty-five years. The Japanese caused many
children to become orphans. I was most unfortunate to be or-
phaned by them myself."

The interpreter whipped the information across the seat.

"Really? You seem to have done very well." The official was
impressed.

"I was claimed by a kind benefactor. He fed me, provided me
a bed. I was more fortunate than most." He dropped his eyes sadly.
"My brothers died."

The American received the news sadly, pityingly. "You were
fortunate, I suppose, if one can term such an extraordinary tragedy
a turn of fortune."

Chi looked at him through the interpreter, as though the man
were a windowpane. "I was most fortunate, but my situation was
far from extraordinary. It was common. It was more extraordinary
to have a complete family."

"What has been done to care for them?"

Chi shrugged. "Ours is a poor nation. We have never been

able to construct facilities to care for our unfortunates." He gesticulated with his crippled arm. "The Japanese created no programs at all for their care. We were allowed to set up no programs of our own. As a result, many thousands have starved, frozen to death, fallen to disease. It is a heartbreaking situation. He bowed his head for a moment of effect, then straightened. "I was very grateful when I was appointed to this position. I have known the terror in which they live. Now I hope I shall be able to assist them."

"I was about to ask, Mr. Chi, about your qualifications. What exactly is the educational background which qualifies you for this position?"

Chi maintained a calm facade over his inner panic. "As I have said, a kind benefactor took me in and cared for me. He taught me." He looked plaintively at the American. "A favored few of our children were educated under the Japanese. Orphans could not be considered."

"Strange," replied the American. "I had understood there was no educational system before the annexation. It was only the coming of the Japanese which generated the school system."

"This was true," admitted Chi reluctantly. "However, it was merely a gesture, an advertisement to the world of their ostensible humanity." Suddenly he was struck with inspiration. "It was that program which made our problem so very great. From no educational system we progressed to one which was partial to those loyal to Japan. Unless parents feigned loyalty to the Japanese their children harvested rice. They received no education." He grimaced. "Of course, orphans had no parents. Indeed, many of them became orphans as a result of their parents' resistance to the Japanese."

The interpreter was beginning to perspire but kept up with the pace.

"So your generous benefactor taught you in the beginning. He must have enrolled you in a university when you were older."

"I am sorry, but no. The Japanese said since I was a cripple, unfit to fight, I was unfit to study."

The American was perplexed. "Then we have come back to my original question. What are your qualifications for your position?"

"Experience," Chi shot back quickly. "In your country it is necessary to read of such problems in books. You do not see the problem lying before you in the gutter every time you turn a corner on the street. You have asked my qualifications. I have spent time in that gutter as a child. After my benefactor had rescued me I remembered what it was like. I cannot forget the hunger, the cold. When the Japanese refused me an education I spent my time caring for others from the gutters." He felt confident now. "I think you must say while the Americans were reading about such things in books I was working in a laboratory. I was learning in the gutters." He kept repeating the phrase, liking it, noticing the official flinch each time he said it.

The interpreter, impressed, was translating now with animation. The State Department official was sympathetic, consoling. "You have made your point well, Mr. Chi. I believe your government has made an excellent choice in appointing you."

Chi, inwardly elated, forged on. "You have seen the problem only in Seoul today. I must warn you it is minor compared with that in the provinces. We shall go out there tomorrow. We must visit smaller towns and villages. There the problem is more pronounced. They do not have the resources which are available here in Seoul."

The American shook his head in dejection. "I have to be very frank with you, I'm shocked. We've been together all day, yet I have seen no attempt at institutional care, even in the process of being generated. I haven't seen even the beginning of an organized effort."

"You must not be so quick to consider us wrong," replied Chi aggressively. "We have been under the control of the Japanese. We have had our own government for only three months. I have been appointed for only five weeks. I think in five weeks one cannot go beyond one's home neighborhood, find the nests of bodies, learn

the extent of this curse throughout our country. We were not allowed to travel freely under the Japanese. We seldom knew what
was happening in the other places. Word passed slowly from one
village to the next." He looked at the American in feigned disgust.
"You wonder why we have no programs. It is most obvious we do
not have them because we have not been allowed the opportunity." His voice became softer, more reasonable. "Now the United
States is giving us an opportunity we have never before had during
our history. I am attempting to plan programs but we have no
money."

The American moved quickly into the defensive position in
which Chi wanted him. "Please forgive me. I did not mean to
imply you were remiss in not having done these things. It is the
shock. I have never seen children, so many of them, in such bad
condition without having been invaded. I have recently toured
Europe. There the bombs have been exploding in their faces for
several years. One can easily understand seeing orphans, wounded
children. The problem is that I was not prepared for it here to the
extent it exists."

Next morning, the jin behind the wheel, they took the road
north toward Uijongbu. Gradually the broad plain became a valley, ever narrowing between towering peaks which hovered over
them in regal beauty. Beside them a river flowed serenely southward, as though nature were totally detached from the devastated
spirits which fed on her. When the valley reached its narrowest
point the jin turned off the road and into the streets of a moder-
ately large town. There was no pavement and the buildings were
overgrown shacks.

The Americans looked up at the nearly vertical cliffs. Deeply
sliced gorges led out of town in the four cardinal directions. The
weather was cold, unfriendly. The car stopped and they got out.
People stopped to stare in wonder at the Americans, so much larger
than they, their clothes finely tailored, their hands and faces clean.

They strolled down an alley strewn with trash. From the rear
the buildings looked even worse than along their facades. Chil-

dren played in the dirt, poorly protected from the cold by ragged undershirts, torn trousers. Few wore anything on their feet. Those who did shuffled along in rubber slippers. They were dirty and thin.

"These are some of the more fortunate of our children," said Chi. "Uijongbu is a provincial seat. There is a greater degree of social order than in the other towns."

The Americans were silent.

"When we begin I shall have a director in each province to oversee the orphanage operations. As you can see, however, it will be very difficult for him to control the problem alone."

"Of course," agreed the American. "He'll need a staff for his orphanage."

Chi shook his head slowly. "He will have need of much more than that."

"More? But surely the orphanage should be sufficient to cure the problem. These urchins will have a roof over their heads, clothes on their backs."

Chi looked at him quickly, affecting surprise. "These urchins? I think few of these children are orphans. These are the fortunate ones." He led them farther into the maze of crates, castoff tin. He knew what he was seeking. "There," he said, pointing. Beneath a piece of cardboard leaning against a fence lay a tiny skeleton covered with skin. They removed the sagging shelter and knelt down. The child was breathing, but not awake. "This is an example of an orphan as we know them." He paused to let them absorb the horror. "How long have we been in Uijongbu? I think perhaps fifteen minutes. If we were to spend the day we would find fifty. If it were a week we would locate five hundred." He watched the shock on their faces. "I must remind you, this is the seat of the province. The outer villages are much worse. I think we must have many more than one orphanage in each province."

The American reached out for the child.

"I think you must leave her," cautioned Chi. "We have no place to take her."

"Well, my God, man! We can't leave her here to die."

Chi shook his head. "Are we three to tour the country and collect all the derelicts we see? I think if you take this one today there will be three tomorrow to replace her. Come."

The American ignored him, picking the child up and cradling her in his arms. "We shall take her to the police."

"They have many problems."

"Then to the provincial government."

Chi shook his head sadly. "There is no director of orphanages here yet. There are no facilities to care for her."

"Then a hospital. A doctor."

Chi's eyes fell. "I am most sorry."

The American shuddered. "Well, I'm damned if I'll see her left here. She'll go with us."

"There is no place to take her. We have no facilities to care for her."

"For today she'll go with us," snapped the American, frustrated. "We have to take her with us. Can't you see? If she doesn't get medical attention she'll die." His voice conveyed the edge of disgust. "She's already unconscious."

Chi realized it was futile. "Then we shall return to Seoul with her."

"Do you mean in a city this size there are no doctors?" The official was incredulous. "I can't believe it."

The Director of Orphanages looked at him helplessly. "There are no facilities to care for her properly." He could not chance their seeing his country's customs in operation. If they took her to a local doctor he would merely invoke the code of responsibility for the dead and abandoned. Whoever first touched the victim accepted full responsibility for care or burial. He became, in effect, the next of kin. Chi knew the entire support effort would be in jeopardy if the custom were bared now. "I think we must take her to Seoul most quickly."

They hurried, almost ran to the car. The interpreter reached out for the child but the State Department official shook his head.

"Just tell them to hurry. This child may not survive the trip." He lay the child on the seat of the car, removed his coat and wrapped her. Then, sitting, he lifted the bundle gently into his lap.

They sped southward, speaking little. The American kept lifting the child, holding his ear near her face. "The breathing is shallower," he snapped to the interpreter. "Tell them to hell with their doctors. Take her to the American compound. We'll do it with our own doctors."

They raced through the East Gate into the city. The jin was as active with the horn as the accelerator. At last they arrived at the American compound. A military policeman at the gate raised his hand and the jin slowed to stop. "Dammit," shouted the American, "we have a dying child." The military policeman, recognizing him, quickly waved them through.

The doctor was thorough, but the odds were heavily against him. "Would you please wait outside?" he asked, immediately ignoring them. They filed out, helpless.

"I wish to thank you for bringing her here," offered Chi. "Even in Seoul our doctors are not as knowledgeable as yours."

The American, pacing, merely grunted.

"Tomorrow we shall return to the countryside," ventured Chi. "I wish for you to see conditions in the smaller villages."

The door opened before he could reply and the doctor emerged. "I'm sorry, Sir. It was too late to treat her effectively."

"You mean she died?"

The doctor nodded silently.

Chi knew the American would expect remorse. He produced a bowed head and a sad face. "Thank you," he said to the doctor through the interpreter. He looked at the State Department official. "I am most sorry. I wish you could have been spared such a sad experience. I wish I could merely have told you about such things." He was inspired to emotion. "I see it daily but I am helpless." He turned away and stood with his head bowed, waiting. The consoling hand touched his shoulder almost immediately. He knew he had won.

THE NORTH—HYESAN

"Everyone will come out." The order was more insistent than usual.

Taejin stirred and opened his eyes. Outside there was a churning activity.

"Everyone will come out," the call was repeated. The other men in the hut began to scramble from their mats. Taejin pulled himself to his feet and went to the doorway. In June at that latitude dawn comes early. Today there was no light in the eastern sky.

"Do not stand there, prisoner. Hurry. Move quickly. There is no time to be wasted." The guard was looking at him.

He stepped quickly out to the dirt of the compound. Around him the other men were looking at each other with sly glances of apprehension. The entire compound was frenzied activity.

"What is happening?" whispered one prisoner. "It is too early to go to the pits."

"Quiet," cautioned another. "They will hear you."

Across from them a line was beginning to move. They were going in the wrong direction for the mine. Then, from far down their own line there were shouts and their group began to spread out and follow the other.

"Quickly. Do not waste time." The voice was high and excited. Taejin had heard it before. "Run. You are wasting my time. Run."

The line broke into a labored trot, some reacting with the suddenness of fear, others with the boredom of repetition.

"I shall not forget the faces of those who do not hurry," the guard screamed. Now Taejin remembered him. He was the one who had killed the old man on the day of Taejin's arrival. They had not seen him since. Now he danced along the line. "Hurry, I say. I will not be kept waiting."

They had almost reached the barrier. Glancing ahead, Taejin saw a line of railroad cars in the floodlights.

"Evacuation! We are being evacuated." He choked back the words.

"What did you say?" screamed the little guard. "Did you say something to me?"

"No, comrade Guard. I coughed." He expected to climb the stump.

The guard sneered. "Be careful how you cough, prisoner. Do not cough words again."

"Yes, Comrade Guard."

To Taejin's surprise the guard was off again, running forward along the line to a cattle car. Throughout the compound there were the usual screamed reprimands, but punishment was conspicuously avoided.

They were packed into the cars so tightly there was no room to sit or lie down. They stood as close together as bundles of sticks and heard the screech of the door rails. The heavy barriers were rolled shut, followed by the snap of the locks. Outside they could still hear the screams of the guards as more and more of the prisoners were loaded onto the train. Finally the sounds subsided. There were a few lurches, then the gradually increasing sway as the train accelerated.

They rolled the remainder of the night and all day, stopping only to fuel and water the engine. Those near the walls of the cars reported back to those in the center it appeared they were moving south. Sighs of relief rippled through the train. Many had feared they were being transferred north into Manchuria.

At one stop the door was opened and a tub of rice was shoved through into their midst. There were no bowls and no chopsticks with which to eat. Only by shifting position and sliding around each other were they able to reach down and scoop up a handful with their bare hands. Some got nothing at all.

Daylight was fading as the train resumed its journey. Taejin had managed to work his way to a position near the door. Now he watched the occasional flicker of lights through the slats. He bent close and saw the signs on the shacks in the outskirts of the city. Suddenly the whole trip took perspective in his mind. A gloomy board on the front of one shack read "Anju." They were drawing as close to Hochon as they would come. After the next few miles they would roll steadily away to the south. Whatever their destination, he knew he must escape now or he would be lost in the mountains even if he did get free.

He whispered to the man next to him. "They are going to kill us, you know."

The man looked at him suspiciously and said nothing.

"They are taking us south to kill us," Taejin repeated.

The man stared straight ahead. "How do you know what they are going to do?"

Taejin waited a moment. "They have many workers in this part of the country. They have no need of prisoners. The only reason they would bring us here is to do something too dangerous for their own kind."

The man shrugged. "What does it matter? We have long been dead. None of us will ever be freed."

"You are right," continued Taejin. "They will never free us. But suppose we were to escape?"

The man snorted and still looked straight ahead.

"We could do it."

There was no answer.

"We could cause the train to crash."

The man looked at him again. "How can we do that? We are cattle. There is no way out of this thing."

"If we started the car swaying it would jump the rail."

"When the train stopped they would shoot all of us."

"They would not shoot us if they need us badly in the south."

"If they thought the train would jump the track they would stop it. They would kill the ones who started the swaying."

"Suppose we caused it to jump the track before they could stop."

"Then most of us would be killed in the crash. The army would hunt down the rest." He resumed staring ahead of him. "We are better off the way we are."

"Why? If we stay the way we are they are going to kill us at our destination. If we can wreck the train perhaps some would escape. We could hide in the mountains. It would cost them much time and effort to track us down."

The man was silent again.

"Some of us might be successful. Some might get through to the other half of the country."

Some of the others near them were becoming restless now. "How can we do what you suggest?" asked one.

Taejin glanced at him in interest. "Begin an easy swaying from one side to the other. Tell your neighbor to do the same."

"Do not do it!" The first man looked frightened. "We will all be killed."

"What does it matter?" laughed the other. "Are we alive now?"

Taejin said nothing further, but began shifting from one foot to the other. Soon others were doing the same. The car began to echo their motion, creaking from side to side on the track.

"Prisoners," came a shout from above, on the roof of the car. "What are you doing down there?"

"You see?" said the first man. "Now they will stop the train and shoot all of us."

Taejin said nothing, continuing his swaying. Some of the others looked confused but kept up the motion. A prisoner near the end of the car looked through the slats. "They are climbing down the ladder."

"What good will that do them?" asked another. "They cannot

reach us without opening the door. They cannot open the door until the train stops."

There was no sign of the train slowing. Outside two guards hung at the bottom of the ladder while a third made his way along the side of the car, holding the slats. His progress was slow, the lurching car almost pitching him off at every oscillation. At last he reached the door. "Stop swaying," he shouted. "Stop the swaying in my carriage."

The motion continued. The lurching was becoming more pronounced with every cycle. The guard's knuckles were white as he clung desperately to the door. "I have told you to stop," he screamed. "If you do not stop I shall open the door and shoot you all."

The train did not slow. It became apparent to Taejin there was no communication between the guards and the engineer. From his location in the engine he was unaware of the problem near the end of his long train.

Taejin peeked through the slats. The guard had slung his rifle over his head and shoulders and gripped the side of the car more firmly. In one hand he held a key which he was trying frantically to insert in the lock.

"You are troublemakers. We are going to shoot you."

He fumbled with the lock. "Do you hear what I say? You are making trouble in my carriage. I shall open this door and shoot you all." His voice was weak, frenzied.

The man next to Taejin was wildeyed. "You see what I told you? Now you have finished us. He is going to kill us all."

Taejin said nothing, but watched the guard intently through the slats. The man had inserted the key in the lock, but now he faced the problem of rolling the heavy door open against the increasing oscillations of the car. He called for help and another guard worked his way forward from the ladder. Together they heaved against the door. Gradually it began to move, a little at a time, until the first guard swung back and motioned his companion into the opening. As the man swung up and in, the car lurched violently in the opposite direction, sending him sprawling into the midst of the prisoners. They were on him immediately. The first guard peered in and panic shone on his features.

"Stop!" he screamed. "All of you will die."

He swung himself upward. As he did so Taejin's knee caught him full in the throat. There was only a momentary grunt and he disappeared in the darkness. Taejin leaped after him. There were shouts from the receding train and a single shot. He was vaguely aware of other bodies flying in desperation from the train farther down the track but he never saw them again. The clatter of the wheels faded busily off into the night.

Taejin rolled as he landed, coming up cut and bruised. He dove immediately at the guard. The man lay still. Working quickly, Taejin took the man's bayonet and struck his temple with the grip. Then, lifting him, he carried him off into the underbrush.

Having dressed himself in the guard's uniform, he slept. Next morning he studied the weapon. Once he was certain he knew its operation he buried the guard and began the long climb up a nearby mountain. From there he would be able to view the surrounding landscape, perhaps determine his location.

The scene from the peak was breathtaking. Spread below him to the west was the gentle curve of the coastline wrapping itself protectively around the multitude of tiny bays and inlets which dotted South Pyongan province. Closer was the patchwork of countless rice paddies and, nearer the mountains, the drier land where other grain crops flourished.

He saw the towns of Sukchon and Sunan, with smaller villages interspersed between them along the highway. Almost hypnotized by the beauty, a thing so foreign to him now, he gazed for a long time. Finally, realizing he must move on, he began retracing his steps downward to the level plain of human abundance.

He considered moving only at night and resting by day, but sensed he would be more noticeable if he did so. His best cover would be a bold traveling of the roads by day, maintaining as military a bearing as possible and assuming an authoritative attitude with anyone with whom he came in contact. Yet, looking down at his uniform, he knew its poor fit would be likely to attract attention.

He decided to search for a military compound. They were not difficult to find. He watched the guards at night and timed the marching of their posts. By the second night he was ready. He had fashioned himself a garrotte of communications wire, and when a lone guard of the proper size passed near him he quickly ambushed him, taking the man's uniform, weapons and ammunition. Safely distant, he examined the automatic rifle and found it to be more modern than the one he had taken from the prison guard. He buried the other and remained under cover for several miles. Then, stepping into the road, he strode boldly off in the direction of Hochon.

As he neared the village he picked his way again into the underbrush to reconnoiter. He was on the outskirts of the town, perhaps two hundred yards and around a bend in the road from the first houses, when he heard men's voices. He shrank into his cover and waited.

"This will be the place," announced one, an officer.

The soldiers with him nodded.

"We shall line them up along the one side and dump them into the ditch over there. If it is done correctly they should fall there as they die."

"But Comrade, what if the criminal is not found? We may find ourselves executing the entire village."

The officer was unconcerned. "They matter little to us. This village has been a problem for many years."

"How many will die per day?"

"Ten. Each day we will shoot ten. Sooner or later he is sure to come here. When he does I think the people will be most anxious to turn him in."

"He has been in prison for over two years now. They say both his father and mother are dead. He has no other relatives. Why would he even return to Hochon?"

The officer shrugged. "We have received our orders." He beckoned and the soldiers turned toward the village. When they were out of sight Taejin raised his head and looked around. His only hope was to find a place where he had cover and a field of fire. He would have time for only one burst. If the villagers responded and grabbed the soldiers' weapons he could lead them into the hills and plan the next move.

He noted an outcropping of rocks some fifty feet down the road from where the soldiers had been standing. It was a perfect location for his mission but had no protection from the rear. He decided he would have to chance anyone coming along the road toward the town at the critical time. His crucial mission was to stop the executions before they began.

Crossing the road to the rocks, he viewed his field of fire. As he had expected, it was excellent. He made himself a hiding place in some nearby bushes and settled down to await the morning.

He was alert with the first light of day. Moving closer to the rocks he measured with his eye the distance to his target. Even with his lack of experience he was sure he could hit them. He began his wait with a knot of anxiety in the pit of his stomach.

It was not long. He heard voices down the road toward the village and settled tensely into his firing position. As they were herded into view he was horrified to see three women and a child among the allotted ten. Some of the six men were old acquaintances. As they were lined up along the ditch the women and child began whimpering. The men were stoical, standing straight and proud.

"You are the first of many who will die for Taejin," announced the officer. He stared at them for a moment, then turned to his men. They had arranged themselves in a line along the opposite side of the road.

As the officer stepped back into line with them there was a burst of fire and the victims cringed. Bodies wilted and weapons clattered to the roadbed. Then there was silence.

Slowly the people looked up in shocked surprise as a soldier darted into their midst. "Come, take their weapons. Dump the bodies in the ditch and come with me. Quickly."

The men sprang into action. Stripping the soldiers of their armament, they shoved the bodies off the road. Taejin, in the meantime, had led the women and child off the road into the brush. Wordlessly, the men joined them and they burrowed back farther from the road.

They traveled southeast, moving always by night. Once they were far enough from Hochon, Taejin began to reconnoiter during the morning hours to locate food and check their location. Then he returned to their hiding place and slept while the men took turns standing guard. They skirted Songnim and Sariwon, then followed the peaks north of the rail line to the Yesong River.

"How are we to cross?" they asked.

Taejin gazed at the winding stream, its length dotted with barges and scows drifting southward. Each was laden with military equipment. "We have come too far to give up hope now," he replied.

The group made a shelter in the mountain and Taejin began daily trips down to the river valley in search of a bridge, a boat, any means of crossing. Near Singye he found the answer in a large pile of logs. He hurried back to his small band.

"I have found a solution but it will require much work. I think the women cannot help with this because there will be much heavy lifting."

They looked at him expectantly, not speaking.

"We shall have to build a raft."

The others were doubtful. "How can we build a raft on the banks of such a river? It would take too long and there are many troop convoys heading south. We would be captured."

Taejin lapsed into silence. They were right. It was a poor plan, a product of futility. "There are many small boats crossing," said one of the men. "We have watched them from here. We have the weapons. Perhaps we could ambush one at night. We could cross the river and be away before they knew it was gone. If we could somehow destroy it they would never know where it went."

"It would not be a difficult deduction," replied Taejin. "They would have only to search the other side of the river."

"I agree," nodded the man. "But if they search the other side of the river and find nothing they may give up. They appear busy. Perhaps they are too busy to be concerned for one stolen boat. They may decide one of their own defected."

"You have observed well," agreed another. "It is most obvious they are preparing for battle."

Taejin gasped, the future suddenly clear. The train transporting the prisoners south, all the troops moving toward the border with the capitalist south. The invasion, the great unification of the masses about which Kim had preached was about to begin. "I shall go out again tomorrow and try to find a boat," he said, hiding his inner turmoil. "If we must ambush to get it, we shall. But perhaps there will be another way. Perhaps some soldiers may wish to join us. We need more men and only I am in uniform."

They agreed. Next morning Taejin set out toward the river bank. No small boats were to be seen, even on the river. He settled into some bushes on the bank and waited.

By midafternoon he had almost given up hope. Traffic along the road had been heavy. Long convoys of trucks and tanks lumbered past his position all day. Each time, he hugged the bushes a little closer and watched nervously.

Suddenly there was a loud report. He blinked, startled. Before him, one of the trucks swerved and skidded into the ditch, its front tire flat. The driver opened the door and dropped to the road, circling to look at the damage. Then he straightened and looked around.

A staff car rolled up and stopped. "What has happened?" asked an officer.

"The tire is flat, Comrade," answered the driver.

"You will repair it and join us. We will cross the river five miles ahead. We shall eat in two hours."

"Yes, Comrade."

"Do you wish someone to help you?"

"It will not be necessary, Comrade. I can do it."

The officer shrugged. "It is your problem. Be most certain you are there when we eat. The ammunition cargo is valuable."

"Yes, Comrade."

The staff car drove off to rejoin the rest of the convoy.

The man went to the rear of his truck and tugged the spare tire from its well under the truck bed. Then, circling once more to the front of the vehicle, he dropped to his knees and peered under the fender. The truck was hopelessly canted, making the use of a jack impossible. He cursed and rose.

Taejin had bolted across the road while the man was bent down and now ran gasping up the hill. "Come quickly," he ordered. "We have an opportunity to cross if we hurry."

They leaped to their feet and followed him down the slope. "I shall pose as a soldier marching prisoners of the people. We will come upon a truck with a flat tire. I will offer your labor to help the driver get it out of the ditch and change the tire. It will be a simple matter to take the truck."

"How can that help us? We still must cross the river."

"There is a bridge which crosses the river five miles south of here. We will cross there."

They were at the roadbed now. They slowed to a walk, Taejin in the rear, the others with their weapons under their clothes.

"Greetings, Comrade. Do you need help?"

The driver looked at Taejin. "I need more than people. I think I must have a retriever." He had found a log and tried to work it under the front end of the truck. It was not clear what he had intended to do with it once he had it in place.

"My prisoners will solve your problem," said Taejin.

The driver looked warily at the others, then back at Taejin. "Where are you coming from?"

"We have been sent from the Suan area. My commander requires these people farther south."

"Every commander requires people farther south," the man snorted with disgust.

Taejin appeared to ignore the remark. He turned to his clan. "Come with me. We shall need a boulder." He led them into the brush at the side of the road. "Hide your weapons here. We can retrieve them quickly when this is over. Now we must find a large boulder. We will need something to use as a fulcrum with that log if we are to remove the truck from the ditch."

They fanned out. In a few minutes he heard a call from one of the men. "I have found one."

Taejin arrived at his side. "I hope we are able to move it," the man said apologetically.

"Find a log," said Taejin. "If we can pry it loose it should roll down the hill. Perhaps we can aim it to come to rest near the front of the truck."

"We will be most fortunate if no other troops stop to assist him."

"If they see enough people working they will not. They must meet their own schedules."

They found a log and wrestled it to the boulder. Soon they had it pried free. It rolled, crashing through the underbrush toward the road. A short time later they had it positioned near the front bumper.

"Let us try it now," suggested Taejin.

The driver was staring at the truck dejectedly. "It will not work," he lamented. "The truck is too heavy. It is loaded with ammunition. How can we move it up to the road?"

"You will drive it."

"I cannot drive it with a flat tire," scoffed the driver.

"We shall change the tire first."

"How can that be done?" he asked in amazement.

Taejin was calmly instructive. "We must lift the front end of the truck anyway. Loosen the nuts and be ready to work quickly. My prisoners will hold the front of the truck up with the log. As soon as it is free of the ground you must pull the old tire off and replace it. Then we will let it down. You can drive it out."

The driver looked doubtful, but took the wrench and loosened the lug nuts. "I am ready," he called.

"Remember," called Taejin. "You must move quickly, Comrade. They cannot hold it very long."

"Do not waste time talking," replied the driver, irritated. "Lift it."

Taejin's band set the log across the boulder and pressed downward. There was a slight shifting of the truck but no elevation.

"It will not work," groaned the driver.

"Do not be a pessimist," cautioned Taejin. "We will move the boulder closer and try again."

They pried the boulder and it scuffed closer to the bumper. Then, with a warning call to the driver, they pressed down on the end of the log. Slowly, the front end of the truck rose in the air.

The driver worked frantically. In a moment he had the bad tire off and the new one in place.

"Put the nuts in place," ordered Taejin.

The driver spun them furiously.

Taejin turned and looked at his people. They were purple with the exertion. "Let it down slowly."

The front of the truck settled gently to the ditch. The driver, a look of relief on his face, took the flat tire around to the rear of the truck and slid it into its cradle. When he returned to the cab he was surrounded.

Shock crossed his face. "What are you doing?" he demanded.

"We are waiting for you to thank us," replied Taejin.

The driver looked around at the weapons. "You are agents from the south."

"We are friends of the people," replied Taejin evenly. "If you wish, you may help us."

The driver nodded nervously. A few moments later they were driving down the road, Taejin seated in the cab with the driver, the rest of his party crouched among the ammunition boxes in the rear. They crossed the river at the bridge. A short distance beyond they saw the convoy drawn up at the side of the road.

"This is where I must stop," said the driver.

"Do you wish to stop?"

"I think it does not matter what I wish to do. I will be shot if I do not stop."

"They can shoot you only if they catch you," suggested Taejin.

The man cast him a quick glance.

Taejin continued. "If you join us we can be far along the road before anyone begins chasing us. We will park the truck in the brush, take what ammunition we can and climb into the mountains. When they find the truck we will be miles away."

"Where do you plan to go?" asked the driver.

"Across the border."

The driver's eyes grew wide. "Such a thing is impossible. There are too many troops preparing for the invasion."

"When will the invasion begin?"

"I do not know. It could be tomorrow."

"Then we shall hide until after it has begun. It will be easier to cross the lines if they are fighting."

They were beside the convoy now. The driver hesitated, then continued past. Little notice was taken of their progress until they were almost all the way past the line. Then there was a shout from somewhere behind them.

The driver drove his foot to the floor and the truck leaped forward. Taejin looked in his rear view mirror. There was running in the camp but no vehicles were following them yet. They roared around a bend in the road, out of sight of the camp, and wound through the heightening mountains. Then Taejin shouted. "There. Up ahead."

The driver followed his finger and veered into a cartpath on the left. Then, turning sharply, he swerved into a thicket to his right. The ground was covered with pine needles.

Those in the rear were out of the truck before it stopped, gathering needles and covering the tracks. Taejin and the driver pulled the bushes together where they had entered. Within two minutes a passerby would never have noticed anything had happened.

Out on the road they heard several vehicles pass at high speed. As quickly as the sound rose it died away. They climbed into the rear of the truck and began sorting through the ammunition cases. The rifle cartridges were packed in bandoliers which they draped about their shoulders until the weight was about to crush them. Then they broke open a crate of grenades, some fragmentation and others white phosphorus. Clipping as many as they could to each bandolier, they abandoned the truck and made their way through the underbrush toward higher ground.

Below them they heard the pursuers return, this time at a slower speed. After passing back and forth along the road several times the vehicles turned into the path the driver had taken. The group cringed. Engines labored past the thicket where the truck was hidden. Proceeding up the mountain trail, they finally ground to a halt. In the distance they heard the shouts. "Look carefully for wheel tracks. The truck was heavy with ammunition."

"There are no tracks up here, Comrade," shouted one soldier.

"We can see only our tracks behind our truck, Comrade," followed another.

There was a curse. "I told you they went farther along the road. I think they are at the Imjin River by now."

"Comrade, they cannot travel that fast with a truck so heavily loaded."

"You are a fool. They did not need much lead to be far ahead of us. They are riding along and laughing somewhere miles from here by now."

"Comrade, I think we must radio ahead."

"Do you realize what they do to units which breed defectors?"

"I suggested it only as a means to catch them, Comrade. We could save our face by capturing them."

"I shall not do it by announcing to higher headquarters that we lost them in the first place. Sooner or later they will be caught.

We must hope that by then we will all be heroes in combat. Heroism may save us."

The engines started again and there was a whine of transmissions as the vehicles backed down the trail toward the main road. Moments later they were gone.

THE SOUTH—GAPYONG

The tapping of Min's walking stick forecast his arrival. Inside the bungalow, Shin was gathering his belongings. He looked up as the older man entered.

Min stopped, seeing the bundle. "What is happening?"

"It is time for me to go, Schoolmaster. I shall seek a commission in the new army. If I delay longer they will have their quotas filled. I would not wish to enter this army at a lower rank." He picked up the satchel. "By going to them now I may even achieve a higher appointment. It appears you have been correct in your prediction. The Americans are more concerned with the communists to the north than the Japanese of the past war. They will be more interested in enlistment than punishment.

Min pouted. "I had hoped you would consider joining me in my venture here. Your agility would be a most welcome asset to an aging man."

Shin walked to him slowly, placing a hand on his shoulder. "I shall not forget you, Schoolmaster. I merely believe your security and that of our nation must rest on those who have learned to conduct themselves efficiently in combat. If we are ready we may never be called upon to fight. If not," he shrugged, "there may be no wealth for anyone."

Min relented, but hesitantly. "If you must go, it is for the best. But please do not forget me. I may need your assistance in the future."

The chill of late autumn was biting. The smoke of thousands of coal fires permeated the city, leaving a soft gray dust across them. Shin moved quickly, anxiously, not very familiar with Seoul.

At the army headquarters Americans were as numerous as his countrymen. A desire to hesitate gripped him, yet he hurried faster, much as fear often had driven him into greater valor at war. Then the desk was before him.

The clerk looked up in bureaucratic boredom. "Have you brought your credentials?"

Shin reached into the satchel, removing his personnel file. The man took the papers, riffled through them carelessly. "You have been an officer?"

"Yes."

"You must go to the next section," replied the clerk, relieved at escaping work.

Shin followed the man's motion. The new man worked his way more carefully through the file. Suddenly he looked up. "Captain Shin."

"Yes."

The man smirked. "Do you plan to ban the baths in our army as you did at Inchon?"

Shin's face went blank. "I think I do not know what you are talking about."

"You know. It is here in your file. You served as the guard commander at the prison of Inchon." The man was glaring at him now. "I was a member of the guard there. Perhaps you can explain to me why you ran away from the prison."

"I was reassigned," said Shin quietly. "The past is of no consequence now. I was a good soldier and was decorated many times for heroism in combat. I think that must be the most important part of my file to you. Rear area actions at the end of a war do not matter."

"But you were a deserter."

"My reassignment was merely not recorded because the war was over before I reached my new unit."

"That was not the announcement at Inchon. The general announced that you had deserted."

Shin went cold. "He lied. He said that only to regain the loyalty of the guards. He knew I was very strict and the guards did not like me for that." His hands were clammy. "He lied."

The clerk now smiled openly. "I think there are others who would wish to speak with you. I think you will be a celebrity for us to process." He turned and called to others at desks nearby. "Come. We have a celebrity. I think you will not want to miss meeting such a hero as I have found."

They gathered, expectant smiles on their faces.

"This," announced the clerk in front of Shin, "is Captain Shin, the deserter of Inchon."

A murmur passed through them.

"I think you must look at my combat record," insisted Shin. "I think you are not interested in the proper things about my record."

Two officers approached, one an American. "What is the trouble?"

The clerk rose importantly. "I have known this man."

The officers took the records and began reviewing them.

"I can tell you much about him," added the clerk.

"You can be still," countered the Korean officer. Shin watched nervously as they continued paging through his record. They stepped off a few steps and talked quietly. Finally the Korean officer returned the record to the clerk. "Process him."

"But. . . ."

"As a major." The officer glared at the clerk and his neighbors for a moment, then walked away.

"Where can you be contacted?" asked the clerk curtly.

"I have been staying near Chunchon, my home. I can arrange to stay in Seoul if you think I shall be needed soon." His manner had become at once superior, condescending.

"You will be called when it is convenient for us," snapped the clerk, still bruised that his game had been rebuffed. "You may stay where you wish. It is required only that you keep us informed."

"I shall provide you with an address as soon as I have one." He turned and marched proudly through the door into the cold air. Outside, he hurried along the broad avenue which ran through Itaewon and Yongsan. There was much traffic, most of it military. He watched those about him carefully, wondering if more recognition would be forthcoming. At last, restless, he set out for the other end of the city.

The government buildings were a motley collection of those left over from various periods. Some had been used during the Yi Dynasty. Others, more modern but equally austere, had been constructed during the period of annexation. He wandered aimlessly through a garden, then approached a teahouse.

"Shin."

He wheeled, alarmed at the sharpness of the call on the heels of his recent confrontation. Then, joyously, he recognized Hong. He broke into a trot, reaching out. "Hong." Then, noticing a reserve in the other's attitude, he slowed. His friend's clothes were western, well tailored. In his hand he carried a fine leather attache case. "Hong. I think you have done something very important. What has happened?"

Hong smiled, warmly but still with an edge of superiority. "I have been appointed a cabinet minister."

Shin drew in his breath, admiration sweeping his face. He bowed. "I wish you good fortune, Hong. I am most honored to have been your friend."

Hong laughed now. "Shin, you still are my friend. Government does not change that." He looked at Shin's worn clothes. "What has happened to you, my friend? I thought you went into the army."

Shin nodded. "I became an officer."

"But now," replied Hong, nodding toward the clothes. "You do not look prosperous." He passed it off. "Come. We shall have some tea. There is a better teahouse in the next street."

Their conversation ranged across many subjects.

"The clothes are those of Schoolmaster Min," apologized Shin. "When I returned he felt it ill advised that I be seen in my uniform. I earned many medals. Min worried for me."

Hong scoffed. "No one would harm you. We would prefer to put you to use in our army now. We are concerned about the Russian presence in the north. We must work toward reunification. You would be very welcome in our army."

Shin smiled. "I have made application only today."

Hong nodded. "Then you have seen. It is settled. What was your rank?"

"I was a captain with the Japanese, but I am to be a major now."

"Yes. I think their policy is to increase one grade for those with combat experience. The most senior officers are being trained in the United States." He paused, thinking for a moment. "You need not go into the army at all, Shin."

Shin looked at him quickly. "I think I cannot do anything else. I know only one thing well."

"You have become a good leader. You would be a good manager. I have many ventures."

"But did you not say you were in government? You are a cabinet minister."

Hong laughed. "Those in power have most positive influence throughout the nation. We control everything which happens. We even control the money the Americans are giving the nation." He wagged a finger. "You could become a wealthy man by working for me."

"Everyone talks of the American money," replied Shin pensively. "The schoolmaster has made careful plans to become wealthy from them."

"Min?" He shook his head. "I would not have thought he would be preparing such plans." Then he laughed. "But why should he not? I shall plan to make a trip to see him. Perhaps I can be of help to him."

"Or he to you."

Hong looked at him sharply. "He to me?"

"Hong, you should remember he is a most intelligent and perceptive man."

"Shin, I am the cabinet minister, not the schoolmaster. I shall offer him my assistance." He looked at his watch. "I must leave. I have a very important meeting."

Shin stood with him. They bowed, and Hong stalked importantly away.

THE NORTH—BORDER

Taejin's group looked at each other with relief.

"It is most regrettable we cannot return for more of the ammunition," said the driver.

"How would we carry it?" asked Taejin. "No, we have all we shall need. We must not fight unless we are cornered. We are not that many. If we must shoot our way through them we have enough for that."

The driver hesitated. "I have wished to do this for a long time," he confessed. "Many men in our unit wish to defect."

Taejin smiled. "We welcome you to our party."

"What will we do when we arrive in the south?"

"We shall go our separate ways."

"What if they will not have us? What if they consider us infiltrators, agents?"

"We must do our best to convince them we are not."

"The Americans will be the most difficult to convince if they enter the fighting. Our leaders say the Americans are butchers."

"We have been told that all our lives," replied Taejin. "Perhaps the Americans say the same of us."

The driver reached into his pocket and brought forth a booklet. "I shall be as well prepared as possible. I have saved this to use if I am captured." He handed the booklet to Taejin. It was a basic handbook of conversational English.

Taejin thumbed through it with interest. "Where could we get more of these?"

"Only some of the soldiers have them. We stole them. I have two."

"Give one of them to me."

The driver reached willingly into his pocket and brought forth the other, handing it to Taejin. They set off again through the mountains. The journey was slow, difficult now. The mountains were higher, their loads heavier. The women remained strong but the child tired easily. Finally she was so ill she could not travel at all.

"Each of us will carry one more bandolier," announced Taejin. "That will free one man to carry her."

One of the men scoffed., "What will that accomplish?" he asked.

"We cannot leave her here alone," replied Taejin, attempting to be reasonable.

"Food is too difficult to find. I think we must abandon her for the good of the others. We cannot continue to take her with us."

Taejin looked at him in disgust. "You are as bad as those we are fleeing."

The man looked only slightly uncomfortable. "I am trying. . . ."

"Do not try," snapped Taejin.

The man looked away in frustration.

"I have a suggestion," said one of the women.

Taejin looked at her without speaking. She returned his look, then beckoned him away from the group.

* * * * * *

The unit had pulled into bivouac outside Tosan on the Imjin River. Infantry, they would march from this point forward while the trucks returned north to bring up more troops. They were allowed one night of rest before beginning the move south to the front.

The road was dusty. The hot June sun sent a shimmer of heat waves rising from its surface. The two guards scuffed back and forth along their posts, bored and hungry. Each time they met at the central point of their posts they exchanged quick words of speculation.

The woman rounded a bend in the road, saw the sentry and spoke to the child. The girl began to cry.

The sentry looked up, at first warily, then with a bored expression. "Woman, what are you doing here?"

"Please, my daughter is sick. I have been walking a long time."

"Go home. No one is allowed to be in this sector."

She looked at him and motioned to the girl. "Do you have a doctor?"

The soldier laughed. "Our business is taking bodies apart, not putting them together."

"She is very ill. We have come many miles."

"You had better return, wherever it is."

"Seoul," she said emotionlessly.

The soldier was instantly alert. "How did you get here, woman?" He had brought his weapon from his shoulder.

"I have told you. I walked." She motioned over her shoulder, back down the road. "I wished to keep her away from them."

"From whom would you keep her?"

"The capitalists."

The soldier brightened. "What were they doing to her?"

"They planned to make her a prostitute. They said they would take her in two years and begin training her."

He smiled. "What is wrong with her now?"

"I must see a doctor," she replied evasively. "She must be helped."

Plainly, the problem was too great for the sentry. "You should talk with one of the officers." He turned. "Come with me."

He led them off the road, through the underbrush to an encampment area filled with resting soldiers. As they entered the area there were many looks but few comments. After an initial study of the woman and the girl they looked back to the weapons they were cleaning, resumed their conversations.

Near the center of the bivouac an officer looked up. "What are you doing here?" he demanded of the soldier. "You were assigned to sentry duty."

The sentry nodded. "Yes, Comrade. I will return immediately, but this woman says she came here from Seoul."

The officer snapped a quick glance at the woman, then turned back to the sentry. "Return to your post. I shall attend to her."

"Yes, Comrade."

The officer looked again at the woman. "You told him you came from Seoul?"

"Yes. I must have a doctor for my daughter."

The officer ignored the statement. "How did you come here from Seoul?"

"We walked."

His eyes widened in mock surprise. "Just like that. You walked here from Seoul?"

"Yes."

"And I suppose you also walked right through the border. Or did you fly over that?"

"We sneaked through at night."

He scoffed. "That is impossible. No one can sneak through the border. You would have been blown up by the mines, even if you were able to avoid the gunners."

"Please," she repeated. "I must have a doctor for my daughter."

The officer looked at the girl. "What for? What is wrong with her?"

"I do not know. She is very weak. It was necessary for me to carry her much of the way here."

"Why did you not take her to a doctor in Seoul?"

"I was afraid. They said they would take her soon to train her as a prostitute. I was afraid they would take her away from me."

"Then why did you not take her to some of our soldiers closer to the border?"

"I was afraid they would send us back."

"And do you think I will not send you back?"

A look of fear flashed quickly across her face. "Please. Do not make us go back. I want my daughter to be free."

The officer said nothing for several minutes, but looked at them intently. After his assessment he said, "You know there are to be no civilians in this area?"

She still looked frightened. "I did not know. I have not talked with anyone until I saw your sentry. He told me, but I did not know it before."

He looked over his shoulder and beckoned to one of the men. "Take her to the road. Stop the first truck which goes by. Put them in it and send them back to the rear. The higher headquarters can handle it."

"Yes, Comrade." The soldier turned to the woman and motioned her to her feet. They walked together out of the clearing and once more onto the road. The sentries continued to march. In the distance they heard the sound of trucks. The sound grew louder and soon a convoy passed them going south. Then the roar receded and they stood again in the silence of the roadbed. Finally a staff car rounded the bend from the south. The soldier waved his hand for it to stop.

"These women are to be taken to the rear for questioning."

The driver looked at them. "Who are they?"

"Refugees from Seoul, Comrade."

The driver looked at them again with more interest. "Get in," he ordered.

The woman helped the girl carefully into the staff car, then climbed in herself.

The soldier watched them disappear up the road, the dust rising in a cloud behind them.

* * * * * *

Their number reduced, Taejin and his followers were able to move faster. They crossed the vast open plain, moving stealthily, and approached the town of Chorwon. The military buildup was very heavy now. With his group hidden in the foothills, Taejin and the driver slid through the shadows and waited. Above them rose the majesty of the Kumaksan, a towering cone of a mountain standing as a silent sentinel over the valley floor and the tragedy about to unfold there.

All the conversations they heard were of imminent combat. They returned to the band and worked their way southward. Finally, only a short distance from the border, they went into deep hiding, intent on letting the inevitable conflict and its resultant confusion assist their defection to the south.

They did not wait long. Next morning they were awakened before sunrise by the thunder of explosives on the valley floor below them. Taejin crept forward to a vantage point. The valley was a steady glow of fire from the detonations. In the flashes he could make out huge rollers moving slowly southward across the plain. As dawn brightened the sky he shrank back in horror. Each of the rollers was being moved forward across the minefields by dozens of struggling men. They were dressed in the clothing he had worn so long in the mine. Every few moments one of the rollers would explode, rising high in the air to shower the landscape with the water which had been trapped inside. Amid the sprays flew the limbs and torsos of the men. Immediately, another roller would be shifted into position to replace the one lost.

Taejin shuddered. Behind the rollers were line upon line of tanks surrounded by infantrymen. As they proceeded through the minefield their progress was slow, held up by the advancing human sweepers.

At last they broke through. The explosions stopped and a tentative cheer went up from the men pushing the rollers which remained intact. Behind them the tanks and infantry accelerated. As

they passed between the rollers there were rapid, insistent bursts
from the automatic weapons. The prisoners fell like ants. The tanks
moved on, the dust from their treads settling over the bodies in a
final and thankless farewell.

There was heavier firing to the south now. In the low hills the
southern forces were laying down a constant blanket of protective
fires. They were ineffective and soon stopped. The tanks clattered
on into the valleys which pointed toward Seoul.

There was a constant roar of engines in the valley throughout
the day. Long columns of trucks ground southward, laden with
supplies for the advancing army.

Taejin and his companions began moving again. They followed
the invaders south through Pochon, and within a day they had
joined the confused masses of refugees near Uijongbu. Taejin and
the driver shed their uniforms and stripped civilian attire from
bodies which lay along their path. Then, their group disbanded,
they bade each other farewell and turned their eyes toward their
individual dreams of freedom.

THE SOUTH—TAEGU

The new government formed, the nation limped into the new decade. Then, however, the lightning strike from the north plunged the peninsula once more into turmoil.

The road to Taegu was a teeming mass of broken and strained humanity. Women struggled. Children wailed. Men received the questioning glances of the old, the injured and each other.

"I am attempting to rejoin my unit."

The old woman looked at him. "I have watched you all the way from Seoul. I think your unit runs faster than you."

Nambae snapped at her icily. "It is most difficult if one stays to fight. The roads become clogged with the likes of you. I think the communists must drive us into the sea before this is over."

She looked sadly at his civilian clothes but said nothing more.

"I know what you are thinking."

"I think nothing."

He sidled over to her. "It is always the same. We who do something more are credited with less. You think me a deserter."

"I think nothing," she hissed again, moving away from him.

Nambae snorted. "Would you have me captured? Must I be killed because of the slow ones?"

"Would you have it a woman or child instead?" She continued hobbling along as she spoke. "I think they will have no mercy on women or children. No more than. . . ." Her voice trailed off in disgust.

Nambae walked along at her side, looking over the crowd of people. Then he began working his way ahead through the tightly packed bodies.

"Deserter," grumbled an old man.

Nambae ignored him, pushing ahead.

"What is a deserter?" asked a small boy holding the old man's hand.

"A man who has no courage. He would see women and children die rather than fight to save them."

The crowd opened slightly. Nambae tried to shoulder his way through but the hole closed as the refugees weaved from side to side.

"Deserter!" shouted the boy, pointing at him.

Nambae moved toward the side of the road, trying desperately now to escape the stares.

Others were picking up the cry. "Deserter. He is a deserter," they chanted, as if to rid themselves of one more occupant of road space, to claim more for themselves.

He was running down along the side of the road, stumbling in the ditch. The calls were becoming louder, more insistent as they wiggled down the column like the spark on a fuse. Then the first rock struck him. It landed between his shoulders, high up. Pain shot through him but it only drove him faster.

"He is a deserter. Get him."

More rocks and sticks followed the first. He dove for a dike stretching out across the rice paddies abutting the road. "I am not," he protested, calling back over his shoulder. "I must find someone."

"Deserter," they shouted after him scornfully. Some of the older children, brave now at his flight, started after him. Their parents and friends called them back.

Nambae sprang from one dike to another, then slowed. The column was behind him now, crawling along like an enormous worm. He shuddered and began paralleling them. He was able to move faster than they. By sundown he had outdistanced his tormentors. He returned to the road, afraid he would become lost in the darkness.

The movement did not stop at night. They shuffled along in the darkness, daring not stop lest the advancing army behind them catch up. Nambae, tired now, scurried from one to another, peering into faces. At the surprised looks he would grunt and move on to another.

"Why do you stare?" The woman was young and carrying a child.

"I am seeking my wife. I have not seen my wife in many miles."

The woman moved away from him. "I am not your wife. Go away. Bother someone else."

Morning brought the heat again. It was sticky. There were many by the roadside, exhausted, hungry, ill. Occasionally a truck would approach them from the rear, honking its horn steadily as it crept through the throng. The people moved aside slowly, glaring hatefully at those fortunate enough to ride. That they were soldiers made no difference. The soldiers looked out over the crowd in superiority, shouting curses at those who reached for the slats and tried to pull themselves up.

Nambae heard the horn and glanced quickly around. The truck was far back in the sea of people, surrounded but advancing steadily. Worried, he turned to the front again. He had seen one the day before, its occupants plucking young men from the crowd at random. They were treated roughly. He began limping, but still hurried forward. Gradually, so that no one in the group immediately around him would notice, the limp became more pronounced. By the time the truck reached his position he could hardly walk. He ignored them and still kept a searching eye on the crowd ahead.

The truck stopped and two soldiers dropped to the ground, running toward him. He limped on.

"You," shouted one. "Stop."

He looked around in alarm just as an arm reached out toward him and grasped the shoulder of a man next to him.

"What are you doing here?" they demanded.

"I am wounded," protested the man.

"Many are wounded. Come." They dragged him toward the truck.

"Please. I was wounded in the fighting," the man wailed.

"Where?"

"Munsan."

"Where?"

"At Munsan-ni. At the Imjin crossing."

"You must tell us in the truck." They thrust him forward and pointed to the truck bed.

Those around him took no notice. Nambae bowed his head and limped on, working gradually to the side of the road. The truck started forward again. Coming even with him again, it slowed.

"Where is your home?"

Nambae kept moving. He could hear the groans of the other man coming from the truck.

"You. The limping one. Where is your home?"

He looked up slowly, staring at them vacantly.

They dropped to the roadbed. "We have asked you a question. Where is your home?"

He continued to stare vacantly at them, as if not understanding. Slowly, he rubbed his hip.

One soldier reached out and shook him. "You must answer us."

Nambae was aware of the others still pushing by him. He let himself go limp, his head bobbing back and forth uncontrollably.

"What is wrong with him?" asked the other soldier. "Is he ill?"

"Who knows? Who cares?" He shook Nambae again and he closed his eyes, falling to the road.

The soldiers looked perplexed. He was lying in front of the wheel.

"Come. This one is a waste of our time." They started back toward the rear of the truck.

Nambae felt a wave of panic. Would they merely drive over him? He had hoped they would drop him in the ditch.

He felt hands on him and remained limp. Slowly he was towed a few feet to the side by the other refugees. The truck roared off, its horn sounding ominously through the heat.

He lay there a long time, feeling the jolts of feet as people tripped over him. A few kicked him, trying to move the obstruction to the roadside without touching it. Gradually he found himself rolled into the ditch. He tried to relax, then felt himself drifting into sleep.

It was dusk when he awoke. Her hands were on him, shaking him. "Nambae."

He opened his eyes. It was Song. "I was looking for you," he said.

"I thought I saw you in the night. I could not be certain." She glanced down his body. "What has happened?"

"A truck. Soldiers," he whispered.

She leaned closer.

"They have been taking all the young men. They are calling them deserters," he continued.

She nodded. "There have been many. How did you escape them?"

"They beat me," he replied. "I was tired from looking for you. They beat me and threw me here."

She had the child strapped on her back, frail but quiet. "Taegu is not far from us now."

He was morose. "It will be useless. There are many people."

She shrugged. "I think we must get there first. Then it will be time enough to worry about the people."

They waited until it was completely dark and he lay still, Song hovered over him. Then, gradually, he sat up. He climbed unsteadily to his feet and they rejoined those on the road. A day later they were in the city. The sky was black, cloudy. Finally it began to rain, lightly at first. Then the drops were big, heavy. They nestled tightly against the side of a building and waited. The rain did not stop. People were everywhere. No one had a place to go. There was no food.

"The government has moved here," they heard someone say.

"Are they under a roof and eating?" The voice was contemptuous.

"I think they are asking the Americans to feed us and give us tents."

"It is obvious they have done nothing else. Why should they do that?"

"The Americans are landing soldiers in Pusan."

"It is too late. They probably will be pushed into the sea."

"Then why have we come here? If you believe that why have we walked so many miles?"

He did not answer.

Nambae and Song looked at each other, listening.

The woman gestured. "Answer me. Why have we come here?"

The man sneered. "Everyone said they would be stopped. I believed it."

His wife cast a quick glance at Nambae and Song, then lowered her voice. Their words were no longer intelligible through the roar of the rain.

Nambae motioned to Song. "Come."

"Wait," she protested, motioning to the baby. "Where are we going?"

"I think we must find food and shelter."

"I shall keep her here," she replied. "Perhaps I can keep her dry. Come back for us."

"I cannot," he answered. "There are too many people. We must stay together."

She took a worn shawl from her shoulders and wrapped it carefully but ineffectively around the child. "Would you carry her?"

"She is your bastard daughter. I have told you I will not carry her."

"I wish I had not stopped for you," she hissed. "I wish the soldiers had taken you."

He grasped her arm and twisted it. "You will watch your

tongue." He looked around furtively. "I am trying to learn where we can find shelter."

She sneered. "If you had performed your assignment when we came from the north we would have shelter."

He twisted the arm again, sharply.

"Would you have me cry out?" she spat. "I think people would come to help a woman and child being molested by a deserter."

"I am not a deserter," he growled. "You know that."

"They would think you so."

He groaned in anger but released her arm.

"Your brother has done as he was told. He has become established as an officer in the army. I think he must be helping the people's effort greatly now." She laughed at him derisively. "You have done nothing. I think your father must be pleased. Perhaps he would recall you so he could express his pleasure."

"My father!" he shot back. "What do I care for my father? He has done nothing for me."

"What would you have him do? He allowed you to escape to the south. Is that not enough?"

"He forced me to keep you," he replied coldly. "He forced me to keep a whore with a bastard child. I do not care what he thinks."

She smiled, but without humor. "He will think you lazy, ineffective. You will care what he thinks when they arrest you."

"He has betrayed me," he snapped. "Come."

They started off through the rain, droplets pelting their shoulders in fury.

"Where are we going?" she asked again.

"I think we must find government buildings. They will have food and news there first."

"They will not let us in," she taunted, confident now of her advantage, knowing he dared not hurt her. "If you had infiltrated the government as you were ordered we would now be inside. We would have been brought here in an airplane."

They lapsed into silence. The water was deepening. They waded on, Nambae continuing his heavy limp to discourage suspicion.

An hour later they were near a compound. The crowds were heavy, unprotected. There was little movement now. Ahead, the people were packed tightly against the gates. There were cries of pain, mingled with moans of hopelessness.

"Attention!" blared a loudspeaker. "I must have your attention."

The crowd shifted uneasily and the noise did not subside.

"The American soldiers have landed in force at Pusan. The communist offensive has stalled. Food and shelter are being transported here to Taegu. You must disperse and be patient."

Mixed emotions echoed through the crowd. Nambae looked anxiously at his wife.

"The offensive has stalled," repeated the loudspeaker. "Food and shelter. . . ."

"Do you suppose it is true?" Song was clearly worried.

"I think they do not know. Perhaps they are merely trying to avoid a riot. There are too many people here. They are hungry and cold from the rain. It would not be difficult for a riot to be started."

"What will it mean if it is true?"

He looked at her glumly, water pouring from his face, but said nothing.

"Perhaps it will end it," she ventured.

"It will not end it. They may put food in our bellies, but it will not end it."

The loudspeaker was repeating its message over and over. They did not hear it. The rain closed like a curtain around their hate and speculation.

* * * * * *

Hong walked wearily into the small apartment. "I am tired."

Yong Cha looked at him, only slightly with understanding. "I think many are tired. We must consider those in the streets. They have no shelter, no food."

It made no impression. "Many of them are deserters. They

wail that conditions are bad but I see no one carrying weapons to fight off the invaders from the north." He crossed to the bed. "They are merely leeches awaiting a gift of food or shelter."

"If they had not come here I think the communists would have them by now. The men would be dead, the women raped."

"They are not the only tired ones, my wife. We have been attending meetings and conferences all day and half the night planning the survival of our nation."

"But we did not walk to Taegu. We came here by airplane." She shuddered. "I do not like to ride airplanes."

"There are most valuable benefits in my position. As a senior member of the government I am dry and eating. You are my wife and may thereby share such benefits." He stretched out on the pad. "When the Americans. . . ."

"The Americans," she spat, ignoring the obvious hint for a massage. "I think you worship the Americans. They have made us wealthy but they could not protect us. I am sick of hearing about the Americans. Where are they now?"

"They have landed at Pusan."

"It is always the same story. They are doing something for us in another place. I have not seen one since the invasion."

Hong was laboriously patient. "The first secretary has told me himself. We shall return to Seoul soon." His enthusiasm was building. "I think there must be much more work than before. Seoul is a shambles from the communists. All of it must be rebuilt."

Her silence conveyed her skepticism.

"And the orphans," he exhilarated, not noticing. "An American was here touring with Chi in the beginning. He was most curious how we could have so many orphans without having a shooting war. Yet he has given us much money on principle." He laughed. "Now we have his shooting war. He should be satisfied. I think the Americans will create many orphans through all of this."

She was unmoved. "Will some of them be ours?"

He ignored the question in his exhausted giddiness. "Look out the window," he urged. "Look at them, the sick and wounded displaced in this rain. Many of them will die." He waved tiredly at the pane. "There are dead out there even now. There they lie, covered with water and being trampled by those still standing. Who is causing such suffering? It is the Americans you say I worship." He scoffed. "I do not worship the Americans. I am happy they are here because they have made me a wealthy man. My home will always be a place of beauty, my children educated. But, ah, the Americans. Now they must do more. They have not armed us well enough and our people have been driven to become refugees. Because they have not brought food and shelter to us our people die in the streets." He smiled with satisfaction. "This time I think there can be little question. It shall not be necessary for us to tell them what someone else has done to orphan our children. We shall have only to remind them of their own negligence."

"I think we may never see Seoul again," she said, unconvinced.

"Of course we shall see Seoul again," he snapped. "The one thing the Americans fear more than anything else is communism. They have constructed some very important bases in Japan. They cannot afford to have the communists surrounding those bases by owning this entire peninsula. They must have this buffer, this place to fight which is away from their expensive bases. Korea, to them, is a place with which to purchase time." He shook his head. "They will be willing to spend much money regaining our nation. They will purchase the friendship of our people." He rose from the bed and began pacing the floor. "After the fighting is over there will be many more American dollars. They are learning a most bitter lesson. Next time they will arm us properly to prevent it happening again. They will save their face by giving us everything. We will be able to ask for anything and receive it."

Yong Cha looked at him anxiously. "Suppose they do not win. Suppose the communists really do push our armies into the sea, ours and the Americans. There will be nothing left for us. As a senior member of the government, as you call yourself, you will be imprisoned at the very least. More than likely you will be shot."

Her husband smiled at her confidently. "They flew very few of us here from Seoul. Those who flew here are to be evacuated if we lose."

"Where would we go?" she asked, aghast.

"They would take us to the United States."

Her eyes widened. "The United States? And what would we do there? All our money would be gone. We would be simple refugees like those in the square. What would we do?"

"We would live most comfortably. I have much money invested outside our country. If the Americans lose our land for us I think they will be most generous with reparation funds for those of us who are displaced. We shall live very well, as did other members of our government during the past war. They were most comfortable in the United States."

Yong Cha was confused. "And what of them?" she asked, motioning toward the throng in the streets.

Hong shrugged. "They do nothing useful now. I think they are little good to anyone."

She was shocked. "How can you speak in such a way?" She stared at him, at a loss for words.

"Are they fighting to keep themselves free? No. They look for a handout. They wail their fear of the communists, nothing more.

She walked slowly to the window, looking down at the milling sea of faces. Near the wall she focused on one woman, water pouring down her face as she looked up at the window. The baby on her back was slumped to one side. Yong Cha wondered if it were still alive. Silently, she lifted her hand and waved to the woman. The woman seemed to brighten for a moment as she slowly lifted her arm to wave in return. Then she merely stared at Yong Cha. Hong's wife gasped in surprise and tears began running down her cheeks. "My friend," she said, quietly, then louder. "It is one of the attendants from my bath an Inchon."

Hong remained where he was. "You must come away from the window."

"But it is my friend. She is there in the square."

He seemed not to care. "There are many people in the square.

You have seen it. Now you will come away from the window. I wish a massage."

She turned and looked back down at her old friend. The woman's look was pleading. Yong Cha ran to her husband. "She was my friend, our friend. We must not leave her there with no one to help her. Please?"

"My wife, there are many out there who are friends of those in here. Many of them have relatives in here. It is one of the realities each of us must face. We are at war."

"Then you will not bring her in?"

"I cannot bring her in." He beckoned. "Come. I would like a massage."

She stared at him for a long moment, then reached for a shawl. "Where are you going?"

"I shall go to her." She started for the door.

"You will stay here."

"She has a baby on her back."

He was unmoved. "You will stay here in this room. I have said I wish a massage."

She began to cry harder. "If it were not for the bath I would not be your wife." She watched him for a softening which did not come. Sadly she walked back to the window, the shawl dragging hopelessly behind her. She looked down at the place in the crowd once more. Her friend was gone.

"I have told you to come away from the window," said Hong again.

She turned to him, flashing anger now. "How can you care so little for them? You have become a very cold man."

"I have told you to come here."

"When I first knew you it was different. You had compassion for those not as fortunate as you. You cared for the sorrow of the people at the basin." The tears still poured from her eyes. "You no longer have love."

He rose. "You will come and massage me. I have worked hard for them. Now I am tired."

"You are an animal. I will not come to you."

He sprang at her, equally angry now. "Stop this talk. I have given you much." He grabbed her, shoving her to the mat.

She rolled away, trying to escape his rage, but he threw her back.

"No," she cried. "You must not."

He tore at her clothes, then at his own. "You call me an animal. You will be taken by an animal!"

"No!"

She bit him and he slapped her, hard. Then, with grunts of exertion, he forced her back, plunging into her. She tried to dislodge him but he was too powerful. Finally, she closed her eyes and felt his explosion, insistent, consuming. It seemed forever before he was spent. He rolled off her, panting.

Quickly she drew her torn clothing over her, covering her nakedness. "You are an animal," she hissed. "I hate you, Hong."

"Then go!" he raged. "Go out to the vermin in the gutter. I will have you no more. You are no longer my wife." He grabbed other of her clothes and thrust them at her. "Get out! I am well rid of you."

She stood and dressed, slowly, pensively. Then, a small bundle tucked under her arm, she walked sadly from the building into the rain.

* * * * * *

"But I am a national director." Chi was outraged.

"I am most sorry. My orders are to let no one in." The soldier was embarrassed but firm.

Chi made a move to push by but the heavy gate clanked closed in his face. He stood back, shaking, wet, now lost of his face. "The heads of our government will hear of this," he shouted. With a wave of his good fist he shoved his way violently back to the car and ordered the jin to leave the square.

The jin blew the horn and started to inch forward.

"I have said you must hurry," shouted Chi.

"I cannot run over these people."

"Run over them if you must," replied Chi. "I shall go to the Taegu Orphanage immediately."

The jin rolled forward, still sounding the horn. Occasionally he bumped a pedestrian, but gently. The people moved to one side, looking hatefully at the car and its occupants. It took almost an hour to get free of the inner city. Even then the crowds remained about them, sloshing aimlessly toward unknown destinations.

At the orphanage a huge mob waited, as if congealed, in front of the gate. The jin blew the horn incessantly as they crept through and up to the opening. Chi got out and banged on the gate.

"No one may come in," shouted a frantic voice from inside.

"I may come in," replied Chi testily, angrily, above the splashing of the rain. "I am Director Chi."

There was a long pause. At last the gate sneaked open a crack and a face peered out at him through the rain. With a look of surprise the man spread the opening slightly wider to admit him.

He squeezed through. "My car must come in also."

The man shook his head vehemently. "If we do I think everyone in the crowd will force his way in."

"If we leave it out there," snapped the director, "they will steal it. They will kill my driver and steal my car. You will bring it in."

The man, confused, motioned for some others and moved toward the gate. Two slipped out when it was barely open and began pushing the wading crowd to the rear. Then, motioning to the jin, they swung the gate wider. The car splashed forward through the opening, the crowd close behind. The men tried to push the gate closed. It was no use. The standing water slowed its swing and the refugees surged into the courtyard, racing for the cover of the building. The leaders darted for the kitchen house. The staff was too small to stop them.

"You see?" shouted the orphanage manager to Chi above the roar of the people and the rain. Now we must lose everything."

Chi was seething. "Where is your telephone?"

"It is in my office. I think we will be unable to reach it now."

"Take me there," ordered Chi.

They began elbowing their way to the office in the main building. Those in the crowd treated them no differently from others. When they pushed they were pushed in return. It took a long time to reach the building and longer, once there, to fight their way down the corridor to the office. The door was jammed open, people dripping water on the floor. The desk was a shambles, much of the furniture broken.

Grunting angrily, Chi forced his way to the desk and reached for the phone. "I wish to be connected with the military compound," he shouted into the receiver.

"You must have a priority call to be connected," advised a voice.

"I am the National Director of Orphanages," shouted Chi authoritatively. "You will connect me with the compound."

It was fifteen minutes before he had Hong on the line.

"Where are you?" asked Hong.

"I am in the Taegu Orphanage. We have been overrun."

There was a hesitant silence on the other end. "Are they communists?"

"They are the thieves who are vandalizing the city. They have broken in and taken over the orphanage. They have stolen the food and are jammed into every room in the buildings."

Hong was irritated. "Why have you allowed this to happen? You reported to me in Seoul that each of your institutions was most secure against thieves and vandals."

"But I cannot guard against riots," shouted Chi. "I think you must send me soldiers to drive them out of here."

There was silence for some moments on the other end of the line.

"Are you there, Hong?"

"Yes, Chi, I am here. I am trying to decide what you must do about your mess."

"I have told you. You must send me soldiers."

"I think it is not that easy," answered Hong. "Perhaps you should make an announcement. You must tell them the Americans are setting up tents and serving food to the refugees in Taegu. Tell them the relief is on the other side of the city."

"And if they refuse to go?"

"Are you serving them food there?"

"Already it has been stolen and eaten by these insurgents. They captured the kitchen first."

"Chi, you must be calm. You must act sensibly. Tell them food and shelter is being provided on the other side of the city. Be certain to tell them the Americans are doing it. If they arrive there and find nothing they will blame the Americans, not our government. By the time most of them have departed your staff should be able to eject the ones who remain. I think you must make them understand there will be no more food coming to the orphanage."

"I shall do it. Now, after they have gone when may I expect more food for the children and the staff?"

Hong paused on the other end. "I have just said, Chi. There will be no more food for the orphanage until the Americans supply it."

Chi shrugged inconsequentially, certain he would be elsewhere. "I have one other problem. I must enter that compound. I must talk with you. I have tried to enter but they would not allow me through the gate."

"I am sorry, Chi. I have no control over such things."

"Do you mean I cannot get inside to see you?"

"I think you cannot until the Americans remove these refugees. If you have any other questions you must ask me by telephone."

"Are the Americans really coming?"

"Chi, I am told they are landing in Pusan now. I know nothing more. I think the first troops must go directly into the fighting."

"How am I to eat in the meantime?"

"I think you must eat just as the children for whom you are caring."

Chi, dejected, cradled the receiver. "I must have your attention," he shouted. "I must have your attention."

The buzz of the milling people continued, enveloping and ignoring him.

* * * * * *

A vast sea of tents had been pitched in the valley south of Taegu, cradled protectively by the soaring peaks. The thousands of refugees had migrated to their shelter, anxious for a bed away from the rains, a semblance of order in their chaotic lives.

Convoys rolled by relentlessly from Pusan, carrying fresh troops northward toward the front. The refugees waited, resigned to the routines of the camp until they would be allowed to return to their homes and lives by the retreat of the communist armies.

Order came gradually, with housekeeping tasks assigned liberally, yet accepted willingly. Inherently an industrious people, they had been ill at ease with idleness, thirsted in their discomfort for a means to progress, improve their woeful condition.

Song was one of the first to be assigned duty in an enormous kitchen tent. She had been reluctant to leave her daughter with Nambae while she worked, so was relieved when he, too, was placed on a work detail digging sanitation pits. Her daughter was placed in the care of another work detail, made up of women assigned for that purpose.

She arrived at the mess tent early. She had only begun to fill a tub in which to steam rice when she heard his voice.

"Song!" It was called across the tent from the other side, away from her.

She turned quickly, surprised that anyone would know her here. Waving, hurrying through the fire pits toward her, she saw him. "Taejin!"

Slowly she lowered the pail with which she had been ladling, tears welling into her eyes.

He slowed as he approached her. "Song." He looked around warily. "How have you come here?"

She led him to the side, away from the others. "It has been so long. I have walked here from Seoul."

Their hands touched, but only briefly. He looked around again, then back at her. "And what of the brothers? Is Nambae here?"

"Yes, but he is working on the other side of the camp. He will not be here now, but I think he must come here later to eat." Her eyes searched his face. "How can you be here? You were sent away to prison."

He shook his head. "I was told you had come to the south, but that you had come with the farmer's sons."

"Yes. The farmer arranged for us to be transported to Seoul. We were to become agents for the north."

"And the farmer was tried. Did you know that? He was tried in the courts and sentenced to prison, but it was all a trick. The truth was that he was rewarded."

"Rewarded? How was he rewarded?" She was searching his face.

"He was promoted from the People's Committee in Hochon. He became the warden of the prison at Hyesan where I was sent."

Her face twisted with anxiety. "Did he see you? Was he cruel to you?"

"He did not know I was there until my mother came to visit me."

"Your mother?" She was incredulous. "How could your mother have visited you?"

"It was forbidden, but she was allowed to think she was sneaking in. It was another trick. The farmer heard the whole conversation. She was murdered after she left, and my father was executed in his prison."

Her eyes filled with tears. "Then how have you come here? I do not understand."

"They put us on a train, all the prisoners. They brought us to the border. They used the prisoners to clear the mine fields when they attacked. All the prisoners were killed."

"But you were not."

"Yes, I was not. I was fortunate and escaped from the train. After that I worked my way to the south behind the invading army."

She smiled, one of the first, she realized, in many months. "I had thought I would never see you again, Taejin. I had thought you would never see your daughter."

His mouth fell open. "My daughter?"

Now a twinkle shone across her face. "Oh, Taejin. I think I have never been so happy in my life. Yes, you have a daughter, a happy memory from the day in my father's warehouse."

"What is her name?"

"Her name is Sookee."

He gazed at her, his eyes damp with emotion. "That was my mother's name."

"I know."

"Where is she? I must see her."

"She is with the *yumos*. The nurses." She paused a moment and her face became serious. "It may be difficult for you to see her. I think Nambae would cause you trouble if he knew you were here."

"Yes. After I escaped they put a price on my head in the north. I think they would like to execute me." He reached and touched her arm. "I must see her. There must be a way for it to happen."

"Nambae has given me much trouble because of her," she blurted. "He did not know until after I was forced to marry him. He was very angry. He tried to have his father annul the marriage."

"And the farmer would not?"

"Yes. He would not. He would not jeopardize his career with the People's Committee."

Taejin's questioning became more intense now. "You said you were brought to the south to become agents. Have you done it?"

"My husband's brother, Kwon, has done it. He had documents forged and became an officer in the army of the south. I think he must cause much trouble in the war. He will cause many of the southern soldiers to die."

"And what of you? What of Nambae?"

"No. Nambae was to infiltrate their government, become an informer. He has not done it."

"Why?"

"He is not intelligent. He cannot think of a way to do it. Each time he devised a plan it was bad. I told him each of the plans was bad."

"But if he had been caught. . . ."

"I would have been sent to prison too. I feared for my. . . ." She paused and smiled. "I feared for our daughter." She became serious again. "I feared that if they arrested me because I was Nambae's wife I might never see her again. I was afraid Sookee would die from neglect."

He nodded.

"I wish I could have done it," she moaned. "I wish I could have let him be arrested. I would have been free of him."

"No. You did the right thing. Our daughter is more important." He grinned. "After all, if he does not perform his mission perhaps he will be taken back to the north by the other agents and disciplined."

"But would they not take me back, too?"

"Perhaps so. We must think about this. We must be certain you and Sookee are safe."

"We must also think of your safety. If Nambae were able to have you returned to the north I think his father would not be as angry that he has not infiltrated their government."

It had brought him back to the present. "Yes," he said, looking around cautiously again. "I must be careful that Nambae does not see me."

More of the other workers were arriving now, the tent becoming a bustle of activity. Song watched them. "I think I must begin working. I do not know what they will do if I am a shirker. What work do you do?"

"They have me preparing the meat, but if Nambae will come here I think I must ask for different work. I cannot risk him seeing me."

"He cannot harm you here, Taejin. He is alone. He has no contact with other agents here. If he had them I would know. His contacts are only in Seoul."

"But still he would make things difficult for you. And for Sookee."

Now Song became anxious. "Please do not ask them to put you to work far from me."

"No. I shall only ask for work which is out of sight when the people come to eat." He thought for a moment. "I have been learning English."

"How have you done that?"

"A friend gave me a book they were issuing the soldiers who would invade the south. It teaches the Koreans to speak English." He was talking rapidly now, a ray of hope on his face. "Perhaps I could get work with the Americans who are supplying our food."

She saw a foreman coming toward her. "Yes. Try it, Taejin. But tell me where I may find you."

The foreman had reached them now. "You must work, woman. You cannot stay in the camp if you do not work."

She nodded obediently and returned to her work.

After the next meal Taejin returned. "I saw him. I saw Nambae."

"Did he see you?" she asked, cautious.

"No. I have been given new work. The Americans call me a 'KATUSA,' an assistant to their army. I will work with the Americans who bring the food in the trucks. I will help our people understand them."

"Do you know English that well?"

"No, but I know a little now. If I work with them I will learn more. I think not many of our people can talk with them now. I can do more than most."

She smiled, proud of him.

"Where is your tent?" he asked.

"I think you must not go there."

"Yes. I must not. But I must know where it is so I may avoid it."

She described it.

"Good. Mine is on the other side of the camp. And Nambae. Where does he work?"

"He digs sanitation pits. They are doing it beyond my tent."

"I will watch them. If they move I will know."

"Yes. You said it would be best for Sookee and me if he does not see you. You are right. I had not thought of that. I thought only of the danger to you."

He was quiet for a long moment. "I am a happy man, Song. Finding you has made me a happy man."

"I am happy too, Taejin, but I will be happier when you can see your daughter."

"I must see her soon," he said emphatically. Then, reaching out, he touched her hand quickly, looked longingly into her eyes, and left the kitchen.

In the ensuing days they saw each other regularly. He was moved to another tent closer to the mess tent so that he could be awakened whenever the American supply trucks arrived. While it meant he worked irregular hours, he was able to be off duty at odd times, thereby enabling him to keep track of Nambae and his work location. His pursuit of the English language, though laborious, paid dividends. He studied hard and displayed good adaptability. The Americans who came regularly to the camp grew to like him, to admire him.

"Nambae has formed a habit pattern," said Song several days after their reunion. "It is time to begin planning how you may see your daughter."

He laughed, excited. "Tell me. What is Nambae doing?"

"He has made friends with some of the refugees on his work team. They have found a place to get *maekju*, beer. When their work is finished each day they go together and drink." She smiled, then broke into a giggle. "Always I have not liked it when he would drink beer, but now I think it gives us the opportunity for you to see her. We can meet when he is drinking with his friends."

"Can we do it today?"

"Wait here at the end of the work. I will bring Sookee here with me. We must be alert, though. We cannot afford for Nambae to catch us together."

Taejin was at the kitchen when Song finished her shift. She merely glanced at him as she made her way quickly into the throng of tents.

He waited more than an hour. At last he was certain she would not come. He shuffled back and forth in the walkway, frustrated that Nambae might not have had his customary rendezvous with his friends. At last he began walking away toward his tent. He had gone only a few steps when she called quietly to him from between two tents.

His heart leaped as he caught first sight of the child beside her holding tightly to her hand. She looked up at her mother. Song smiled and nodded to her, dropping her hand. The child looked again at Taejin, then reached up for her mother's hand once more, drawing close to her leg.

Taejin stood where he was lest he alarm her. Song began walking toward Taejin, the girl hanging back uncertainly.

"It is all right. He is a good man," said her mother reassuringly. "Come."

At last the child allowed herself to be led to him. He knelt and smiled at her. "Sookee, *Anyanghashimnika.*"

She started to smile, then hid her face quickly in her mother's robe.

"Hello, Sookee," he said again.

She peeked at him, now the hint of a smile broadening for a moment into a wide grin.

He held out his arms to her and she looked again up at her

mother's face. Song was smiling. "It is all right, Sookee," she said
again.

Finally, reassured, she took the three tentative steps to him.
He enveloped her in his arms, burying his face in her hair. "I love
you, Sookee," he whispered.

Her arms gripped him, but only for a moment. Then, looking
back at her mother, she turned and fled to the comfort and safety
of her robe.

Still kneeling, he looked up into Song's face and tears were
running down his cheeks.

"Tomorrow we shall meet again," said Song. "We will come
here again at the same time and we can have a few more minutes
together."

He nodded, rising. "Thank you, Song."

Each day they repeated the visits. Then, one evening, he asked
her, "Does she know? Have you told her who I am?"

She shook her head. "Not yet. I am afraid she may speak of
you at the wrong time."

The child was sitting atop his shoulders, giggling happily. "It
is good," he replied. "But one day she must know. One day we
must take her away together and have her to ourselves."

A look of apprehension flitted across her face. "I think the
farmer's sons would seek me out. When they found me with you
they would send us back to the north. The farmer would kill us
all."

He slid his arm about her shoulder. "We shall not be in Taegu
forever. One day we shall all return to Seoul. That is the day we
must plan for. We can make our plans now."

She leaned against him and her arm was around his waist.
Sookee sensed the closeness and reached for her mother's hair. Song
reached up and took the child's hand with her other hand. They
stood there, caught in the odd embrace for several minutes. At last
Taejin reached up and lifted Sookee off his shoulders.

"Where is your home in Seoul?"

"We lived near the East Gate. I do not know where we will live when we return. I think the home we had may not be there any longer. I think Nambae will try harder to make a contact when we return."

Taejin agreed. "I think he must. With the fighting they need his help. But we must plan. How are we to find each other in Seoul?"

"You do not know the city."

"Yes. I do not."

"Then we must pick a landmark. A major one."

He listened, not answering.

"Nambae will have to go to the government every day. If I can live near the East Gate I can watch for you while he is away."

"I do not know when I will get there."

"I will watch for you, Taejin. I will not give up."

"Yes. We must never give up. I must never lose you again."

"Good," she smiled. "If I must I shall watch for you every day for the rest of my life."

THE SOUTH—RETURN TO SEOUL

The parade had gradually formed once more. The long lines, so recently creeping to the safety of Taegu and Pusan, began weaving their way northward again.

Chi sat in the rear of his car, shouting incessantly at the jin to hurry, sometimes leaning from the window to scream a refugee from their path. Snow was falling. Only the thousands of feet scuffing it away kept the road visible.

"Hurry," shouted Chi.

"I am trying, Chi. They refuse to move."

Chi leaned from his window again. "If you do not move aside we shall shoot you. I am a national director. You must allow us to pass."

The shouts made little impression.

"We shall shoot. Do you hear?"

Suddenly a hand reached out and grabbed him. "Whom would you shoot? I think you must shoot half our nation."

Chi looked uncertainly into the angry face. The man was dirty, his clothes mere rags. "I must go to Seoul quickly," he replied, uneasy. "I am a national director. The government needs me in Seoul."

"If they needed you badly I think they would have flown you to Seoul with the others." The man gripped him more tightly.

"Perhaps it is more a matter of you needing the government to protect you."

Chi swallowed hard. The man was trotting along at the same speed as the car, still gripping him tightly.

"Today you need the protection of Seoul so you threaten to shoot us because we walk. I remember you well, Chi. Ten years ago you wished to escape the quay wall at Inchon. You made demands on us then. You made promises, and people were shot." The man turned his glare on the jin. "Stop. Stop the car."

The jin glanced back uncertainly at the man.

"Tell him to stop," the man growled at Chi.

"Stop," squealed Chi in the terror of his recognition. The car ground from its crawl to a stop and the man reached for the door handle.

"What are you doing?"

"I shall help you out." The door swung open and Chi was yanked from the seat to the roadbed. The jin had leaped from behind the wheel and circled the car. "I am most sorry, Chi, but I must agree with them. You are no longer interested in the oppressed people. You have interest only in Chi." He did not wait, but turned and disappeared into the crowd.

The man was leering down at Chi. "Now, I think it is time for you to begin shooting."

Chi flinched with lost face. "I have no weapon."

"Oh," laughed the man. "He has planned to shoot us without a weapon." He looked back at the cripple. "I think you must plan for the soldiers to do it as before."

A crowd had formed about them, enjoying the diversion.

"Please," whined Chi. "I must go to Seoul quickly. I am needed there."

"Then I think you must walk quickly. Perhaps you should run. You will be very late arriving if you continue to lie in the road."

The people laughed.

"Where are the sick ones?" shouted the man. "Bring the sick ones to me. They shall ride in this fine car."

A buzz of voices washed through the crowd and some came limping forward.

"No. You cannot take my car."

"Already I have taken it," snapped the man. "It is not yours any longer."

"But it belongs to the government," protested Chi.

"Then I think the government will wish to help these people return to their homes." He was assisting the tattered derelicts into the car.

"I shall report you to the government," threatened Chi.

The man ignored him, circling the car and sliding behind the wheel.

"What is your name?" Chi shouted in frustration.

"Remember Inchon," replied the man. "You had no difficulty remembering any of us there." The car rolled forward, the crowd parting freely to let it through.

Chi scrambled to his feet and looked around for the jin. The man was nowhere to be seen. The people pressed around him, laughing, chiding. "Where have you stolen the car?"

Chi looked about him in alarm. "I have not stolen it. The car was issued to me. I am a national director."

"You are a thief," cried someone back in the crowd.

"A thief," they chanted, picking up the accusation. "He is a thief."

Chi was frantic, casting about wildly for an escape.

"A thief," the people continued.

He broke and tried to push through, away from the ring of faces. They shoved him back.

"You must allow me to go," he screamed. "You have stolen my car. Now you must leave me alone."

"We have stolen his car. We have stolen from a thief," laughed one of those shoving him.

Chi shrank back, now afraid they meant to kill him. They pressed in.

"This way." It was whispered close to his ear. "Come." He felt the tug on his arm and backed away with it, still watching them. "Down now. Quickly."

He dropped to his knees as the group surged forward. There was a tangle of bodies over him, then past him. "Follow me," whispered the voice again.

Chi scrambled to his feet and began running, aware now of the other as man more than voice. They dashed back along the road toward Taegu. Gradually the shouts fell away behind them. The faces of those through whom they ran were open, questioning. At last they slowed and Chi looked at his rescuer.

"I am not a thief," he asserted. "I am a national director."

The man shrugged. "I think it does not matter. Would you have been more dead, or less, because of what you may be?"

"Who are you?"

"My name is Nambae."

"Why did you rescue me from them?"

Nambae shrugged again. "I have been chased. They stoned me in the summer."

"What did you do?"

"I ran."

"But what did you do that caused them to stone you?"

Nambae looked at him levelly. "I have not asked you if their charges were true."

Chi was apologetic. "I am most sorry. They would have killed me."

"What is your name?"

"I am Chi. I am the National Director of Orphanages."

Nambae nodded, neither believing nor questioning, yet interested that Chi might be legitimate. Perhaps this could be his gate into the government. "I think now you are Chi, a refugee no different from the rest of us."

"How shall I go to Seoul?"

Nambae laughed. "I think you must walk like everyone else."

"We shall stay together," said Chi. "We shall be safer if there are two of us."

"Four."

Chi looked around them, then glanced over his shoulder. No one looked at them. "Four?"

"My wife and her daughter are with me."

"Where are they?"

"They are ahead, where you lost your car. They will wait for us."

"They saw what happened?"

"Yes."

They walked on in silence, then saw Song coming toward them, the child on her back. "Is he hurt?"

"No."

She looked at Chi. "They are animals."

"Yes."

She looked at his clothes, fine but now dirty, stained.

"They have stolen my car."

"I saw." She turned to Nambae. "They are far along the road now. I think we may go safely."

Nambae shook his head. "I think we must wait."

They sat in the snow by the roadside and watched the end of day. The grayness of the storm reached gradually into the night. There were no lights to illuminate the falling flakes. It was cold and the road was friendless. At last Nambae rose. "We shall go now. They should be far ahead and we must move or freeze."

They climbed from the ditch in which they had rested, Song clutching her daughter tightly against the cold.

"How long must we walk to reach Seoul?" asked Chi.

"Perhaps a week. Perhaps longer."

"How do we eat?"

Nambae laughed in scorn. "When the American trucks come past they throw us food. It is not enough."

"And what of sleep? How do we sleep?"

Nambae looked at him incredulously. "What do you expect?"

"I have only asked."

We rest by the roadside, just as we did back there. Some take longer for the trip than others." He paused. "Many will never get there at all."

They plodded through the rest of the night in silence. As daylight came they heard the sound of the trucks to their rear.

"Food," said Nambae.

Chi looked back. The crowd was swarming around each of the trucks, everyone trying to be first, get a double ration. As the trucks rolled forward the people grasped at the hoops or rigging trying to feel, if only for a moment, the warmth of the exhaust.

Nambae took Song's elbow, pointing. "There. Beside that tree. Wait there."

She nodded and walked faster to get into position.

"We have tried many things. This has worked most effectively before. When you get a ration, throw it to her."

"What about mine?"

"She will give to us from what we throw."

"What will it be?"

"American food. They give us cans of American food."

"Cans?"

Nambae looked at him as if at a child. "If you do not know I think you must wait and see."

"I know what they are. We receive them at the orphanages. How do you open them here?"

"You must not worry about it," said Nambae, looking back over his shoulder. The lead truck was close now, began to slow. "Get hold of the tailgate and hang on," ordered Nambae. "We must be among the first when they stop."

The horn blared and the truck rumbled by, the white star insignia on the doors.

"Now." Nambae reached out and grabbed a chain hanging from the rear of the vehicle. "Come."

Chi reached up, missed, and tried again. Nambae reached back and grabbed his collar. "Hold on!"

The truck continued on for several yards. The tree was close, over beside the road. The refugees grunted and inched closer. Men in the rear of the truck began handing down cans of combat rations, one can per person.

"You!" one of them shouted to a woman. "No more. You're hiding them."

The woman looked up at him and spat. The soldier looked over at her ominously. As he did, Nambae reached up boldly, scooping half a dozen cans toward Chi. With the return motion he swept up as many more for himself.

"Down," he shouted. Chi was confused, but dove quickly under the truck.

"Where the hell did they go?" shouted the American in disgust.

"Food," cried the crowd, in English. "Food."

The soldier shrugged and began again, handing out one can per person in the snowy dawn.

Nambae and Chi crept forward under the truck until they were under the cab. Nambae motioned obliquely forward. "Behind them. We must go behind the crowd. Meet me at the tree. Quickly." He rolled out and scrambled up to run for the roadside ahead, then doubled back for the tree. The refugees ignored him.

"Get those two." It was a voice from the cab. The call was useless for he shouted in English.

Chi was running hard, afraid the American would follow him. He dove across the ditch, then looked back. No one was near him, even noticing. He stopped, caught his breath and walked to the tree. Nambae already was there, opening a can and gulping down the contents. Song was helping Sookee.

Nambae looked up and smiled fleetingly as Chi approached. "She has the opener."

Chi looked at Song. She held out a can to him. "Here."

"Thank you." He took it and began drinking a cold stew from the container.

"You must wait before eating more," cautioned Nambae. "They come only once each day. If you eat it all now I think you will be hungry later and have nothing."

Chi did not reply. The food was strange to his taste, almost unpalatable. When he was finished Nambae handed him two more cans.

"Carry them in your pocket. They are for later."

They set out again, working their way through the people on the road.

"I have a suggestion," said Chi late in the day.

They looked at him, waiting.

"I have an orphanage in Gimchon. It is on this side road. We shall go there. They will provide us a good meal. We shall sleep on a hot floor tonight. Tomorrow perhaps their vehicle can take us all the way into Seoul."

Song looked hopeful.

"What will we do when the refugees take that one away from us tomorrow?" asked Nambae.

"They will not. We shall go to Seoul by another route."

"Do you know this part of the country well?'

Chi nodded. "We shall go north to Wonju, then on near Chunchon. From there we shall go west to Seoul. I think there will be very few people on the road if we go that way."

Song nodded silently.

Without a word they turned off the route of the refugees and began making their way between the mountains toward Gimchon. The sky became darker and the weather developed a wind which cut through them as it whirled down the valley from the north. Then, before them, they saw the town. They stopped, looking at it briefly, then Chi stepped out in the lead, beckoning. Half an hour later he was knocking on a large wooden gate.

"Who is there?" The voice was young, frightened.

"I am Chi, National Director of Orphanages."

There was some scuffing of feet in the courtyard and they could hear the bolt being released.

"Wait." It was a call from farther back, probably at the building. "What are you doing?" The voice was that of a woman.

"Director Chi is outside," replied the child.

"Wait," the woman called again. There was silence inside the gate, then the sound of approaching footsteps. "I have told you never to open the gate to anyone without asking me," she admonished. "There are many bandits."

The gate opened only a crack and a crudely bandaged face peeked out at them. At sight of Chi a choked cry issued from its folds and the gate swung wide. One sleeve of the woman's torn sweater hung limp and empty.

The three walked in and Nambae secured the gate behind him.

"Where is my manager?" demanded Chi with hardly a look at the woman.

"Gone," she replied.

He wheeled on her. "Gone? Do you mean he has run off?"

"No. The communists came." She was crying, weaving in weakness. The bandage on her face was dirty and crusted with dried blood.

"Did they kill him?"

Song approached the woman and began helping her toward the building. "Come. I think we must talk inside. She is not well."

Chi moved up beside them. "Did they kill him?" he asked again.

"No," sobbed the woman. "They took him, but I think he is probably dead by now."

They climbed the steps into the building, a group of small children hovering quietly around them, watching and listening.

"Then who is managing the orphanage?"

The woman stopped, steadying herself with her one arm on Song. "I am."

"And the others? There were four besides the manager."

The woman looked at him, a note of dislike replacing her earlier relief at seeing him. "When the communists came they turned the children out. They raped and killed two of the other women. They took the manager and the third woman when they left."

"And you?"

"They believed me dead. They were most cruel." She turned

and hobbled with Song to a room filled with the stench of human waste. "They have raped and killed the older orphans."

"Why have they taken the one?"

"One of them wished to take her."

Chi looked about the room. "You are doing most ineffective work. This place smells."

Song had become more and more anxious. "I think she can do nothing more," she protested. "She has only one arm. They have thought her dead. She has no help." She was unwinding the bandages from the woman's face. "I think you are not the only one with difficulty. You are not the only cripple."

He was stung. "The children must help. If they were trained properly they would be helping with such things."

"They have been very frightened. The older ones are gone. There is no one to help." The woman's face was bared now, grotesque wounds bulging out at them. "I thought you had come here because you wished to help us."

Chi backed off from his aggressiveness. "I do. I am merely surprised to find such confusion."

Song started to speak, then glanced at Nambae and remained silent.

"Do you have food?"

"A little. Only rice. I steam rice for them twice each day."

"And your vehicle. Is your vehicle still here?"

The woman whimpered as Song gently washed the wounds. "Yes," she replied at last. "They were going to destroy it but the Americans were coming. They had to leave too quickly."

"I shall need it," said Chi. "I must go to Seoul." He rose. "Where do we sleep tonight?"

"In the next room. It is cleaner than this. Only the babies sleep here."

"Fine. We shall eat a bowl of rice tonight and sleep well. We shall depart in the morning." He began to walk out.

"Must we leave so soon?" asked Song. "There is much to be done here."

"Of course we must leave. I must return to. . . ."

"And you, Nambae?"

Nambae looked from one to another. "Our friend has said we must go."

"I will not. Not now."

Chi started to speak but she cut him off. "If you were still walking the road I think it would take you many days to reach Seoul. Now you have a vehicle."

"Then we shall arrive there sooner." He started to leave again.

"We shall not go until we help clean up here." Song said it with finality. "I think two days will make little difference in Seoul, but they could mean a great difference here."

"But. . . ."

"If you were on the road from Taegu I think you would be dead."

Chi watched her, speechless, then walked from the room.

Two days later the truck swung through Wonju and labored into the hills to the north. Chi drove easily despite his arm. He felt confident for the first time since he had met his companions. Song huddled between Chi and Nambae, Sookee on her lap.

"What will you do when you return to Seoul?" asked Chi.

Nambae tensed, instantly alert for new information, contacts. "I think I must seek new employment," he replied.

"What work do you do?" Chi looked across the cab at him. "What was your work before the invasion?"

"I have done many things. In my last task before the invasion I was a clerk. I have no friends to place me in a better position."

"I do not understand," said Chi. "Have you not said you are from Seoul?"

"Yes," lied Nambae, "but my parents were killed by the Japanese. I have no influence."

Chi smiled. "Perhaps I may be of help to you. You have helped me. You saved my life."

Nambae stared at the road ahead. "Perhaps I could make a

new beginning. I was most unhappy in my former work. My employers offered me no opportunities to better myself."

"I wish you to meet my friends. They are most influential."

"Thank you," replied Nambae. "I think perhaps they can help me find a more important position."

"What are your qualifications?"

"A merchant," blurted Song. "His father was a merchant."

"Oh?" Chi showed his surprise. "I thought you said you were an orphan, that you worked as a clerk."

"We were both orphans," continued the woman. "But he was an orphan only after the Japanese murdered his parents. They decided his parents were too successful. They accused them of black marketing. They were executed."

Chi glanced quickly at Nambae. A look of discomfort had crossed the other man's face. "I am most sorry," he said. "I had much the same experience."

They rode on in silence for several miles, winding through the frigid hills. Forested peaks rose above them and away into the grayness. Finally Chi turned westward along better roads toward the capital. They saw many military vehicles, few refugees. Chi was reflecting on Hong. He had wanted to corner as many sources of money in their new nation as possible, yet he had not succeeded with merchandising. Other factions had monopolized the marketplace. Chi wondered if the invasion had disrupted that monopoly. If he could present Hong with an opportunity to expand his influence he could recover from the embarrassments of Taegu. "I think perhaps I could assist you in starting as a merchant."

"No. I think it would be most difficult. The large markets are closed to those wishing to begin. They demand too much money from new people."

Song looked at Nambae, anxious. "Perhaps we could get started. We could work together."

"I would prefer a position with the government," said Nambae, leveling a warning look at Song. She returned it with equal animosity.

"That is most difficult," objected Chi, attempting to dissuade him. "There are many with influence. I think you could not obtain a very good appointment. As a merchant perhaps you could open your own market. Reconstruction is certain to be coming. The government would be most helpful."

Nambae squirmed, but Song smiled, pleased. "Then I think we could control the others the way they have been denying us. We could require such deposits from them. We could demand a percentage of their profits."

"You are most observant," said Chi with enthusiasm. "I must talk with my friends. They have much influence in the government." He smiled at Song. "I think they would be very profitable friends for you."

"If your friends have such influence why can they not assist me in obtaining a government position? I think they could arrange a comfortable appointment."

"Such positions would be menial," replied Chi. "Most menial things. Those in government are anxious to help if you can assist them in obtaining something they desire in return. Surely you can understand that." He looked at Nambae. "If you were a merchant, if you controlled a number of other merchants, you could be of help to these people. I think they would be most willing to help you become established. It is very simple."

Nambae lapsed into silence as they rolled slowly into Seoul through the East Gate. They looked at the gutted homes, the wandering, emaciated children.

"I think you will be very busy," said Song. "There are many more orphans than when you left."

"Many will never be found," he replied without remorse. "However, the Americans will pay us much more than before." He gestured to the wasted buildings. "They will also pay generously to reconstruct the markets and to restore the economy."

"Yes," said Nambae. "But will not the people who receive the money be the ones who were merchants before?"

"The people who receive the money will be those who rebuild, not those who were torn down. The government will decide who may rebuild. We must be certain you are there first."

They were near the center of the city. "Where can we stay?" asked Song. "We would be lost in a refugee camp."

"You will stay at an orphanage, of course. I have told you before. I have much influence."

He turned slowly through the streets and finally came to a stop before a hastily repaired gate. Damage was everywhere, but the orphanage remained. An elderly man hobbled from the building. "Director. You should have seen it. It was horrible."

"I know," said Chi. "I have been seeing it all over the country."

The old man led the way into the building, its walls torn away in places, the windows shattered. "They have taken the girls," he said. "They lived here, and when they left they made the girls go with them."

"There are many more," said Chi dispassionately. "I think your orphanage will become much larger after restoration."

They had entered what once had been an office. A demolished desk lay in the corner, discarded. A board stretched between two boxes served as the manager's table.

"These people are my friends and business associates. They have now returned from Taegu and are in need of a place to stay until they restore their lives."

The old man nodded to Nambae, then turned back to Chi. "When will the repairs begin?"

"I cannot say. I must attend meetings with the government. Is there enough food?"

"It is scarce."

"I shall do the best I can." He motioned to Nambae and Song. "Show my friends to a room. Prepare one also for me in the event my home has been ruined. I shall return later."

They were alone in the small room. It was sparsely furnished but the floor was warm. Sookee had fallen asleep.

"Why did you say such things about becoming merchants? It

is not within my assignment." Nambae's voice was soft but menacing.

"Becoming a clerk in the government would serve no purpose. You would be better carrying information as you did before. Much more is expected of you by your father."

"It is not for me to decide. I have received an assignment. If I begin doing something different they will begin asking many questions." He looked about the room in disgust. "I have no business being here."

She was cryptic. "You must seek ways to do more for your father if you would be considered effective. I think you fear too much and lead too little."

He wanted to strike her but dared not. "Such remarks will cause you much discomfort, Song. You must be more aware of your precarious position. Were others to hear you, severe discipline surely would follow."

"They would discipline you as well," she hissed. "I have been forced to follow you. It is very difficult to follow a poor leader, a man without courage."

He growled, advanced toward her.

"The People's Republic will soon be lost. What will you do then?"

"Stop it," he ordered. "You will attract the attention of the others if you speak of such things."

She sneered. "Is that why you do not strike me as you wish? You fear attracting the others?"

He moved to her side and shook her, firmly, angrily.

"Stop it or I shall cry out," she warned.

He backed off, seething. "What do you want?"

"I want to escape from them and from you. I want to have a life where I may be free."

"That is not possible. You had best forget it."

"It is possible. They are losing. Already the armies of freedom are approaching Pyongyang. In another month they will be at the Yalu River. There will be no more People's Republic."

"I still must deal with the other agents here."

"You have been only a messenger, a runner. You have never seen Kwon, your own brother. You have never even heard from him since we landed at Inchon."

"He could contact us at any time."

"After two years?" She scoffed. "I think he is busier attending to his own advancement. He has no time for you."

He brushed it off. "Time means nothing for the victory of the masses."

"Time means too much," she objected. "You should be preparing for the fall of the People's Republic. You should be doing something of greater value to them if you believe they will continue to exist. But you should be doing something which will be of benefit to yourself if they lose."

"There. You see? You wish both winter and summer at the same time."

"I wish nothing for you," she snapped. "I wish only for my daughter and myself."

He groaned again, fighting a desire to strike her.

"You must do something positive," she urged. "Chi has offered you control of a market. If you deal with Chi you can become an influential merchant. The others must come to you. Chi has influence. Use him. The people from the government will come to you. Once you have become established they will do much to gain your favor."

"And if my father's friends come before I have accomplished it I shall be in much trouble."

"Tell them why you have done it. You are making friends in influential places. Soon you will be ready to deliver important information."

"That is not my mission."

"You have been forced to improvise. Tell them whatever you must to delay them."

"You would make me a capitalist!" he hissed. He looked at her, long and silently. Then, unwilling to argue further, he settled to the floor and slept.

* * * * *

Hong looked up tiredly as Chi hurried into his office.

Chi bowed with respect. "Hong. I am most happy to see you once more."

"What do you want, Chi? I have told you on the telephone I will meet with your friends. I think there is nothing more to discuss."

Chi smiled, ignoring Hong's indifference toward him. "We must discuss the rebuilding program for the orphanages."

Hong merely stared at him impassively, saying nothing.

"There must be much money given to the orphanages by the Americans." Chi swung his good arm in a wide arc. "I have visited several of the houses throughout the country. They are most sadly ruined."

"I think you helped with the ruining," replied Hong evenly.

Chi's face showed his shock. "I?" He scoffed. "No, Hong. I have merely inspected them. I have gone to several of them, and always the situation is the same. The buildings are a shambles, the people injured. Some are even gone. The soldiers of the north have taken some of the girls with them for their pleasure."

"And what of the orphanage in Taegu?" countered Hong. "I think the soldiers of the north did not ruin the orphanage at Taegu."

"No," spat Chi. "It was the mobs. I called you for assistance, but you would not listen to me." He fixed a reproachful glare on the other man.

"Chi," said Hong, the boredom becoming more pronounced, "I merely told you I expected you to take care of the situation. You did not. Now you come here scolding me." He shook his head sadly. "Your arrogance is insufferable."

"But I have done nothing wrong, Hong," protested Chi.

Hong was now glaring at him. "You allowed the orphanage at

Taegu to be overrun. You lost their food and the buildings were ruined. You lost your car on the road. You went to the orphanage at Gimchon. Your friends insisted on cleaning the orphanage and all the while you insisted on coming directly to Seoul. You did none of the work. You ate while the children went hungry. You took their truck." He wagged a finger at him accusingly. "You are more interested in your belly than you are in the orphans."

"Wait!" squeaked Chi. "Who has told you these lies?" His face contorted with hate. "I think you have talked with Nambae. I think he has told you these lies."

Hong raised an eyebrow in surprise. "Nambae? I thought he was your friend. Why would he tell me such things? No, Chi, I have not talked with Nambae yet. And when I do it will be concerning the markets."

"Then who has told you these things?" demanded Chi.

"Many people. I have talked with many people from the Taegu Orphanage, from Gimchon, from here in Seoul."

Chi groaned. "I think Yong Cha has made up these stories." He nodded, having convinced himself. "Yes. It was Yong Cha. She has been too good for the rest of us since she has become your wife. She would wish to ruin us all and be the only victor from the quay wall."

Hong scoffed. "She is gone."

"Gone?"

"She is no longer my wife. I sent her away."

"But why?"

"She was another of the leeches. You are a leech. The first day I came to the quay wall you attached yourself to me as a leech. Then it was the jin. Then it was the woman. You are all vermin." He lit a cigarette and watched the smoke curl upward. "I am well rid of you all."

Chi's jaw dropped. "I do not understand you, Hong."

Hong continued. "I do not speak in riddles, Chi. I am replacing you. The next director will do a more effective job. I think he will show me more respect."

"You will not!" growled Chi, rising. "If you replace me I shall talk with people about Hong." He lowered his voice, whispering passionately. "I think you would not wish people in our government to know of your past. I know very intimate things about you, Hong. You are making much money from your graft. You are using your position to make yourself rich. If they knew these things about you I think you would not remain in the government for long."

Hong sprang from his chair and slapped his desk. "Get out. Do not ever let me see you again."

Chi backed away warily toward the door. "I shall talk, then. I shall see the leaders of our nation. You have forgotten all I did for you at the quay wall in Inchon."

Hong started around his desk, but the door slammed and Chi was gone. Hong stared at the door for some moments, then wheeled and returned to his chair. He made some notes, then picked up the telephone and dialed.

"This is Hong," he said when the party answered. "I have just removed Chi as the National Director of Orphanages."

He waited, listening to the person at the other end of the line.

"He has been ignorant of the needs of his position so I have had no choice. He threatens to go to the government leaders and tell them lies about me. These stories are not true, of course, but conditions are unstable now. We cannot take chances with the lies of Chi." He took a deep breath. "If he becomes troublesome it may be necessary for him to meet with an accident."

There was more conversation from the other end of the line.

Hong nodded at the receiver. "In the meantime, I shall be seeing applicants for the vacant position."

THE NORTH—PYONGYANG

The jeep pounded northward over roads which were rough, often even nonexistent.

"I am told the Americans are entering the outskirts of Pyongyang," shouted Colonel Kwon. "I hope we arrive there before they do anything significant. I know you must agree with that, Shin."

Shin said nothing, holding on tightly in the rear of the bouncing vehicle.

"I was surprised," continued Kwon. "A promotion for each of us." He laughed. "I predicted it, but I wondered if they would really do it. It was most entertaining the way we stole the stage from the Americans in that last action. We proved the Koreans are an effective army. I tell you, that is the biggest reason we were promoted. There are many in our army who were ecstatic to see us beat the Americans to the objective in such a way. I had not realized how very much it meant to them."

The jeep struck a rut, veered, then straightened.

Kwon laughed again, childishly gleeful. "I congratulate you, Shin. One day a liaison officer, an errand boy for the Americans, the next, a battalion commander, a lieutenant colonel." He shook his head, then looked back at Shin. "Even the Japanese did not promote you that quickly."

"The Japanese were not my countrymen. That was not my army."

"Ah, but it was. Any army is your army, Shin. Any nation is your nation. Yesterday you fought for the horrid Japanese. Today you fight with us. Tomorrow you could as easily fight for the United States or the Soviet Union. I think it makes little difference to a man like you."

"I do not understand such a comment. You received a promotion as well. One day a lieutenant colonel, the next a regimental commander, a full colonel. I see no difference. We are the same. You outranked me then and you outrank me now."

"It is not exactly the same. I did not fight for the Japanese."

"You were not old enough. If you had been old enough you would have been taken in the conscription as were the rest of us."

"I am a loyalist, faithful to the people," continued Kwon, ignoring him. "You must consider it this way, Shin. You are more a mercenary than a soldier. You are not concerned for a cause so long as you are fighting, playing the hero. You are more of a pet dog than a soldier for your country. The general staff is aware of your attitude. You fought for the Japanese but you were not a firm believer in the Japanese. You performed feats so you could gather medals, so you would be promoted. You hated the prison at Inchon, not because it was a prison, but more because it offered you no opportunity to earn a medal. You wished to become a general, but you could not continue such a campaign at Inchon." He grinned, knowing Shin was cornered, could say nothing. "There are rumors you took retribution through brutality to your men, your subordinates. Then, when you were exposed, you deserted. You ran away from the Japanese army because they denied you the chance to continue being the hero."

Shin ached to protest, but knew it was useless. Kwon had achieved promotions rapidly. It was obvious he had developed close friends on the general staff. And yet, he had paradoxically and repeatedly selected Shin to serve under him despite his obvious disdain for his past. Shin was curious at being assigned to lead a battalion in combat, again in close proximity to Kwon. What did the promotion mean? He wondered if he had enemies on the gen-

eral staff, if his assignment to Kwon were merely a means of pun-
ishing him for the guards at Inchon. He dismissed the thought as
paranoia. Officers were not promoted for such reasons. Still the
thought lingered. He could not understand being requested again
by a man whose dislike of him was so obvious. Suddenly he was
certain that as he led his battalion under the regimental command
of Kwon he would be assigned the most difficult objectives, draw
the most suicidal missions. Until he was free of Kwon he would be
fighting two enemies the rest of his life.

"When we arrive," Kwon was saying, "there will be changes,
Shin. We shall fight as a unit, not as individuals. I selected you
personally because, renegade or not, you are a most effective fighter.
But we shall not engage in personal heroics. You must remember
that. We shall go forward and fight this war as we are told to fight
it. If I see even the slightest hint of your former tendencies toward
individual heroics you shall be disciplined. I wish you to fight and
fight hard, but you shall do so under my orders. I am certain you
understand that." He turned and shot a warning glance at the
back seat.

"Yes, Sir," said Shin. "I believe I have demonstrated my will-
ingness to fight under your command."

"Not really," snapped Kwon. "You have fought well, I agree.
But it has been fight or die. You know that. And you have quietly
questioned my judgment. That is not to happen again. You must
remember we are fighting for the reunification of our nation. Do
you understand what I am saying?"

"Yes, Sir."

They rode on, spoke no more. At Hwangju the hills gave way
to the broad Pyongyang Plain. The railroad tracks paced beside
them, following every turn of the river and road they paralleled.
Occasionally a bridgehead appeared, the clustered pontoons frozen into the ice. Above them the crumbled abutments of the former
span were as mutely testimonial as a temple ruins, unused and
forgotten in the destruction. The jeep wove its way through shell
craters, remnants of barbed wire. The clouds hung over them, po-

tent but waiting. The snow stretched ahead for miles, flat, cold, spattered with mud and soot.

At Junghwa they came upon elements of corps headquarters. The air was still, and thin, formless poles of smoke rose almost vertically from the stovepipes poking secretively through the tops of the tents. Military policemen stood along the route, scrutinizing each vehicle for authenticity.

"Take us to the headquarters," ordered Kwon. "We must talk with the liaison."

The driver, questioning, stopped beside a military policeman. The soldier, an American, started to motion for his counterpart.

"Come, come," said Kwon impatiently. "We speak English. direct us to the liaison."

The soldier pointed. "The tent next to the bunker, Sir."

"Thank you," said Kwon. The soldier saluted stiffly as they drove off.

Three hours later, extensively briefed, they began the trip to their regiment. Somewhere above the clouds the sun had set, and with it a brisk and chilling wind had begun whipping across the plain. They huddled within the side curtains while the gusts buffeted the vehicle. Ahead, they saw flashes in the sky, low against the horizon. Their light reflected off the low clouds, lending an aura of hell to the bleak loneliness of the night. They could not hear the rumbling over the noise of the engine.

Kwon was in a foul mood. "You have heard the briefing, Shin. The Americans wish to make an airborne attack to capture Pyongyang." He glanced over his shoulder. "I shall be most anxious to progress rapidly into the city. It is, as I have said before, our war. I would prefer a capture of Pyongyang by our army, not the Americans."

They were within five miles of their destination when they came upon the first roadblock. The military policeman held up his hand. The jeep ground to a halt.

"I'm sorry, Sir, but you're entering the tactical area. All canvas must be down and windshields flat."

Kwon sniffed. "I shall decide when to put my side curtains down. I am a regimental commander."

The military policeman stood firm. "Sir, I'm under orders not to move the barriers for any vehicle wearing canvas." He looked at his Korean counterpart, who stepped forward and repeated the instructions in Hangul.

"I speak English quite well," replied Kwon.

"Sir, may we help you with the canvas?"

Kwon glared ahead at the barriers, knowing he must relent. Finally, with an impatient grunt, he dismounted. "Do it quickly," he ordered. "We have no time to waste."

Shin's headquarters was close to the action. They were on a pincer drive which took them around and into Pyongyang from the east along the south bank of the Namgang River. They filtered through a sea of refugees, many wounded, who smiled and cheered as they picked their way ever deeper into the city. Another battalion was situated to their left, advancing parallel to them. The regimental reserves were located to the rear, plugging the gap between the two forward battalions. Throughout the night the advance was slow, mainly because of the darkness. There was only sporadic defensive fire from the enemy.

"Sir, we have received a change from the regiment." It was his adjutant, a young, highly alert officer.

"What kind of change?"

"The regiment has ordered us to establish a bridgehead across the Namgang River at this point." He held out a map and pointed to a section some half a mile from their position.

"Assemble the staff."

"Yes, Sir."

"Please leave the map with me."

"Yes, Sir." He held out the map and darted off into the night.

Shin bent and studied it. A bridge had existed at the objective some time in the past. That it was still there was doubtful. He looked up at the sound of footsteps and saw the forms of his staff in the gloom.

"Who has been ordered to hold the area we are occupying now?" he asked the adjutant.

"The reserves, Sir. They are to move up and fill the gap. We have been ordered to place some men across the river and keep others on this side to hold a sector extending to here." He pointed to the map again."

"What are the new regimental boundaries?"

"They remain the same on the left, Sir. Actually, the regiment is merely extending the right boundary."

"They are doubling our battalion's area while splitting our command down the middle with a river," said Shin with disgust.

"Yes, Sir."

Kwon had wasted no time. The situation would have been difficult to control with no opposition on a summer afternoon. In winter darkness, such a penetration of hostile territory was an invitation to disaster. He turned to his executive officer. "How long have you served with this battalion?"

"One month, Sir."

"Which is the best company?"

"A Company is the best, Sir, but they are also the weakest now. They have only forty percent of their strength. They have received many casualties."

"Tell me of the others."

"They have greater strength, Sir, but they have not as much experience."

Shin nodded. "I wish the strongest. They shall gain some experience tonight."

"Yes, Sir. I shall assign C Company."

He nodded. "C Company will establish the bridgehead with supporting fires from A Company. B Company will continue and maintain our sector on the south bank. Once the bridgehead is established, A company must stand by in reserve. Please prepare the operations order."

"Yes, Sir." The staff huddled together, murmuring among themselves.

"Adjutant."

"Yes, Sir.,"

"How far forward are our points?"

"They are almost to the bridge, Sir."

"That is excellent. You and I shall go forward for a look. Executive officer, please advise me when the battalion is prepared. You will then stand by to make the assault on my command."

"Yes, Sir."

Shin ducked from the shelter and started forward. Artillery was screaming over their heads, thumping into the inner city far ahead. They picked their way carefully, keeping covered and advancing in short, quick dashes. At last they were among the dark forms of their troops.

"What company is this, Adjutant?"

"A Company, Sir."

"If they are so depleted why have they been placed at the point?"

"I do not know, Sir."

Shin nodded and moved off to the right toward the river. Below, the water was still, hardly moving along the narrow channel where the surface was not frozen. Near the bank the ice was littered with debris and patches of snow.

"Tell me your name, Adjutant."

"I am Captain Kwak, Sir."

"All right, Kwak. You and I shall go to the bridge."

"Now, Sir?"

"Of course," he snapped. "We are planning to send a company across that river. I think we must learn what its condition is before we kill a hundred men."

Kwak nodded uncertainly. "Yes, Sir."

Shin left the cover, creeping along the escarpment. Behind him he could hear the captain panting in pursuit.

The bridge lay before them, still intact. Shin dropped to his belly and crept forward, Kwak close behind.

"Look, Sir. There."

Shin glanced at the adjutant, then followed his point. Below, among the piers, he could discern movement in the flashes of the artillery.

"I think they are preparing to destroy it," he said.

"I think so," replied Kwak.

Shin watched for a moment, then motioned Kwak forward. "Take them under fire. I shall go out on the span over them. We must stop them."

"But, Sir. . . ." It was too late. He was gone.

Shin crawled forward quickly. Reaching the roadbed, he leaped up and ran along the concrete rail onto the span. Kwak had opened fire on the figures under the bridge. The attention of those guarding the crossing had been attracted to the source of the fire and they were now raining a heavy volley in return.

Shin raced forward, tugging at a grenade as he went. He glanced quickly over the side, advanced a few more yards and looked again. Seeing the pier below he pulled the pin, released the spring, and held the lethal ball for a count of three. Then, dropping it over the side, he dove to his stomach. The explosion came almost instantly, close to the pier. There were muffled cries, followed by thuds below, the cracking of river ice. He raised his head and looked along the bridge. The enemy bridge guards were peering over the rail, not fifty feet from him. He took aim and emptied his carbine at them. They danced in the ecstasy of dying, then slumped. Instantly he was on his feet, running forward. Stooping, he retrieved a weapon, then dove for the escarpment on the northern end of the span. Crawling along, he peered down at the piers again. There was no movement. His gaze dropped farther to the frozen Namgang. The remnants of three men were scattered across the snow.

He reached for his hand radio. "Send the assault team now. The bridgehead has been secured."

There was a moment of silence, then the set crackled in his hand. "The assault force will begin the attack in five minutes, over."

"I say again, send the force across now. Immediately. The bridge-head has been secured. The bridgehead has been secured."

Moments later he saw the shadows moving cautiously out onto the span. Gingerly at first, they gained confidence as they advanced. By the time they reached him they were running, streaking for cover as they reached the land again. Small arms fire erupted from a building behind him. It was inconsequential and soon fell silent.

Shin stood upright now, and approached the company commander. The man looked at him in surprise. "Sir, how have you come here? Who has secured the bridge? It was to be our mission."

"It does not matter," he snapped. "Spread out and begin clearing the sector. A Company will be arriving to keep the bridge secure."

The officer hurried into the night without a reply.

Wearily, Shin spoke briefly once more by radio to his headquarters, then started back across the bridge. By the time he had reached the south bank the battalion staff was waiting.

"Who secured it, Sir?" It was the executive officer.

"It does not matter. They were preparing to destroy it. Deploy A Company as security and come with me." He stopped and looked around. "Where is Kwak?"

"He was wounded, Sir."

"How badly?"

"He is with the medics. I think it is not serious. He should be back shortly."

Shin nodded and began once more to cross the bridge. Looking ahead he saw a group of figures moving onto the span from the north bank. He stopped, watching them in alarm, then relaxed. They were not running, not being evasive. Refugees. "Remove them," he ordered in a low voice. "Remove them from the bridge until we have advanced farther. There may be a counterattack."

"Yes, Sir."

Shin quickened his pace. The staff was behind him. Reaching the north bank, they followed the source of the refugees back to a highway some two blocks from the river. It was broad, crowded with people plodding toward the countryside, a faint hope for safety. Small arms fire was chattering, occasionally heavy. The sounds were to their left rear.

"Sir, we have outdistanced the battalion."

"They have been ordered to move westward, toward the city."

"They are doing so, Sir."

"I merely wished to look at our flank. The enemy may bring armor along this route. I think we must place rocket launchers on this flank."

"Yes, Sir."

"I think tanks will have difficulty passing through the refugees."

"They will not, Colonel. If the people do not move they run over them. They crush them."

Shin was unimpressed. Then, through the gloom, they saw a car approaching. The people dove for the ditch. The vehicle did not slow. "What is this?"

"It appears someone is trying to escape the city, Sir. He must be most wealthy to have a car."

"Perhaps he is not wealthy at all," observed Shin. "Perhaps he is influential. Quickly. We must capture him."

They took cover and waited, their weapons ready.

* * * * * *

"I think you have been misinformed. The others have been flown out? I was told we would go very early in the morning."

"The plans have been changed, Comrade. The defense is weak, the enemy forces strong. They are fighting in the southern and eastern outskirts of the city now."

"How close are they?" Secretary Kim attempted to conceal his fear with aggressiveness.

"It is most difficult to say, Comrade."

"Do you mean you will not tell me? What are the field commanders doing? You must tell me." He rose and stalked angrily across the room, then wheeled on his assistant. "So they have flown off and left me. I am a secretary of the Party!" He dove for his desk and began assembling papers, placing them in a briefcase. "Order me an airplane. We shall drive to the airfield. I, too, shall be flown out."

"Excuse me, Comrade Secretary, but there may be no more airplanes."

Kim wheeled and slammed his fist down hard on the desk. "You shall not tell me that," he hissed. "I will not hear such talk. You will take me out of this city." He turned back to the papers.

The assistant shuffled uncomfortably for a moment.

"I shall arrange things for them," grumbled Kim. "My secretariat is a most powerful one. Corrections." He looked up at the other man. "I have the power to arrange prison for anyone in the People's Republic. It is a most educational experience." He fixed an appraising gaze on the assistant. The man blanched and hurried from the office. Moments later he was back. "A car has been made ready, Comrade Secretary."

Kim grabbed his case. "And the airplane?"

"We shall go to the airfield. By the time we arrive I think one will be ready."

"It would be most unfortunate for those who disappoint me," rasped Kim.

The artillery was tearing into the city with increasing intensity. Several times as the car dashed through the streets they found their way blocked by rubble. The flashes were sudden, came without warning, casting an eerie glow for fleeting instants through the darkness. Fires were burning. In the smoke they could smell the occasional acrid remains of human agony, bodies charring in the ruins.

Refugees were everywhere, scurrying from alleys, plodding along thoroughfares, ducking with the crash of artillery or stoically shuffling onward, unmoved or not perceiving the peril.

"You must blow your horn," screamed Kim. "Urge them out

of the way. If they do not move run over them." Kim sat in the back of the car, glowering out at the dismemberment of his world.

They were on a highway leading eastward when it happened. "Where is the airfield?" he demanded.

"It is ahead of us, Comrade. We must go about a mile farther."

Suddenly there was a cracking explosion. He felt himself thrown violently against the door of the car. Then, still pressed against it, he was floating as if through space. It seemed an eternity before the pavement tore into him, lashing, scraping. The door bounded away, and he watched it go, marveling in his loss of time at its resemblance to a fallen leaf blowing in the breeze. He slept, it seemed, yet when he awoke the door was still bounding away, end over end.

"Here," shouted a voice. "The passenger is here, Sir."

Slowly, he rolled his eyes upward toward the soldier. "The airfield. I must go to the airfield."

Another man had elbowed his way in to look down on him. "Why?" he demanded.

"The airplane is. . . ." His voice trailed off.

"You must check the wreckage," ordered Shin. "We must examine what is left."

"Yes, Sir." The other scrambled back to the smoldering car. In a moment he was back, the split briefcase hugged protectively in his arms. "This is all that remains, Colonel."

"Were there other passengers?"

"Only the driver and another passenger in the front seat. Both are dead."

Shin nodded. "Take this one across the bridge. Bring the papers. I wish to have a look at them."

* * * * * *

"You have done what?" Colonel Kwon stared unbelievingly at the field telephone in his hand.

"I have secured the bridgehead, Sir, and taken a prisoner. He appears to be a government leader."

"Have you questioned him?" You must obtain my permission before such questioning, Shin. I shall do the questioning at my headquarters."

"We have not questioned him, Sir." Shin's voice was clipped in irritation. "We have captured a briefcase of documents with him."

"Have you examined them?"

"The case was split open in the explosion, Sir."

"What explosion?"

"We stopped him with an antitank rocket, Sir."

"Was he riding in a tank? I think high government officials do not travel in tanks, Shin. I think you are attempting to make yourself into a hero again. You have been there only twelve hours and already you are ignoring my advice to you."

Shin disregarded the reprimand. "Our prisoner was in a car, Sir. They were running over refugees to get out of the city. Before he became unconscious he was delirious. He ordered us to take him to the airfield right away."

"And the papers. What have you done with the papers?"

"I think he is a People's Secretary, Sir. I think he could be Kim, the Secretary of Corrections. At least, most of the papers are signed with that name and title."

There was a long silence at the other end of the line.

"Are you there, Colonel Kwon?"

Kwon sighed, his stomach urging him to vomit. "Yes," he replied, almost inaudibly. "I am here. You are to bring the prisoner and the papers to me at once."

"Yes, Sir."

"And Shin."

"Yes, Sir?"

"I wish you to bring him to me personally. Do not send a messenger or guard detail with this one."

"Yes, Sir. I shall be there as soon as possible."

R.H. Brady

Kwon dropped the receiver into the hole in the field telephone case and stared into space.

Secretary Kim had regained consciousness. Realizing his predicament, he listened cautiously, keeping his eyes closed. Apparently the soldiers were readying a litter. He sensed others standing over him, watching.

"You must be most careful placing him on the litter," said Shin.

"What does it matter, Sir?" grinned a soldier. "He is a communist. Would he be so cautious with one of us?"

"That is not our concern," snapped Shin. "We wish to know everything possible about this one. He is to be questioned most thoroughly."

"Yes, Sir."

As they hurried him to the rear Kim pretended to sleep. If he were unconscious or delirious they could not question him.

"Be most careful not to lose any of those papers," warned Shin. "They may be very important documents."

Kim's heart pounded. They had his briefcase. He had hoped it had been destroyed in the explosion.

At last they slowed and he heard bodies chafing against canvas as they carried him into a tent.

"Sir, here is your prisoner. I shall place the papers here on the table."

"Have you questioned him?" Kwon seemed anxious.

The secretary's ears rang at the sound of the voice. Still, he kept his eyes tightly closed.

"No, Sir. You have said you wished to do that yourself."

"Good. That will be all, Shin. You may return to your unit."

"Yes, Sir."

The sound of the footsteps receded and they were alone, the only sound the distant whump of artillery still pounding the city. Kwon looked down at his father, remembering. The old man was sleeping. Gently, he reached out and touched his hand, feeling a futility at the predicament, and yet relief that his regiment had been the one to make the capture.

The secretary listened for sounds. There were none. He felt the hand touch his, and when it remained he knew there would be no others present. He opened his eyes.

"Father," whispered the colonel.

The secretary smiled. "You have done well, my son. I am most fortunate to have found you. Others might have killed me."

"Yes. I was afraid it would happen before I could have you brought here. Are you hurt badly?"

The secretary snorted. "Of course not. I am merely bruised but I thought it best I pretend unconsciousness. It is most effective at discouraging questions."

"Yes. You were wise."

"They know. I think they know."

"They know you are a People's Secretary named Kim. Only that."

"And you?"

"Only that I am their colonel. I am their regimental commander."

"They have run off and left me. They flew away last night."

"Who, my father?"

"The others of the government." The secretary's voice rasped with hate. "There will be a most thorough purge when this is over. They shall regret leaving me."

The colonel pursed his lips. "I doubt it was intentional. I am told you have most important papers with you. If it was their intention to abandon you they would have taken or destroyed such papers. They would have attempted to shield your identity to prevent your being forced to talk during interrogations."

The secretary's face had become pale, his eyes anxious. "The papers. Where are the papers?"

The colonel smiled reassuringly. "I have them here. You have nothing to fear."

"I must return. How am I to return?"

"We shall devise a plan."

"You cannot turn me loose without compromising your cover. That cannot be done. You are too valuable." He shook his head. "There must be a different way."

"It is most simple. You shall escape."

"How?" scoffed the father. "At night it could have happened. Dawn is coming. I think I cannot escape in daylight. Besides, it would be most unprofessional of you to permit the escape of so important a prisoner."

His son smiled. "Then I suppose I shall have to declare you too ill to travel farther back. I may find it necessary to interrogate you for the entire day."

The secretary's attention riveted on his son's features. "I have not been told of this latest promotion. You have done well."

"Thank you, Father."

"What of your brother? I keep waiting for news of great things regarding him. Nothing has ever come."

"He has been serving as a messenger."

"A task for schoolboys and misfits," replied the father scornfully. "I think he has not tried. He could have remained in the north and become an errand boy."

"I am told he has met with much difficulty arranging contacts."

"I think so. Or perhaps he has made his defection a bit more real than was expected. Have you seen him?"

"Not at all. I have been most busily engaged in my own assignment. Such a meeting could have been too easily observed and hasty conclusions drawn."

The father nodded in agreement. "Perhaps he shall be able to accomplish more now. I visited Seoul in August. There is much turmoil there. I am told there was much more destruction in the counteroffensive. Perhaps he can make his way into the government with the reorganization."

"Perhaps so. I shall try to arrange a discussion with him when I return to the south. I think now we must determine a means of reversing this war. There must be a second offensive by the People's Republic."

His father was unconcerned. "The second offensive is to begin very soon."

"I think it will be most difficult. The south has the help of the United States. They have much momentum, and the People's Army is crumbling. They are defecting by the thousands."

"The second offensive will reverse the trend. Comrade Chairman Mao has promised to enter the war."

Colonel Kwon's eyebrows shot up. "The Chinese? How soon will it begin?"

"Most soon. He is merely waiting for the proper justification."

"The People's Republic is being thoroughly mauled," exploded the colonel. "What further justification does he require?"

"There are great hydroelectric plants along the Yalu River. When they become threatened he will enter the war."

"Why can he not do it now? Are we not sister republics?"

"I think MacArthur expects him to do it now. If he were to do so at this time they would be ready for him. If he waits they will think he has no strength. They will think him a weakling. They will become overconfident. That is when he will strike." He laughed. "It should be a very great blow to the Americans. They consider themselves invincible."

"Can we expect no assistance from the Soviets?"

The secretary shook his head. "No, the Chinese are a greater threat to world socialism. It is wiser to use them."

"Why? If they pose a threat. . . ."

"We can resist the Chinese from within, the Soviets from without. A vigorous fight with the Americans should sap the Chinese strength sufficiently that the rest of the world may deal with them more reasonably."

"But do you not think Comrade Mao can perceive this?"

"A cocky oaf! He has been out of Yenan only four years. His only opposition was Chiang. He has beaten a weakling and thinks he is ready to conquer the world. We have talked with the Soviets and we all agree. Comrade Mao should be encouraged to enter this war. We shall win it and invite him to leave."

"I think he may refuse."

"If he does the Soviets will come to our aid." He looked at his son and changed the subject. "I think today is the first time you have seen your father as a People's Secretary."

"Yes. You were still the chairman in Hochon when we departed. You have advanced far."

"It has been most difficult. I spent a very demanding period of time at Hyesan. They assigned me as warden of the prison there."

"I think now we are faced with a more immediate problem. We must arrange your return to the people's government before they appoint a successor for you."

"Yes, and that must occur before the fall of Pyongyang. If I have not appeared once the city has fallen I shall be presumed dead."

The colonel was deep in thought. "There is one possible solution." Gradually he began smiling. "Yes, of course. It is a most perfect answer."

His father watched him with increasing interest.

The son leaned forward. "We shall return you as you came."

"I do not understand."

"The officer who brought you here will return you to the northern forces."

"I do not understand," repeated his father.

"This officer is most obedient to me. I made him a lieutenant colonel only a week ago. He was serving as a major, a liaison officer with the Americans. He built a most impressive combat record with the Japanese during World War II. He became an officer in their army."

"Why would you promote such a man?" The secretary was disgusted.

"I intend to use him for our ends. He is a most obedient officer. He will perform whatever mission I assign him with great efficiency."

"And he is a Japanese sympathizer," spat his father. "I think I have taught you better values."

Kwon held up his hand, smiling confidently. "The more important thing you have taught me is that the end justifies the means. I shall use him to further our cause. Consider the lawyer, Chung. You purged his entire family to arrange your promotion out of Hochon. Did you succeed in killing them all?"

"The father and mother."

"What of Taejin? Did he die in Hyesan?"

The secretary became agitated. "No. It is my one great shame. He escaped."

"Escaped? How? When?"

"I had arranged for the prisoners of Hyesan to open the Chorwon minefields at the start of the invasion. He escaped from the train on the journey south. He has never been recaptured."

"Most interesting," mused the colonel. "Regardless, I am using this Shin simply to do my bidding."

"He is loyal to you, then?"

"He is terrified of me. He has lost his face because of an incident at the close of World War II. I am merely taking advantage of that. He must obey me or be humiliated further. He is most ambitious. I think he would find such a situation too much to bear."

"How do you plan to return me to the People's Republic?"

The colonel smiled, stepped to his door and issued an order. Then, removing his father's shirt, he began wrapping his packets of documents and taping them to the old man's torso. By the time Shin arrived the father was ready.

"It appears," said Kwon to Shin, "you have committed a grave error. Corps headquarters has advised me you have managed to capture and injure one of our most valuable agents in the north. They are most unhappy about it. Naturally, I am not pleased with the embarrassment you have caused me." He glared emphasis at his subordinate.

"I am most sorry, Sir. I had no way to know." Shin groaned in frustration. "You gave me specific orders not to question him. I did not." He looked at the secretary,. "He appears to be in much better health than he was when I brought him here."

"It was necessary for me to feign unconsciousness, Colonel, until I could get to a higher headquarters." The secretary smiled disarmingly. "You must not worry about it."

"Sir, have you called me back only for this reprimand?"

"I have called you back to assign you a mission. You are to return our friend to enemy territory as quickly and safely as possible."

Shin looked uncertainly at the old man. "Can you move well? What of your injuries?"

"I shall cause you no delay, Colonel."

"I think we must wait until darkness," said Shin, turning to Kwon.

"Shin, it cannot wait that long. The city is about to fall. I think in such an eventuality your problem must be much greater. Corps will be most unhappy. The next logical step must be to the chiefs of staff, perhaps the Blue House. Certainly the heads of government need not become involved." He shook his head. "No, I think this must be done in all possible haste."

Shin shrugged, looking at the secretary. "It will be much more dangerous for you but I shall do my best."

"Shin," interrupted Colonel Kwon. "You would be well advised to make your best most successful."

"Yes, Sir." He saluted, motioned to the secretary and they departed.

There was no conversation as they moved closer to the front. With daylight, plumes of smoke were visible, billowing busily up to join the cloud cover. Their balance upset by the particles in the smoke, the clouds had in their turn begun dusting the city with snow once more. Visibility became sharply reduced.

"We are fortunate," observed Shin as they dismounted. "The snow is not as effective as darkness, but it will provide a measure of concealment."

The secretary stepped to the ground. "What is your plan?"

Shin ignored the question. "Kwak," he called.

The bandaged adjutant stepped forward. "Yes, Sir."

"Assemble two platoons from A Company for a raiding party."

"Yes, Sir." He turned and headed for the communications desk.

"Operations officer," called Shin.

A major stepped forward.

"We shall be penetrating approximately three blocks into the softest point in the sector. We must move quickly to take advantage of the snow."

"Sir, we have penetrated deeply now. The enemy has reinforced his defenses across our entire front. When you returned I had just finished drafting a request for tank support to assist us."

"We cannot wait. Corps wishes our friend returned through the lines as quickly as possible."

The operations officer was agitated. "It will be most costly, Sir. We will lose many men."

"Then you must plan a diversion," said Shin. "Launch a concentrated assault on the south bank of the river. Call in heavy concentrations of artillery. Take every man you have into an attack there. If you make it believable they will withdraw some of their people from the north bank as reserves. Then send the raiding party out on the extreme right flank. I need only a few minutes. If they penetrate and withdraw immediately we may succeed. We shall be following them closely in the assault."

The operations officer was dubious. "If we could await the tanks it would be successful. Without them it will be suicide."

"We have received our orders. We must follow them."

"Yes, Sir." The operations officer returned to his charts.

The snow was falling more heavily. Details across the street were difficult to recognize. Artillery and mortars pounded into the sector immediately forward of their position. At last the battalion moved ahead on the south bank of the Namgang.

Automatic weapons greeted them. There was little advance, yet they crawled forward slowly, giving the appearance they meant to claw their way into an advanced position. Across the river the patrol lay poised, ready for the order to advance.

Shin looked at the secretary. "I hope you are worth what is happening over there."

"I am. What is happening across the river will be most successful."

A soldier scampered up to them. "Sir, the observation post reports troops pulling out of positions to our front."

Shin nodded. "Good. We shall move in five minutes. Tell the patrol leader to advance only three blocks, then fall back. Tell him we shall start in five minutes."

"Yes, Sir." The soldier scrambled away. The sounds of the combat across the river were deafening. The ground beneath them trembled with the reverberations of high explosives. Then, through the swirling flakes, they saw the patrol rise and start forward.

"Come," he ordered, nudging the secretary's arm. They began picking their way quickly but unobtrusively through the debris. When they had advanced little more than a block a piercing crash erupted immediately to their front. It was followed instantly by a second. A scream echoed through the snow, followed by another explosion.

"It is an antitank weapon," shouted Shin. "Quickly. This way." He pointed off to their right, urging the old man to hurry. They advanced obliquely, found an alley, and scurried into its protection.

"Here," said Shin. "Hide in this debris. We shall withdraw beyond our former lines to draw them to us. After the enemy has passed you in pursuit of our forces you will be able to proceed farther into their territory."

The secretary nodded, smiling triumphantly.

Shin gave him a long look. "I wish you good fortune." Then, the reports of small arms fire drawing closer with his patrol's retreat, he ran breathlessly to the rear.

Secretary Kim waited, watching. The patrol backed past his alley, then his own army followed. Finally he was alone, the sounds of the battle receding to the east. He rose and, looking carefully about him, hurried from the alley and made his way toward the inner city.

* * * * * *

"Who are you, Comrade?" The officer looked up distrustfully.

"I am People's Secretary Kim. I was trapped on an inspection and have missed the government evacuation." The room was disorganized but showed little damage as a result of the siege.

The officer was doubtful. "What identification do you have?"

Kim braced. "I shall not justify myself to you, Comrade. Take me to higher headquarters, to people I can trust with the people's secrets."

"Very well, Comrade," the officer replied, a note of petulance in his voice. He turned to another officer. "Take our people's secretary to army headquarters for further proof. Guard him well." He smiled humorlessly. "We are most anxious that he not come to harm."

"Yes, Comrade." He motioned to a squad of soldiers, took Kim by the elbow and led him from the room.

They were far from the battle now. The staff car raced along pavement marred only by the deepening snow. At last they turned off, entering what had once been a large municipal building. The car stopped and two guards watched carefully as Kim stepped importantly from the rear. He glanced quickly around, then straightened and limped toward the entrance.

Inside, the activity bordered on the frantic. Clerks did not walk, but ran. Everyone carried weapons. Grenades dangled from their harnesses like apples awaiting the reaper. Kim was urged quickly along the corridors and into a staff office.

"What have we here?" asked a colonel.

"A man who claims to be the People's Secretary of Corrections, Comrade."

"I am impressed," replied the colonel dryly. "Has he identification?"

"He has refused to talk with anyone below this headquarters."

"Then he shall talk with me."

Kim maintained his air of importance. "Comrade, I will talk with the commanding general. No one less."

"I think you are in a difficult position to decide such things. Perhaps you should show me your identification. Then we shall decide whether or not you will see the general."

The secretary's eyes narrowed. "Do you realize, Comrade Colonel, how many have been purged because they resisted my requests? I am a simple man, a worker for the people. I wish to see the general. Sooner or later I will." His voice was almost a whisper, chilling in its implied threat. "It would be most unfortunate if it became later because of your proletarian obstructionism."

The colonel gulped, then stood. "Yes, Comrade. Please follow me."

They walked to a door, knocked and entered.

The general looked up, an expression of surprise crossing his face. "Comrade Secretary," he said as he stood up. "I am most surprised. I thought you had left yesterday."

Kim glanced triumphantly at the uncomfortable colonel.

"I would have departed, Comrade General, but I was unavoidably detained. Some of your units, it appears, are reluctant to extend hospitality to a secretary of the people."

THE SOUTH—SUWON

"Taejin." The mess sergeant approached the mess boy.

Taejin turned from his sweeping. "Yes, Sir?" He put down the broom, walking toward the sergeant.

"Get into a clean uniform and come with me." The sergeant turned and started away.

"Have I done something wrong, Sergeant?"

"The commanding officer wants to talk with you."

Taejin hurried along at his side. Then, turning abruptly, he darted into his small cubicle and began changing into a clean set of kitchen whites.

The headquarters, though hastily built, was comfortable, neat. The adjutant looked up, said nothing, but got up and stepped into the inner office. Moments later Taejin was ushered in.

The officer wasted no time. "Your name is Taejin?"

"Yes, Sir."

"I understand you're from the north."

"I was born in the village of Hochon, Sir."

"Why are you in the south?"

"I escaped, Sir."

"Escaped? You mean you defected."

"No, Sir. I escaped. I was a prisoner."

"Why were you in prison?"

"I was convicted of sedition against the communist regime, Sir."

"How did you escape?"

"I was sent to the prison mine at Hyesan. Before the invasion they placed the prisoners on a train and moved us south. I escaped from the train."

"Do you have a family anywhere?"

He brightened. "I have a daughter," he announced proudly.

"Only a daughter? No wife?"

"I have a wife also," he replied quickly.

"Are they in the north?"

"I think they have escaped to the south. I think they would go to Seoul."

"But you aren't sure?"

"No, Sir. I only hope they are in Seoul. If they are there I will find them again someday."

"Any other family?"

"No, Sir. My mother and father were murdered by the communists in the north."

"Your English is unusually good. Where did you learn it?"

Taejin was still standing stiffly before the desk. "I stole a book from the north soon after my escape. I studied it in a cave near Pyongtaek during the communist drive to the south. When the Americans came I had learned enough to begin working for them."

"What did you do?"

"I was a KATUSA, a mess boy for the infantry."

"Then how did you arrive here at Suwon?"

"I was wounded, Sir. A mortar round hit the mess tent where I was working."

The officer nodded, smiled for the first time. "Sit down, Taejin. Relax."

"Thank you, Sir." He sat.

"They brought you to our hospital?"

"Yes, Sir. The sergeant with the infantry had helped me with my English. The medic at the hospital taught me more."

"You've covered a lot of ground in a short time."

"I study every night, Sir. When I am not working I study."

"Do you have a goal for all this study? What do you hope to do with your knowledge of the English language?"

"I would like to stay working for the Americans, Sir."

"Why is that, Taejin?"

"I think I would not have good opportunities with the Koreans. There are many refugees."

"But not that many who speak English as well as you." The officer was watching him closely.

"Many are very intelligent," countered Taejin. "It is only a matter of them having the chance to learn. Those who wish to escape the communists are usually more intelligent than those who stay in the north. They have more ambition."

The officer smiled. "Well said, Taejin." He glanced at some papers on his desk. "How would you like an opportunity to move up?"

Taejin tensed. "I do not understand, Sir."

"I mean, if you had a chance to move to another job where you could use your English language would you take it?"

He brightened. "Oh, yes, Sir. I would be very grateful if I could use the language more."

The officer leaned back in his chair. "We have a very great shortage of interpreters with our forces here. Of course, we have a number of our own people who are school trained in Hangul, but they're never enough. Particularly now, with as many new people entering the country as we have, there are a lot of instances where those interpreters we have are far too busy to handle all the requirements." He waved a pencil pensively in Taejin's direction. "A request has come down for us to keep our eye open for capable people we think can be trusted. When we find one, we've been asked to send them on for further screening. I'd like to send you."

Taejin's eyes widened. "Where would I be sent, Sir?"

"To Seoul, initially. But you would have to move wherever the command went, depending where you were assigned."

"When would this happen?"

"Very soon." He rose from his chair. "I've screened you. I think you'd be a good candidate. The rest will be taken care of by my staff."

Taejin had risen with him. "Thank you, Sir. Thank you very much," he grinned.

Next morning he was loaded aboard a truck and driven to Seoul. He was interrogated extensively, always in English.

"Congratulations," said an officer finally. "You've done very well."

"Thank you, Sir."

"I hope you'll like your assignment. We've tried to place younger men like you in the more mobile commands, but you've been through a lot. The medics have taken a long hard look at your past injuries. Their recommendation is a less mobile assignment." He riffled through some papers. "We're going to put you with the headquarters staff."

"Here? In Seoul?"

"Yes." He paused. "It will mean long hours, but the living conditions will be better than in the field."

He was whisked off quickly, only to spend two days in processing. Finally, however, he was issued clothing, assigned living quarters and shown where to report for work next morning.

He looked at his bunk. It was his first stable home since Hochon, since the coming of the communists. Slowly, he sat, then lay on its soft comfort. Finally, rolling over, he buried his head in the pillow and wept.

THE SOUTH—GAPYONG

Headmaster Min looked at the messenger in shock. "What do you mean? Who has told you this?"

The young man cringed. "Everyone in Gapyong is talking about it. They are saying the Chinese have entered the war to assist the army of the north."

Min looked about him fearfully. "What else do they say?"

"That the Chinese will kill the Americans and make us slaves. They are much stronger than the armies from the north."

"Why do you say that? Because they have won in China? Because they have beat the weakling Chiang?"

"The people are saying they have many thousands of soldiers in Manchuria. Already they have crossed the Yalu and are fighting against the Americans and our army."

"The Americans will beat them," said Min flatly. "The Americans will drive them all the way back to Manchuria." He scoffed. "I think it is only another rumor. There have been many."

"I think it is not rumor," said the messenger. "The Chinese are driving the Americans back. All along the front they are winning battles. They have beaten the Americans badly at the Chosin reservoir."

"Then I think the Americans must bring in more soldiers. They must make more of a sacrifice."

"The people in the town have asked for you. They do not know what to do."

"Tell them they must have faith."

"Faith? Headmaster, they wish your advice. Am I to return and offer them only faith? In what must they have this faith?"

"I think in themselves and in the Americans."

The other shook his head. "They cannot have faith in either. They cannot believe in themselves because they have never learned to make decisions. They cannot have faith in the Americans because the Americans are losing. Please, Headmaster, you must come and talk to the people."

"You have told me they cannot have faith. Without that they cannot dream. Is a dreamer to stand before them and tell them their desires? Am I to go there and describe a school, a plan, and not even know beyond the faith in my own heart if it can ever be? I have had my dream for years, yet what do I have but a cottage? The answer to my dream is the Americans, yet I have worked for the Japanese. Now you have told me the Americans are losing, that my dream may never come true. And you say, 'the people need you.' I think they must have little need of me."

"Headmaster, consider your life. You were a Korean schoolmaster who determined to head a Japanese school. You accomplished it, Headmaster. And when the Japanese were determined to execute you? You held fast to your dream then. Any other man in Gapyong would have gone far away and never returned. But you did not. You returned, knowing most surely they were setting a trap. Why did you return? Because you refused to run away from your people. Your courage brought you back. For that the people of Gapyong respect you. Only you have given the people of Gapyong a hope for more than a bed tonight and rice tomorrow."

"Do you think they are alone? Do they? I think people the world around live with the same fears. Even in the great America I understand there are many who starve, many others who have no clothes. Do they dream? I think you must tell me, my friend. I do not know. I know only that if I am to continue living I must have a dream, clear and warm and peaceful as the sunrise. That is what sustains me. It brought me to Gapyong many years ago."

The man interrupted him. "Headmaster, you should be telling these things to the people. You should be setting the example for them. Too many have died in this war. Too many have been left homeless."

Min paused and looked out over his field, this tauntingly beautiful place which had drawn him inexorably through the years. Was it to be but his mountain, attainable only at his death, once he had invested all his life and energies to achieve it? He shuddered and turned to the messenger. "Come. I shall talk with the people."

They walked together, an aging schoolmaster and a lost man, plowing silently through the snow. Trees beside the road bent their ice-encrusted branches low, as if echoing the hearts of those passing by. The village was bleak, seeming to draw itself ever more closely into the hills in search of protection.

They entered the town. The people left their houses by twos and threes, following closely but silently behind the pair as they made their way to the school.

At the foot of the steps Min stopped and turned, looking over the people, not in evaluation or pity, but with an attitude bordering on fear. They stood there, saying nothing, waiting. He ascended the steps and opened the building.

"I am told the Chinese have entered the war," he said.

They did not reply.

"I am told the people of Gapyong are waiting for my reaction, my feeling about what the future holds for us." He looked at the crowded room, wondering how he would ease their hurt, relieve their worry.

"I have had a dream for Gapyong. It has sustained me for many years. It began long before I came here, and I have never forgotten it. Quite simply, my dream is to make of Gapyong the town which will rebuild our nation. The Japanese came. I resisted them. They wished to kill me for it. The communists came last summer and we were oppressed once more. My goal appeared impossible but I did not give up. I have kept believing in my dream for you and Gapyong through all the adversity."

The faces of the people were stone, emotionless. There was no visible sign that his words were either heard or understood.

"The Chinese may be fighting, they may be winning for the moment. But I tell you, there can be no dream worth the mind's labor without the will to make it true. Without strong will it is fantasy, a game for children. My will tells me not to fear, that the Chinese cannot win."

A man coughed and several in the room cast nervous glances at one another.

"I think you do not believe me." His spirit was rising. "I do not ask that you believe me. You have asked me to come here, to tell you how I feel, what I think. I have done it. My belief need not be yours. But it must be mine. I must live with it, work for it, and one day, perhaps, die for it."

Still not a word had been spoken by the others. Min looked about, knowing the faces and their individual fears.

"What will happen if they do come?" It was a voice far back in the room.

"Then I think we must rely on the soldiers to stop them, to drive them away."

"And if they cannot?"

"If we believe that I think we must carry each other to the happy mountain, to our graves, and let them have all Gapyong."

"What will you do, Headmaster?"

"I? I am building a new school. I worked at it yesterday. If you look at it tomorrow you will see me working at it still."

"Why?"

"Why? For you, for the people of Gapyong."

"But I think you cannot finish it without the Americans."

Min's normal attitude was fully recovered. He spaced out the words for force. "I will build our school!"

The people looked around, shaken, then glanced uncertainly back at Min. He stood, frozen in his importance. He raised his hand as if to continue but they were already filing through the door.

When they were gone Min looked hesitantly about the empty room. "I will," he announced, "build my school." Turning back to his desk, he groped absently for a pencil. He held it poised, as if to contemplate words which could convey his feelings. Then, suddenly realizing forlornly that he had none, he dropped it back to the surface and braced himself for the long, cold walk home.

THE SOUTH—SEOUL

After Chi's dismissal by Hong, Nambae and Song never saw him again. Summarily evicted from the orphanage, they gravitated back to the area of the East Gate. They had no means of support, and thus burrowed once more into one of the teeming refugee camps. Nambae again began trying to infiltrate the government, but lacking credentials he was turned away.

"Have you tried to contact this Hong?" asked Song, frustrated.

"I will not become a merchant," he snapped.

"Neither will you become a civil servant," she retorted. "You know no one. You have no friends. You have no home. You have nothing to offer them."

He pouted, but said nothing.

"You could ask your cell leader for assistance. I think you are ashamed to ask him for help. He will only make you a messenger again." She sneered disgustedly at him. "I think you fear him."

"I do not fear him."

"Then why have you not asked for help? Others of our comrades are in the government. You are not seeking to be the first. How have the others done it? I think the cell leader has helped them. He could help you."

"They were better prepared by our comrades in Pyongyang," he replied angrily. "They were provided with documents, with names of people to contact." He grimaced. "Even my brother was given documents. He had no difficulty penetrating their army."

"You should have thought of that in Pyongyang. I think it is very late to complain about that now. You have been given a mission and you are not accomplishing it."

"I was not given documents because I believe they wanted me to fail."

"Such a statement is ridiculous."

"It is not. I believe I am being punished."

She raised an eyebrow. "Yes. And for what would you be punished? Did you report back on the route we took to get to the south? I think you did not. You could have reported to our comrades on the way we came here and you would have been a hero. Yes. Perhaps you are being punished. Why would they give documents to one who did not report back as he was ordered?"

"My brother did not report back either. I think he was given his documents in Pyongyang. He had no need to report back."

"That is ridiculous. He would not have gotten documents before we moved south. What if those who brought us had searched us and found them? No, he would have gotten them from the cell leader once we were in the south. You could have requested them." She snorted. "I think you are afraid."

"It is not these things for which they punish me. I am being punished because of you. I have married a tainted woman, a whore. It has caused my family much embarrassment. You are the cause of my punishment."

"Then you should not have insisted on making me marry you. I did not want to marry you. You have no cause to blame me."

"But you were tainted. You did not wait until you were married. I think you sold yourself to many men."

"Do you think such talk will put food in your belly? Do you think it will find you an entry into the government? I think you cannot infiltrate the government unless you talk with the cell leader. I think you are afraid of him."

"He will not give me documents."

"You have not asked him. You would rather continue to feel sorry for yourself and place the blame on someone else."

Nambae bounded to his feet. "Again I am taunted by the whore! Again you resort to your insults. I will not stay here and listen to you."

"Yes," she shouted. "Run from me. Feel sorry for yourself and continue fearing the cell leader." She had not risen, but glared up at him. "I think you will never be able to infiltrate the government. You are a coward."

He reached down and struck her, knocking her into a corner of the tent. "I will go now. When I return you will see. I will have the documents."

She laughed derisively through her pain. "You are a coward," she screamed again.

He stormed from the tent. Song rose slowly, rubbing her face. Sookee crawled to her, trying to comfort her mother. Song reached out and cuddled the child to her, stroking her hair. Then, almost in a daze, she took the small hand and together they walked from the maze of tents.

Activity at the South Gate was frenetic. They walked through the crowds of people, coming at last to the shell of what had once been the market. Workmen were scurrying around, reconstructing from the rubble. Song watched them, Sookee holding tightly to her hand.

Two men emerged from the building, one young and well dressed, the other aging, moving slowly. The elder man spoke to one of the workmen, obviously directing his efforts.

"You must oversee their work carefully while I am away," he said. "This is your opportunity to prove yourself a worthy foreman."

"Yes, Headmaster," replied the man, hurrying back into the structure.

The old man turned to his younger companion. "I think it will be finished in only a few days, Hong. My students will make you happy that you have come to Min."

Hong nodded. "Schoolmaster, you had best hope they do.

The future of your work for me will be determined by their performance here."

Song, upon hearing the name, shrank back. This was the man
of whom Chi had spoken, she was sure. Her mind whirled with
the impulse to approach him, tell him who she was. She realized,
however, that she would be more prudent to wait, watch for an
opportunity to approach him once his conversation was over. She
did not have long to wait. A few minutes later the two men bowed
low to each other and parted. Hong walked quickly toward a waiting car.

She hurried forward, her daughter almost dancing to keep up
with her. "Minister Hong," she called.

He turned and looked at her, saying nothing.

She smiled. "I am Song."

He sniffed. "I know no Song."

"I think Chi has mentioned my name to you."

He drew himself up, indignant that she should accost him. "I
have no use for acquaintances of Chi." He turned to continue toward the car.

"I am not his friend," she said quickly. "He is a most cruel
man."

"He is an animal." He continued walking.

"He was so at the orphanage at Gimchon," she added, watching him closely for a hint of softening.

Hong slowed, then stopped. "What do you know of the orphanage at Gimchon?" He was glaring at her now.

"We befriended him. We saved Chi's life on the road from
Taegu. We went to the orphanage in Gimchon with him."

Now the recognition crept into his eyes. "Yes. I have heard of
you. You are the one who insisted on cleaning the place. You cared
for the old woman."

She dropped her eyes. "She was most seriously wounded but
Chi did not care. He only wished to return to Seoul quickly. I
think he feared for his own life and comfort. He did not like the

filth at the orphanage." She looked pleadingly into his face. "Yes. You are right. Chi is an animal."

"Why do you approach me here? Why are you here at the market?"

"I came here to see it. I suppose I was dreaming." She paused for a moment. "I had a dream that I might become a part of the markets."

Hong looked at her appearance and that of her daughter. "You do not look the part of the merchant," he observed.

She hesitated, then forged ahead with resolve. "I have become a refugee. I am no different from any of the other thousands who have been left homeless by the war. But I have been a merchant. I know the markets."

He raised an eyebrow. "Oh? I had thought Chi told me it was your husband who knew the markets. His father had been a merchant and he had learned from his father."

She shook her head vigorously, now determined to tell him the truth, to take that step which would free her of Nambae. "He has lied. I think Chi told a great many lies. He did not like women. He would always give a man the credit." She looked imploringly at Hong. "My husband is nothing. He has no knowledge of the markets. It was my father who was the merchant."

Hong motioned them to the car and leaned comfortably against it. "But I am a cabinet minister. Why would you approach me to discuss the markets?"

"Chi told me you wished to control the markets. He said you would take over all the markets in Seoul when you returned from Taegu. I would like to work with you."

He looked around quickly, then back at her. "We cannot talk here," he said quietly. "Come. Ride with me. We will talk elsewhere."

They entered the car and his driver began weaving his way deeper into the city.

"What would you seek from me in the markets? I do not understand why you would come to me. I have told you, I am a cabinet minister. I do not control the markets."

"Chi said you would have people who would manage them for you. He said you would not want to be known as the man who controlled them, but that you would have others manage them and report to you."

"I think you would wish a stall. Nothing more."

"I could manage the entire market for you."

"You do not look the part. You would not be convincing as a manager."

She was stung, downcast. "I do not look the part because I have lost everything. I would not look this poor if I were to become your manager."

"The person who manages must have an investment. I think you have nothing to invest."

"I would gain my investment from those who bought stalls from me."

"I think you would need the investment first."

"Minister Hong, this is not the only market in Seoul. I think if you plan to control the markets you must wish to own the ones at Itaewon, the South Gate and Changdok as well. Unless you controlled them all the others would squeeze you out. They would ruin you. They would talk to the government and tell them you were controlling one of the markets."

He looked at her with new interest. "How have you known these things?"

She cocked her head. "It is simple. A merchant must always watch the competition. He must always seek to eliminate the competition. I think the others must wish to do that to you."

"And what of your husband? What would you do with him? If he knows nothing of marketing I think you must not want him to be involved."

"Yes. I do not." She motioned her head toward her daughter. "I must be free of him for her. There is no future for her or for me as long as we are with him."

"Then you would leave him?" He was surprised.

"For the good of my daughter I must leave him." She grimaced. "He beat me this morning. I have left him because of it."

"And what if he finds you? Would he not come and seek you and take you back?"

She smiled evasively, but without humor. "I think he has many problems. I think he will not have time to come and seek me." Her face became serious. "You must not worry about him."

He nodded. "What do you know of me?"

"I know only that you are a cabinet minister. That you wish to control the markets. I think you cannot do this in public because of your position, so you must have associates who will run them for you."

"But why could I not own them publicly? I think there would be little problem if I were an astute businessman. I could be that and a cabinet minister as well."

She shook her head. "I think much of the money for the reconstruction of the markets must come from the Americans. They would not be as willing to give the money to a cabinet minister in the government. They would say it was graft." She watched him for a reaction, but there was none. "It would be better for you and for your fortunes if the Americans did not know of your investments."

A slight hint of a smile creased the corner of his mouth. "You are more observant than your appearance would suggest."

"It only seems this would be the case."

He changed course. "What would you do with the markets?"

"I suggest you not open all of them at once. You should create a need for the people to visit each one. If they all opened at the same time most of the people would visit only one."

"Yes. You are right. But so long as many people went to each one to trade I think it would not be necessary for everyone to go to each of them."

She nodded, but not in agreement. "If you did not have the

same products in each market the people would have to visit all of them."

"What do you mean?"

"If you had only fabrics at the East Gate, and only lacquered goods at Itaewon, people would be forced to visit both. If other markets dealt only with brass or with inlays you would have even greater control of their shopping."

"But the people would then have to travel all over the city." He was dubious. "I think each merchant would see fewer people each day."

She smiled. "Then you must have a different agreement with your merchants. Your fee from each merchant must not be based on his sales. Instead, you should obtain your fees from the merchants collectively based on the number of people who enter each market each day. It will cause the merchants to work harder at selling their goods."

"That is not the way it is done."

"But it would be much more profitable." She was excited. "If you do it as it has always been done, you would receive only a percentage of the sales of each merchant. If one did not sell as much, you would lose. But if you tax the entire market prorated on the number of customers who enter the building, I think they must try harder to sell their goods so as to make up for the amount they have to pay in the tax. Each market would be much more profitable for you. And by having each market a specialty market, all the people of Seoul would have to go to each one. More people would enter each building. Their entry tax, which the merchants would have to pay, would be what you would earn."

"A most profitable thought," mused Hong. "I can see that you have learned your lessons well from your father." He smiled at her. "Is he in Seoul?"

She shook her head sadly. "He was murdered."

"I am sorry." He quieted for a moment. "What would you do with your daughter? If you are working in the markets I think you must have a way to care for her."

"I shall have to leave her with a *yumo*, a nurse."

Hong leaned forward and motioned to the driver. "We must find you clothes," he said, leaning back again. "If you are to manage the markets you must look the part."

She looked at him in concern. "I have no money now to buy them. I cannot even pay a nurse now."

"But if I were to loan you money now you could take care of such things. You could pay me back later from what you tax the merchants."

Song brightened. "Yes. I could do that."

"And where do you live?"

Again she showed her concern. "We have lived in the refugee camp near the East Gate. I have left my husband this morning, so I have no place to go."

He waved a hand, dismissing the problem. "We shall find you a place to live. It shall be a place where you will have no need to worry."

Late in the day she returned to the East Gate, the scene of her triumph. She gazed at the market, now awed that she had finally achieved her dream.

THE SOUTH—PUSAN

With the new invasion Nambae fled beyond Taegu to Pusan, then to Chinhae, a seaport on the southern coast west of Pusan. He was terrified that the invading communists would catch him, would return him to his father.

This far south, he felt safe and moved freely about the city. More and more troops arrived daily, unloading hastily from ships which hardly touched the quays while the soldiers debarked, then put to sea again. The soldiers were marched into the city. There they were loaded into trucks and trains for the trip up the peninsula and into the combat.

It was at Chinhae the soldiers found him.

"Is your name Nambae?"

He looked up in alarm at the group. "What do you want with me?"

"You will come with us."

"But I have done nothing. I do not wish to go with you."

"Our colonel has said you must come. He will be most unhappy if you give us trouble." The speaker reached out as if to grasp him.

"Please do not harm me," blurted Nambae. "I shall go with you."

The leader smirked. They led him to a truck. The streets were slush, wet and cold. He climbed into the rear with two of the soldiers. They sped through a city marked in its contrast with

Seoul, the cities which had been touched by the war. The driver turned south. Soon they were speeding along piers crowded with American and Korean combat troops. They pulled to a stop in front of a headquarters building.

He was beckoned down from the truck bed. "Where are we?" he demanded. "I do not understand what you are doing."

They said nothing, hurrying him up the steps and into the building.

"Here," said the leader. "Go in here."

Nambae looked at him questioningly, then reached slowly for the door handle and entered the room.

"Well," said Colonel Kwon. "I thought you had forgotten us, Brother."

Nambae stared in disbelief, a mixture of joy and apprehension gripping him. "I cannot believe it," he breathed. "It has been a long time."

"I think it has been too long," replied his brother, smiling disarmingly. "I saw you in the city today. At first I could not believe my eyes. I thought you had been assigned to Seoul when we arrived at Inchon. But then, I think one does not forget his own brother." He rose and pointed to a chair. "This should be a most opportune time to become reacquainted. Do you not agree, Nambae?"

The younger brother instinctively moved to avert trouble by changing the subject. "A colonel! Brother, our father would be most pleased with you. I think he did not expect you would rise so high in such a short time."

"With the war of liberation being fought it was a simple matter to obtain promotions. This army of the south is a most ineffective mob. There are few good leaders. Few of their officers are able to think for themselves."

Nambae nodded, smiling. "Your point has been proven by their constant losses in the field. The People's Republic has been beating them consistently."

"Yes. It is true. But you must tell me of yourself. I have heard little of your activities."

"I was not as fortunate as you in the beginning."

"We suspected that when we learned you were merely a messenger."

"I attempted to join the government. It was most depressing. Every post of value or influence was filled."

"Please tell me what you have done." The colonel was maintaining an air of uncharacteristic calm. "Your personal problems are of no concern to the people. Each of us was assigned a mission. Mine was to enter the army, yours, to enter the government. Instead, I think you have spent much time worrying about a whore and her baby. Now you have run away to Chinhae." He lit a cigarette, slowly, not taking his eyes off the younger man. "Perhaps you thought you would not be found here, so far away from your assignment."

"Wait. Your assumption is wrong."

"Wrong? How is it wrong? You have told me yourself you were unable to enter the government. You could have been a messenger in the north. The People's Republic needs messengers."

"I have told you I worked as a messenger. But I was not as fortunate as you, Brother." Nambae became aggressive, dealing from imagined strength. "They did not provide me with forged documents as they did you."

"And Chinhae. Why are you here?"

"I have come to seek a new start. Still I try to enter the government. I have followed my cell leader here."

"And what of your wife, the harlot?"

"I do not know. She disappeared after our return to Seoul. No matter. I am the better off to be rid of her."

"Of what assistance is that to the masses? You are rid of a whore. How does that help us reunify our nation? How does that serve the People's Republic?"

"I think it is of greater assistance than killing the masses. My brother has become a colonel leading the soldiers of an enemy army against our people. How many of our people have you killed, Brother? I think no army promotes officers for losing battles."

"My activities are not of concern to you. I am performing my assigned mission and you are not performing yours. You have been here over two years with no visible results. Our father is unhappy. I am ashamed of you. I would not waste my time talking with you had our father not ordered me to do so."

"You have talked with him?" asked Nambae in surprise.

"We visited during the battle of Pyongyang. He is convinced you have become a real defector. He is considering recalling you for punishment."

Nambae flushed. "It is not true. If our comrades in Pyongyang had provided me with false documents, as they did you, I would have been able to infiltrate their government. In truth, Brother, you are a lie."

"A lie?" The colonel was cold. "I think it is your wife who is a lie."

"I have no wife."

"But you do. She has become a business associate of a cabinet minister." He fixed his brother with a gloating stare. "You see? You could not penetrate their government. You cry and sob that you did not receive documents, but she has done it. She is a close associate of one of their cabinet ministers." He paused. "But she has become a capitalist in the process. What must our father think? His son sleeps with a capitalist."

Nambae recoiled in shock. "I did not know."

"But you should have known," continued his brother. "If you had been more diligent I think you could have engaged this cabinet minister in conversation. Knowing such a man is valuable because you may harvest information. I think you have only one source so you must use it diligently. You must obtain and report all the information you can."

"But I do not know him. Only now have I learned she is involved. You have told me only now."

The colonel laughed sardonically. "What a magnificent agent for the people! You cannot even keep track of your decadent wife."

"What is this business arrangement she has developed?"

"The markets of Seoul. She will soon control all the markets." The colonel smiled. "And you did not know? I think you have contrived to dupe the masses. I think you are very much a part of this deception."

"When Seoul is retaken I shall confront her. I shall force her to provide information to me and to the People's Republic. You shall see. I am most loyal to the masses."

The colonel brought his fist down hard on the arm of his chair. "I think you must not call yourself loyal to the masses. You have said, 'when Seoul is retaken.' Already you are planning for the south to recapture Seoul." He glared. "We have taken Seoul. In a month we shall have Taejon, Taegu. By the time the snow is gone there will be but one nation here. The People's Republic."

"I hope you are correct. But what will happen if the Americans bring in more soldiers? What will happen if other nations join them? Our armies could be stopped, driven back. This war could continue longer. I think no one can say how long it will last."

"And your wife would wish to see it go on indefinitely?"

"She is most greedy. If what you are telling me is true she will become wealthy as a result of this war."

"I think if you are her husband you must become wealthy as well."

Nambae was perspiring profusely. "It does not matter to me. I could not obtain an appointment in the government because our comrades did not provide for me as they did for you." He glared at his brother accusingly. "This may be my best opportunity. I could become close enough to this high official to be effective."

"I think one's effectiveness must be measured by one's reports. There have been no reports from you in other matters."

"There will be many reports from me."

"Only if the south recaptures Seoul. That will be your only opportunity to meet all these powerful men. I think you cannot increase your wealth unless you return to Seoul. You cannot expand your capitalist empire unless Seoul falls to their decadent forces again." His standing up indicated the visit was ended. "I believe you have become a capitalist. I believe you knew your wife was doing this. I believe you are scheming to defeat the People's Republic. You are plotting against the masses, capitalist. It is most clear why we have received no reports from you."

"You are wrong, Brother," protested Nambae.

"Do not call me that again." he pivoted angrily toward the desk. "Get out!"

THE NORTH—PYONGYANG

Secretary Kim read the note, then exploded in rage. "Why does he summon me to his office? Does he think he is the chairman? I will not dignify him. It is a play for power." He glared at the messenger. "You may tell him if he wishes to talk with me he must call for an appointment."

The messenger shifted his feet nervously. "I understand, Comrade Secretary, but he has told me I am to bring you back with me."

"Why?" shouted Kim. "Do you mean I am under arrest? No, I shall not go."

"Perhaps he intends it as a courtesy, Comrade."

"A courtesy? I think he knows nothing of courtesies. He knows only ambition." He reached nervously for a stack of papers on his desk, rearranging them absently. "You may go back and tell him I shall be most happy to arrange an appointment if he wishes to see me."

As soon as the man had gone Kim pressed a buzzer. His deputy entered. "Yes, Comrade?"

"I have had a visit from the investigative service." His voice was quiet, but the anger was still apparent. "The secretary has had the audacity to send a messenger to me. Here," he continued, thrusting the note toward the deputy. "Look at what he has brought me."

The deputy picked it up, read it quickly, returned it to the desk. "Has he been watching you, Comrade?"

"He has no reason to watch me. I have done nothing wrong."

Then perhaps we should begin investigating it, Comrade. Obviously it is not a social matter. The note is most strong."

"Then be on with it. Waste no time. I shall not be intimidated by this upstart."

An hour later an aide entered his office. "Comrade, the People's Secretary of Investigation is outside. He demands to talk with you."

Kim sat back, a slight smile of satisfaction creasing the corners of his mouth. "I think he has learned his lesson. Send him in." He riveted his eyes on the door in anticipation.

The man was small, energetic, considerably younger than Kim. "Comrade Kim," he said, speaking even as he entered the room. "I am sorry you found it necessary to call me from my duties. I am a very busy man." He pulled up a chair and sat, not waiting for an invitation.

"I think you are no busier than I," countered Kim. "You arrest them, I punish them. What do you wish to discuss with me?"

"It appears we have a problem, Comrade. Perhaps I should say you have a problem. I think that would be more accurate."

Kim felt an impulse to bark, reprimand him. He waited.

"It seems your absence when the other secretariats were evacuated from Pyongyang raised some questions. You did not rejoin the government for two days."

"I was left. . . ."

"Naturally," continued the other, ignoring him, "when we returned I had no choice but to begin an investigation."

"I have done nothing wrong," stormed Kim. "You are manufacturing. You have nothing against me."

"That remains to be seen, Comrade. The investigation is not yet complete. However, some interesting facts have already been discovered." He sat back and folded his arms, watching Kim.

"To what facts do you refer?"

"As you know, I control our agents in the south."

Kim's stomach knotted. He remained expressionless.

"Kwon has made amazing progress in the capitalist army. But

then, you knew that, did you not? You have learned he is a colonel."

Kim looked triumphant. "It was his assignment. He was ordered to infiltrate their army."

"Yes. I am aware of that. But to have advanced so rapidly is most unusual. One day he was merely a liaison officer, the next a full colonel. A week after that he was in command of a regiment in the battle of Pyongyang." He lit a cigarette. "Such progress is most amazing. One wonders how he has achieved it. Would it not raise a question in your mind, Comrade?"

"He achieved it because that was his mission," snapped Kim.

"And then, when our government was evacuated, his father was among the missing for two days. Such coincidence. Father and son on different sides of the war, both loose in Pyongyang for two days. Would such a coincidence not alarm you, Comrade?"

"I am never alarmed by coincidence. The only thing which alarms me is a deliberately planned crime against the masses."

"You have stated my point exactly, Comrade." The visitor was smiling. "That is the way I feel. I think too many things are shrugged off as coincidence when they are not really that at all. Generally, when we look more closely we find there has been a most carefully planned scheme behind things which appear coincidental to the casual observer."

"I do not know what you are talking about."

"Do you not, Comrade? Then does it surprise you that your son's regiment was attacking the People's Republic along the Namgang River in the eastern sector of the city? Does it surprise you to learn they established a bridgehead across that river? Now consider your movements during that period. The government departed, yet you did not. One would have suspected you would travel north when you and your assistant departed in the car. Ah, but other questions have arisen. We have found the remains of your car in the eastern sector. It was found at precisely the location in which the bridgehead was established. Not only that, Comrade, but it is most apparent from the time of your disappearance that you were in that locality at approximately that time. Your assistant was found, what was left of him, by our agents who remained here in the city."

Kim elected to remain silent.

The visitor rose and strolled slowly to the window, gazing out at the city. "I wonder if we have a situation of disloyalty in our midst. I wonder if we have stumbled across a cell of capitalist agents among the People's Secretaries. I wonder if Kwon was promoted because of some service he might have performed for the capitalists which made it easier for them to drive northward. Could there have been exchanges of greetings in the eastern sector that day? I wonder if something more than greetings might have been exchanged."

Kim bounded from his chair. "Lies. They are all lies," he screamed. "You are far too new in your secretariat to know what happened. You are a schoolboy."

"I am merely a servant of the masses. I am new, but I read voraciously. Most particularly I enjoy mysteries. I enjoy contemplating the circumstances surrounding missing persons. There is one now, as a matter of fact, which I find most intriguing. There was a comrade who wished to be an agent for the People's Republic. The government trained him. He seemed a bright young man, full of promise. He had amassed a most impressive record of digging out enemies of the masses. He came from a small village west of here." He turned away calmly from the window and looked at his adversary. "His name was Nambae."

"He has had difficulty becoming established. He was assigned to infiltrate their government."

"Ah, you know about this missing person." Delight danced across the younger man's face. "How could you possibly have obtained such information?"

"I have my sources, just as you have yours."

"A prison warden. Nothing more," scoffed the other. "Did you know he has worked as a messenger? That is a strange way to infiltrate a government. Did you know that he has now decided to become a capitalist? A merchant?"

Kim recoiled. "What are you talking about? Yes, he has been only a messenger, but this last is not true. I have facts you do not know. He has not become a merchant."

"Comrade, my investigation is only beginning. I am certain I shall turn up far more interesting information concerning you and your renegade sons." He turned to leave the room.

"Wait."

He stopped, still facing the door. "Is it time for a confession so soon?"

"You know better than that, Comrade." Kim's attitude had calmed. "Please sit down. We have much to discuss."

The investigator strode hungrily back to the chair and sat. "On the contrary, Comrade, I believe there is much to be confessed."

"I think there is no basis for confession," replied Kim hastily. "I admit there are things you do not know, but they are not crimes against the people. As for Nambae, I have issued instructions for him to be brought to Pyongyang for exposure."

"But Comrade, I think that is not your function. It is my business to expose, yours to punish."

Kim nodded. "I know, Comrade. But this is a most embarrassing situation for me, my son's poor performance."

The other leaned forward. "What about Kwon?"

"I did meet him," admitted Kim in a low voice. "It was a chance thing. A chance of war."

"Really?" sneered the investigator. "I find that most difficult to believe."

"It is true," protested Kim. "I was not told the government was leaving earlier than planned. By the time I learned of the change everyone was gone. I arranged immediately for an airplane to take me out, to help me rejoin the others. They were to depart from an airfield east of the city. We got into the car, that assistant and I, and started for the airfield. It was night. The snow was heavy and we could not see. Then there was an explosion and I was thrown clear of the car." He thought for a moment. "I was injured, bruised at least. I remember flying through the air with the force of the explosion. I was captured. The enemy carried me back into their rear and their battalion commander called his regiment. He told his colonel he had captured what appeared to be a high socialist official."

"Did they not attempt to question you there and then?" He was dubious.

"I was in shock from the blast, but even when I awakened I feigned unconsciousness to avoid interrogation."

"What happened then?"

"I did not know it at the time, but Kwon was the regimental commander. They took me to him. The moment he saw me he dismissed them and sent them back to the front."

"Did they not think that strange?"

"Why should they think it strange? He was the regimental commander. He told them he would take care of the situation. I think they could not question it."

The investigator nodded. "Please continue."

"We talked for several hours. That was the first I had known of his being a colonel." He looked accusingly at his antagonist. "Your secretariat has not kept me informed concerning the welfare of my sons."

"How was he promoted so quickly?"

"He exposed another officer, a former Japanese sympathizer."

"Comrade, I know that is not true. Do·not lie to me again. You have been doing rather well."

Kim looked at him, cornered, trying to imagine the man's sources of information. "He has an officer in his command. He is the commander of the battalion which captured me."

"Lieutenant Colonel Shin," prompted the secretary.

Kim looked at him sharply. "I do not know."

"Then permit me to educate you. He was a captain in the Japanese army. He commanded the guards at the Inchon prison.

He was a major while Kwon was a lieutenant colonel. When your son was made a colonel he arranged for Shin to become a lieutenant colonel."

"Yes," said Kim. "Now I remember. My son told me that."

"Of course he did. He then had Shin insert you back through the lines under the guise of your being an agent of the south."

"Yes. How do you know these things? How do you know about this Shin?"

"Order of battle is also my business," replied the investigator. "Knowing what units we are facing and who their commanders are. Knowing each commander's strong and weak points. My people are aware of everything."

"Then why do you ask me?" growled Kim. "You have known of the entire event."

"Because, Comrade, I wished to see how truthful you could be. Because I wished to hear what you would say about Nambae." He smiled. "You see? You have lied to me."

"I have told you everything."

"You have lied to me."

"How have I lied? I have told you the truth."

"I shall give you the opportunity to make it the truth."

"I do not know what you are talking about."

The secretary studied him, his face serious. "You have said you ordered the criminal brought to Pyongyang for exposure. I know that you have not."

"I have ordered it. Whether they can find him or not is another matter."

"You have not ordered it yet, Comrade. That is the lie. But we shall now purge that lie from your record and your conscience. We shall make it the truth." He reached for Kim's desk buzzer and pressed the button. "And since you do not seem to know where he is I shall advise you."

An aide entered the room, looking expectantly from one to the other of the two secretaries.

"I am not ready for you yet," snapped Kim to the aide.

"I believe you are, Comrade. He may take notes." He looked meaningfully at the aide. "I believe the information I shall give you now will greatly assist in the apprehension of this criminal."

Kim looked at the aide and nodded. The man took a notebook from his smock and stood ready to write.

"The man we seek is attempting to enter a business arrangement in Seoul with a cabinet minister by the name of Hong. This criminal has an unusual relationship with the manager of the market at the East Gate in Seoul. He is married to this manager. She is also a prostitute. When our second offensive entered the city he evacuated to Pusan, then moved on to Chinhae. There, he met with his brother. They argued and he left. Later, he returned to Seoul. With the assistance of the Americans the prostitute resumed her capitalist ways, reconstructing the market at the East Gate. Our criminal now plans to move into the operation and expand it to the South Gate, then Itaewon and Changdok. Presently he can most likely be found at the East Gate."

Kim was cold with the realization of the man's thoroughness.

"And this man's name, Comrade Secretary?" asked the aide.

The inquisitor looked at Kim and nodded.

"Nambae," rasped the old man. "Bring him back to Pyongyang for exposure as a defector from the people."

"Yes, Comrade." He left the room.

"There," smiled the Secretary of Investigations. "Was that not most simple? Now you have purged the lie from your lips. You have gained the opportunity to punish a criminal."

"And what will happen if they cannot find him?"

The other man pursed his lips. "The information I recited earlier sounds most incriminating against you, Comrade. I suspect the central committee would be so shocked they would demand immediate retribution."

Kim stared at him without speaking.

"Of course he will be found. You, Comrade Kim, must deal with the situation once he reaches Pyongyang."

"But I am handling it there as well. It is my people who are to arrest him, not yours."

"Already the request for assistance is passing from your people to mine. My agents will arrest him and deliver him to you." He smiled. "You must not worry, Comrade. You shall have ample opportunity to be the hero in this case."

THE SOUTH—REPATRIATION

It was spring, the kind of morning which makes even the most barren land seem heavenly, plucks the winter's burden from heavy hearts, envelopes them in music.

Song was exuberant, effervescent. Seeking a means of expressing her joy, she determined to dress her daughter in consonance with the lightness of her heart.

Elsewhere in the city Nambae waved angrily for a taxi. "Take me to the market at the East Gate," he told the driver. They streaked off through the city, passing burned or crumbled buildings, roadblock barriers only moments before removed from the thoroughfares for the day. And yet commerce had returned. Shops, quickly prepared, were open. Restaurants beckoned passersby. Businessmen strode toward their empires, seemingly oblivious of the stalemated war grumbling less than a hundred miles to the north.

The taxi drew to the curb near the East Gate and Nambae paid the driver. The building had but a single entrance opening not at the front or side, but beveled across a corner. Steps led up to the interior, where already a buzz of activity had developed.

Nambae looked neither right nor left, but headed straight for the steps. As he took his first step upward there was a shout behind him, out in the street. He turned and saw a fight, rapidly being joined by others. People along the sidewalk shrank back, their eyes riveted on the growing brawl. Then, however, the scene rapidly took on the character of an entertaining diversion. The shouts grew louder. Spectators congregated, laughing and cheering.

Nambae felt the grip on his arms clamp tight with a jolt. He looked around wildly, trying to see who held him. They were strangers. Then he felt himself being thrust down the steps and across the sidewalk. He let out a cry but it was lost in the confusion of the fight. A car swerved to the curb and the two men shoved him roughly into the rear. He screamed. The men laughed. The car tore off into the traffic.

As quickly as it had begun the fight was over. Curiously, the combatants helped each other to their feet, smiled and sifted into the crowd.

Pinioned in the rear of the car, Nambae cried out in pain. They had bound him and were holding him on the floor. "You are an enemy of the People's Republic."

"I am not an enemy. I was. . . ."

One of the men kicked him, grinding his heel hard into his face. He let out a groan, then fell silent.

The car raced on, past Kimpo and on toward the sea to the west. At Puchon they pulled into an alley. Nambae was dragged from the car, gagged, and tossed carelessly into the rear of an oxcart. Sacks of rice were stacked neatly on top of him, the weight sending stabs of pain through his body. His captors changed clothes. Moments later the oxcart emerged from the alley, the animal plodding rhythmically toward Inchon with the men shuffling busily alongside.

The agony of his interrogation was excruciating. He was burned until he was hoarse with screaming. He was beaten until he bled. His mind whirled in the confusion of space, time, engines throbbing, rolling seas, and always the pain. There was no light, no darkness. Only pain piercing through his consciousness. Gradually he was aware of nothing else, then nothing at all.

When he awoke he was propped up, standing without effort between two hulking guards. He discerned an office. The soreness remained, throbbing and insistent. His sight was blurred, his hearing rang. Then he recognized his father.

"It is most unfortunate you refused to cooperate with the interrogator," said the old man, slowly walking toward him.

He tried to speak. He was too weak and words would not come.

"I had thought you a good worker, faithful to the party and to me. Instead, you have gone south and done nothing. I am told you have tried to become a capitalist."

The son strained for words, then fell silent.

"Place him in the chair," ordered the father. The guards dragged him to the chair and Kim turned to the Secretary of Investigation, who had been listening in obvious satisfaction. "Does the progress of this case please you, Comrade? Do you enjoy it?"

"I am most happy on behalf of the people, Comrade."

Secretary Kim looked at his watch. "We have a half hour before the public exposure. I wish to spend the time with him as his father. As you know, once we are out there I am the Secretary, he the prisoner. Nothing more."

The other smiled suspiciously, with cunning. "I think you wish to help him escape. No, it cannot happen."

Kim scoffed. "It should be obvious to you, Comrade, he is too weak to escape. He has much difficulty standing. However, if it worries you, place guards on the doors. I merely wish to visit with him."

The other man shrugged, then motioned to the guards.

When they were gone Kim approached his son, squatting beside the chair in the fashion he had used as a young man in the fields. "Why?"

Nambae looked at his father. "I have done no wrong," he whispered hoarsely. "I tried, but the government was full. All the positions had been appointed. I was not provided with documents. They provided them for my brother but I was given nothing. I received no help." He lay his head back, grimacing in pain.

"I am told you have done nothing since."

TAEJIN   391

The son kept his eyes tightly closed. "That is not true, Father. Song made a contact, a cabinet minister whose name is Hong."

"Yes," replied the father. "But you have been trying to become a capitalist with her. The secretary has told me the arrangement."

"That is not true, Father. One day while I was away looking for my cell leader Song deserted me. When I returned she was not there. She has been nothing but a problem to me, and I felt I was well rid of her. Then, when I talked with Kwon at Chinhae, he told me she had become a capitalist, that she was working with this Hong."

"But why did you go to Chinhae?"

"I went there because I was told my cell leader had gone there. I wished to contact him and try to obtain some help, some documents such as my brother was given."

"The secretary has told me none of this."

"When they arrested me I was on my way into the market for the first time. I had just returned from Chinhae. I was on my way to confront Song. I was planning to arrange her return to you for punishment."

"She is of little consequence to us. I think there will be ways, since she is now a friend of this cabinet minister, in which she can be convinced she should help our cause. If we were to bring her here that contact and opportunity would be lost."

Nambae perceived the situation. "Your friend, the secretary," he rasped through the pain. "He has started all this?"

The old man nodded forlornly. "Yes. There was little I could do. He had me placed in such a position that any deviation on my part would have destroyed all of us. Me, your brother, you. Your choice of a harlot wife has made it more difficult for everyone."

"Is that why I was provided with no documents? Was it my punishment?"

The secretary shrugged. "I know nothing of documents. He has forced me to bring you back."

The son rolled his head slowly to the side, looking at his father. He knew now he must pay. He wondered if he could drag this other secretary down with him, this man who would destroy them all. "I think he has not told you of his relationship with Hong," he said carefully.

The old man suddenly sparkled with interest. "What relationship has he with Hong?"

"Hong is an opportunist," continued the son. "He has become most wealthy, yet he cannot be certain which way the war will end. He believes the safest way is to prepare his bed on both sides."

"You talk in riddles," admonished the father anxiously. "Tell me what is happening."

"He is purchasing the favor of your Secretary of Investigation," lied Nambae. "He believes the most certain way to obtain asylum should the People's Republic win is to have the accuser in his debt. He has paid large sums of money to your comrade. The secretary is a most wealthy man. On the other hand, the secretary also is not certain which way the war will end. I think he wishes to be friends with an important person in their government. Then, if the People's Republic loses, he will have an influential person in Seoul to prevent his execution."

The father's eyes narrowed. "That is how he has known these things. He has called you the capitalist, yet he was becoming far more wealthy than you." A smile of satisfaction crept across his face.

"I have wished to report these things to you, Father, but it was very difficult. All reports must pass through this secretary."

"Are you certain the man, this Hong, is not merely an agent?"

"I am very sure. I have learned he is already paying large amounts of money to the Secretary of Investigation. He thinks it most humorous. He believes the money is for the secretary's private use, not for the People's Republic. It is protection money."

Kim was ecstatic. "When have you learned this?"

The son hesitated, feigning thought and trying to select a time frame which would fit with what appeared to have happened in Pyongyang. "I think ten days ago."

The secretary mused. "Ten days ago. Yes, I think that would be correct. He first accosted me five days ago." He stood and walked back to his desk. "He has planned an execution. He shall have one." Smiling with deep satisfaction he prepared to leave for the ceremonies.

"You mean you will execute me?" The son was not surprised, but edgy.

"I think I have no choice. If I save you now it will be viewed as a political trick to spare my son. It is you or everyone. But I think you will not be alone today." He strode to the door without looking at his son again. "It is most late," he snapped. "I have obtained a confession. We must go to the square."

The guards entered the office and dragged Nambae to his feet. Then, the two secretaries leading the way, they walked from the building into the square and ascended the platform. A large crowd had been gathered, not against their will. They watched expectantly, almost in a festive mood as Secretary Kim stepped to the microphone.

"Comrades from the masses," he began. "Fellow workers. It is my duty to stand before you today and report crimes against the People's Republic. No criminal escapes our justice, punishment by the people. You have a right to observe the exposure about to take place, to learn of the crimes, to witness the punishment."

He paused and swept his gaze across the sea of faces. "We have here an enemy of the people. He defected to the south. He defected from you. He defected from the masses because of greed. He wished to become a capitalist, a seeker of wealth and comfort. For this he will die before you today. He will feel your wrath. He will learn from the bullets that the people must not be cheated. He will stand against the wall and we shall not provide him a hood. His shamed face will be visible to the masses to the end."

A weak cheer went up, a shifting of feet. The guards took the prisoner's elbows and began leading him from the platform toward the wall. The secretary held up both his arms.

"Wait," he shouted. "I have not finished. Ever since the rise of the workers I have had only one purpose in my life. That purpose was to dig out your enemies, seek them out and destroy them. It has been my only goal. I care not who the criminal may be. If he is an enemy of the people he is destroyed, and no one may escape because of favoritism. I wish you to believe this. I have proof of this loyalty to the People's Republic today, proof that no criminal will be spared, no matter what his position, no matter who he is. This man," he shouted, his voice rising passionately, "is my son!"

A gasp rippled through the crowd. They stared at him, unable to comprehend such loyalty to them, to the masses of souls he would never know as individuals.

"As I have said," he continued loudly, "There can be no favorites. A man cannot be excused his crimes because of family or position. That is a trick of the capitalists. It is a mark of their decadence. It is the reason our system, equality for all, will soon rule the world. I am very certain you agree."

A cheer rose through the square, the sounds reverberating from the buildings and spiraling skyward. He let them continue, calculating the effect of their exuberance, their belief in him as a hero. When the sounds did not subside he raised his arms once more, intoxicated in his success at manipulating them. They quieted, waiting for more.

"There is a man in the south, a cabinet minister in the capitalist dictatorship. He is a specialist, a specialist at corruption. He is a member of their government, yet he uses that position to become wealthy. He steals from his government, accepts favors from individuals. He receives bribes from the United States, the people who taught him such tricks. He engages in capitalistic enterprises such as selling babies and becomes even more wealthy." He paused, looking over the intent, silent crowd. "We have learned he has also meddled in the affairs of the People's Republic. It was he who corrupted Nambae, who is about to die for his indiscretion. It was this same man who has tried, and still attempts even today, to protect his capitalist skin on that future day when we crush his government. How does he do that?" He smiled. "He bribes members of our government. He is most shrewd, this selfish capitalist. He corrupts only those who can be of value to him. He corrupts those who can protect him when the People's Republic succeeds in beating the capitalists to their knees." His voice rose, vibrating in passion. "He has corrupted one of the highest officials of our government. He has made him wealthy. He has offered him large amounts of money. This high official in the People's Republic has accepted this money. He has become a wealthy man. Yet he has told no one of his connection. If he said anything he would be seen for the capitalist he is. We would realize we have a capitalist in our midst. We would purge him, execute him as we are doing with my son today."

He turned slowly, dramatically, and raised his arm to the remaining guards on the platform. "I direct you," he ordered, loud and clear, "to seize the Secretary of Investigation!"

The secretary started, looking about wildly in disbelief. The guards, all members of Kim's corrections staff, advanced on him quickly, pinioning him roughly. A crescendo of confused, shocked conversation had risen through the crowd.

"Stop," cried the new prisoner. "They are lies. I have not done what he has said." His voice could not be heard beyond the guards surrounding him. Secretary Kim walked quickly to the group. "Gag him. I think the confidence of the workers will be destroyed if they hear his protests. He will lie to implicate others. He will do most terrible things to avoid the firing squad. The masses must not be denied."

They had done it even as he spoke. The young secretary glared at the triumphant Kim through eyes drawn narrow with hate. Kim looked at him and smiled. "Come now, Comrade. You have told me in times past how important it is to keep up one's appearance." He turned and walked back to the microphone. "Let the executions begin," he screamed.

When it was over he returned to his office, then stopped in surprise at the sight before him. The Chairman of the People's Republic was seated, awaiting him.

"Comrade Chairman," he breathed.

The chairman smiled. "Comrade, I have come to congratulate you. In your soul you have the fire of a dragon. Again you have proved your total loyalty to the workers and the People's Republic." He reached out and shook Kim's hand. "Not many would have shot their own son."

Kim shrugged, passing it off. "Comrade Chairman, he was an enemy. It was most necessary that he die."

"And the secretary," continued the chairman. "I knew nothing of such double dealing. You were most perceptive."

"It was not my first investigation and exposure, Comrade Chairman. Under different circumstances I would have sent him to trial, but the court consists of his people. They would have exonerated him out of loyalty to the man. Justice would not have been served and we would have lost an opportunity to educate the masses on the consequences of disloyalty. It was necessary to do it quickly, decisively."

The chairman nodded agreement. "We must always purge those who oppose us. We must keep the Party pure." He stopped and studied Kim. "Comrade, we now have a glaring vacancy. We cannot tolerate a vacancy in so important a position. You have always proved yourself a quick and most effective investigator. I therefore name you to the vacant secretariat."

Kim's knees were weak. He felt a cry of joy rising in his throat, choked it back. Tears streamed from his eyes. "But what of my position in corrections?"

"I have long believed," replied the chairman, "that both secretariats should belong to the same man. I must confess that his youth had led me to believe our late Secretary a most logical choice. But you have proved that service, loyalty and experience are the wealth of the revolution."

When the chairman was gone Kim sat at his desk, churning with the adversary emotions of loss and victory. The sun set and night dusted over the city. Still he remained far into the night, contemplating the busy though empty years to come.

THE SOUTH—DMZ

The fighting had ended months before, yet each man in the long network of fortifications which stretched from coast to coast sensed the urgency of alertness. Divisions deployed along the line were kept at a peak of readiness, belying their meager appearance. Dispersed through the rugged and lonely terrain, huddled in bunkers and listening posts, they sometimes seemed not to be there at all.

A long, high fence was being constructed across the peninsula, each side amply protected by mine fields. For the troops on line, the other side of the zone seemed suddenly foreign, another world, or at least, the end of theirs. The people might as well have spoken a different language, been of a different race. Cousins, perhaps, by blood, they were bitter enemies by ideal. Though many inwardly yearned for peace, reunification, an opportunity to meld together with those on the other side, it took on more the character of a dream. Never in the lifetimes of the soldiers had they known such an existence. Reality was antagonism, threats, danger, and sometimes death.

The night was chilled with early autumn. Clouds blanketed the demilitarized zone, deepening the darkness.

Late, long after midnight, the young soldier leaned forward, peering into the black nothingness before him.

"What is it?" asked his companion quietly.

The other man shook his head. "I cannot be sure."

Together, they strained, at once wishing to hear it again, identify the sound, and hoping it was the first man's imagination.

"Perhaps it was an animal," suggested the one who had not heard the sound.

"I think it was metal," replied the first. "It sounded like digging, cutting."

"Listen carefully. I will call." He reached for the field telephone at his elbow and turned the crank vigorously. He waited a moment, then spoke in whispers, anxious, intense. Then, dropping the receiver into its pocket, he leaned forward beside his companion. "They are alerting the others. Have you heard it again?"

The other man started to shake his head, then stopped. "There! Did you hear it?"

He nodded. "Yes," he whispered, reaching quickly again for the phone. "We heard it again," he reported anxiously. He listened intently for a moment, nodding animatedly at the receiver. "Yes, Sir," he snapped. He repocketed the receiver and leaned forward again. "The headquarters will send troops into the trenches."

"Have the other outposts heard the sounds?"

"Yes. Two."

There was a busy, scraping sound behind them. They turned abruptly, alarmed, then relaxed as an officer and a sergeant bustled in beside them.

"Where?" asked the officer.

"To the front," replied the first soldier, pointing. "Perhaps a little to the left, Sir."

The officer looked quickly at the sergeant. "Tell the others. We will fire as soon as the flare illuminates them."

The sergeant scurried off in the darkness.

"There," said the first soldier, waving his hand excitedly. "Did you hear it?"

The officer nodded quickly. "Yes. I heard it. I think they are trying to breach the wire."

Suddenly there was a muffled pop, high above them to their front. An eerie glow radiated over the starkness of the terrain as the parachute flare began floating slowly downward.

In the openness of the truce land before them, dozens of men suddenly turned, clambering for cover. The men in the listening posts and trenches began firing, raining their concentration across the sea of grass.

One by one, the enemy soldiers began dropping. More flares were dangling above them now, and mortar rounds whumped into the glade.

The fire was not returned from the northern sector, and finally, all movement having ceased to their front, the southern forces stopped firing.

A constant parade of flares continued to oscillate their glow over the grotesque scene, one after another, until dawn.

THE NORTH—PYONGYANG

"I came as quickly as possible, Comrade. Is something wrong?"
The deputy was tired, yet alert despite the darkness. It was three
o'clock.

"We have been humiliated again," said Secretary Kim softly.

"What do you mean, Comrade?" asked the deputy, his curiosity rising.

"I mean," growled Kim, his venom surfacing, "that yet another border action has failed. We have been defeated in an action
only one hour ago." He glared at the deputy meaningfully. "You
see? It proves my analysis of our intelligence system. It is totally
ineffective." The secretary had looked down again as he said it.
"These reports indicate most clearly the uselessness of our former
comrade." He shoved the papers away in disgust and pulled himself from his chair. "We have a fine network of agents in the south,
yet their direction from here has been totally blind. They have
been providing us with the wrong information."

"Perhaps we should recall their leaders. Punish only a few and
the remainder will begin to perform better."

"I think it is not their error, Comrade. The error lies in
Pyongyang." Kim's manner was calm, yet menacing. "We have
been assigned this secretariat. The Secretariat of Investigation is a
most important organization. It is our duty to provide the best
and most useful information to our army. We must purge the errors from the system. We must correct the crimes of our predeces-

sor." He circled back to his desk and sat once more. "His goals were wrong. He assumed we did not drive the capitalists into the sea because we were too weak. That was a most grave error. It placed us in a defensive frame of mind. But we cannot remain defensive if we would reunite our nation. We must change our thinking. We must be the attackers. We must not allow our soldiers to think in defensive terms. They must not think negative thoughts, and defensive thinking is negative thinking." He gazed calmly at the deputy. "You see? They were not prepared to undertake an offensive thrust at the enemy. Because of that, they failed. We failed, and the People's Republic has been humiliated."

"What do you suggest, Comrade?" asked the deputy, more in the manner of an apprentice.

"This action has failed because we did not have enough information about our brothers to the south. Military information! My predecessor, the criminal, wished to think our program of reunification could be brought about by political means. He expected them to wake up one morning and take a vote. I think he placed a great many people in their government for that purpose. It is as though he were preparing their assembly to accept us. You see? It became a matter of waiting to see if they would accept us, not whether we would accept them. His every thought was defensive. He worried too much of their national assembly and not enough of their military."

"We have excellent people in their military," protested the deputy. "Even your son is there. He is one of their generals."

"Yes, of course we have some people there, too. But I think we do not know enough about them. We have lost the initiative. He should have spent as much effort placing people in their military as he did in their national assembly."

"I think there will be little opportunity to place more people with their army now, Comrade. The fighting is over and the open access we once had has been closed off."

"Comrade, no initiative is lost forever. The fighting is over, as you have said, but the war will never be over until we have reunified our land under the People's Republic. We shall purge the errors from our system. We must change the things our people in their army do."

Comrade, we have most accurate figures on their strength."

"Yes, on their strengths. We have counted their noses. We know how many people they have."

"And we have informed our commanders. Our forces have been aligned very efficiently against them. I cannot understand the defeat you have mentioned. We have superior numbers on our side in every case."

"Precisely," replied the secretary, ignoring the deputy's consternation. "Numbers. We play a game of mathematics with them. They place two, we place three. They place three more so we hurry into the area with four more." He looked at the other man. "What does that tell you of our inefficiency?"

"We have been maintaining a stronger posture," replied the deputy, without conviction.

"Have we?" asked the secretary, becoming triumphant. "The question we should be asking ourselves, Comrade, is whether we are maintaining a more intelligent posture. Our recent comrade has given them the initiative. They act, we react. Our every move is an answer to something they have done. That is the error of our program. We must present the surprises, not the capitalists."

"I think we must merely begin making the first move," replied the deputy tiredly.

The secretary watched him for a moment, unmoved.

"It is very simple, Comrade," added the deputy.

"Would you merely step up and make a move? That is what has happened this morning. And our army has failed. Comrade, my point is that we do not know where or how to make a first move effectively with the information he has provided us. We do not know because he has concentrated only on their strengths, and now we have learned he failed at that. He has done nothing to seek out their weaknesses. When we have properly identified their weaknesses we shall begin causing uncomfortable situations for them. We shall strike only at the weaknesses, but strike often. I think if we armed our minds properly, if we had the information we require, we would soon enough have them thinking defensively instead of offensively. Each of our thrusts need only be a small thing, yet each one will make its mark. In a matter of time we shall have them believing they are most weak indeed. They will be less confident and will suddenly find themselves reacting so frequently to our actions they will have no time to create new problems for us."

The deputy was sitting forward in his chair, listening intently. "Who began this morning's action, Comrade?"

"Our army began it," rasped the secretary. "I ordered it so, to prove my point."

The deputy sat back, clearly shaken.

"Our goals must be changed, Comrade," summarized the secretary. "Our agents must work harder. They must inform us of every weak link in the capitalist chain."

"Comrade, that places a very difficult burden on them. They have been directed to gather information, to send it to us. We must interpret it here. If we now ask them to seek information they consider weaknesses they must interpret it there. They must become much more selective in the information they send us." He paused, as though afraid of the next statement. "If we have found so few weaknesses in them perhaps they are stronger than we think."

"Coward!" exploded the secretary. "Where is your imagination?" He became calm as quickly. "We must be creative, Comrade. Our first goal is to learn about their commanders, their order of battle. Our former comrade boasted to me of knowing their order of battle most intimately. I think he did not know the meaning of the term. We must ask for all information on every commander they have on the line. We shall not be content with hearing they have a specialist in defense or offense commanding a division. Our interest must be also in what he cannot do. In what his subordinate commanders cannot do. Perhaps we must not listen only to what our agents say. Perhaps we must hear more important messages in what they do not say."

"Then must we purge our people here?"

"We must ask better questions. We must tell our people in the south most specifically what we desire. We must be certain we receive all the information, not only those things against which we must defend. We must decide what we must have and demand it. We shall soon enough place them on the defensive."

"I shall send an order immediately, Comrade."

"I have not finished, though this last will come later."

The deputy stopped.

"I wish to obtain complete order of battle information on the Americans as well. It would be foolhardy to plan a threat against a man's weakness only to learn he is being assisted by an American who specializes in that weakness. We shall avoid much frustration by being thorough, Comrade. Another thing we shall obtain is information on their state of preparedness and their morale. That is a most basic difference between them and us. We say little about our strength, yet we have much better capabilities than they suspect. They crow to the world about their power. Most frequently, closer inspection reveals they do not have the strength they claim. Their morale wavers. I think their soldiers are not as capable as they claim. They are much less willing to sacrifice. I shall have very detailed reports on their preparedness and the morale of their men. I want the information to come from the soldiers themselves, not their officers, not even their sergeants."

"Would you have our people purchase such information?"

"No. We must be more careful. We must overhear their conversations, see their confrontations, be aware of their grumbling." He looked sharply at the other man. "There is a very greedy man in their government. He is a cabinet minister named Hong. I think it would be most appropriate if our people were to use his vast influence."

"Is he not the man who corrupted our former secretary?"

Kim growled the words. "He corrupted the thoughts of my son."

The deputy watched him, cautious of his temper.

"He began with a woman and corrupted her," continued the secretary. "She was married to my son. They were trained together as agents before they were inserted into the south." He shook his head. "Once they were there she did less than Nambae. At least he became a messenger, but she has done nothing at all. I think it is time for her to assist the masses."

"But how could she do that, Comrade? If she has done nothing in all this time perhaps she would not wish to help. I think it would be merely another case of retrieving one of them for punishment."

The secretary's excitement was building. "Ah, but she will wish very much to assist us. You see, she has close access to this Hong. He has corrupted her. As a result she has abandoned our thought and is working with Hong. She manages his great markets in Seoul." He grinned impishly. "It will be most satisfying to me when she begins extracting information from him for us, for our cause. She will be a great contributor to the reunification of our land."

"If she has become imbued with capitalist thought it could be risky. If she is approached she may refuse and we would then be forced to retrieve her. If we do not bring her back she could turn on us. She could tell this Hong about our network there." He shook his head in concern. "It could be very dangerous for our agents. She could expose them all."

"But she will not," smiled Kim confidently. "There are ways to ensure she will be most anxious to practice obedience. She has been absent from socialist thought for quite long enough. It is time for a new dedication."

"How can it be done?"

"We must merely tell the cell leader. Have him assign the task to my son, Kwon. He will know how to control her."

THE SOUTH—SEOUL

As Song departed the market she heard his call. Taejin hurried up to her, trim in his uniform, and grasped her outstretched hands.

"I saw you yesterday," he said, "but I could not get to you before you were gone. I was afraid Nambae would be near."

She smiled. "He is gone."

He raised an eyebrow. "Gone?"

"Yes. I took Sookee and left him soon after we returned to Seoul from Taegu. He was too cruel. He had not been able to infiltrate the government. He went to see his cell leader and I took Sookee away while he was gone. I have never seen him again." She turned back up the steps. "Come. I have an office here. Let me show it to you."

"And Sookee?" he asked, following her. "How is Sookee?"

She laughed back over her shoulder. "She is fine, and growing very fast. You will be pleased when you see her. She knows about you now. She knows you are her father." She led him through the packed aisles and into a small but neat office. "This is where I work."

"This is very nice. Do you work for the manager?"

She looked at him quietly, demurely. "I am the manager," she replied. At last she noticed his uniform. "Are you in the army?"

"No. I am an interpreter for the Americans. I work at the United Nations Command in Yongsan." He stood tall, proud.

"Then your study of English has served you well." She affected a pout. "I thought you would come and find me sooner."

He hung his head, but could not conceal his happy smile. "You must not be angry with me, Song. I came many times, but there were many people. I saw you yesterday for the first time."

"Did you come here directly from Taegu?"

"No. I continued to work as a mess boy. They took me into the fighting with them." He shrugged happily. "They helped me with my English."

"Did you come to Seoul then?" She was gazing at him, hungrily filling the lost years.

He sobered. "No. I was wounded and they sent me to a hospital at Suwon. While I was. . . ."

"How were you wounded?" she interrupted, concerned now.

He waved it off. "It was not serious."

"If you were in a hospital I think it was serious." She put her arms around him, but gently. "How were you wounded, Taejin?"

He returned the embrace. "The enemy artillery shelled our position. The mess tent was hit and I was wounded by the shrapnel." He brightened. "But it was good fortune. While I was in the hospital they taught me more English. It was better English, not the colloquial language they spoke at the front. As I recovered I was allowed to stay with them. I worked in their kitchen but I studied hard. They arranged for me to become an interpreter in Seoul." He stepped back, his hands holding her shoulders as he studied her face. "Now you must tell me of Song."

She laughed. "We must go. You must see Sookee. I will tell you my story on the way." She busied herself closing the office.

"Where is your home?"

"I live in Itaewon. It is close to your Yongsan compound." They were outside. "We will take a taxi."

He stepped to the curb and waved.

"Now you must tell me of Song," he said again as they crowded into the converted jeep.

"It is a long story. When we left Taegu we were walking with the refugees. It was very difficult, but we had good fortune. We met a man who was being beaten. We rescued him. He was the orphanage director for the government. We walked to Gimchon and he drove us the rest of the way to Seoul."

"That saved you many miles of walking."

"Yes, but it was more than that. He told us of his friend, a cabinet minister, Hong. He said Hong would control the large markets when Seoul was rebuilt. I wanted Nambae to meet with Hong but he refused."

"Why? A cabinet minister is a very powerful man."

"Yes, but the orphanage director wanted to arrange a situation for us in the markets. Nambae was trying to find a position in the government."

"A cabinet minister could have arranged that."

"Of course. You must remember that Nambae is not very intelligent. He would not meet Hong because he was afraid he would be forced into the markets."

"Tell me about when you left Nambae. You said you left him when you returned to Seoul."

"We had no place to live. We had no money to buy food, clothes. We went to a refugee camp and he was cruel. He beat me. He was angry that his leader had not provided him documents so he could infiltrate the government, but in his anger he beat me. One day when he went to find his leader I took Sookee and left the camp."

"Nambae is an animal," moaned Taejin. "You are well rid of him." He spurred her on. "But how did you get into the markets?"

She smiled. "I went to the East Gate. I hoped to find you there, but as I searched I found the market. Hong was there talking with a man who was rebuilding it."

"How did you know it was Hong?"

"I heard his name as he talked. I knew the orphanage director had told him of Nambae and me so I spoke with him as he was leaving."

Taejin was surprised. "And he gave you a position? Just like that?"

"No. He did not want to talk with me at first, so it was necessary to convince him."

"How did you do that?"

"You must remember that my father was a merchant. Hong is not. I suggested ways to organize the markets and he realized he could become very wealthy. He invited me to manage them for him."

"Song, you are a very intelligent woman."

She leaned forward and told the driver to stop. "This is my home."

Taejin paid the driver and they walked to the door. "Now you shall see your daughter again."

Sookee had grown. Now seven, she attacked Taejin with the exuberance of love. Taejin clasped her, tears of joy running down his face. "I am happy to see you again, Sookee."

Please do not leave us again, Father," she murmured.

"He did not wish to leave us before," Song reminded her. "It is important that he has returned."

Taejin and his daughter talked and played together while Song prepared food. Later, he tucked the child into her pallet and hummed to her softly as she drifted into sleep.

"Do you live at the compound?" asked Song.

"Yes," he replied, stroking her.

"Must you return there tonight?"

"I must return in the morning."

"Please stay with me," she whispered. "I want you to stay with me."

He nodded. "Yes, I must stay."

She reached up, loosening his shirt. "At last," she giggled, "I can be the wife of Taejin."

They undressed each other, slowly, tenderly. Then, with gentle insistence, they relived a beautiful moment from long ago.

* * * * * *

General Kwon sat in the taxi, watching the traffic but listening intently to the message being relayed by the driver. "I cannot understand him," he wailed. "We have produced every piece of information they have ordered."

"They want more, Comrade," replied the driver.

"But morale? Preparedness? American commanders?" He sucked air through his teeth with a loud hiss. "I think he is asking more and more difficult questions."

"He believes in your ability to produce results for the reunification, Comrade. You are a general. Such information should be very simple for you to obtain."

"He is asking that I risk exposure," replied the general disgustedly. "If I request such information people will wonder why. If our people approach Americans requesting preparedness and morale information someone will wonder about that. It is too obvious."

"They wish you to accomplish it by more surreptitious means. There is to be no obvious direct contact."

"Then it will be even more difficult," agonized the general.

"You have many contacts," observed the driver quietly. "Use them."

General Kwon watched the passing scenery. They were working their way around the perimeter of Seoul, occasionally turning off main thoroughfares to wind through narrow back streets. Then, certain they were still alone, they would emerge once more on the main route by way of a different intersection and continue on their way to the next convenient burrough. The confusion maneuver was repeated frequently.

"I have several contacts," said Kwon finally. "I have not yet used them extensively for basic information. They have never organized an operation of the size required for this mission. They may not be effective."

"The secretary suggests Hong," replied the driver. "He is a most decadent man. His principal motivation is greed, his greatest fear, exposure. He could be used very effectively."

"He is a dedicated capitalist."

"He is more dedicated to what capitalism can do for him than he is to the system. I think he would work fervently to escape pain or poverty." The driver looked quickly over his shoulder, then back at the road. "He has many obedient contacts. His friends are influential. I think he will find a way for them to provide the help he requires. It is very important, however, that he become deeply involved. He must believe it will result in great future rewards."

"I think this must become a very large network. I must rely on you to provide much manpower."

The driver shook his head. "More of our agents cannot be made available. They have other assignments. You must accomplish this with your own resources. You must use your initiative and imagination."

Kwon leaned forward, now anxious. "None? Will you provide me no help?"

"Yes. None."

"But what will happen if I encounter difficulty? he asked petulantly.

"You must solve such problems with your ingenuity. You have accomplished equally difficult things before."

"Take me back to my headquarters," said Kwon impatiently. "It is possible to go directly across the city from here."

The driver smiled. "You are not the great general with me, Kwon. You must remember that. In reality, you are not a general and I am not a taxi driver. Such things are but games for the public to see. They mean nothing other than to provide us with a means of accomplishing our tasks. You may order your soldiers to do your bidding, but please remember your true place. I must discuss other things with you."

"I am most sorry, Comrade," replied the general. "I meant no disrespect. I was merely anxious to proceed with my assignment. It will require much planning."

"I think there is more planning than you now understand," replied the driver, turning into yet another side street and watching his rear view mirror. "You are to activate Song. The secretary is most disturbed that she is not an active participant with us. Much effort was expended in her training and transport to the south. You shall use her or she will be returned as was her husband."

"I do not know where to find her," objected Kwon.

"I had an interesting fare two days ago. A man and a woman rode with me from the market at the South Gate to Itaewon. They talked of Nambae. The woman was Song."

Kwon was startled. "Who was the man?"

"His name was not mentioned. He wore a uniform."

"Was it an army uniform?"

"It was not. I have never seen one like it before."

"But you are certain it was Song."

"Yes. I am certain."

"And you know where she lives?"

"Yes."

Kwon smiled now, relieved to find an amusing facet to his mission. "I shall be most pleased to educate her, Comrade," he replied.

* * * * * *

It was raining as Song made her way home from the market. Her spirits were low. Taejin would be working and would not be able to visit her this evening. She huddled under her umbrella, admitting to herself that she had become spoiled by his presence for the past three days.

As she turned from the street toward her house she felt a hand grip her arm. She let out a cry and turned quickly to stare into the face of General Kwon.

"Kwon," she gasped. "How have you found me?"

He ignored the question. "I think we must talk together, Song."

She pulled, trying to free herself from his grip, but he would not let go.

"Come. It is raining. Let us go into your house where we may stay dry."

"You are not welcome in my house," she retorted. "I do not want to talk with you."

"Ah, but you will. I merely wish to talk with you about the future."

"Then we will talk here. I do not want to take you into my house."

"You must not be so inhospitable to me, Song." He smiled. "Did you know that your husband has been returned to Pyongyang?"

"Are you now to do the same with me?" she asked, suddenly weak, cold.

"I did not take your husband. He was assisted in his return to Pyongyang by others, by those whom our father requested to invite him home. My function is merely to look into your welfare. I wish to see if you are comfortable and have received enough to eat."

"I am doing very well. I shall continue to do well without your assistance. Leave me alone."

"Yes," he leered. "I understand you have made a very comfortable capitalist bed for yourself. You have followed in the footsteps of your worthless father."

She tried again to free herself, but it was useless.

"It is a shame, Song. Your father was an enemy of the people of Hochon. He took from them and made himself a parasite, a toad of the Japanese. Now you would do the same. You would rebel against the masses by becoming wealthy at the expense of the people." He motioned toward the house. "And in the future you would lead your daughter along the same foolhardy path."

"That is not your concern, Kwon. I am her mother. I shall be concerned for her welfare."

"And your husband. Are you not concerned about him?"

"Nambae is no longer my husband. He did nothing to establish himself, and now you have told me he is in Pyongyang. I have no need to be concerned for him. He can take care of himself."

"Your husband is dead," he said, his voice casual. "He was educated very carefully by the People's Republic, yet he chose to forget his training. His forgetfulness proved to be most tragic." He smiled icily at her. "Others should learn from the errors of Nambae. It would be unfortunate for such events to have to be repeated."

She stared at him, terrified. "What do you want with me?"

"I seem to recall others," he said softly, "who received the benefit of extensive schooling at the time Nambae received his. Yet these others have done nothing with such training. I think it would be very beneficial if you reconsidered your position and came with me. I have much work for you to perform. It will be most healthy for your daughter if you work for me. She will remain safe."

"And if I do not?" There was a tremor in her voice. "What will happen if I refuse to work for you?"

"Then I should cease to be concerned for the safety and welfare of your daughter. She is, after all, a symbol of my family's disgrace. Seoul is a most dangerous city in which to live. Many horrible events occur regularly here, particularly among the cutthroat capitalist merchants. I think I could not continue to look after her and assure you of her health."

"I think I am able to assure myself of her health. I need no assistance from you."

"Please accept my apologies, Song, but I think you will be much too busy to look after her welfare. We shall arrange for others to care for her. Of course, I shall continue to inform you of her condition when you make your regular reports to me."

"No," she screamed. "You cannot take my daughter!"

He said nothing, but motioned toward the house, releasing her arm. She stared at him in horror, then dashed past him and through the door. The house was empty, the child nowhere to be seen.

Kwon had followed her into the house, grinning.

"Where is she?" she demanded, her voice hoarse.

He ignored her. "You will be expected to stand at the South Gate tomorrow morning. Carry a basket in your left hand and a shawl in your right. You must count regularly to ten, then look upward to the top of the South Gate. Keep your eyes on the crest of the gate for a count of five, then look down at your feet. Keep repeating the process until you are approached by a taxi. The driver will ask you if you wish to purchase a paper lantern. You will reply that it must be orange. He will then take you to your destination."

"And will I then see my daughter?"

"You must stop asking such questions," he replied curtly. "Each time you ask such things I shall become antagonized. An antagonistic man is very difficult as a taskmaster. Do you not agree?"

She stood, motionless, and the tears poured from the corners of her eyes. By the time her vision had cleared he was gone.

THE SOUTH—
TONGDUCHON-NI

The highway wound northward from Seoul, following a placid valley which was crowded on each side by towering, craggy mountains. The boundary between the valley and mountains lay in a pattern much like gear teeth, with finger valleys probing their way into the ruggedness, only to surrender to the ridges on either side. Into these tiny draws were crowded rice paddies, and along their edges crouched the occasional homes of the farmers, lonely and isolated.

In the center of one such draw stood an old farmhouse, uncharacteristically sturdy in its spaciousness and structure. A masonry wall ten feet high surrounded it, enclosing a broad courtyard and two buildings. The larger building, once the home of the landowner, now housed an orphanage for some fifty children. Numerous large rooms opened onto a central corridor which lay along the center of the structure, depressed one step down from the level of the rooms. Most rooms were used as sleeping quarters for the various age groups. One room served as an office. At the rear of the building, another room was the kitchen.

The second building, considerably smaller, was of less substantial construction. It cowered against the wall at the rear of the compound and housed the orphanage director and his family.

There was no moon, though the night was clear, starry. Three men trudged along the highway, talking only occasionally and softly. Two carried heavy satchels, the other a rope which was coiled about his shoulder. Drooping below the rope was a useless, deformed arm.

As they approached the midpoint of the valley's opening they turned abruptly from the highway and hurried their pace along the dike between the paddies. At last, reaching an intersection of two dikes, they stopped. The two carrying the satchels set them carefully on the path and the three squatted together, glancing appraisingly at the wall which rose in the darkness only a few yards away.

"We must discuss our plan now, for one final time," whispered the cripple, sliding the rope from his shoulder.

"Quickness." said one of the others. "We must rely on quickness, Chi."

Chi nodded. "If we do it as planned we shall be most successful." He glanced at the one who had spoken. "You will be first on the wall. Once you are inside you cannot linger. Go immediately for the director." He turned to the other man. "You will go over the wall next. You will open the gate for me immediately."

The other man nodded.

"We cannot talk once we reach the wall," continued Chi. "Do you have any questions now?"

There was a pause. The three looked at each other silently.

"Then we will do it," said Chi finally. He rose, gathering the rope with his good arm and scurrying off toward the wall. Behind him, his companions lifted the satchels and followed. At the wall, the satchels were deposited next to the gate.

Chi was uncoiling the rope, at the end of which now dangled a grappling hook crudely wrapped with rags. As the two men reached him he swung the hook in a looping arc. It struck the top of the wall with a dull thud, started to slip, then caught. Chi gave the rope a quick yank. The hook slipped slightly, but then the rope became taut.

Chi stepped back and nodded. The first man gripped the rope, gave it a test tug, then scampered up into the night. They watched as he swung his leg over the top, then dropped from view. In an instant, the second man scrambled behind the first.

Instantly, Chi moved to the gate. There were scuffling sounds from inside the wall, then the muffled clank of the bar being lifted from the gate. It swung open with a grating squawk. Chi's companion darted through and grabbed one of the satchels, dragging it through the gate, then reaching back for the other. Chi had scurried through, and now stood looking quickly about the courtyard. The other man had begun swinging the gate closed once more.

Suddenly, from the other side of the courtyard, in the direction of the director's house, there arose the sound of voices, shouting. Then, a man's voice echoed in an agonizing groan and a woman screamed. Footsteps pounded across the courtyard.

Chi and his companion dropped into the shadows close to the wall and watched. Lights went on in the small house and the woman continued to scream. Then the first man over the wall appeared, breathless.

"Why does the woman continue screaming?" demanded Chi.

"Her husband is dead," replied the man.

"If she had died with him she would not scream so," snapped Chi.

"She can do us no harm," answered the man. "Come. Let us do our work."

Lights began blinking on in the main building. The three men crouched low, running along close to the wall and circling behind the orphanage. The two men with the satchels dispersed to opposite ends of the building. Chi approached the door of the kitchen.

A dim light glowed inside, sending a soft ray through the window. He stopped, glancing cautiously through the window. Off to his left, the screams of the woman continued.

Inside, an adolescent girl stood in the kitchen, confused and frightened. As Chi's face appeared in the window she shrank back, whimpering in alarm. Chi darted from the window and through the door.

"No!" screamed the girl as Chi grabbed her. "Do not hurt me!"

"You must leave," rasped Chi. "Do not stay here. Tell the people Hong must pay for his crimes."

The girl's face contorted with pain from his grip on her arm. He drew her close, staring passionately into her terrified eyes. "Do you hear?" he growled. "Tell them Hong has destroyed your home." He dragged her to the door, thrusting her from the building. "Go!"

She rose hesitantly from the heap in which she had fallen, looked terror at Chi, and dashed off toward the gate.

Chi heard shouts and footsteps behind him in the corridor. He hesitated only long enough to see they were children, their questioning looks filled with panic. He bounded out of the building.

Coming toward him were his two companions.

"Come!" shouted one. "We must hurry."

He joined them as they raced for the courtyard and the front gate. Suddenly, from behind them, there was a shattering roar. Heat swirled about their shoulders, and Chi felt himself falling with the force of the explosion. As he bounced, he could smell fire, and looked up to see the entire courtyard enveloped in an eerie, orange glow.

His companions were already back on their feet and running. He scrambled up and ran after them, almost breathless with the success of the mission. Behind him, the screams of the injured reverberated through the night. As he turned the corner to race through the gate, he glanced quickly back over his shoulder.

The orphanage was a mass of flame, the walls crumbled and broken. From the door and windows, children were leaping, crawling, stumbling. Many had become mobile torches, dropping as they attempted to flee. Then he was gone into the coolness of the valley air. He did not look back again.

THE SOUTH—SEOUL

Taejin turned the corner, approached her house. Having been on duty the evening before, he had been released early today as compensation. He had changed his clothes quickly, anticipating time to play with Sookee before Song's arrival home.

He approached the door and knocked. There was no sound from within. He knocked again, but still it was unanswered. Now curious, he pounded with the heel of his fist, the heavy thuds reverberating through the walls. There was no response.

It was still early in the afternoon. He wondered that the nurse and Sookee were not at home, then decided the child probably had gone to the market with her mother. Still light at heart, he turned away and began the trip to the South Gate.

The city was alive, crawling with activity. He smiled happily at strangers. Suddenly, all the world was his friend, everyone he saw, his brother.

He bounced up the steps and into the market, apologizing politely as he squeezed his way through the crowded aisles. When he reached her office he found it closed, locked. Disappointed, he turned to the nearest stall.

"Where is Song?"

The merchant was busy, bartering with a customer.

"Excuse me," he said, louder. "Have you seen Song, the manager?"

The man looked at him in mild annoyance. "She is not here. If her office is closed it means she is away." He turned back to his customer, proffering goods, talking rapidly.

Taejin shrugged and elbowed his way to the counter of a stall across the aisle. He took the corner of a display fabric in his fingers, feeling its texture. The merchant turned to him quickly. "It is very rich. It will be beautiful on your woman."

Taejin nodded. "I have come to find Song, the manager."

The merchant flipped the bolt of material, exposing more of its richness. "You see? It is finely woven."

Taejin dropped the corner. "Song. The manager. Have you seen her?"

The man urged the fabric toward him. "I have not." He held up the cloth, the better to display the colors. "You need search no longer. This is the finest in the market."

"When did she leave?" he asked, brushing the merchandise aside. "Did she have a child with her?"

The merchant lost interest. "She has not come here today." He turned away to another customer.

"Are you sure?" pressed Taejin. "Are you certain she has not been here?"

The man was measuring the new shopper. "Go away. I have not seen her today. I am busy." He quickly painted a smile for the new customer, now ignoring Taejin.

He turned back to the office and tried the door once more. Then, disappointed, he worked his way through the crowd, his eyes alert for any sight of her.

By the time he had searched her other markets the hour was late. He turned back toward her Itaewon home.

It was still closed. Anxious now, he thumped on the door, then listened intently for any sound from within. He knocked again, without response. At last, slowly, he sank to the step and sat, his back resting against the door, to await their return. Gradually the chill of the night crept through him. He dozed, then awakened, cramped, apprehensive. At last, past midnight, he rose.

He knocked again, gently now, but when there was no response he gathered his doubt about him and made his way to Yongsan.

He returned each night, knocking, waiting. Nothing. Now descending into a deeper chasm of emptiness than he had ever before known, he became a near automaton, working by day, seeking them by night, and ever more firmly embraced by his growing, pervasive fear.

* * * * * *

It was early when General Kwon arrived at the restaurant. His special waitress approached him. "Do you have particular requirements, Comrade?"

"When you are not serving you must remain close to the door. Allow no one to enter or approach close enough to overhear. We shall remain all evening, but there is much to plan. Hong is about to pay his dues to our cause."

"You must work quickly, Comrade," she whispered. "Our cell leader contacted me this afternoon. He is most anxious for results."

"He will obtain quicker results, and better, if he practices patience. A running tiger foolishly bypasses an agile prey."

She nodded and padded into the winding corridors leading toward the kitchen.

"General Kwon?" The voice was terse, authoritative.

"'Yes. Are you Hong?"

"Yes." They bowed and shook hands. Hong removed his shoes and stepped up into the tiny room. They squatted at the low table.

"It is interesting that you should contact me now," said Hong. "I have become most concerned about the activities of agents and saboteurs from the north." He eyed the general carefully. "Now your aide has said you have information which will interest me. I hope it concerns the recent disaster."

Kwon, caught totally off guard, fought to maintain his composure. He fed Hong a smile, sparring for time to regain control of the conversation. "It is comforting to know a cabinet minister will extend me the honor of his time," he oozed.

Hong continued, impatient. "Has the army apprehended the agents?" he demanded.

"We apprehend many," countered the communist.

Hong scoffed. "Do not parry me with platitudes, General. I am most concerned about last night's disaster. An orphanage was bombed. Many children were destroyed. Before that, a market manager disappeared. I believe she was kidnapped."

Kwon felt an immediate wave of relief, now aware of the disaster which concerned Hong. "I think it will not be long," he replied, "before we have the culprits. Our people are most capable in situations of that nature." He spread his hands. "Of course, it is as much a task for the National Police as it is for the army, however."

Hong shook his head in disgust. "I would prefer the army's involvement."

Kwon watched him, waiting. Hong made no move to clarify the statement, but turned the conversation back to Kwon. "If the subject of our meeting is not the orphanage disaster or the missing manager, why did you ask me to meet with you?"

"We have many problems in the military," began Kwon, his voice low, cautious. "We have received very little help from the government. You are the one minister who has treated us differently. I think you have appreciated our efforts. It is very difficult to provide an effective army in the face of constant opposition."

"Some of the cabinet are most dictatorial," agreed Hong. "They talk of freedom, reunifying our nation, yet they would create a nation of slaves. I have attempted to avoid such pomposity." He studied his host. "What difficulty have they caused you?"

Kwon became supplicant. "I am most humble when I ask you to hear my entire conversation this evening. We have selected you because of your attitude. Some things I say would not be appreciated if they are known in the government."

"The matters we discuss here will be kept in the most strict confidence," assured Hong.

The communist spread his hands. "We believe the Americans hold our military forces as hostages." He paused, watching for any reaction to the statement. Hong's expression was implacable. "Of course, they have given us arms, but they watch us closely. They inspect us constantly."

"That is because of the joint command status. I think the United Nations Command inspects all troops in our country." Hong was not challenging, merely interested.

General Kwon scoffed. "I think the name joint command implies each of the armies, each of the nations is represented. Yet, the United Nations commander is an American. His staff is American. We have only liaison officers on his staff, here in our nation. We have the largest armed force in this joint command on our soil. The American Eighth Army is merely one of the parts of this joint command, just as are the British, the Turks, and of course our own First Army and Second Army. They should be equal, yet the inspections constantly being conducted on our troops and installations are made not by the United Nations liaison staff, but by the staff of the American Eighth Army. Equals judging equals?" He lowered his voice menacingly, viciously enthusiastic now to make the impression, to capture this man. "No, I think it is not equality at all. Our staff never inspects the American forces. We are not allowed in their areas, their compounds. The Americans merely tell the world it is an equal partnership in defense. In reality we have the most soldiers and they retain all the control. If we do not operate as they dictate we shall be threatened with a cessation of military assistance."

"I think such a thing will not happen," objected Hong. "If the Americans withdraw their assistance the north shall soon provide theirs. The Americans will not wish the north to be so close to Japan."

The general smiled. "For that reason, I think we are in a position to demand more from them." He sat back and glared expectantly at the other. "I think you must help us."

"How would you have me help you?" asked Hong, surprised.

"You are a cabinet minister. You are a friend of our military forces."

Hong remained silent, waiting for the general to state his point.

"We wish to inspect their readiness," hissed Kwon. "We suspect they are not as ready, as powerful as they would have us and the rest of the world believe."

Hong raised an eyebrow. "Would you have me demand of them that our staff be permitted to inspect them? I think such a request would generate an economic incident. We would lose much more than we would gain with such a maneuver."

Kwon nodded enthusiastically. "But if they were not aware of the inspections they would have no cause for complaint."

Hong snorted. "Such a thing is impossible."

Kwon leaned forward and lowered his voice. "We have chosen to discuss this with you because we hold you in the highest esteem. We want to save you much embarrassment and discomfort."

The cabinet minister recoiled. "What are you talking about? What embarrassment and discomfort would you save me? You are a general, a general with but one star on your shoulder." Suddenly he began to rise. "I will not remain here and hear threats."

"Do not be too hasty, Hong. You agreed to hear my entire conversation, so do not try to bluff as the Americans bluff." He emphasized his words with a wagging finger. "If we did not hold you in such esteem we would permit you to share in the fate the other cabinet ministers are soon to suffer."

Hong hesitated, his eyes wide. "I do not know what you are talking about," he snapped.

"Then listen carefully to my words," said the communist calmly. "Remember, you were invited here as a friend."

Hong sank back to the floor. "I said I would listen," he murmured.

"You also promised your confidence," reminded Kwon, now sure of his control.

"Yes."

The prelude now past, Kwon paused for a long moment of

reflection before continuing. He would soon learn how accurately his father had judged this man, how great his loyalty was to his nation, or to himself. The nation was on the brink of a coup, an upheaval of which Kwon had learned only hours before. At first, he had not been close to the men at the core of the plan. Now, with greater numbers of military men being included, he had been recruited.

The move had played conveniently into his scheme. He could use the upcoming events as a countermeasure against any loyalty Hong might exhibit for the present regime. If no loyalty existed, on the other hand, the cabinet minister might prove a powerful ally from within, aiding the coup and solidifying Kwon's own stature with the military leaders. Therefore, Kwon could win personally, whichever way the upheaval ended. He felt his pulse quicken with his inner exuberance, and he froze his features against any outward expression.

"The present government will not be in power much longer," resumed Kwon. "Most of them will soon be imprisoned or flee for their lives." He nodded to Hong. "You are more fortunate. Because you have been our friend we have determined to remain yours. When the change comes, when the military junta takes control, you will remain in your post. You will be as important in the new government as you have been in the last."

"Then you are the leader of this band of rebels of which we have heard?"

A knot formed in the pit of Kwon's stomach. If he lied, claiming leadership, Hong would soon enough learn the difference. Then Kwon would lose control over him. On the other hand, if he denied leadership, Hong might not trust Kwon's assurances of protection. He reverted to his thoughts of a few moments before and resolved to use Hong to elevate himself in the eyes of the junta. He shook his head, smiling. "No, I am merely held in high regard by our general staff. I have been loyal to the army." He gestured. "Such faithfulness has its rewards, just as it does for our friends outside the military services."

"And you want me to arrange these inspections for you as the price of my freedom?"

"We should not discuss your position in terms of freedom. You are a wealthy man, Hong. You have kept it well hidden. We admire the manner in which you have constructed your kingdom of enterprises. Naturally, when you remain a part of the government you will be permitted to retain all of them. We have no interest in taking them from you, in depriving you the opportunity to develop them further." He laughed. "Why would we strip wealth from a man who has been shrewd and intelligent enough to bypass the Americans and amass a fortune?"

"Tell me what you consider the extent of my fortune to be," bristled Hong. "It is a strong allegation."

"Perhaps we could discuss it better in terms of its sources," countered Kwon. "It is the sources in which we are most interested, not the revenues. In future years you may well discover new ways in which to increase your wealth even further. We applaud such ingenuity, as I have said before."

"Then what about those sources?" Hong was clearly uncomfortable, anxious to learn the extent of their knowledge.

"Hong, I understood immediately your concern at the destruction of the orphanage." He was staring unblinkingly at the minister. "You control them. You derive much personal wealth from the contributions to these institutions. If a man wants to become an orphanage director he swears allegiance to you, makes a contribution to your personal fortune, and he is duly appointed."

Hong opened his mouth to protest, but Kwon waved impatiently and continued.

"This is not our concern. That you become wealthy by such means is not of interest to us. But it is a fact we know of the operation. We know of the source of wealth. Then, of course, there are your many markets. There is the vast network of massage parlors in the American compounds." He smiled conspiratorially. "You see? We really know a great deal about your activities, Hong. And it is these sources which will permit us to inspect the American forces. I think you must not be blind to the possibilities. Your orphanages are most attractive to the American soldiers. They go there frequently. Then there are the massage parlors in the American compounds. The girls spend many hours soothing the soldiers. I think there is much interesting conversation on the tables."

Hong shook his head. "Such sources would be of no assistance to you at all. You should know that. You are a general. Those who go to such facilities are merely the soldiers. They are not the officers, the ones who know best the condition of their divisions."

"My apologies, Hong, but we disagree. Officers, if questioned, would provide the answers which their generals, their government, wish us to hear. The soldiers have not been so instructed. They are told they must not discuss matters of military activity with our people. They are very careful in the villages. However, when they are at the orphanages they talk among themselves. When they are in the massage they are relaxed. They seem not to think of such places as dangerous to their security. They are within enclosures controlled by Americans. They are not as careful as they would be in the villages or in the bars of Seoul."

"What would you learn from such encounters?" asked Hong.

"We would become more aware of their state of morale," smiled Kwon. "We would know of the petty problems they encounter in their everyday existence."

"It would be very difficult to gain any accurate reports of such conversations," replied Hong. "The people who operate the orphanages do not understand English that well. The girls who massage them know only bedroom English. Other subjects are above their mentality."

"Are their duties above the mentalities of others?" suggested the communist. "Could not others, people who understand English better, be installed in such positions? We must, after all, consider our goal realistically."

"The wages would be much higher," countered Hong. "The girl who gives a massage is not of the highest social class."

"Perhaps such wages need not be higher for all, however. I

think a few carefully chosen girls could well serve a large facility. Our purpose, we must remember, is to monitor, not to canvass every man."

"It appears you have planned well, General. However, I believe more information would be to your advantage."

Kwon waited, curious at the man's perception.

"Perhaps information could be gained from their officers in a similar manner."

Kwon's spirits churned at his success in changing Hong's attitude. Suddenly he was talking as an ally, a conspirator. "What is your plan?" he asked hungrily.

"I must think about it further," replied Hong. "For instance, the Americans have a golf course in Yongsan. They use our young women as their caddies. There may be ways in which we can use such situations to obtain more information from them without their suspecting us."

Kwon nodded. "Then you have much work to do. You must arrange for the new people to be placed in your agencies."

"Can you provide the people?" asked Hong. "I think if I provide them there will be questions. It could prove embarrassing to our cause."

"Then the arrangements will require time," replied Kwon evenly. "We will talk again when they are ready. Your only remaining problem is that of obtaining the money to support our operation. So many enterprises will require much funding." Kwon looked at him carefully.

Hong's stomach churned. "Naturally, I shall be willing to assist financially. However, if another source of funds can be found it will make it easier for me."

"Hong," said Kwon, his voice low, almost in a whisper, "you are being provided with a generous opportunity. You shall remain free to pursue your enterprises as diligently as your ingenuity permits. Do you not believe the comfort of your continued life and appointment worth some investment?"

"Investment," moaned Hong. "My investments have suffered

a serious blow with the destruction of the orphanage only last night." He looked up quickly at the communist. "It would be a great comfort to me if you, if the army could provide some protection for the orphanages and the markets."

Kwon shook his head. "Such a thing would be very difficult."

"But you want me to provide information about the Americans. Information from the orphanages." He looked pleadingly at the general. "It will be very difficult if the Americans stop visiting them."

Kwon's eyes snapped at the dilemma. "I shall see what we can do," he replied tersely.

Hong swallowed. "When is your coup to take place, General? I certainly want to be prepared to join you when it occurs."

Kwon smiled now. "I think you have joined us already. You have no need to worry of time and dates, only the performance of your tasks. For you the coup is a reality now."

"How may I contact you?" he asked. "Should I contact you at your headquarters?"

"No," replied the general. "Take note of the woman at the end of the corridor as you leave. She is wearing a red shawl. You will make all your reports to her. She will relay them to me."

Hong merely nodded. They stood. "Thank you, General," he said, bowing low. "I am grateful for this opportunity."

Kwon nodded, silent and without expression as his guest departed.

Moments later the waitress entered. "Is that all you need of me, comrade?"

"Please sit down," he said, motioning.

She sat, looking at him curiously. "Is there a problem?"

"No," he answered, smiling. "Things have developed much better than I had hoped. He will prove to be very useful."

She nodded. "That is good, Comrade. Our leaders will be pleased."

"Hong is a great curiosity to me," continued Kwon. "I think he will be a profitable ally. I expected him to be willing to cooperate with me, of course. It was natural, since it would provide him a means of preserving his wealth. But I did not expect him to be so inventive or so willing to provide funds. Of course, he has another problem. An orphanage was sabotaged last night. Also, he believes the disappearance of Song was a kidnapping as a threat to his markets. It has bruised his capitalist heart. Now he wishes the army to provide him with protection."

"Can you do such a thing?" she asked, surprised. "Can you order the army to protect so many orphanages and markets?"

"There is no need," he replied. "So long as I agreed, Hong will take comfort. Once he has provided information to us I think he will no longer be in a position to complain of anything to me."

* * * * * *

The briefing room was quietly ornate, its decor discouraging loud conversation as effectively as that of a tabernacle. Situated on the second floor of the command building in the Yongsan compound, it served as the briefing center for the United Nations forces. The corridor leading to its highly polished double doors was carpeted with thick, heavily padded loop which muffled voices as well as footsteps. Inside, the lighting was subdued, the chairs comfortably cushioned, the stage commanding. At one corner stood the podium, an extravagantly engineered nerve center which provided the speaker with total control of his and his audience's environment. A bank of pushbuttons and dials permitted him to manipulate lights, sound, screens, projectors and, it seemed, the very thoughts of the listener.

Like most of his companions, it was General Kwon's first visit to the gigantic headquarters. He swept along the corridor, proudly erect in his new rank of lieutenant general, and kept his eyes straight ahead. Before and behind him marched the other members of the new general staff which had been appointed during the coup.

"Perhaps we should have something like this," said the officer beside him quietly.

"Like what?" asked Kwon, his face totally expressionless.

"This is a most beautiful building," replied the other. "It is more like a palace than a military headquarters."

Kwon sniffed. "I think the money spent for such opulence will be better spent on arms for our defense. Our new government would never engage itself in such useless expenditures merely for the comfort of the staff." He looked meaningfully at the other man as they turned through the door and into the hushed conversations of the briefing room.

The lights dimmed and a spot light stabbed through the room to illuminate the podium. "Good morning, gentlemen," began the speaker. "My name is Taejin, an interpreter for the liaison staff in this headquarters. It is my duty this morning to assist you, on behalf of the United Nations Command, concerning the defense posture being maintained by our joint forces for the defense against invasion from the north. If you have any questions or any need for further translation, please raise your hand. I will assist you."

Kwon's eyes widened as he recognized Taejin. He straightened slightly, now more interested in the speaker than in what he had to say. The escapee had been found. He could imagine his father's pleasure, its reward. In the course of the briefing, however, or immediately thereafter, he knew he was vulnerable to being seen by Taejin.

"It is most important," continued Taejin, "that each of you understand fully the missions which exist in our several contingency plans, along with the reasons for the plans themselves. The commander-in-chief has asked me to interpret in this briefing for him in order to reduce the possibility of any misunderstanding resulting from the differences of language between our army and the Americans. At the conclusion of the briefing the lights will be raised and anyone wishing to ask a question directly of the United Nations commander-in-chief will have an opportunity to do so."

Now Kwon slumped down in his seat, certain he must escape the room before the lights were turned up. Taejin must not see him yet.

The briefing droned on, the officers listening intently and sig-
naling their aides when they wished notes regarding a specific item
of information. Finally, Kwon began to shift uncomfortably in his
seat. Within minutes he was leaning toward the officer next to
him. "I must leave."

The other officer leaned closer. "Why? Is there a problem? I
think it would be most insulting to leave now."

"I am very ill," said Kwon. "I must leave."

"But what of the briefing?" asked the other. "You must have
the information they are providing in order to produce your portion of our plans."

"I shall arrange to be briefed later. What has this interpreter
said his name is?" Kwon leaned a little closer, as if anxious not to
miss the name.

"Taejin. He is member of their liaison staff."

"Thank you," said Kwon, rising from his chair and moving
with stooped shoulders toward the end of the row. The other officers looked up at him in surprise.

"I am most sorry," he said as he shuffled along the row. "I
must leave. I am ill."

They nodded, moving their legs to let him pass. Reaching the
aisle, he hurried to the rear of the room, taking the steps quickly.
An aide approached him. "Is there a problem, Sir?"

"Yes. I am very ill. I must leave to avoid embarrassment."

"Is there something we can do to help?" asked the American.

Kwon looked about them quickly, affecting concern. "We must
step outside," he said in a low voice. They moved through the
black curtains at the doorway, into the light trap and out to the
corridor.

"Is there something we can do to help?" asked the American
again.

"I am suddenly very weak," answered Kwon, wiping his forehead. "My stomach is giving me trouble." He appeared to wait,
then looked at the officer as an afterthought. "I think you may do
one thing, if it would not cause difficulty."

"Yes, Sir?"

"I am missing a very important briefing. I cannot afford to be without the information. Would it be possible for a private briefing to be arranged for me?"

The officer hesitated.

"I do not wish to cause difficulty for you," Kwon hastened to add. "Perhaps this interpreter, Taejin, could come to my office and brief me. He seems to be most knowledgeable."

The officer shook his head. "Taejin is only an interpreter. He is in no position to brief you. Our command will be happy to provide a briefing officer for you. Would tomorrow morning be satisfactory, or would you prefer to wait until you have recovered your health?"

"I think we could do it immediately after this briefing. Then I shall put my staff to work right away." He smiled weakly. "I hope you understand, but this Taejin seems very knowledgeable. I would not wish to inconvenience a briefing officer."

The American stood firm. "I'm sorry, General. I cannot make such a decision. I'll be happy to refer your request to the commander-in-chief. I'm sure he can work out an understanding with your general staff."

Kwon drew himself up. "That will not be necessary. I will discuss it with the Minister of National Defense." He stroked his brow. "I must return to my headquarters now."

Kwon seethed all the way back to his office. The moment he arrived he motioned his aide into his office. "I am not well," he snapped. "Cancel my appointments for the rest of the day."

"Yes, Sir."

"I do not wish to be disturbed at my home. I shall be sleeping."

"Yes, Sir," replied the aide.

An hour later a disheveled old man was shuffling along the thoroughfare outside the Yongsan compound. He walked the length of the block near the gate, crossed the street, and returned to his starting point. The path was repeated slowly, almost absently, throughout the afternoon. Traffic entered and departed the huge gate. The old man seemed not to notice. Then, late in the day he stopped, uncharacteristically alert. Taejin, now out of uniform, walked from the gate and flagged a passing taxi. Immediately, the old man did the same, springing agilely into the vehicle.

"Please follow that taxi," he said quietly to the driver. "You must not lose him."

The driver nodded. They sped from Yongsan, climbing the gentle rise into Itaewon. Taejin's taxi turned off the main highway into smaller streets, finally slowing to a stop.

"Pass him," said the old man excitedly, looking at his watch. "Take me back to Yongsan."

The driver cast him a quick glance, but continued past. Looking back, his passenger watched as Taejin hurried to the door of Song's home.

Next afternoon Taejin again rode the taxi to the home of Song. Paying the driver, he went to the door and knocked.

"Are you Taejin?" asked a man's voice.

Taejin wheeled to stare in alarm into the face of a soldier. Behind the man stood another, his hand on a holstered weapon at his waist.

"What do you want with me?" he asked, his voice tense with fright.

"You will come with us."

"I will not come with you."

The soldier was emphatic. "I am sorry, Taejin. You must come with us."

"Why? I have done nothing!"

The second soldier unsnapped the holster, withdrawing his weapon.

Taejin eyed him warily. "Why am I under arrest?"

"You are not under arrest, Taejin. You are only being taken to a meeting."

He resigned himself to the inevitable. They led him to the car and drove off into the city.

A half hour later the sedan pulled from the thoroughfare into the southern army headquarters compound and came to a stop. Taejin shook off the offers of assistance from the sentries and walked without protest into the building. The corridor was long, somewhat barren except for the various section designations and the names of their heads. Most of the names were strange.

His escort turned into an office and Taejin looked over the door instinctively for a name sign. There was none. Moments later he was ushered into an inner office and the door closed. Kwon sat smiling at the doorway, expectantly, as if he had painted the expression there hours before.

Taejin was startled as he recognized the son of Farmer Kim. He froze, staring in disbelief.

"Welcome, Taejin," said Kwon softly.

"Why are you here? How have you managed this?" blurted Taejin, confused.

"I believe it is customary for a mere interpreter to practice greater courtesy when addressing a general," smile Kwon.

"But you. . . ."

"I am a general. Yes. And you are merely an interpreter. Actually, that is an error. You are a fugitive."

"You are an enemy agent, a communist," snarled Taejin, moving toward the door.

Kwon stared at him. "I think it would be most wise of you to sit down. If you talk with me for a few minutes you may decide against doing anything rash," said the general.

Taejin stopped and turned. "Exposing a communist agent is not considered a rash action."

Kwon laughed. "I think you should consider your position, Taejin. I have studied your file carefully. You are an interpreter, nothing more. You are far from your protectors here. Would you walk out there and tell people that I am an enemy agent?" He shook his head pleasantly. "No, I would think that a most rash move on your part. I would consider you far wiser to sit down and talk with me for a few minutes."

Taejin fought a nausea of anger mixed with fear. "You and your brother came here as agents."

"News travels quickly to the prisons," countered Kwon. "How did you learn?"

"My mother told me before your father had her murdered."

Kwon raised his finger to his lips. "Come. Sit down and do not speak so much in anger. It will convince no one. My people are most loyal to me. It would do you no good to run out there or shout or do any of those other foolish things the cornered so frequently do." He motioned to a chair. "Sit down."

Taejin sat.

"The first thing I wish to do is to educate you, my old friend. I think there is not any animosity between you and me. There should be none. After all, we are both Hochonese, are we not?"

"You and your brother. . . ."

"My brother is dead."

Taejin stared at him in silence.

"Did you not know that my brother had died?" Kwon waited for an answer. There was none. "He died because he did some foolish things. We tolerate foolish behavior in no one, even our own sons and brothers. We would do no less in the case of a mere boyhood friend."

Taejin sat staring at him, certain he would soon be on his way to a reunion with the farmer.

"You are a fugitive, Taejin. I dislike the need to be so abrupt, but facts are facts. You are a fugitive. You escaped from a prison train, murdered a number of people throughout the countryside, including soldiers. You defected to the south. Those are merely your crimes against the northern half of our nation. I think we must now consider the south. Here, you have lied about your origin and evaded the conscription of men to fight in the war. You have allied yourself with the Americans to the point you take their side in differences of opinion with our own people. There are those here in the south who could be convinced you are guilty of sedition against them. I think you would be most deserving of prosecution from either half of our nation." He smiled once more, confident and cunning, then continued. "I could do either of two things in such a situation as this. There is always the possibility of arranging your transport back to my father. Then, on the other hand, there is also the option of turning you over to this government for prosecution. I think you would not find either of those options pleasant."

Taejin merely waited, silent.

"Now," smiled Kwon, "there is the third alternative. I think you and I must arrange to be friends. We must remember we are both Hochonese. After all, are we not interested in our own welfare? Are we not interested in improving our own position, our own condition in life? I think we must assist each other. Do you agree?"

Taejin shifted uneasily. "What will happen to me if I do not? What will happen to our nation if I give in to you?"

Kwon raised an eyebrow in mock despair. "If you elect not to be my friend I shall be forced to arrange transport for you to visit my father. I think he would be most anxious to see you."

"Is that what you did for your brother? For Nambae?"

"I have told you Nambae is dead. I attempted to reason with him, just as I am attempting now to reason with you." He shook his head sadly. "He was stubborn. He would not take my brotherly advice. His wife and your bastard daughter were reduced to living alone in this terrible city. It is a very sad situation, but Nambae would not listen to my brotherly advice."

"So you arranged it?" Taejin looked at him in disgust. "You arranged the murder of your own brother."

Kwon shook his head. "His death was arranged by others, but it is most incorrect to refer to it as murder. It was not murder at all, but punishment. It was a corrective measure. It was a message to all others who would ignore suggestions. The same could be arranged for them if they failed to follow suggestions. It is very simple." He leaned back and folded his hands, smiling paternally at his prey.

"What do you wish from me?" asked Taejin, his voice in a desperate whisper. "What are you telling me I must do?"

"I think you must be my friend." The communist pursed his lips, then nodded. "Yes, that is all I ask. For instance, if you were to remain silent with regard to my past, I would be most willing to remain silent about yours. If you were willing to do certain favors for me, I would be willing to do the same for you. I think I would do such a thing for a true and loyal friend."

"What favors do you wish from me?" asked Taejin cautiously.

"I wish to be briefed regularly. I think I must not receive superficial briefings such as the Americans are accustomed to giving our people. They insult us. They plan war contingencies in our land and they do not even consult us until after they have prepared their plans. It would be most helpful if I were to be briefed more thoroughly than that. As an interpreter for them I think you are aware of their plans." He leaned forward and stared calmly at Taejin. "You may begin by telling me the information from yesterday's briefing at the Yongsan headquarters. It will be interesting to hear what you have to say about the defensive posture of the United Nations command."

"I cannot do such a thing," retorted Taejin. "You know I cannot do that."

Kwon nodded. "Then, of course, there is the case of your daughter." He said it simply, not with the air of a threat. "We are caring for her, you know. Perhaps I should tell my friends how anxious you are that she remain free from harm." He reached for the phone.

"Wait!"

The hand paused.

Taejin looked disconsolately down at his feet, thinking for a long moment. He wished desperately that he could go to someone, that he could tell of Kwon's past as well as his present affiliations. And yet, what Kwon had said was true, to an extent. Taejin knew that Farmer Kim would welcome the opportunity to execute him, yet that concerned him less than the danger to Sookee. Kwon's statements about Taejin's offenses in the south had been less accurate. The charge that he had lied was ridiculous, for he had been open about his past from the start. However, he knew that Kwon, from his position as a general, would be able to use lies and half truths to ruin him. Nothing could be gained, then, by going to them. No one would believe an interpreter against a general. Kwon would remain free, still operating as an agent, still enjoying his army rank. Taejin would have suffered for his daughter.

At last he looked up. "I think there is not much choice for me. When do you wish me to begin?"

"I think we must not waste time. We shall begin now. I shall expect the information to be very complete. Do not attempt to leave anything out. And," he added, puncturing the air with his finger for emphasis, "I shall be very interested in the condition of the American forces. I wish to know their plans most intimately. Of course," he said quietly, "we must observe all the rules of close friendship."

"I do not understand you."

"When you return to your American friends you must remember that Kwon is your very close friend. You must not do anything which would place me in an uncomfortable position. Were that to happen, others of my father's friends might find it necessary to arrange for your daughter not to be so healthy."

Taejin went cold. He thought of Sookee and of Song. "General, it is my duty this evening to brief you, on behalf of. . . ."

* * * * * *

The old woman hobbled purposefully up the steps and into the market at the East Gate. On her only visible arm she carried a basket. Her head, shrouded in a faded shawl, bobbed back and forth as she made her way into the crowd of shoppers.

The aisles were narrow, crowded. Customers, jostling for positions at the crude counters, paid little heed to the woman, and she edged her way between them, working ever farther back toward the rear of the building. The merchants, competing aggressively with their neighbors for each sale, ignored her as she worked her way to the corner of a counter far at the rear. On the boards were heaped bolts of cloth, colorful and rich.

She looked around her, not appearing to wish service, but more interested in the people crowded next to her. They were feeling the fabrics, conversing with the merchant, bartering the price.

Drawing the shawl more tightly about her face, she reached busily into the basket. Then, her back turned to the others, her unusually broad shoulders shook as she tugged at the contents of the basket. Finally, bending low, she worked her way around the corner of the stall and into a crossing aisle.

Still, the passersby ignored her. She looked furtively about, quickly studying the crowd of people, then struck a match and touched it to a string which she had fed around the corner. Suddenly straightening, she started for the door, taking great, rapid strides and shouldering through the shoppers.

Someone shouted back at the stall where she had stood. Then there was a scream, followed by a dull explosion. Instantly, the market was engulfed in flames, screaming and moaning people in panic. Shoving their way to the entrance, they found it blocked with bodies of those who had already been trampled while trying to flee. There were more screams now, as they realized the futility of their predicament. They were hopelessly trapped, entombed.

It was over quickly. Within five minutes the building had become a furnace, sending huge, billowing clouds of smoke upward to drift toward the sports stadium only a short distance away. Crowds gathered across the street, gaping at the disaster and shuddering with the horror of death they knew had struck within the old walls.

At the edge of the crowd stood the old woman. She watched the building and the crowd with equal interest, a faint smile playing devilishly about her craggy lips. Then, hobbling once more, she stepped into an alley, away from the crowd. No one noticed. Moments later, Chi stepped out. He blended into the people, watching, seeming to measure the effect of his handiwork. Then, saying nothing to those who were chattering around him, he hurried away.

* * * * * *

The sighting was coincident. It occurred on one of the few days Song had been allowed to see Sookee. The communist agents had taken her to a busy restaurant deep in the heart of the city. There, the woman and the child had sipped tea and talked. The matron sat stiffly, listening intently to every word. The child could not understand. Her mother could not explain.

The visit had progressed only a few minutes when Song saw Hong enter. With him were two other men, one old, his clothes tattered and dirty. His head, not covered, was sparse of hair. A wispy beard wilted from his chin. He hobbled along, looking neither right nor left, between Hong and a brigadier general she had not seen before. Suddenly she remembered. He was the old man who had been with Hong at the South Gate market the day of her first meeting with Hong.

She bent more earnestly toward her daughter, anxious to cover her sudden preoccupation. It was nothing, she told herself. The argument failed. Like numerous other agents from the north, she had been instructed to be watchful of Hong. Yet, though others might have missed his entry here, not recognizing him readily, Song's previous association with Hong forced instant awareness.

Then the thought struck her. Why would Hong be with another general and the old man? Was he betraying his relationship with Kwon? If he were and she reported the fact to Kwon, she might be rewarded with a more free access to her daughter. If Hong's activity were not a betrayal, perhaps Kwon still would be impressed with her alertness and loyalty.

She looked quickly at the matron. "I must talk with Kwon at once."

The matron grinned, not having seen the men. "Of what must

you talk with him? Do you now plan tricks to escape with her?" Her eyes dropped to the child.

"A man has entered and gone to a back room. He is of great interest to Kwon. He should be told."

"Is he one who is wanted at home?"

"He is Hong, the cabinet minister who works for Kwon, but today he is with an old man and a different general. I have not seen the other general before."

"I shall leave with the child," said the matron. "You may call Kwon. Do it quickly."

Song nodded and reached out a tender hand, brushing the cheek of her daughter. "I hope I shall see you again soon," she said softly. "Today has been much too short."

Sookee looked at her, tears in her eyes. She said nothing as the matron led her quickly away.

"Why have you called me at my office?" snapped Kwon.

"It is most urgent. I must speak with you."

"Where are you? I will meet you."

Song identified the restaurant. "Cabinet Minister Hong has entered with two other men."

"Who are the others?" Kwon's voice was sharp through the telephone.

"I do not know the others. I have not seen them before." She paused. "One of them is a general."

"What general?" Kwon demanded. "Did he wear a name tag?"

"I could not see it. His back was toward me. They were walking away from me to a private dining room."

"Is the room visible to you?"

"The door."

"You must move closer. I think we must be aware of their conversation."

"I cannot. Hong knows me. If he sees me as the door opens I think it will be troublesome for your liaison with him."

Kwon cursed. "You must remain there and see that no one leaves."

Inside the room the three spoke in soft voices. "Schoolmaster, I have asked you to come here because I must have your help," said Hong.

Min's old eyes crackled. "For many years you were too busy to remember your schoolmaster. Now, each time you need help, you remember where to find me." He turned, looking fondly at Shin. "Shin has been busy, too. But he has not forgotten to visit with me. Even now, as a general, he visits me often. That is why I have asked him to be with us today."

Hong became contrite. "I am most sorry I have neglected you, Schoolmaster."

"It does not matter," muttered Min, passing it off now that he had made his point. "Why have you called for the help of Min?"

Hong took a deep breath, relieved that the old man apparently would hold no grudge. "I have built up a number of investments over the years. These, of course, must not be discussed openly, for I am a cabinet minister. However, recently I have been suffering most serious losses."

Min leaned forward with interest. "What sort of investments have you made, Hong?"

"You know of my markets, but I have other services as well."

"I think you must be more specific with me. Do you not trust me?" Min was becoming petulant again.

"I have the highest admiration for you, Schoolmaster. That is why I contacted you."

"Then you must not hide behind generalities, Hong. What sort of other services do you offer?"

"I control the massage parlors for the American compounds. I control the orphanages throughout our country."

Min's eyes were alert, almost admiring. "Then you have become a wealthy man, Hong. I commend you."

"I listened to your lessons many years ago, Schoolmaster. I have merely tried to do as you suggested."

Min smiled, flattered. "Then you honor me more than if you had visited with me often."

"But now I must have your help," repeated Hong.

"Help? How can I help a cabinet minister further?" asked Min.

"Two of my ventures have been sabotaged recently," growled Hong. "It was the work of agents from the north, of course, but rebuilding will require much effort."

"What has been destroyed?" asked Min quickly.

"The first was an orphanage. It was in a valley at Tong-du-chon-ni. Many enemy agents operate throughout that zone. It is the tactical area. Late one night the orphanage was bombed."

"Airplanes?" asked Min, surprised.

Hong shook his head. "No. The agents entered the courtyard and demolished the building with explosives. The orphanage director was murdered."

"And what of the children?" asked the schoolmaster.

"Many were killed. Others escaped, but were badly burned."

"And your other loss?" asked Min, passing the orphanage off.

"The market you reconstructed at the East Gate was burned by an arsonist yesterday. Everything was lost. Many people were killed."

Min nodded. "I read of this disaster in the newspaper. It is most unfortunate." He paused for a moment, then looked back at Hong. "But how can I help you?"

Hong spread his hands. "You said you would rebuild our nation from your school in Gapyong. You have trained your students in the building trades." He took a deep breath. "It will be expensive for me to hire tradesmen to reconstruct the orphanage and the East Gate market. Can we not make their reconstruction another training task for your students?"

Min glanced quickly at Shin, but did not answer immediately. Hong started to speak, then thought better of it and waited.

At last the old man spoke. "Have you planned to request further reconstruction funds?"

Now Hong smiled. "Yes, Schoolmaster. Already I have requested funds both from our government and from the Americans." He sobered. "But if I contract for the work, all the funds will go to the pockets of the workers."

"And if my students do the work?" asked Min.

"Then I think we may be able to recognize profits."

Min's eyes twinkled. "Hong, you are a good student." He turned excitedly to Shin. "Have I not told you of the pride I take in Hong?" He did not wait for a reply, but addressed Hong again. "Naturally, since my students will do the work, a greater percentage of the profit will go to my school."

Hong's face fell. "Greater percentage? Min, I too have many expenses."

"Everyone has expenses," admonished Min. "If my students do the work I think they must receive the greater part of the profits."

Hong hung his head in despair, searching for words.

"Do you not agree with me?" prodded the old man.

The cabinet minister took a deep breath. "Min, I must tell you a secret. It is a sensitive matter. We must not discuss it except between the three of us." He looked from one to the other of his companions. They said nothing, waiting.

"Our army has been subordinated to the Americans for many years. The Americans know much about our forces, but our people know little of the Americans. We know little of the Americans' true strengths."

Min looked quickly at Shin. "Is this true, Shin?"

Shin had been caught unawares. "Hong is a cabinet minister of our government. He was the only cabinet minister from the previous government to be retained. I think it is because he knows our people and our defensive posture most intimately," he replied.

The old man turned back to Hong. "What has this to do with reconstruction?"

"I have been approached by one of the generals in our army. Several months ago he explained this problem to me. Through the orphanages and the massages I have been gathering information on the Americans for our army. It is a most expensive undertaking."

Shin was more intense now, watching his old classmate's face as the story unfolded.

"Does the army not take care of the expenses of such things?" asked Min, surprised.

Hong shook his head. "We cannot afford to have the Americans learn we do such things," he replied. "I do this as a patriotic gesture for our nation. However, if I were to receive half of the profits from the reconstruction I would have funds with which to pay these high expenses of patriotism." He turned to Shin. "You, too, are a general, Shin. Have you not known of our army's lack of information about the Americans?"

Shin avoided the issue. "Who is the general who approached you?" he asked.

"General Kwon."

Shin raised an eyebrow. "I know him well. We served together during the fighting. He has arranged my promotions."

"Do you work with him?" asked Hong.

"I am a member of his staff. I have worked under him since I was a major."

Hong nodded. "He is a very influential man. Perhaps you have worked with the information I have provided to Kwon."

Shin shook his head. "I know nothing of these matters. Perhaps he is gathering such information for another portion of his staff."

Min cleared his throat. "Hong, I think you have come to me as a tax collector. If my students do the work on the market and the orphanage, I want them to gain the funds for the school. I apologize, but I cannot give the funds to the government to learn about the Americans." He looked reproachfully at the cabinet minister. "You are foolish to pay for these things, Hong. They will never repay you."

Hong leaned back, beaten. "What percentage do you demand for the school?" he asked quietly.

Min stroked his scraggly beard. "I think the school should receive eighty percent. But of course," he hastened to add, "my students will be doing the work. Their skill is great. I shall send only the best to your projects. You will still receive twenty percent to engage in your game of espionage."

"But, Schoolmaster," began Hong, "I. . . ."

Min waved his hand impatiently. "I do not wish to discuss the matter further," he snapped. "Now, when you have received the funds for the reconstruction, contact me. I shall put my students to work as soon as you do."

He got up, painfully, indicating the session was closed. They slid back the door, unaware of Song and her companion, and walked quickly to the street.

* * * * * *

"Shin?" scowled Kwon. "He is a constant source of trouble to me. He is an opportunist. Are you certain the other was Hong?"

"I do not know Hong, Comrade. Song has said he is Hong. I know only Shin."

Kwon cast a look of disgust about the room. They were sitting in an obscure house deep in the Inwang section of the city.

"What was the subject of their conversation?"

"It was impossible for us to overhear," said the woman apologetically. "We were unable to move near the door to the room without danger of discovery. Our only recourse was the troubling and unsatisfactory business of sitting and attempting to identify them as they departed."

"You are correct," snapped Kwon. "You have produced a most unsatisfactory performance. Of what good is such information to me? Three people have decided to conduct a meeting. They are people who should not even be acquainted with each other. I place two operatives on the scene for purposes of observation. Afterward they are able to advise me of the names of only two of the men and not a word of their discussion." He pushed himself petulantly from his seat. "I will have to do such things for myself. If that is the case, perhaps you must consider carefully the measure of your usefulness in the south. Women are in great demand at home." He turned and stormed from the house.

By the time he had reached the restaurant Hong was waiting. "You wished to talk with me, General?"

"Yes. I wanted to thank you for the information I am receiving from your sources. In the early days it was difficult to derive much value from the bits and pieces which were delivered to me by the messenger. However, as the data began accumulating it became easier to keep a watchful eye on the Americans and their activities." He smiled. "I have brought you here to offer my congratulations."

Hong bowed in gratitude. "It has been a long and very difficult endeavor. However, I believe we may feel satisfaction."

"I was interested to learn," remarked Kwon, changing course abruptly, "that you know a member of my staff. His name is Shin."

Hong's mind raced, hoping Shin had not reported his indiscreet discussion to Kwon. "Shin and I have been friends since we were boys," he said.

"Do you see him frequently now?" probed Kwon.

The cabinet minister shook his head. "Our work keeps us much too busy."

Kwon eyed him calculatingly. "But you have seen him today," he prompted. "You ate together only two hours ago."

"Yes," replied Hong. "We had some important business to discuss."

"What business?"

"That is of concern to me and to Shin," retorted Hong, becoming slightly irritated.

"I must point out to you, Hong, that Shin is a member of my staff. He works for me. Therefore, you see, his business is my business." He smiled, but there was no pleasantness now. "As a matter of fact," he added, indicating Hong casually, "you work for me, too. I think your business becomes my business as well." His expression became suddenly hard. "What have you discussed of our arrangement?" he demanded.

Thoughts raced through Hong's mind. If Shin had reported their conversation to Kwon, the general would hardly be probing now, he thought. He decided Kwon was speculating.

"We discussed reconstruction," he countered resentfully. "Have you not heard? A market was destroyed yesterday. Agents from the north have burned my market at the East Gate."

"Shin has nothing to do with reconstruction," snapped Kwon, ignoring the disaster. "Why would you discuss such matters with him?"

"We discussed the problem as friends," shot back Hong. "With a mutual friend."

"Yes," said Kwon. "The old man. The disheveled one." His expression became dubious. "Why would a general and a cabinet minister discuss these matters with such a person?"

Hong felt a wave of relief. It was obvious now that Shin had not mentioned their meeting, but that Kwon or others had observed them together. "The old man is Min. He was our schoolmaster when we were boys."

"A schoolmaster?" Kwon snorted. "I think he must know as little of reconstruction as you or Shin." He took a deep, bored breath. "Perhaps I must remind you, Hong, that you can be destroyed as effectively now as during the coup. It would take little to convince our leaders that certain facts were overlooked previously."

The cabinet minister bristled. "Would you threaten me again with the loss of my wealth? You are stripping it from me. What have you done? What has the army done to protect my investments? I have lost a great deal in the bombings."

"Your losses are but a grain in a field of rice," replied Kwon. "We could arrange for you to relinquish the entire field."

"And you would lose the information I provide," snapped Hong. "You have told me it is valuable. You would not want to have to begin again, to face a reconstruction program of your own."

He paused, and Kwon started to speak, but the minister cut him off.

"General Kwon, it is pointless for us to argue. It changes nothing." His tone softened. "Perhaps we should concentrate on solving problems, not fighting them."

He watched for the general's reaction, but it was merely silence, waiting.

"The reconstruction of my orphanage and the market will be very expensive."

"But you could receive funds to assist you," reminded Kwon.

"Yes," agreed Hong. "But did you not say when we made our arrangement that I should continue my inventiveness?"

Kwon nodded, saying nothing.

"If I rebuild in the normal manner, all the reconstruction funds will go into the pockets of the workers. But I am left with a need to pay the costs of gathering information for you." He spread his hands and smiled. "Min has provided a simple solution."

"The schoolmaster?" asked Kwon.

"Yes. Min is a very successful man."

"He dresses in rags."

"It is a part of his method," explained Hong. "Many years ago, Min determined to leave the government school and construct a private school. It stands today at Gapyong. His students are trained in construction. The students of Min will reconstruct my orphanage and market as a training project."

"Then the reconstruction funds will go to Min and his school," reasoned Kwon. "You will be unable to retain these funds."

"If Min could be convinced of our need, perhaps all the funds need not find their way to Gapyong," suggested the cabinet minister.

"Then you must convince him," stated Kwon. "The need is not ours, but yours. You said he is your friend, your old schoolmaster."

"You could be of assistance to me," said Hong.

"Why should I assist you?" asked the communist. "I am a busy man."

Hong became supplicant. "I cannot discuss our need with Min," he agonized. "Even if I could he would not understand our need."

"Your need," corrected Kwon again.

"I think we must consider the need ours," suggested Hong. "We could gain more than you realize from Min."

"More?" asked Kwon.

"Much more," replied Hong, baiting him.

"But you are a cabinet minister," reasoned Kwon. "Is he not impressed that his former student has become a cabinet minister?"

"He is not impressed enough," replied Hong, annoyed at the memory of Min's rejection. "He thinks of me still as a boy, his student. This is why I am asking you to assist me."

"But what could I do?"

"Min met me first as a boy. He would meet you first as a lieutenant general. I think the impression would be quite different."

Kwon pursed his lips, dubious.

"He really has a great deal of money," prodded Hong.

"From selling a school's services?" Kwon shook his head. "I think Min would be of little value to our cause."

"My apologies, Kwon, but Min has a great many sources of funds." He looked earnestly at the general. "He charges tuition from his students. He obtains government grants, not only from our government, but from the Americans."

"The Americans?" asked Kwon, surprised. "How has he arranged such a thing?"

"He named his school after an American soldier who was killed in action early in the fighting. The Americans were impressed."

"Most ingenious," mused Kwon.

"Also, he receives private contributions from the family and friends of the dead soldier. And from those who served with the man." He nodded. "And, yes, he sells the school's services."

Kwon clicked his tongue in apparent admiration.

"General Kwon, any one of these many methods would support Min's school. But the schoolmaster dresses in rags, remains silent about the many sources of revenue, and places much excess money in his own pockets."

"Do you want me to point out to him he has been found out? Do you want me to confiscate his fortune?"

"I think," replied Hong softly, "that if we made Min aware of other sources of funds he could be convinced to share the profits with us. He is a very greedy man."

"What sources would you suggest?" asked Kwon.

"Min has the method," replied Hong, becoming more enthusiastic now. "Also, he has the school. It is attractive bait for the altruism of the Americans. If we can provide him with more numerous avenues to the American pocket, I think he will be grateful to us."

Kwon's interest glowed across his features.

"Many Americans come to our nation," continued Hong. "Many of them are businessmen who want to establish contacts here. Many of them visit the headquarters of the United Nations Command."

"And you believe Min is unaware of these visitors," inserted Kwon.

"I think he is unaware of most such visits."

Kwon leaned back, touching his fingertips together thoughtfully. "Yes," he said at last. "I think we may be able to provide great assistance to this Min." He smiled. "We shall educate the educator."

Hong was exuberant. "Then you will go with me to Gapyong?"

"Tomorrow," replied Kwon. "We shall go to Gapyong tomorrow morning."

"I shall arrange the visit," said the cabinet minister.

"I want to take another man with us," added Kwon.

Hong stopped, looking at him expectantly.

"I shall take an interpreter from the United Nations Command."

The cabinet minister was cautious. "Do you think it wise to include him now? It may become necessary to discuss our reason for needing funds. If this interpreter is assigned at the United Nations Command, he may have American friends."

"He does," said Kwon emphatically, smiling broadly, "but he is a much closer friend to me. You see, he and I were boyhood friends, much as you and Shin. He is very loyal to that friendship. And he will be the one who will provide the information about the Americans who visit their headquarters."

Hong nodded. "I shall arrange a driver."

"No. I think we must not have any others with us."

"Then what is your plan?"

"You will drive."

THE SOUTH—GAPYONG

They climbed into the elevations east of Seoul with little conversation. Then, at the top of the pass which began winding down toward the river and Gapyong, Kwon signaled Hong to stop. "I want to discuss some of the finer points of our visit with Taejin," he said amiably.

Hong pulled to the side of the road and stopped.

"Taejin has been a close friend to me since we were boys," he said to Hong. "We went to school together, much as you and Shin." He turned to Taejin. "It is now time for us to discuss the reason for your accompanying us on our journey into the countryside. We are to visit an old and very influential man. He is a schoolmaster. Today, we shall permit him to join our cause. Your function, Taejin, is to be present and to listen. You must be attentive, yet you must not speak at all. You must be alert to all the finer elements of the plans to be discussed. From that point on your task will begin." He smiled knowingly at Taejin. "Naturally, you will say nothing of the trip, the conversations or the plans to the Americans when you return. It would cause us the greatest concern." His expression became serious, threatening, as he awaited the reply.

"I shall listen and say nothing," said Taejin softly. "What will be the remainder of my assignment?"

"We shall be in a more favorable position to discuss that once this visit has ended." He nodded to Hong and the minister guided the car down from the pass and along beside the gentle river.

Min turned quickly and looked from his office window at the sound of the vehicle. Seeing Hong and the two others, he pivoted back to the desk, stuffing papers into the drawers. Then, grabbing for his cane, he stumped his way from his office and out to the front entrance of the school. A wary smile creased his old face as the three ascended the steps.

"Hong," he greeted. "Am I to be honored again so soon?"

The minister smiled, bowing low. "Schoolmaster, I want you to meet my good friend, General Kwon."

Min turned to Kwon. The two exchanged bows of greeting. Min then preceded them into his office and poured tea.

Kwon, glancing about the group, assured himself that his team was ready. "Min, I am very impressed with what Minister Hong and General Shin have told me of your school. I was unaware of its existence before."

Min merely nodded, suspicious of their motive.

"Naturally, I was happy when they told me you had agreed to have your students repair his damaged facilities. It will be a great help to the people of Korea."

"I am happy to help, General," said Min finally.

"Of course, it will not be as costly for your students to do these things as it would be for other workmen," continued Kwon smoothly.

Min said nothing.

"We have a disturbing problem in our military forces." The communist was watching Min's face carefully for a reaction. "It seems the Americans persist in inspecting our defense posture very carefully, yet we are never allowed to do the same with theirs. Hong is graciously helping us to correct this inequality in our land."

Taejin looked quickly at Hong. The minister was obviously ill at ease, but silent.

"We are not in a position to allow such matters to appear in our budgets," explained Kwon. "Were we to do so, the Americans would know of our efforts to learn their posture. It would prove very embarrassing for our people." He sighed and looked benevolently at Hong. "Hong is contributing from his own enterprises so that we may continue our program. Do you not consider your former student most generous for making such a sacrifice, Min?"

Hong was a very good student," replied Min noncommittally. He cast a suspicious glance at the motionless Hong.

"We have been concerned for his personal sacrifice," continued Kwon evenly. "Therefore, we have asked him if there were some way in which we could repay him. It was then that he told us of your school. He is anxious for us to devise a means to help your institution."

Min smiled faintly, nodding hopeful assent.

Kwon returned the smile pleasantly. "How do you finance your programs, Schoolmaster?"

Min bowed his head. "I rely on the kindness and generosity of those for whom we perform our training projects," he replied softly.

Kwon raised an eyebrow. "Is that your only means of support?" he asked, surprised.

"I receive an occasional grant from our government," admitted Min. "Such grants usually are small."

"Ah," exclaimed Kwon. "Then I think we have perceived a way in which we may help you. Our plan should provide sizable amounts of money for you, Min."

Throughout the revelation Min's pulse had quickened, his face lighting with a broad grin. "Such concern for my humble school pleases me," he replied. He looked now at Hong. "You are kind to have remembered me, Hong."

The cabinet minister's stomach churned as he smiled weakly in the old man's direction.

Kwon now became businesslike, kind but driving. "Have you considered seeking support contributions from the Americans, Schoolmaster?"

"Such things are difficult," parried Min, neither admitting nor denying his practices.

"But it is a great source of funds," pressed Kwon. "Why, your school bears an American name."

"The American died in action on this land where I built my school."

"Yes. I have been told of this," agreed Kwon. "This fact should prove very attractive to the Americans. Did you realize businessmen from the United States are frequent visitors in Seoul?"

"I have no access to such people," replied Min evasively.

Kwon grinned. "But now you shall, Min. We shall see to it."

Min's eyes widened. "But how will you do such a thing?" he asked quickly.

"It is simple," explained Kwon. "These businessmen are anxious to establish commercial relationships in our land. Such arrangements are of great value to them. They must be anxious also to contribute to an institution which so honors one of their countrymen."

"It would be difficult for me to approach such people," moaned Min, his joyous smile fading. "I am only a poor schoolmaster in a country village. They would not be interested in me or my school."

"Forgive me, Min," objected Kwon. "I believe you are wrong."

"Schoolmaster," said Hong, breaking his silence. "General Kwon is anxious to help you, to help your school. We shall all participate."

Min looked quickly at Taejin. "And you. How will you participate in this venture to improve the lot of Min?"

Kwon shot a warning glance at Taejin. "The interpreter," he said, "will provide much of the coordination for our program. He works closely with the Americans. I asked him to accompany us today so that he could gain a better understanding of you and your institution." He nodded emphatically. "He will work very diligently under my direction." The general paused, studying Min. "Will you accept our assistance, Schoolmaster?"

Min bowed his head again with his gratitude. "I am most honored by your consideration, Kwon."

Kwon sat back, radiating pleasure. "Fine," he breathed. "I am certain our arrangement will prove profitable to you." He gazed at Min, but only for a moment, then sobered. "Of course, I am sure you will want to be as helpful to Hong as he has been to you?" he asked.

The smile of pleasure faded gradually from the old man's face. "How? Already I have agreed to rebuild his orphanage and his market. There is little else a humble schoolmaster can do to assist a powerful cabinet minister."

"Ah, but there is, Min," corrected Kwon. "You will receive much money from our program of assistance. And yet, Hong still makes great personal sacrifices for us all." He stared hard at the old man. "Do you not feel that your gratitude to him could be expressed in terms of sharing?"

Min's joy was gone as he realized how thoroughly he had been duped by his own greed. "But I have many expenses," he whispered lamely. Then, looking quickly from one to the other of the men, he added, "Perhaps the school could be expanded."

Kwon painted disappointment across his countenance. "Are you saying, Schoolmaster, that you do not wish to be equally helpful to Hong and our nation?"

"I do not mean that at all," protested Min, "but. . . ."

"If you are saying such a thing, Min, perhaps we should reconsider our desire to help you." He paused for the words to strike home. "You must agree that fifty percent of something is more to be desired than one hundred percent of nothing, Schoolmaster."

Min wilted, thoroughly beaten. "I shall help Hong in return," he murmured.

Kwon contemplated him for a moment, then added his parting blow. "Excellent. Then you will be satisfied to receive fifty percent of the reconstruction funds Hong is able to obtain for the reconstruction of the orphanage and the market. I am certain that should suffice for your school. Of course, you will be receiving more from our new venture together, so that will offset any losses you sustain now." He looked at his watch. "We are busy men," he observed. "We must return to Seoul. I am happy to have met you, Min. You are a very perceptive and generous man."

Min bade them goodbye at the door of his office, too dejected to accompany them to the car.

"It progressed well," observed Kwon when they were on the highway. "Are you not pleased, Hong?"

Hong beamed. "Yes," he replied. "I thank you for your assistance, General Kwon."

"I trust you will find your twenty-five percent of the contributions helpful in financing our intelligence-gathering operation," added Kwon.

"Twenty-five percent?" asked Hong in dismay. "You negotiated for Min to provide me with fifty percent."

Kwon smiled at him without warmth. "Of course. But I am certain you will consider fifty percent of your share more beneficial than one hundred percent of nothing. You must remember, Hong, that I have many programs for which I am responsible. They, too, require funding."

Hong swallowed hard, nodded and said nothing further.

Taejin, from his place in the front seat, looked out in despair at the passing woodlands. The vultures, he thought, would fight each other to the death over the carrion of their greed.

THE SOUTH—SEOUL

"I believe you should not eat so heavily of this American food," whispered the voice. "It will rot your stomach."

Taejin, reaching for hors d'oeuvres at the enormous table, did not look up. "I did not know you planned to attend this reception, General Kwon."

"I have never before availed myself of an opportunity to attend one of their receptions," replied the general. "I have heard many tales of their opulence. I decided to see one for myself."

Taejin did not reply.

"You should escort me on a tour of this palace as a matter of courtesy."

"This is the Mess of the Commander in Chief of the United Nations Command," said Taejin. "It is one of two assigned. The other is smaller. It is used only by the most senior officers."

Kwon affected surprise. "Why does he require two? Is this not regal enough for him?"

Taejin turned. "We must not speak so loudly here. There are many ears."

Kwon smiled with satisfaction, following him. "I agree. It would be more desirable to view the terrace."

They walked slowly through the crush of uniforms, nodding and smiling but avoiding any conversations, and through the glass doors to a broad patio which reached out toward a smoothly tailored expanse of lawn beyond. The gardens bordering the scene were lush with summer, yet few people had strayed outside to take in their beauty. Kwon led the way to the distant end of the paving and stopped.

"It is time for us to develop our friendship further." He was standing with his back to the building. "Come. Stand in front of me. Face me so that you may warn me of anyone approaching."

Taejin made the move. "I have briefed you thoroughly at each request. I have not omitted information. Now I have agreed to inform you regarding their important visitors. There is nothing more I am capable of doing."

"I am pleased with your performances," agreed Kwon amiably. "However, an inventive mind and a desire for closer friendship are interesting bedfellows. They devise further ways to serve one another."

Taejin saw others step onto the patio. He looked at Kwon and smiled pleasantly, as if enjoying the conversation. The others moved away to a far corner of the gardens without noticing them.

"You said you have another requirement for me. Tell me what it is. I want to go inside and be free of you for the remainder of the evening."

"Free of me?" Kwon shook his head. "Again you have done what I have told you irritates me greatly. That is a most disrespectful manner in which to speak to a general." He reached into his pocket and withdrew a cigarette, lighting it slowly and watching the interpreter. "One does not talk with a friend in such a way, especially a friend who is doing so much to save the life of your bastard daughter every day. Please be more cautious in the future."

"Tell me your next requirement," pressed Taejin, ignoring the reprimand.

"Photographs," replied Kwon softly. "I want to obtain a constant supply of photographs from American compounds all over the land. Wherever there are the Americans I must have photographs in the most intimate detail."

"You have asked the impossible, Kwon. Such a thing is not possible," answered Taejin, relieved.

"Taejin." The general's tone was fatherly. "You lack inventiveness, imagination. However, because we are so close I shall explain to you how such an assignment may be carried out. The results should begin arriving in a matter of days."

Taejin sneered. "I said it is impossible. You have seen how carefully they guard their compounds."

"Yes. An outside observer would meet with a great deal of frustration were he to attempt such a task. However, you are in a position to accomplish my request indefinitely with no frustration at all. It is simple. You will merely use the American soldiers as your photographers."

Taejin smiled, confident. "You flatter me, Kwon. I am sorry to disappoint you, but I do not have the authority to order their photographers into the field to record their compounds."

"But you work for a general."

"Yes, but he does not permit me such powers."

"The common American soldier is a strange man," mused Kwon. "He feels he must photograph everyone he knows, every place he frequents. He delights in sending such photographs home to his family, to illustrate to them not only the difficult conditions under which he lives, but the equipment he uses, the men with whom he works, even the quaint qualities of this land in which he is required to live. He takes each roll of film to the exchange system and pays for them to be developed." He paused, smiling happily. "You shall arrange for the exchange concessionaire to make an extra print of each of these photographs for us."

"Such a plan is very expensive. He would not do it."

"The concessionaire brings all these films to Seoul. His processing laboratory is here. There would be but one point from which such prints must be collected each day."

"The cost of extra prints in such volume would be too high. He would not do it," repeated Taejin.

"I believe you are correct. If you, or even I, were to go to him and request such a service he would most certainly refuse. However, he receives great profits from his concession. He is becoming a wealthy man. I think he would be very disappointed if he were to lose his concession, if he were no longer permitted to operate his business." He wagged his finger. "The laboratory, all the equipment, belongs to the Americans. He would have no way to establish a firm to service the needs of our nation's people without great expenditure. It would cost much more than providing the extra prints."

"I could not convince the general to issue such an order to him."

"I agree," answered Kwon quickly. "However, you carry many of the general's requests about our city. It is your function. You must merely approach him and advise him of the general's request. You must allow him to see how difficult it is for you to make such a request, but that you have no choice."

"He will go to the Americans and complain."

"You will prevent his doing so. You will point out to him that his position is very precarious. Tell him others are seeking to replace him as the concessionaire. They have offered such a service. He will wonder why such prints are needed, but you can tell him the Americans wish to learn quietly if their men are photographing only those things which are allowed. It must be quiet, then, or the checking program will not work. You see? He will not only be cornered, but he will feel a sense of intrigue with the importance of what he is being told to do. He will soon become convinced that protest would cause him to lose the concession."

Taejin bit his lip. "How are such large volumes of photographs to be transported each day?"

"I have assigned you a mission, Taejin. I have explained to you the matter of executing your task. You must develop your own delivery plan. I have more important things to consider." He paused. "One of those is your next mission."

Taejin was rapidly becoming depressed. "I suspect the next will be equally demanding. You demand much, Kwon, but produce little."

Kwon surprised him by ignoring the insult. "Do you understand order of battle?"

Taejin scoffed in disgust. "Of course I understand order of
battle. I am not a schoolboy, Kwon. It is not necessary for you to
talk down to me."

"I want the entire order of battle for the American forces in
our country."

"You have as much access to that as I."

"They will not make the complete file available," cut in Kwon.
"I want everything, all the information on every commander they
have in our country, their histories as people, military background,
the way they think, their specialties, whether it be defense or offense, what kind of attacks they are most likely to mount, what
kind of defense they feel most comfortable establishing. Everything. I do not have access to such information from my office."
He smiled. "Now I shall know. You shall tell me. It should be a
large document, since I want everything down to and including
battalion level all over our land. I want the same information on
their advisors to our army. And do not forget to include the staff
officers along with the commanders of each unit. The staff officers
are important to me as well."

"That is impossible. You know it is impossible," retorted Taejin.
"They have a very large force here. The commanders are not that
stable. They rotate home in little more than a year after their arrival. Any document I could provide you would be obsolete before
you read it."

"That is inconsequential. I know I can rely on you to maintain
it in a current state for me. We shall revise it each week."

Taejin's jaw dropped. "I would be unable to compile such up-
dates."

"Taejin, there will be ways. You will find them."

"You have other ways of obtaining such information. Use them."

"But why should I use others when I have you, my close friend,
in such an influential, such a perfect position to obtain it for me?"

"I am not in a perfect position."

"I said you must find a way. That is your assignment." Kwon oozed his hate. "I shall expect information within a week. Every week thereafter I shall expect more." He smiled and ground out his cigarette on the stones of the patio. "It would be shameful for you to disappoint me, and dangerous."

As Kwon spoke, an aide emerged from inside the building and walked toward them purposefully.

"We have company," interrupted Taejin.

General Kwon stopped and waited for the aide to reach his side.

"General Kwon?"

"Yes," snapped Kwon importantly. "What is it?"

"You have a telephone call, Sir."

Kwon merely cast a glance at Taejin as he followed the man away. "General Kwon," he said, picking up the instrument.

"General, this is Hong," said the voice, strained, anxious.

"Why have you called me here?" demanded Kwon.

"Do not speak so angrily with me," replied Hong testily. "I must see you immediately."

"I am busy now," began Kwon, but Hong cut him off.

"I said I must see you. It is urgent."

Kwon sighed deeply. "I shall see you early in the morning."

Hong was adamant. "I must insist, General, that you come at once."

"Very well," replied Kwon. "Where are you?"

"I am at the Itaewon market," announced Hong. "Come at once." The line went dead.

Kwon set the receiver down thoughtfully, then turned and went to the cloakroom for his hat. "Please extend my apologies," he said to the aide at the door. "I have been called for an emergency."

As his sedan approached the market in the Itaewon section of the city, traffic was snarled and police were diverting all vehicles away from their destination. Kwon's driver came to a stop next to a policeman.

"I am sorry, General, but we must detour all traffic," said the police officer apologetically.

"What has happened?" demanded Kwon.

"The Itaewon market has been bombed," replied the officer.

"Then I must go there immediately," snapped Kwon. "Move aside."

"But. . . ."

Kwon waved at his driver impatiently. The car crept forward and the policeman looked uncertainly at his companions on the barricade, then motioned for them to allow the sedan to pass.

As they pulled to a stop, fire crews were playing streams of water over a massive heap of rubble. Kwon got out of the car and walked forward, amazed. The firemen merely glanced at him and returned to their work. He wandered through the mass of hoses, coughing with the smoke.

"General Kwon!"

He heard the shout and turned, squinting through the haze and lights.

"General Kwon!" the call came again, and a moment later Hong appeared, his face and clothes filthy with soot, soaked with water.

"Hong," said Kwon calmly, immediately assuming his composure.

"General, I thought you were going to protect my markets. My investments are being ruined with this obvious sabotage." Hong was highly distraught. "How can this have happened?"

Kwon steeled his features. "Hong, I said we would attempt to protect your orphanages from harm. We cannot place the army around each of your many investments to protect them. We would be required to abandon the protection of our nation to do so."

Hong snorted. "You promised an empty basket. Perhaps I should reconsider our relationship."

"Hong!" growled Kwon. "Be more cautious, my friend. You would be most embarrassed were people to learn you are engaging in espionage."

Hong's eyes widened. "Espionage?"

Kwon smiled. "Yes, Hong. Oh, of course, you and I know what you are doing is for the good of our nation. However, were people to learn that a cabinet minister was becoming a wealthy man through all these business ventures, and were the Americans to learn you were spying on them, I think there would be an embarrassing investigation. Naturally, your control over these ventures would come to an abrupt end. And who knows? Perhaps your continuation as a cabinet minister would be questioned." He reached out a hand and placed it paternally on Hong's shoulder. "I would be unhappy to be part of such a purge, but for the good of our nation such a move might become expedient."

Hong was glaring at him hatefully. "We must not discuss such things here." He looked quickly about them. "We should not be overheard. There are too many people here."

"I agree," replied Kwon, still smiling. "There is no need for us to discuss them at all." He reached calmly into his pocket, withdrew another cigarette, and lit it. "Now, you called me here. What did you want to discuss with me?" He looked tiredly at the rubble.

Hong opened his mouth to speak, then stopped, realizing it was useless. He was hopelessly involved. Espionage? He shuddered.

"Excuse me, Minister Hong."

He turned at the voice. It was a fire marshal. "I was told you may know some of the bodies."

"I? Why would I know them?" he scoffed. "I was merely passing by when I saw there had been a catastrophe. I am a cabinet minister. I thought I might be of some help."

The marshal nodded. "One of my men said you were asking if any bodies had been found." He paused. "We have found one."

Hong's eyes darted over the man's shoulder. The streams of water continued to pour into the smoldering ruins. "I shall come with you." He turned. "General Kwon. Will you come with me?"

More from curiosity than interest, Kwon matched his stride to Hong's. They wound through the confusion, stepping over hoses and around pieces of equipment.

"Over here, Sir," said the marshal, pointing.

A small group of men had gathered near a crumbled pile of bricks. Hong and Kwon followed the marshal into their midst.

"Do you know this person?' asked the marshal, pointing.

Hong looked down at the body, almost unable to conceal his gasp. "No. I do not. Who is it?"

"We do not know," replied the marshal. "There is no identification."

"Then perhaps it was a worker," sniffed Hong. "I have never seen this person before." He turned to leave, but stopped and turned back for one last look at the twisted, torn remains of Chi.

＊ ＊ ＊ ＊ ＊ ＊

The curfew was near. Taejin steered the jeep slowly, despondently, through the summer night. Then, stopped at a signal light, he saw her.

Song was haggard, her clothes threadbare. He hardly recognized her, yet the stirrings of his love for her trembled through. He leaned out, started to call to her, then choked it off. As he drew back she looked up, her eyes widening. He saw her lips form his name, the hand start upward in greeting, then stop.

Carefully, from behind the wheel, he pointed to the side street. She watched him, seeming not to notice. He pointed once more, and slowly, apparently without concern, she turned, gazing vacantly at the side street. It was empty.

The light changed and Taejin accelerated, suddenly alert, wishing for he knew not what. He proceeded straight, trying desperately to drive as he had before seeing her. Then, two blocks farther, he turned into a side street. At the next corner he paused, watching for followers. There were none. Now anxious, he turned the corner and doubled back, away from the main thoroughfare. His heart was pounding as he reached the side street to which he had pointed. He slowed to a crawl, looking. Then, in the deep shadows, he saw her move. Quickly turning off his lights, he pivoted and motioned her in beside him.

"Taejin," she whispered. "Taejin."

He jerked his thumb impatiently toward the rear of the vehicle and she climbed back. "Get down," he ordered. "No one must see you."

She nodded, melting to the floor close against the seat. He rolled forward and turned deeper into the winding alleys, watching carefully for followers. Still there was no one. "Song," he said at last, softly. "What happened to you and Sookee?"

She spoke back without moving. "We were taken by Kwon. He has Sookee now."

"And if you do not work for him he threatens to harm her," he added. "We have the same problem."

"Has he found you?" she asked, feeling a surge of panic.

"Yes. He is making difficult demands." He reached back between the seats and touched her shoulder, gently, with reassurance. "The curfew is near. We must find a place to hide for tonight."

"There is no place," she moaned. "If we are found together we will both be killed, and Sookee with us."

"No. He will do nothing. He will only make more demands." He turned a corner. "We will go to your home."

Safely in Itaewon, he parked and stretched, scanning the area carefully. At last, sure they were not being watched, he motioned her from the vehicle. They entered the house.

"I have not come here since he took Sookee," she said.

"I know. I came here every night to wait for you." He gathered her into his arms. "What do you do for him?"

"I do what I am told."

"What does that mean? There must be a specific thing you do."

"Yes. I am an informer. I am to watch people. I am to report to him and watch those he does not trust." Her look was pensive as he lighted a lamp. "There is very little for me to do. I think he took us only to be cruel, to spoil the life I was building. It is punishment."

"Then I am more a spy for him than you are."

"What do you do?" she asked, fearful of the reply.

"I brief him on the American plans. I am now to provide him with information on American visitors. Tonight he has given me two more assignments. They are too difficult. I cannot do them and still perform my job at the United Nations Command, but I need the job in order to fulfill his demands."

"We must rescue Sookee and escape from him."

"He will harm you and Sookee."

"You see?" she exploded. "He does the same to each of us. And even if we could escape, where could we go? We lived in the north and we know it is bad. Is there greater freedom in the south?" She looked at him with an expression of anger mixed with sadness. "I think it is useless. There is no good in all Korea. The south is as bad as the north."

"There is an entire nation here," he replied. "It is a good nation. Not everyone is decadent."

She tried to hide her disgust with the situation, but could not. "Remember the refugees on the Taegu road? There were deaths, tramplings. I watched beatings for a container of American food. The people were animals and our government did nothing to help." She shook her head. "There is much in our nation for the leaders, but little for anyone else."

"Then why should we bother with escape?" he retorted in equal disgust. "Why do we talk of rescue for Sookee? If you think that, there can be no hope. If there is no hope there is little use to talk of rescue and escape."

Her head was bowed and she said nothing further.

"Song, when I was in Hochon I was arrested and sent to Hyesan. I was meant to die there. Many did die there, and I could have given up hope and died also. I did not. Later, we were placed on a train and sent to the south. We were packed into cars like cattle, so close we could do nothing but stand. The situation appeared hopeless, but I would not, I could not accept such hopelessness. I devised a means of escape. A man next to me, a prisoner like myself, begged me not to carry out my plan. He was willing to accept what they did to him because he believed there was no hope. He could not face immediate danger so that his future might be better."

He reached out gently with his hand and raised her head until she looked at him. "That other prisoner died at Chorwon. He refused to have hope, so he died. Song, I cannot believe as he did. I cannot believe as you say you believe now. If we can rescue Sookee we will not be rescuing one child. We will be doing it for all the sons and daughters of our nation. If we are willing to try, to fight them, it can be a new beginning for Korea. There must be hope or there can be no life. You must believe that or you would not want to rescue her at all."

Quietly the tears had begun welling from her eyes once more. "And you have such hope for Korea now?"

"Yes. I believe we must have hope for our children, now and tomorrow and for all time."

"It is easy to talk of tomorrow, but how can it be any different?" She reeked pessimism.

"Our greatest problem is our division. All our energy is spent worrying about the north. And in the north they worry about the south. Someday we must reunite. We must cast off our differences and become one nation again. Perhaps that must become the greatest dream of all for our people. But without courage it cannot happen."

"It is a beautiful dream, Taejin, but it will be very difficult. In the north they believe in communism. They will want to reunite, but only under communist rule. In the south we have free enterprise, but what does that mean? We want to reunite with the north, but with free enterprise. Neither side will give in."

"But there is a difference, Song. In the south, free enterprise offers everyone a chance to succeed, to make his life better. In the north I think there are very few of their people who want or believe in communism. If they ever have the chance they will reject it. It will take time, but as the years go by we will build a strong economy

in the south. We will develop industries and enter the world market." His enthusiasm was growing.

"We have industry now. We have textiles. We have brass. We
have furniture." Her tone was flat, not matching his passion. "We
also have poverty."

"We will have new industries. Already a steel factory is planned.
It will be built at Ulsan, near Pusan. When such heavy industry is
developed we will be able to build cars, ships. With such industries there will be much more work for our people. They will be
able to escape their poverty."

Her eyes had widened. "But how can this help reunification?
How can it do anything but widen the differences between the
north and the south?"

He spread his hands. "If we are the stronger economy I think
it will help our cause. There will come a time when the north will
not pose the threat they do today."

"But they do today, not only to our half of the nation but to
us. To Sookee."

He deflated. "Yes. We must think of a way to rescue Sookee
and escape Kwon and his friends."

"I suspect he does not have as many friends as he would have
others believe."

Taejin looked at her and raised an eyebrow. "How many?" he
asked.

"Only one man that I know. He drives a taxi in the city. I
think he is Kwon's boss. He gives Kwon his orders. Remember,
Kwon is a general only in the south. In the north, where his true
loyalty lies, he is not so important."

"Are you sure the taxi driver is his only contact?"

"The others I know are women."

"Women?"

"Waitresses. Bar women. The matron who keeps Sookee. I know
nothing of any others."

"I think he keeps others who are well hidden."

"No. It is an organization of paper. Many of those who work

for him do not realize what they are doing. They do not know he is a communist agent."

"I have not seen the taxi driver," said Taejin.

"He does not want to be seen," she replied.

"He must know of me."

"I doubt that he does. If the taxi driver knew of you I think he would demand your return to Pyongyang. Kwon merely reports the information you provide for him. He would not reveal the source, for it would weaken his position with his superiors."

Taejin fell silent. If Kwon were not as powerful as he had said, he was more vulnerable than Taejin had thought. Perhaps she was right. Perhaps the taxi driver did not know of him. "Then it may be easier to escape from him," he said.

Her eyes fell. "You said yourself they have Sookee and they will harm her if either of us makes a move."

"Then Sookee must be rescued."

"And what if they kill you? What if they kill us all?"

"Then we must die trying. We must not stop for fear. If I would have stopped for fear I would have died at Chorwon with those others."

They quieted and the chill of the night crept in. Gently he reached across and drew her to him. She did not resist, but lay her head on his chest. The sobs were gone.

He squeezed her shoulder. "It all revolves about Kwon. When we get Kwon we will have eliminated them all."

"And the taxi driver and the matron. We cannot forget them."

Taejin lapsed into a pensive silence, trying to sort out the intricacies of the relationships. "Do you know of a general by the name of Shin?" he asked at last.

"Yes, I know of him," she answered in surprise.

"Is he involved in this situation?"

"I do not think he is, but I cannot be sure. I know Kwon hates him, but he has some control over Shin. I do not know what it is."

"Then I shall learn," promised Taejin. "He may be our means of getting to Kwon."

"I do not understand."

"Trust me," he replied. "Have hope and trust me."

"How can we meet again?" she blurted suddenly. "Where will I see you?"

"We will meet here."

"It is dangerous."

"It is not as dangerous as you think. Remember, Kwon needs the information he is getting from me. If he harms us there will be no more. In the meantime we can work out a plan. If each of us is alone we can do nothing. But working together we may be able to set a trap for him."

"Just remember Sookee. We must not do anything if it will bring her harm."

He smiled in the darkness, holding her close against him. At last he became aware of her steady breathing. Then he, too, drifted into a sleep punctuated by dreams of Kwon, a taxi driver, General Shin, and Kwon, Kwon, Kwon.

* * * * * *

The American aide motioned Taejin into his office and closed the door. "You asked me about General Shin," he said.

Taejin brightened. "Yes. Have you learned of him so soon?"

The American smiled and nodded toward a chair. "He's quite a heroic type. Helluva fighter, but he hates staff work."

"Does he have a relationship with General Kwon?" Taejin's heart was pounding.

The American glanced at his notes. "That's a strange thing. Shin's been riding Kwon's coattails ever since the early days of the war. Before that he was heavily decorated by the Japanese. He performed with outstanding valor in the fighting here under Kwon. But there's a curious note. Sort of an appendix to the file. It cautions of possible personality conflicts between the two but no specifics are mentioned. Merely urges caution."

Taejin sat back and took a deep breath.

"What's up, Taejin?" The American was studying him.

Taejin continued staring straight ahead, then shook his head and stood. "I am not sure. I think there is something wrong, but I cannot identify it now." He gazed through the window, then shrugged. "I shall keep you informed," he said, turning toward the door. "Thank you for your help."

"Taejin."

He stopped and faced the officer, saying nothing.

"Come on back, Taejin. Let it out. What's bugging you about Shin?"

Taejin hesitated. "I cannot say." He thought for a moment. "I think you may be able to help, if you would."

"Of course. What can I do?"

Taejin sat, bowed his head and took a deep breath. "I must talk privately with General Shin," he said, looking pleadingly at the American.

"And how can I help with that? Why don't you just go over there and see him?"

"I cannot talk with him in that compound. I cannot let our army know I have talked with him."

"Why not?"

"I think it involves espionage." His expression had not changed. "I cannot talk there because if it is true they would arrest me to keep me quiet and there would be no solution to the problem."

The American had become much more somber at the mention of espionage. "Then by all means you may call him over here."

Taejin shook his head. "No. I cannot request it. They would expect me to go to the general. He would not come to me. I am only an interpreter."

"Then we'll request it."

"But please do not mention my name." Taejin was clearly agitated.

"Why not? You're the one with the suspicions. We can't. . . ."

"I will talk with him once he is here. But he must be called here by the American command. I cannot be involved until he arrives here."

The American sat back slowly in his chair. "Is Shin the one involved in espionage?"

"I hope he is not one of them," replied Taejin evenly. "If he is involved they will destroy me very soon. If what I think is true, he will be happy to have had the conference, for he will be able to expose the entire scheme."

"But there's no way they can destroy you if we know of this thing. Obviously, we'll protect you."

Taejin shook his head again. "No. I must talk with him alone. If he is involved you will know only when I am destroyed. It will happen without warning."

The American slapped the desk. "Dammit, Taejin, this is stupid. Why in hell would you accept destruction rather than let us protect you? It just doesn't make sense."

"Because there are others," shot back Taejin. "There are two others they would destroy in my place if they could not get to me. I must gamble that I am right, and if I am, the other two will be safe. If I am not, the others may be able to escape in time."

"Then why not do it the simple way and let us get these other people into our hands, too? That way all of you will be safe."

"No. It is too complicated to explain. It must happen the way I have told you. When it is over you will understand."

"Damned oriental mystique," muttered the American. "Why in hell does everything have to be shrouded in the mystique?"

"It is not mystique," retorted Taejin. "It is a matter of lives, and their agents have one of those in custody now. We must do this my way if there is a chance to save her."

"Ah, so it's a woman!"

"It is a child."

The American stopped and studied him once more. "Okay. We'll see if they'll do it your way, but I think we're going to have to go in and talk with the general about it. He may go along with it and he may not. You'd better come with me. He's sure going to have a lot of questions."

Taejin nodded silently and came to his feet. "I am ready."

* * * * * *

General Shin strode warily into the corridor, then turned sharply through the highly polished door and looked about him. The only man in the room was Taejin.

Taejin rose and snapped to attention.

"I was told the general wished to discuss a matter with me," snorted Shin. "Where is he?"

Taejin bowed and tried to smile. It was useless. "Sir, I am the one with whom you have come to talk."

"You? I am summoned across the city to meet with an interpreter? This is ridiculous." He turned and started toward the door.

"Sir, I have requested that the Americans invite you here because it is a matter of the greatest urgency. I did not dare to approach you at your headquarters."

Shin stopped and glared at him. "And of what is an interpreter so aware that it escapes the general staff?"

"Sir, it involves espionage from the north."

Immediately, Shin's expression changed. "Espionage? You must tell me of this espionage immediately."

"Yes, Sir."

"Do the Americans know of this?" broke in Shin before Taejin could continue.

"I have told them only that it was most important that I talk with you here. I have told them it is a matter of the greatest urgency. Nothing more."

"And just like that they have issued you the office of their generals and made you a commander of General Shin!" His voice was contemptuous. "You had better come with me to our own headquarters and we will discuss this in our own offices."

Taejin hung his head, his heart suddenly turned cold. "Then

you are a part of General Kwon's operation," he said softly. "I did not think it would be true of you, Sir." He started toward the door, but Shin had stopped as though slapped.

"General Kwon?"

"Yes, Sir. Lieutenant General Kwon."

Shin studied him for a moment longer. "We must discuss this openly. Now. What do you know of General Kwon?" He motioned to a pair of chairs and the two sat.

"General Kwon and I knew each other as boys."

Shin said nothing, waiting.

"We were born and raised in the village of Hochon in the north."

Still Shin remained silent.

"Sir, are you aware that General Kwon's father is the Secretary of Investigation and Corrections in the government of the north?"

"Impossible!" snorted Shin. "This is. . . ."

Taejin merely watched him as the voice trailed off to silence.

"What did you say your name is?" asked Shin.

"Taejin, Sir. I am an interpreter in this headquarters.

"How have you come to know so much about General Kwon?"

"I have told you, Sir. We knew each other as boys in Hochon."

"Yes. That tells me only of history. How have you come to know of his activities now? You have made a very serious charge."

"His father had me arrested for sedition against the communist government many years ago. I was sent to the prison at Hyesan. Later, the father had his sons inserted into the south as agents, and an arrest of the father was staged so that if anyone in the south had observed the ploy they would not suspect it was an insertion. Instead of being sentenced to prison for fathering defectors, as was the charge, he was appointed warden of the Hyesan prison, the same one in which I was a prisoner. He hated my father and had him killed. I managed to escape, and came to the south at the outbreak of the war. Kwon has found me and is forcing me to provide him with order of battle information. If I do not, he has threatened to kill my daughter. One of his agents has her in custody."

Shin had lapsed into a thoughtful silence. At last he looked up. "Are you certain his father is the Secretary of Corrections?"

"Yes, Sir."

"That is most interesting." Shin's attitude softened. "Taejin, a strange thing happened during the war. We were fighting for Pyongyang. I was a battalion commander, and General Kwon was my boss, the regimental commander. One night my unit captured a man. He was carrying a packet of papers which indicated he was a very high official of their government. They said he was Kim, the Secretary of Corrections. Kwon had me deliver the man, along with his papers, directly to his headquarters at regiment. He then dismissed me. Later, he called me back and reprimanded me for having arrested one of our agents. He ordered me to insert the prisoner through the lines back to the north. The action cost a number of lives." He stopped and thought once more. "Yes. The father and the son must have enjoyed a visit that day." He turned to Taejin. "What other evidence do you have?"

"There was another person from our village of Hochon who was sent here as an agent, although it was against her will. If she had not come her father would have been executed. She was forced to marry General Kwon's brother, who also was an agent. The brother lost heart once he arrived here and did no meaningful work for them. As a result, he was sent back to the north and executed by his own father. They are most cruel."

Shin nodded sadly. "We are all cruel. I think one day we must begin to live a more civilized existence in this modern world our nation is so slow to recognize."

"This other person is the mother of my daughter. It happened before she was forced to marry General Kwon's brother."

"The birth of your daughter?" asked Shin incredulous.

"No. The conception. The forced marriage happened soon after the conception. They did not know until afterward."

"Then why did they not annul the marriage?'

Taejin grimaced. "General Kwon's father was rising in the Party. He was afraid he would lose his face, and that in turn would end his political career. He made his son continue the marriage."

Shin nodded. "How did General Kwon get custody of the child?'

"When Song, the mother, arrived home from her work one day General Kwon was waiting for her. He talked with her outside her house, but before they talked, our daughter had been kidnapped from the house. Kwon told her that if she worked for the People's Republic our child would remain safe. If she did not, our daughter would be killed. She was most reluctant to agree, but she had no choice. They allow her to see our daughter each week, but the meeting is carefully guarded by the child's matron."

"Are there others involved in this ring?" asked Shin.

"I do not know the others, but I am told there is a taxi driver who is their leader."

"Is he Kwon's leader?"

"I am told that he is."

"Then we must find him as well."

"I think it will be simple once we have Kwon. However, he merely directs the operation and Kwon is the one who is doing the actual work against our nation."

Shin sat back and lighted a cigarette. "I think the moment Kwon is exposed the taxi driver will go into deep hiding. It will be very difficult to find him then."

"I have a plan which may cause him to come out of hiding."

Shin looked at him in surprise.

"If he were told he could return me as an enemy of the People's Republic to Pyongyang, I think he would be most anxious to do so. It would help him save his face after having lost an important agent and the son of the Secretary."

"How would you convey this message to him?"

"It is simple. Song is very anxious to recover our daughter."

"How would giving him a message help to recover your daughter?"

"I think the taxi driver may not know of the hostage situation with our daughter. I think Kwon is keeping that as his own threat to Song and me. Perhaps the taxi driver would be understanding with her if he realized she was telling him things he did not know. He would consider it loyalty to him and to their leaders in the north."

"But perhaps the taxi driver will then merely come after you himself, Taejin."

"He does not know of me yet."

Shin raised an eyebrow. "Why would he not know of you?"

"Kwon has kept me a well guarded secret. If the taxi driver knew of me he would have demanded my return to the north immediately. Kwon has known this, yet without me he would not have had access to the information he is trying to extract from me. He must have the information to make himself appear efficient to his father. He has already seen that his father will most assuredly recall him and dispose of him if he does not perform well."

Shin nodded. "Yes. It is typical of the way General Kwon would operate." He studied Taejin's anxiety. "Tell me your plan."

"I shall have Song go to the taxi driver and tell him she can deliver an enemy of the People's Republic. However, she will point out to the taxi driver that she wishes to recover her daughter. She will tell him if she can see that her daughter is safe she will deliver Taejin to him in exchange for our daughter."

"But you said the taxi driver does not know of you. If you were such an enemy of the People's Republic he must know of you."

"It is not so much that I am an enemy of the People's Republic. The fact which concerns Secretary Kim is his obsession with the annihilation of my family. He has succeeded at killing my mother and father. I am all that is left to completely fulfill his passion."

Shin watched him and said nothing.

"When Song tells the taxi driver she can deliver Taejin to him he will immediately ask the secretary for instructions. Kim will be elated and order the arrest to be made as soon as possible. He will consider it a form of revenge for the loss of his son."

"Then you would sacrifice yourself to this man?"

"I would hope for some assistance from you, General Shin."

"How could I help you?"

"Song will request that our daughter be visible to her as she delivers me to the taxi driver. I humbly ask your assistance in the rescue of our daughter from the matron at that moment when Song turns me over to the driver."

"Where would you have this take place?"

"I have not decided yet. I think we must first concentrate on the arrest of General Kwon."

Shin nodded and stood, reaching out a hand to Taejin. "If all this is true you will have done our country a great service. I shall see that you are properly rewarded when all of this is over."

Taejin bowed soberly. "My greatest reward will be knowing that my daughter and Song are free."

Shin looked at him silently for a long moment, then nodded and left the room.

* * * * * *

General Shin steeled himself, straightened his uniform. Often the hero in combat, he now felt the rapid thudding of his heart at the prospect of a political battle. In the field one knew the enemy, met him, measured him, fought him, defeated him. In the lacquered offices of the Ministry of National Defense the enemy was more likely to be a shadow, unrecognized until the battle had already been lost. Perhaps he could gain strength in imagining the musty odor of canvas, the pulsed whir of artillery lacing the sky above him, the acrid aftermath of exploding ordnance. . . .

He raised his hand and knocked on the door. It was opened immediately by an aide, who then stepped outside and closed it behind him.

Shin's eyes focused quickly on the man before him, four stars gleaming on his epaulets. He snapped rigidly to attention and saluted. "Major General Shin reporting as ordered, Sir."

The Minister of National Defense returned the salute perfunctorily. "I am told you know of a traitor among us. A member of the General Staff."

"I believe it to be true, General."

"You have served under General Kwon in a number of assignments through the years. Why do you now decide to expose him?"

Shin paused, measuring his words. "I have always considered him a difficult but very effective commander. I have not until now believed him disloyal."

The Minister of National Defense eyed Shin for a moment, then slowly circled to his desk and sat, leaving Shin at attention. "Do you realize, General Shin, the seriousness of your charge?"

"Yes, Sir."

"Perhaps you are a patriot." The man watched Shin carefully, alert to his reactions. "And yet," he continued, "perhaps there is another motive."

A wave of uneasiness coursed through Shin.

"Perhaps," said the minister, "by casting doubt on a senior officer you feel there is something to be gained for Shin." He folded his hands and pursed his lips, awaiting a response.

Shin braced for the worst. "General I believe what I now suspect can be substantiated. I am a soldier, a loyal soldier. I owe much to many people, including General Kwon. But I owe more to our nation. I fought battles with and under General Kwon, but I did not fight them for him. I fought them for our people."

The minister was unimpressed. "You have not told me why you come now, Shin. Why is it now different?"

"I have met a person who knows him better."

"A person? Only a person?" The minister's eyebrow curled upward. "And who is this person?"

"His name is Taejin. He is an interpreter."

"Where is he assigned?"

"He is assigned at the United Nations Command."

A moment of recognition flitted across the minister's eyes. "Ah, yes. I recall. He is an American toad."

"I believe he is telling the truth."

"He was discovered and hired by the Americans."

"He has much evidence."

The minister rose abruptly. "Then I think he must show us this evidence. I think he must not hide in the skirts of the Americans."

"He is willing to sacrifice himself," responded Shin quickly. "He will place himself in very great danger, but he is willing to do it if General Kwon will be exposed."

"Has he a plan?"

"Yes, Sir. But he must have assistance."

The minister finally motioned Shin to a seat, then sat in an adjacent chair. "What sort of assistance does he want?"

"General Kwon is merely the figurehead of this group of agents. He is not the leader, but only a soldier with much to lose if he does not produce."

"And what of the others? Who are they?"

Shin grimaced. "I have learned that General Kwon's father is the Secretary of Investigation and Corrections in the communist north. Secretary Kim is General Kwon's father."

"How have you learned this?" exploded the minister. "It must be an error. There are many Kims in Korea."

"Taejin is also from the north," replied Shin easily. "He knew Kwon well when they were boys."

"Then perhaps this Taejin is also in espionage. Perhaps he is not to be trusted either."

"General Kwon's father is ruthless."

"A common knowledge."

"He arranged for the deaths of Taejin's entire family."

"Perhaps it was merely a feud," offered the minister.

"Secretary Kim also executed his own son, General Kwon's brother, as an ineffective agent."

"Have you verified this information?"

"Yes, Sir."

"And who are the others here in the south?"

Taejin believes if Kwon is arrested he can expose the others. He believes the entire cell can be caught."

"And you believe him?"

"Yes, Sir, I believe him."

The minister paused, considering the implications. "You pose an interesting theory, Shin. A very dangerous espionage operation could be erased if you are correct. On the other hand, there is always the possibility we are being duped." He pulled a cigarette from his pocket, lighting it slowly and watching the smoke curl upward. "Shin, what if this is wrong? What if this is only a carefully planned scheme to eliminate General Kwon?"

Shin started to speak, but the minister waved him to silence.

"Who has something to gain from the fall of General Kwon? This Taejin is a candidate. This Taejin has a great deal to gain from this ploy. Suddenly he would become a hero. A lowly interpreter uncovering something we should have known years ago. Our staff would lose its face. The Americans would gloat, and we would have no alternative but to honor Taejin." He drew again on the cigarette. "Yes, it is an interesting theory. Of course, we would not be totally taken in by his allegations. We would investigate very thoroughly. In the meantime, a very important general would live under suspicion. At the same time, if there really were a cell of agents out there, the rest of the animals would have ample time to make their escape."

He rose and walked pensively to a window. "Now let us consider another possibility." He turned to face Shin. "Let us suppose the perpetrator did not turn out to be this Taejin. I think if a lieutenant general were to depart the staff there would be a promotion available for a major general." He watched Shin carefully. "The logical successor would be a man who has worked for General Kwon for many years. A man who knows his operation intimately. Do you not think such a progression would make sense?

Would not such a move cause the least interruption of staff functions?"

Shin shifted uneasily.

The minister returned to his seat, never taking his eyes from Shin. "I think you are nervous, General Shin. I think perhaps you could have schemed against the man who made you what you are. Perhaps avarice has played a part in this provocative escapade."

"But General, I have not done this," blurted Shin. "I have brought the matter to your attention only because I fear for our security."

"Or your own," snapped the minister. "I think we must now undertake an investigation. It will be very involved."

"Excuse me, Sir, but is not time an important factor?"

"More important than truth? I think we must hear from the people you say General Kwon is using. I think we must be very certain that everything they say is investigated." He stubbed out his cigarette. "And I think I must discuss the matter with General Kwon."

Shin went cold with terror. "But General, you cannot! If he learns he has been accused I think several good people will be in very great danger. I think our general will see to them."

The minister stormed from his chair. "And should he not?"

"And what if he is what they say?" ventured Shin heatedly. "Will talking with him not alert them all?"

"Then what do you suggest?" the minister shot back. "You are supposed to be a staff officer. A good staff officer does not present a problem without a good proposed solution."

Shin was stymied. It was obvious the minister was not disposed to face the problem impartially. Were he to bring Taejin and the others to this man their tales might merely be repeated to Kwon. Kwon would create a diversion for the moment and then plot carefully for the elimination of his accusers.

The minister was waiting, his impatience growing. "Well, Shin?"

Suddenly it was clear. "General, I think there may be a way to establish the facts without a long investigation."

The minister's expression changed, but he said nothing.

"I think," continued Shin, "that I must bring Taejin and the others here to your office." From that point he unfolded an elaborate plan.

The minister finally nodded his approval. "If you are correct, Shin, you will have served us well." He rose. "And if you are wrong?" He shrugged. "That will be your error. Whatever the outcome, I think we must waste no more time."

* * * * * *

General Kwon nodded obediently at the telephone. "Yes, Sir. I shall come immediately." He cradled the instrument, staring at it for a long moment, then rose.

Passing through his outer office, he snapped at his aide. "I shall be with the Minister of National Defense."

"Do you wish me to go with you, Sir?" asked the aide.

"No," replied Kwon haughtily. "The minister has said it is a matter of the utmost confidentiality. He wishes me to come alone."

As he hurried through the corridors his mind was a montage of confused thoughts. There had been no hint of the subject of the meeting, making it impossible for him to prepare his input.

Arriving at the suite of the Minister of National Defense, he was ushered quickly into the inner office. He strode grandly forward, his eyes riveted on the general before him, and saluted. The greeting was not returned. Kwon hesitated, disarmed at the rebuff.

"Come, General. I would like to introduce you to some others of my friends." The minister gestured to an area behind Kwon. Kwon turned, then stopped, frozen in disbelief at the people in the group. Before him stood Taejin, General Shin and Minister Hong. Slightly behind them, almost cowering, was Song.

"What is the meaning of this?" roared Kwon.

"Meaning?" echoed the minister. "I think your reaction tells me that you must know them too."

"What an interesting group!" hissed Kwon. "A battalion of raging malcontents." His breathing was labored, his color blanched.

The minister smiled, now truly without feeling. "May I remind you, Kwon, that these people are my guests? You must not treat them so rudely."

Kwon gesticulated, nodding in fury. "I want an investigation," he roared. "Whatever they have told you, an investigation will prove them wrong."

The minister motioned to a chair. "Come, please sit down so that we may have a discussion. Perhaps you can help me to understand."

Kwon faded into a chair, panting, trembling with rage. "There is no reason why this group should be assembled here. An investigation will prove that."

The only response was silence.

Kwon looked across the group, his eyes wide with frustration. "You," he growled at Taejin. "You have done this. You and my brother's wife."

Taejin merely watched him, the hint of a smile creasing his eyes.

"He is a liar," he said, pointing at Taejin but glaring at the minister. "He has lied about his origin. He is really an agent from the north. He has been sent here to discredit our general staff. He was taught well by his scheming father, the man who tried to imprison our entire village. The Japanese heart of Hochon!" He nodded. "But my father saw through him. He brought the lawyer to a fitting downfall." He looked farther around the group. "And Song, the harlot. You disgrace us by even being here." He looked back at the minister again, grinning maliciously. "She will destroy any man you let near her. She destroyed my brother. She was already pregnant, but she lured my brother into a shameful marriage. So coy, so shrewd!" His hand shook as he pointed at her. "The shameless offspring of a timid merchant who became wealthy while the masses starved." He nodded with finality. "Well, you shall never again see your precious daughter. Make no mistake about it." His eyes darted to Hong. "And Hong. Cowering Hong. I have warned you. No longer will we protect you. You will go the way of your comrades. You have been a thorn in the side of the. . . ." His rage left him speechless. He gasped for air, then wheeled on Shin.

"Kwon," said the minister.

Kwon ignored him, rising and moving toward Shin.

"Kwon!" The minister shouted now,. "You will sit down!"

Kwon stopped, turning slowly to face the minister, his eyes wild.

"Sit down, Kwon," repeated the minister.

Kwon sank once more into the chair.

The minister circled his desk and opened a drawer, removing a thick folder. "I would be interested to hear more about your family. Your brother and father are of particular interest to me."

Kwon stared, his jaw dropped.

"And Hochon. You seem to have an inordinate knowledge of Hochon. Why would an orphan from Pusan have such intimate tales to tell of his father and brother in a small village west of Pyongyang?" He tapped the folder. "This is your personnel folder, Kwon." He fixed an unblinking stare at the now shaken Kwon.

"Lies," rasped Kwon. "They are all lies," he cried, leaping from the chair and racing for the door. As he opened it he was faced with two heavily armed guards, with two more immediately behind them.

"Out of my way!" he shouted. Their weapons prodded him back into the room. He turned, looking forlornly at the group, then at the minister. "It was the Americans," he whispered, exhausted. "We could have reunited our country if it were not for the Americans. They have done this. They have been the ones who have corrupted all of us."

The minister finally broke the silence. "General Kwon, you have done this to yourself. It was not the Americans. It was not these people here. They have said nothing to me of your crimes. You merely assumed, because they were here in the room, that they had told me stories of your espionage. You were wrong. I ordered them to tell me nothing, to remain silent and let you talk."

Kwon stared back at him, confused.

"General Kwon," continued the minister, "you are under arrest for the crime of espionage against our country."

"They said nothing?"

"When I first learned of your activities I was very troubled, Kwon. I have checked very thoroughly, and have found these acquaintances who are with us now." He nodded to the soldiers. "Take him away."

They shackled him and led him from the room.

* * * * * *

Min reached for the telephone with a deep groan. The old finger shook almost uncontrollably as he dialed. Then, waiting for the rings, he stared in horror at the newspaper once more. He wondered what he had done, how he had allowed himself to become involved with this man, this criminal the story exposed. And he, Min, had struck a pact with this man to hoodwink the Americans. In his chagrin he contemplated all the things the Americans had provided for him. Yet, he had come to hate them, to hate anyone not Korean. He knew it had not been a single event, a single person. A cascade of thoughts, of events, had brought it about. And here now, today, he was certain to be exposed in his infidelity to Korea, the Americans and himself.

The thought nauseated him. Infidelity? To whom? No, he had practiced no infidelity. He had been true to his goals since long before the Americans came. They were merely the expedient vehicle of his destiny, nothing more. His stomach relaxed with the thought, then knotted again as he realized there would be no recognition of his goal, only of his association. The Americans and his own government would dig deeply. They would find his treasured secrets without ever seeing their true origin.

"General Shin," said the voice at the other end.

"Shin," croaked Min. "Is it true?"

"Is what true? Is that you, Schoolmaster?" His voice showed his alarm at the old man's tone.

"Yes. The newspaper. Is it true about General Kwon?" The color was gone from his face, the wispy beard somehow older, more sparse.

There was a pause. "Yes," replied Shin at last. "It is true. He has been arrested."

"What will that mean for us?" queried Min weakly.

"For us?" Shin was puzzled. "Did you know him?"

"Yes," replied Min quickly. "They have arrested him as a spy, but I did not know he was a spy when he came here. He was with Hong so I believed him loyal."

Shin became irritable, obviously under a strain. "What danger could there be to you? You merely met him."

"We made an agreement." Min's voice rang with panic. "They could discover our plan."

"No, Schoolmaster. I do not think they would arrest you." he paused. "What agreement have you reached with Kwon?"

Min ignored the question in his fright. "I think he will tell them everything about me."

Shin had regained his composure. "Schoolmaster, I think you must not worry so. The situation is no different, except that we know about Kwon today. We fear when we realize the danger. If we are unaware it has no effect on us."

Min's mind was racing. "Shin, what of the Americans? Will they not be angered by this? Will they not seek retribution because of this discovery in our highest offices?"

Shin's voice tightened once more. "There will be problems for those who knew him well, for those who were his accomplices."

"Shin," interrupted the schoolmaster, "they will consider me his accomplice. Hong and I were his. . . ."

There was a swishing sound, then a metronomic click, click, click through the receiver. General Shin listened in alarm, then called out into the telephone. "Schoolmaster! Schoolmaster, are you there?"

Only static hissed through the receiver into his ear.

"Schoolmaster," he shouted at the instrument. There was no reply. Impatiently, he depressed the cradle, then lifted it again and dialed. A series of sounds gurgled deep inside the instrument, then the rhythmic, pulsing buzz of a busy signal.

* * * * * *

Immediately upon Taejin's order, Song made her way to the South Gate and a rendezvous with the taxi driver. She had not long to wait. The vehicle swerved to the curb.

"Why do you wait here so openly?" he demanded. "We must be more cautious. The discovery and arrest of Comrade Kwon has made them more alert."

"It is a most urgent matter, Comrade," she replied. "I want to do something which Comrade Kwon has never allowed me to do."

He merely glanced at her in the mirror as they wove through the traffic.

"I want to prove my loyalty to the masses."

He scoffed. "I think he has given you many assignments. Have you not performed them loyally?"

"Of course. But he never believed it was a loyalty to the workers. He has held my daughter as a hostage and believed I worked to ensure her health and safety."

"Woman, we are in a serious business. We cannot indulge ourselves in sentimentality. If she is with our people your daughter is safe."

"I want to have her with me."

"If Comrade Kwon felt it necessary to hold your daughter I think he had a reason. Perhaps your loyalty is indeed in question."

"What must I do to prove this loyalty to you?" she pleaded.

"You must continue to perform your assignments as you are told."

"And if I do more?"

The driver cast her a quick glance over his shoulder. "What more would you do?"

Her eyes bored back at him. "There is a great enemy of the People's Republic in Seoul."

"There are many enemies of the masses in Seoul."

"This man is of great interest to Comrade Secretary Kim. He would be most anxious to have him returned to Pyongyang."

"Who is this enemy?" asked the driver, curious.

"His name is Taejin."

"I know of no such man."

"Comrade Kwon knew of him. He knew how much the Secretary wanted to retrieve him."

The driver shook his head. "Our comrade would have turned such an enemy over to me for return to the People's Republic."

"I think Comrade Kwon was more interested in his own image. He wanted to advance himself at the expense of the rest of us. He wanted your position."

The driver snorted. "That was impossible. His assignment was to follow my orders."

"Yes. I think so. He followed your orders and played us all for fools in the process. He was determined not to follow the fate of his brother."

"Your husband."

"It does not matter. He knew of Taejin and allowed him to keep his freedom so long as the criminal obeyed him."

"How do you know such things? You are equally guilty for not telling me of this before."

"I could not," she whined. "He threatened to kill my daughter if I exposed him. I could do nothing."

The driver was free of the city now, rolling smoothly along the highway toward Pochon. "And now you would lead me to this Taejin? If he were such a criminal I think I would know of him."

"I can deliver him to you."

The taxi swerved to the side of the road and stopped. The

driver turned in the seat and glared at Song. "How would you do this? Why?"

She shrugged. "Kwon hated me. I could not prove my love of the People's Republic to him because he would not believe me. He was convinced I worked only to save my daughter. I had no way to prove my love was for the workers so long as he held her. Now I want to prove how I really feel."

"And you would do so by delivering to me a criminal of whom I do not know?"

"Ask Secretary Kim," she flashed. "Ask him of the value of Taejin to him."

"And if he wants him?"

"I shall deliver him to you, but we must do it quickly."

"How will you capture him?"

She smiled. "A woman has her ways."

He pursed his lips. "And you want your daughter in return."

She dropped her eyes. "I hope you would reward my action."

He nodded. "When it is done I shall consider it. First we must make our plans and carry out the mission for the Secretary. After it is done we will have time to think about your request for the girl."

Song looked up at him sharply. "There are things we must consider now. I will want to know she is safe when I deliver Taejin."

"She will be safe."

"Perhaps Kwon's matron will kill her. Please have her where I can see her."

"Where will you deliver him?"

She gazed at him evenly. "A schoolmaster has died in the village of Gapyong. Taejin will be among the mourners. The funeral will be tomorrow. When we descend the mountain I shall bring him to you as if to introduce him to a friend. It will be a simple matter to place him in the taxi and drive away."

"I must enlist assistance. I cannot drive and guard a prisoner."

"I will help you," she replied. "I will have a weapon in my shawl. I will ride with you and guard him."

He thought, then nodded. "Fine. You will see your daughter when we return to Seoul."

"No!"

He snapped a wary look at her.

"I must see my daughter there at Gapyong. If you doubt me, have the matron with her to be certain of my loyalty. But I must see my daughter so that I may have courage. Taejin is a very dangerous man."

The driver turned to the wheel and began the drive toward Seoul. "We shall see," he replied noncommittally, "how important this Taejin is to Comrade Secretary Kim."

THE SOUTH—GAPYONG

As Taejin drove the jeep toward Gapyong his pulse was pounding. He had not seen Song since he had sent her to her rendezvous with the taxi driver. Now he was not certain they would not be trapped. Still, he had no alternative but to carry through with the plan and accept the consequences.

He parked the jeep. A large group of people was forming before and behind the bier, preparing for the long climb to the mountain. He looked at them and saw the sampling of a nation, poor, rich, young, old, people from every walk of life. As he drew nearer he saw merchants, tradesmen, farmers. He swept his gaze across the buildings nestled back among the trees, reflecting on the old man's achievement.

At last, with the sound of tambourines and the wailing of the mourners, the crowd began weaving along in procession. The climb was long, slow. They wound their way into the forest and up the majesty of the mountain ridge toward the sky. The sun beat down punishingly, yet the pace did not change. At last, entering an open crown atop the mountain, they drew to a halt.

They gathered in a large group then, the sounds of their moaning concentrated and reverberating across the neighboring burial mounds. Min was raised high, that he might view for the last time the clear blue sky to the east. The peaks of the Sorak Range strutted boldly across the horizon, and below them the lush valley of his youth displayed its peace to the world. Chunchon rested lazily in the sun, as if to guard his joys on the mountain. Then, slowly and gently, the body was lowered, still in a sitting position, into the mound they had prepared for him. The designated mourners established their vigil and the rest of the crowd moved restlessly toward the trail.

The return trip was faster than the ascent, and in little more than an hour Taejin was back at the school. The day was old, the sun low in the sky. He stopped and gazed once more at the school, this monument not to the named American, but more to an old man now safely delivered to the happy mountain. At last he turned to the jeep.

"Taejin!"

He stopped and looked at her, a dichotomy of delight and apprehension sweeping through him. "Song," he replied, forcing a smile.

"Please come with me," she said, her voice clear, confident. "I want you to meet a friend."

They passed through the crowd to a taxi, away on the fringes. The driver dismounted, watching closely.

Suddenly, some yards away, there was a commotion. A man stumbled, falling against a woman. Her eyes grew wide and she opened her mouth to shout. The small girl, whose hand she had held tightly, was wrenched from her as the woman slumped, bleeding profusely.

The taxi driver turned to look, alarmed. Instantly, two squeaks puffed from Song's shawl. The driver recoiled, drawing a weapon as he fell, his eyes now wild. He snapped off three quick shots as he hit the ground. The last two bullets screamed off crazily into the cloudless sky, but the first had slashed its way through Taejin's shirt, barely scratching his arm. He dodged, twisted, and saw Song firing again into the driver. The body recoiled with the impact, then lay still.

Shin raced by Song, the bewildered child in his arms. Behind them was confusion. "Hurry," he urged. "We must be away quickly."

"Taejin," she shouted, tears in her eyes.

"Run, I say!" Shin ordered. "He is coming." He grabbed her arm with his free hand and they dashed for his sedan.

The driver sparked the vehicle forward, Song hugging Taijin and her daughter close.

What will happen now?" she sobbed. "Must we run forever?"

He caressed her determinedly. "We will run no more, Song. We have won."

She rolled her eyes up to him. "Will we now have peace?"

"There will be difficult days ahead for all of us," he replied. "But we have tried, and our nation will continue to try as well." He looked down at her fondly. "You have been strong, Song. I have much pride in you."

Then they were out on the open road, the river flowing placidly beside them as they drove without words toward the distant hills.

Printed in the United States
6245

9 781401 045388